Seeking
Atticus

Seeking Atticus

Norm D'Plume

The Book Guild Ltd

First published in Great Britain in 2018 by
The Book Guild Ltd
9 Priory Business Park
Wistow Road, Kibworth
Leicestershire, LE8 0RX
Freephone: 0800 999 2982
www.bookguild.co.uk
Email: info@bookguild.co.uk
Twitter: @bookguild

Typeset in Garamond

Printed and bound in Great Britain by CPI Group (UK) Ltd, Croydon, CR0 4YY

ISBN 978 1912362 387

British Library Cataloguing in Publication Data.
A catalogue record for this book is available from the British Library.

For Michael…
without whom this book would never have been written.
He wouldn't let it lie!

Deputy Dog's Boarding Kennels

6th August 1987

Dearest Brian,

Humble Bumbles! I felt terrible when I heard you'd phoned last night, or was it morning for you? I can never remember how the time difference thing works. I'm sorry to have worried you but so much has happened and I honestly haven't had the time or the brain cells to write. I'll do my best to bring you up to date with everything and hopefully, you'll understand.

So first of all, let me assure you I am okay. I have to confess though, a couple of weeks ago I thought it was curtains – I'd completely lost it! Honestly Brian, I was a gibbering wreck! I even thought I'd had a stroke! Imagine that – coming this far and then just before the court case that will decide my future – I'm a basket case!

Funnily enough, I'd been trying to make an appointment at the doctors when it all started. I'd made my mind up the night before to get some sleeping tablets. I couldn't stand the thought of yet another night climbing the walls. No wonder they use sleep deprivation as a form of torture – I tell you, too much of it can have you howling at the moon! I needed to make an emergency appointment, but my vision had gone funny and my coordination was all out of whack. I'd had so much trouble dialling the number that when I finally got through, my mind went blank and the receptionist hung up on me – the bitch!

Alison had been calling up the stairs, giving me the hurry up treatment, so feeling horribly weird, I ventured down. She and Jim had an appointment with their accountant and were waiting to

2

leave. She gave me the diary, pointing out the viewing that was booked in for 9 o'clock, and left. (Part of my job here is to show new clients around the kennels prior to booking.) As I waved them off, it felt like only half my face was smiling. I legged it to the bathroom and sure enough — I was definitely all of a droop on one side! I had a comb in my hand and when I lifted it towards my hair, it slowly slipped through my nerveless fingers! I was pretty spooked by then but before I had time to think, there was a car at the gates hooting to come in. The 9 o'clock viewing! The kennel maids were all out, taking the dogs on their early morning walks, so I had no choice but to see to the viewing myself. I was all over the place and to make matters worse, the stroke theory was beginning to formulate in my head.

I left a note for Alison (in old lady, spidery scrawl!) explaining that if she found me collapsed in a heap somewhere, it meant I'd had a stroke. I pulled myself together and went up to the gates to greet the prospective clients. As soon as I started the guided tour, I discovered I had completely lost the power of speech! I began my well rehearsed spiel but to my horror and the embarrassed surprise of the visitors, the sounds that came out of my lopsided mouth were a series of grunts and groans, completely in keeping with a stroke victim! I broke into a sweat. I attempted a smile but succeeded only in alarming them even further with a wild eyed snarl! As my words of apology were equally unintelligible, I abandoned my efforts to speak and decided to just walk them around the building, giving occasional arm signals and energetic gesturings towards places of interest.

To my enormous relief I saw Jim's car coming back up the drive. They'd left an important file behind apparently and had returned to collect it. Do you remember Snagglepuss in The Yogi Bear Show? Well that was me... exit... stage left... running all the way... straight out of the building and towards the house, pausing only to point urgently to the reception area as I pushed past Alison at the door!

After assuring the clients her receptionist was neither mad nor drunk, she handed them over to a returning kennel maid and hot footed it back to find me. She had my note in her hand and soon realised that any form of communication was impossible. She quickly scooped me up and rushed me off to the doctors. I still couldn't speak – I just sat there crying so Alison was called in and she explained everything for me. The doctor said that extreme stress can bring about symptoms of a full blown stroke. She was confident that's all it was but took a blood test to be sure. I left with a short term prescription for Valium to get me through. The doc told me to take two when I got home and I slept for a straight sixteen hours. Wonderful!

Anyway my bestest buddy on the other side of the pond, I really must go. I've taken on an extra job in the evenings to supplement my meagre income. Remember me mentioning the new boarding cattery that's opened nearby? Meet their new driver! Dogs by day and cats by night! Just call me Dr Dolittle! The cattery's owned by the funniest gay couple to ever mince the earth. I can't wait for you

to meet them – Sasha and Mau-reece!
– probably Eric and Norman really! Camp
as Christmas but such a laugh and
you'll never guess what they've called
the cattery – Mrs Slocombe's Pussies
Hotel! I don't know how they got away
with it. I think one of them changed
their name to Mrs Slocombe by deed poll
or something, but anyway, the upshot
is, most evenings I am bombing around
London in a bright pink Rascal van with
the words Mrs Slocombe's Collection
and Delivery Service emblazoned on the
sides!

Will write again soon, I promise. So
much more to tell you but my pink
chariot awaits!

Loads of love,
Brian
x x x

The Life Of Brian

Liv sealed up the airmail letter and was about to nip down to the village post box when the phone rang.

"It's for you-hoo!" called Alison from downstairs. "It's Michael."

"Okay," she called back, "I'll take it in your room if that's alright?"

"No problem," floated up the reply. She picked up the extension in Jim and Alison's bedroom.

"Hello?" She heard the click as Alison replaced the receiver.

"Hi… how you doing?"

"Yeah, good thanks. I was just off to post a letter to Clare. She rang last night – I felt so bad."

"Why, what's up?"

"No… nothing's up, I just felt bad because I haven't written for so long. Poor old Briany… Alison said she was really worried."

"Bryony?"

"Clare."

"So who the hell's Bryony then?"

"Clare!"

"Oh for—"

"Clare is Brian," she chuckled.

"BRIAN! Right, that's it. Stop right there. What *are* you talking about?"

"Okay," said Liv, "I'll explain—"

"Well don't take too long – the phone card will run out!"

"Alright!" laughed Liv. "It's no big deal or anything – we just call each other Brian sometimes, mainly when we write."

"So *she* calls *you* Brian too?"

"Or Briany," she added. "It's kind of morphed into Briany over the years." She heard him sigh. "It's from The Life of Brian, you know, when they're all on the cross claiming to be Brian of Nazareth. *I'm Brian! – No, I'm Brian! – I'm Brian, and so is my wife!*"

"Ah…" said Michael as the penny dropped. "So it's another film-speak thing. Like at my nan's that time."

"Oh God, don't remind me!" laughed Liv. "The look on your face!"

"Yeah well, who could blame me?"

Michael had taken Liv off to meet his beloved nan. He tried to get over to see her at least once a month and had called by Liv's en route to see if she would like to come along. It had been quite early in their friendship and she'd been a bit taken aback at Michael's impromptu invitation.

"Why not?"

"Well… er…"

"You're not doing anything are you?"

"Not really, but…"

"Where's the harm? Come and make an old lady's day."

Before she knew it, she found herself sat in his battered old Alfa with flowers, chocolates and a crate of Guinness on her lap, wending their way to Epping.

"Epping!" she yelped when he casually let it drop that his nan lived near Epping Forest, "I can't go to Epping bloody Forest! Are you nuts? I thought she lived round the corner or something."

"It's not that far. We'll be there in less than an hour," grinned Michael. "Come on, cheer up, we're gonna—"

"Yeah, yeah. I know, we're gonna make her day," she muttered, feeling more than a little aggrieved. "I've been hijacked," she fumed. "That's what this is, a bloody hijack!"

Her annoyance, however, dissolved the moment she saw the look of joy on his nan's face as she peeked through the curtains and saw them at her door. He was right of course – they had made her day.

"I'll get the kettle on then eh?" she beamed as she toddled off to her kitchen. Liv wandered around the cosy sitting room taking in the wealth of photographs on display and enjoyed spotting Michael's young face smiling back at her. From naked baby on a rug right up to the one that had been given pride of place on the mantelpiece, a framed image of Michael, the Royal Marine.

"Salvation Army!" joked Michael as he followed her gaze.

"This is almost exactly like my nan's place – she's even got the same pictures on the wall!" she exclaimed, pointing to prints of The Crying Boy and The Green Lady with the blue face. Michael laughed, saying he thought they must be compulsory. Not *wishing to take his nan's chair, Liv asked Michael where she should sit.*

"Sit anywhere you like," he replied.

Liv joined in Michael's laughter over the phone as they recalled her immortal reply.

"Shall I sit on your face and wriggle?"

She remembered the stunned look on Michael's face just before his nan had shuffled back into the room with the tea tray. Liv's words, her terrible, inappropriate and shocking words had hung in the air between them. She'd sat through all the chit chat and amusing family anecdotes without once meeting Michael's eye. Her burning face had brought concern from his nan.

"You alright dear?" she enquired kindly. "You look a bit flushed. Shall I turn the heating down?"

Finally, after the longest two hours of her life, Michael said it was time to go.

"Airplane!" she said the minute he shut the car door. "It was from the film Airplane! – remember? Elaine, the air stewardess said it to Ted Striker."

"Who's Ted Striker?"

"The bloke in Airplane! You know, 'We have clearance Clarence, roger Roger, What's our vector Victor', and all that? Oh don't tell me you didn't see it?" she said desperately. Michael shook his head, completely in the dark.

"Oh God," she said with an anguished look, "I'd better explain."

"I think you better had," grinned Michael. "I mean, it's not every day I get an offer to sit on my fa—"

"STOP! I didn't mean – Oh God," she groaned again. She

10

gave a hurried account of the film explaining how once they had seen it, just about everyone, herself included, had started peppering their vocabulary with its wacky one liners.

"I *still* can't believe you hadn't seen it," she laughed down the phone. "But surely, you've seen The Life of Brian?"

"Yes I have – I've got the video – and don't call me Shirley!"

As soon as possible after her terrible faux pas, she'd presented him with his own copy of Airplane! Before long he was '*Clearance Clarence*' and '*Vector Victoring*' along with the best of them, his own particular favourite being '*I don't know where I'll be then Doc, but I won't smell too good, that's for sure!*'

"The Life of Brian was a great film," he said once they'd stopped laughing. "Excellent in fact."

"I saw it with Clare when it first came out on the big screen – that's when the whole 'Brian' thing started. You know sometimes when you're part of a really great audience and everyone's laughing out loud? It was like that. So funny."

"Yeah, and it's not until you've seen it a few times that you realise how clever it is – Cleese called it their masterpiece. I don't know what all the fuss was about, do you?"

"No! They were just poking fun at religious zealots. I bet most of the backlash came from people who'd refused to watch it."

"Exactly," agreed Michael, "They believe we were created in God's own likeness right? Well, if that's so, God

11

must have a sense of humour – it stands to reason doesn't it? He probably thinks The Pythons are great!"

"He probably does," laughed Liv, "and I'm sure He appreciates the virtue of being able to laugh at ourselves too." She heard a series of beeps.

"My credit's gonna run out any minute Liv, got to go. You're sure you're okay?"

"Yep, I'm fine, all sorted, just posting this letter and I'll be off to bed."

"You sleeping alright now?"

"Much better thanks."

"Okay, I'll ring you tomorrow."

"Yep," she said again.

"Take the dog with you—" he added just before the line went dead. Smiling at the concern in his voice, she collected the letter from her room and went to find Nosebag, Jim and Alison's overweight St Bernard. Together they moseyed on down to the village. As she dropped Clare's letter into the box, she realised with a pang she'd not really brought her up to date with anything, only the phantom stroke and her extra job at the cattery; nothing about the court case at all.

"I'll write again tomorrow," she told the wagging St Bernard. Nosebag licked her hand and barked. She was getting bored. She had places to go, smells to explore, litter bins to plunder. She was on a strict diet and absolutely ravenous. She had not taken too kindly to the new regime forced upon her; a drastic cut back on rations, no snacks or tit-bits and a foolhardy amount of exercise. She'd even been dragged off to the lake, unceremoniously dumped in from the jetty and made to swim back to the shore. She had wreaked her revenge though, the very next day at the annual village cricket match.

It had begun with the unexpected jingle of her lead. Jim and Alison rarely took her out during daylight hours because she had become too much of a liability. Alison had tried to talk Jim out of taking her but for some reason he'd decided she should accompany them. Nosebag had been delighted and had surprised everyone with her beautiful behaviour. Jim had been smiling away in an *'I told you so'* kind of way when Nosebag decided it was payback time. She had waited until he was at least six pints into the afternoon, the seventh held firmly in his right hand; her lead, wrapped many times around his wrist, was in his left. He had kept her close by his side, enjoying the attention her appearance had brought. He had an unlit cigarette in his mouth and had knelt down on one knee to receive a light from a seated spectator. Just at that moment, there was a lucky connection twixt leather and willow. The umpire's arms shot up and as the crowd roared "SIX!" Nosebag took off across the green with the kneeling Jim in tow and ploughed a perfect furrow straight through the carefully manicured wicket. Banished from the green and barred for life from all future village events, they'd sloped off home, tails between their respective legs, Nosebag chuckling under her breath in true Muttley fashion. No need for medals; revenge had been a sweet enough prize.

Back on that same village green, Liv's attempts at persuading her to jog back up the lane to the kennels were met with disdain. Nosebag had got wind of something delicious in the opposite direction that needed her urgent attention. There would have been no contest but for the trick Liv had up her sleeve, the pepperoni trick that never failed. Ducking to avoid the salvo of saliva fired off in response to the tantalising morsel held inches away from Nosebag's rapturously twitching nose, the pair of them hurtled back to the kennels in double quick time.

As she lay in bed that night, waiting for the Valium to kick in, she went through the mental check list that had become another addition to her countdown to sleep routine. The doctor had suggested a few techniques, some of which she'd found quite helpful, others less so. The deep breathing had been a disaster; she found herself thinking too much about her breathing, concentrating too hard and before she knew it, she'd started hyperventilating. She leapt from the bed gasping for breath and had been in such a state she needed an extra Valium to calm herself down. The relaxation had not gone too well either. She found that tensing and relaxing each body part usually brought about an attack of cramp that sent her hopping round the bedroom clutching either a leg or a foot as they went into painful spasm. The checklist had proved very successful however and she found ticking off the items on her 'things to do' list extremely satisfying. She ticked off '*Write to Clare*' but even as she did so, she knew she was cheating. She closed her eyes and began composing the letter she should have written. She groaned inwardly, it was such hard work. It had been fun telling Clare about Sasha and Maurice but the letter she needed to write was anything but funny. She had to catch her up with the harsh

14

realities of her battle with Carl. '*Battle?*' she thought to herself. No, it wasn't a battle. She'd lost countless battles along the way… but she was strangely confident she was about to win the war.

Doctor Strangelove

Her war with Carl had been raging on and off since the day in 1981 when she'd finally found the courage to ask for a divorce.

"So what is it you're trying to say here?" Carl's voice was cold but his eyes told of the burning anger inside. "What do you want? WHY DON'T YOU JUST CUT THE CRAP AND SAY IT!"

She didn't answer. The tension in the room was unbearable. Carl's fury, which had been visibly building ever since he'd agreed to this discussion, was about to explode. She knew what would happen if she dared voice the unspeakable but he was pushing her closer and closer to the point of no return. It was now or never. She could back down and let things return to normal, whatever that might be, or she could find the courage to see it through.

She had been working towards this moment for so long, rehearsing her speech until it was word perfect. She had tried to second guess his reaction and had logical responses in reserve; reasonable, sensible and absolutely fair suggestions as to where they should go from here. It was clear they couldn't possibly go on as they were; this life could not be lived. She knew the solution, had known it for years, but trying to discuss it with Carl was proving far worse than she could ever have imagined.

No matter how many times she had envisaged this scene, no matter how carefully she had prepared, this was the real thing and finding herself face to face with the certainty that Carl's anger would explode the second she pressed the button, her courage was deserting her. She had deliberately avoided the 'D' word. D for Divorce = D for Detonation. She knew how the Russian and American Heads of State must have felt back in the sixties when they had *their* fingers on the button. Trouble was, she was sitting opposite Dr. Strangelove here and God only knew what he might do. The consequences for her world and the people in it were as potentially catastrophic as a nuclear holocaust had been for theirs. She reached for her cigarettes but he knocked her hand away.

"JUST SAY IT!" he yelled again, almost taunting now, confident she would back down. She stood up, moving away from the table, her eyes held frozen in his glare. She steadied herself against the worktop. She could literally hear the pounding of her heart. She stood quite still, waiting for him to comment, but the pounding was for her ears only. She felt decidedly odd, her every sense heightened.

'Adrenaline,' she thought, *'adrenaline has flooded my body, slowing things down, giving me time to consider my options… fight*

or flight... "No hurry," said Adrenaline, "take your time... this extra time I've bought you... and make your decision!" But here's the thing; adrenaline being adrenaline, with its gung-ho *'Fuck You! Nuke the Bastards!'* persona, when it came to the crunch, surrender was never going to be an option.

"I want a divorce." The slap was instant. She fell back against the wall, cracking her head. He was immediately upon her, his hand pushing her face up into his.

"You want a divorce?" he sneered, his face contorting, incandescent with rage. "That's fine." He twisted her face round and pointed to the door. "Off you fucking go – but the boys stay with me." He pushed her aside and began systematically hurling and smashing everything he could lay his hands on. She stood firm in the eye of the storm, holding him in her gaze now. "You'll lose the boys," he promised and then prodding her chest, his finger punctuated the words, "YOU'LL NEVER – SEE THEM – AGAIN." He stormed out, slamming every door behind him. She heard his car screech away. A cloud of choking dust drifted in through the kitchen window as he snaked down the road in a depressingly familiar display of apoplectic rage. She sank down onto a chair and closed her eyes. As the adrenaline began to leave her body, she started to tremble violently, her teeth chattering so loudly she pictured a set of the joke shop variety and didn't know whether she would laugh or cry. Before any such hysterical reaction could kick in, skidding to a halt amidst a hail of gravel, he was back.

Liv pulled the covers up tight. She was shivering as the memories of that day washed over her. She tip-toed to the bathroom and

18

retrieved a couple of hot water bottles from the airing cupboard. 'What about a hot water bottle Waddle' – the punch line of her favourite joke brought about a shaky smile. Back in bed, she found their warmth comforting and eventually the trembling lessened – the panic attack had been headed off at the pass. Sometimes it was hard to believe she had come this far, surmounted the insurmountable, but the scars she carried bore testimony to that fact. They weren't physical, for up until that day, Carl had never laid a hand upon her. He had always vented his anger by smashing things spectacularly all around her, never once causing bodily harm – but her emotional wounds, although invisible, were grievous just the same.

As he burst through the door, the look of torment on his tearstained face told her she was not in any danger. He fell at her feet, buried his head in her lap and the terrible sobs that racked his body broke her heart. This was so much worse. She sat rigid, not knowing what to do. She couldn't follow her natural instinct to put her arm around him and tell him everything was going to be okay. There were no words of comfort; it was not going to be okay. She sat in silence, patting his back hopelessly, a tableau of abject misery. Eventually, realisation began to dawn, the battle was over. She always found the strength to fight him; the nastier he got, the stronger she became, but her resolve weakened and ultimately collapsed when faced with Carl, the broken man. History was repeating itself. They had been here before, six years before when he'd begged her to stay, pleaded with her to reconsider and promised her the world. Sadly, their marriage was already over, the mortal blow had been struck long ago; it had just taken a very long time to die.

19

Jiminy Cricket

Childhood sweethearts, they had married in 1972, their son Charlie, was born a year later. Like many of his contemporaries in the early seventies, Carl was quite the entrepreneur. He became part of the get rich quick brigade and Liv found herself, quite literally, left at home holding the baby as Carl's life in the fast lane took off. The proprietor of a thriving property development company, he had also invested in a London nightclub. Olivia hardly saw him. At work all day, he would come home only to shower and change, spending most evenings at the club. They lived completely separate lives. She remembered how taken aback Terry, the head of security, had been when they met during a rare visit to the club with Carl. Not only Terry, but everyone connected to the club had had a similar reaction. She couldn't help but feel that for some reason, she wasn't quite what they'd expected. She had sparkled that night and found herself the centre of attention; even Carl had seemed genuinely proud to have her on his arm. She'd been bitterly disappointed when her suggestion of making it a regular thing was met with reluctance; she was back in her box until the next time he allowed her to shine. Unfortunately for Carl, Liv's box had much in common with Pandora's; one opening had been enough. Terry's antennae had picked up on something that night and Liv's fate had been sealed. His instincts were infallible and he had every intention of following them through; MrsVogel was soon to become the latest notch on his legendary bed post.

He set about wooing her in earnest and pursued her relentlessly. After a couple of 'chance' meetings at her local supermarket, he realised she was a complete innocent. His attempts at flirtation and any hint of sexual innuendo had been met with embarrassed silence. She would politely change the subject but her flushed cheeks and her inability to look him in the eye gave her away. He was captivated. His usual line of pursuit, generally so effective, was getting him nowhere. He changed tactics. He found excuses to call round and see Carl at the weekends. He always had a quirky little gift for Charlie; nothing expensive but each was designed to ingratiate himself with both the little boy and his mother. He genuinely loved kids and in no time, he and Charlie were the best of pals. He began dropping in when he knew full well Carl was away 'on business'; well aware of Terry's visits but with typical arrogance, Carl was not worried in any way, in fact he thanked Terry for keeping an eye on his missus and more importantly, keeping her out of his hair.

Their friendship grew and although he was still

incredibly attracted to her, something was troubling him and his plans of seduction had taken a back seat. He was becoming increasingly aggrieved by the whole situation. Sickened by Carl's outrageous disregard for his marriage, he found himself looking inward and recognising the same hedonistic traits that had wrecked his own. It had been almost a decade ago but recent events had dragged up a plague of emotions he could well do without. Ever the pragmatist, he shrugged off the past and worked out his options for the immediate future. His thought process had been typically straight forward. This whole thing had started because he wanted to screw Liv; but now he wanted to screw Carl. What's more, his need to screw Carl had become greater than his desire to screw Liv! This led to the realisation that since meeting Liv, he had unknowingly acquired a conscience. It was quite a blow. He had never had one before and he was not wearing it at all well. The old Terry, without Jiminy Cricket on his shoulder, would have rubbed his hands and relished the prospect of achieving both goals at once. In screwing Liv he would be screwing Carl – fait accompli! However, thanks to the little green insect chirping away in his ear, this was no longer an option.

Perhaps he was seeking redemption, he didn't know, but whatever the reason, he was now Saint Terry the Patron Saint of Marriage and his mission was clear. Huge chunks of his life had been dedicated to the cause. He made Carl a gift of his own fucked up life and cautioned him not to do the same. He offered his wisdom, his time, his support; he gave him the chance to mend his ways, he warned that refusal to mend those ways could prove costly. He wasted his breath. Now Saint Terry did not suffer gladly this wasting of breath; and so it came to pass that he did strike down upon him with great vengeance and furious anger; and in the name of little J.C. (who was, after all, a disciple of the real J.C.) he did blow the whistle upon him.

Once Terry's decision had been made, he realised immediately why no one else had stepped up to the plate. It was the hardest thing he had ever been faced with. Apart from briefly wrestling with the knowledge he was about to commit an act that in a man's world was strictly taboo, his concerns were not connected to Carl in any way. They were all for Liv. It was the thought of sitting down with her, face to face, and telling her – telling her what? Telling her who she was married to? Telling her what everyone else already knew? Telling her that all those fears she had pushed to the back of her mind were about to become a reality? The burden was heavy and so was his heart. He knew that if he gave it too much thought he would buckle, so the next day, he pulled his chair up in front of her and with her hands in his, he laid the truth bare.

He had expected to see confirmation in her eyes; confirmation that she had known all along. Carl was a philanderer of the serial kind and given his reckless disdain for discretion, she had to have seen this coming. This thought had sustained him as he lay sleepless the night before the deed was done – *at least she wouldn't be shocked* – but it was shock that stared him in the face as he blew her world to smithereens. She marvelled at how easy it had been to be the last to know but had to acknowledge she'd been living in denial for years. Carl's behaviour ticked every box in a '*Is your man playing away?*' questionnaire, but she couldn't believe he would do that to her and had been willing to believe his lies. He'd found it all too easy and had openly bragged to friends and acquaintances of his conquests; he'd enjoyed the notoriety as much as the affairs.

Terry stayed with her that day until she convinced him she was okay. She promised him she would not do anything without carefully considering her options. It didn't take long; when Carl came home from work that night, she told him the marriage was over. He had completely fallen apart when she told him she was leaving with Charlie. She had been stunned by his reaction, thinking as she did, that he couldn't possibly love them. The gravity of his situation began to sink in. He begged her to stay. The thing that really tore her up was when he pleaded, "Don't take my son and run away – that's what my mum did! Please Liv, I'm not him – I'm not my father." The truth of it was, when faced with his anguish and total despair she lost the strength to walk away. He agreed to move out to give her some time and space. Not wishing to upset her family she kept the full extent of Carl's treachery away from them, saying only that they were going through a bad patch and a trial separation had been planned.

Everything changed. She felt alienated from everyone and trusted in nothing. Apart from her family, everybody had known and she no longer believed in their friendship. Clare had been devastated. She begged Liv to believe that although she'd had her suspicions, she hadn't known for sure. She and her husband had argued about it constantly. She'd desperately wanted to confront Carl, but Mark had sworn the rumours weren't true and warned that wading in making false accusations would completely destroy their friendship. The two couples had been best friends for years and as the main contractor for all Carl's building projects, Mark was uncomfortably aware that all his eggs were in Carl's basket. He reminded her they could shoot the messenger and insisted that without proof, she shouldn't be saying anything to anyone. Clare explained how she'd agonised over what to do and told of the countless anonymous letters she had written and ultimately destroyed.

Emotionally unhinged, Liv found the only person she could trust was Terry. She was determined to protect him and realising how many people had known, she decided that Clare was not the only one who could have written an anonymous letter. It was a great source of relief to Liv that Carl didn't question the existence of such a letter. Terry's anonymity had been secured. Not that Terry needed protection, far from it; he was a force to be reckoned with and had no problem with Carl knowing he was the whistleblower per se, just a hint of blokey discomfort, nothing more. He was an older guy, ex-army, running his own security firm. His men guarded the portals of every fashionable club in London. Carl had met him on the club circuit and had invited him to take care of the security at his own club. Just six months later he had become the unlikely beacon in Liv's darkness. He also became her lover. He eased her pain and gave her the precious gift of reassurance. She wasn't to blame for Carl's cheating; her femininity and desirability were not in doubt. He restored her confidence, her spirit and her self-esteem, but there was trouble ahead. Terry saw an affair, Liv so much more. He saw the crescent; she saw the whole of the moon. It ended and Liv's fragile world collapsed once more.

Close to a breakdown, her only salvation had been Charlie. She held it together for him but she had been greatly weakened. There were chinks all over her armour and to his enormous relief Carl managed to persuade her to try again. He promised her everything. He'd spend more time at home; he'd be a proper family man; they could move closer to her family; she could get a part-time job; whatever she wanted, he'd agree. So she had stayed and made a go of it, but as anyone who's been in that position can testify, it had not been easy. If Carl had been honest and made a clean breast of it, maybe they could have put it behind them and had some chance of moving on, but he remained resolute in his denial. He admitted he had been a lousy husband and father, agreed he had been living the life of a single man, but swore he'd never actually been unfaithful. She wanted to believe him; tried making herself believe him but she'd lost the knack. Those rose tinted specs were gone forever and there was no going back. Once everyone heard she knew about Carl, those who'd felt guilty about keeping quiet before were compelled to confess everything they had known; it seemed that every man and his dog needed to unburden themselves and Liv was subjected to a great outpouring of information concerning Carl's alter ego. The difficulty was, Carl's alter ego was – Carl! Selfish, uncaring, unloving Carl was also lying, cheating, duplicitous Carl.

Gandhi

Liv wasn't the only one taking a trip down memory lane that night. Driving home from work, Michael had been thinking about the first time the two of them had met, something she later admitted had not even registered on her radar. They had not connected in any way that night, but without doubt, it had been the dawn of a whole new era for both of them. Michael had long since given up asking whether, with the benefit of hindsight, he would have avoided that meeting and taken a different path; it was a rhetorical question after all, and needed no deliberation on his part. He knew that if he could have seen into the future and caught a glimpse of what was to come, he would still have found himself at the Midsummer's Madness bash held at Carl and Olivia's house in the summer of '84.

Ironically, it had been his ex-fiancé Hannah who had talked him into going. He loathed fancy dress parties, they were so bloody predictable; sadly deluded women grabbing the opportunity to let it all hang out, when clearly the kindest thing to do for all concerned was to keep it harnessed, corseted and well tucked in. Strutting their stuff as bunny girls, French maids and the like; togas were ever popular too and it was this same sorry bunch who insisted on wearing those God awful, baggy arsed leggings. What possessed them?

By way of compromise, they went to the party, but not in fancy dress. Carl sent a car, a vintage Rolls Royce driven by Lady Penelope's Parker, to pick them up. It was in full swing by the time they got there a little after eleven. Michael was pleasantly surprised – not a bunny girl in sight! The costumes were fantastic, even their dog, an evil looking bull terrier, had entered into the spirit of things; resplendent in red satin, it sashayed its way through the crowd in a sexy little basque with black suspenders and diamante accessories.

He got a drink from the bar and took up a stool with a view. There was a liberal sprinkling of Druids (no doubt celebrating the Summer Solstice); werewolves, a bumblebee, Robin (no sign of Batman) and a pair of Blues Brothers. He spotted The Incredible Hulk, Uncle Fester with Morticia, Charlie Chaplin, and standing beside him at the bar, leaning on his gnarled walking stick with a nappy type of affair wrapped around his skinny brown body, was a very convincing Gandhi. Michael grinned down at his bald, bespectacled head.

"Alright Mahatma?"

"My faith is brightest in the midst of impenetrable darkness," came the enigmatic reply.

All three Marx Brothers were there; Carl was Groucho

and he found out later that Harpo, the raincoat clad character in a curly wig and battered top hat, was Liv. There was even a horse and a pantomime cow mooching around, heads nodding and rear ends swaying in time to the dance music belting out from the most sophisticated sound system Michael had ever seen. He had to admit that done like this, fancy dress was great. He remembered being introduced to Harpo, who honked her horn in disapproval at his lack of costume and was gone, swallowed up by the heaving mass of merry revellers. He and Hannah didn't stay long; they felt out of place, and not only because of their clothes. They were clearly the only two people there not under the influence of certain mind altering drugs that, courtesy of the druids, were circulating quite freely; nothing too serious, but the air was heavy with the sweet smell of marijuana. Michael had no problem with recreational drugs and enjoyed the odd joint now and then, but Hannah was horrified and kept pestering him to leave. A row had ensued. He had tried persuading her to stay, pointing out it had been her idea to come in the first place, but when Darth Vader offered them a spliff, her tight lipped response of "*No thank you, I abhor the use of illegal substances,*" told him it was time to go. They passed Gandhi on their way out. He had obviously overheard their earlier exchange and murmured a helpful little proverb from The Great Soul himself, "*No one who has wisdom will ever touch opium, liquor or any intoxicants.*"

"*My point exactly!*" agreed Hannah with an air of vindication. Michael heard later that had they stayed to the end of the party, Hannah's solidarity with Mr Mahatma might have wavered. He had most definitely succumbed to some kind of intoxicant. The general consensus was to point an accusatory finger towards 'Portaloo Blue', the strongest home-grown marijuana known to mankind; named thus for its birthplace, a converted Portaloo at the bottom of the local dealer's 'herb garden', and the purpley blueish hue of its freaky looking buds. It was rumoured to have its roots in Hades. Those who'd partaken had been dropping like flies. He was found face down on the floor of the new guest suite; his fake tanned body leaving a perfect little imprint on the pale cream carpet; a sepia version of the white on black outline drawn by forensics in a murder investigation.

As Michael climbed into his bed that night, he was comfortable with his thoughts. It was hard to believe that three years had passed since that first meeting. Becoming entangled in the Vogels' lives had turned his own life upside down but at least he could say he had no regrets. Within minutes, he was fast asleep.

It's A Boy!!

Liv, however, was far from comfortable with her thoughts. She had taken another Valium over an hour ago but was still tossing and turning in her bed, immersed in the misery of 1975.

The marriage limped inexorably on and with the support of her family and close friends, she was getting through. Charlie starting school, however, seriously threatened to undermine her recovery. She had been beset with anxiety from the start and it took a while to settle him in, but settle in he did and before too long, left alone with her thoughts, she found herself going quietly mad.

She began taking classes; she tried Sociology, English and Creative writing. Sociology brought about a brief rekindling of her feminist spirit. She discovered that back in the sixties, far more girls than boys were passing the 11+. The powers that be, *'undoubtedly men'* insisted Liv's rabidly feminist tutor, were worried by the imbalance and decided to lower the pass mark for boys in order to redress this unfortunate situation. Liv was shocked. She was particularly incensed by this because she had narrowly missed a place at the county grammar herself. Although she had been placed in the A stream at her local secondary modern, it didn't alter the fact she hadn't received anything like a grammar school education. She'd left school at the age of fifteen without a qualification to her name; a fact that Carl never missed an opportunity to point out. Not that he had any qualifications himself; it simply amused him to see how much it bothered her. This flickering flame of feminism was soon extinguished and Sociology bit the dust. English had been her favourite subject at school and she loved reading, so she had been particularly excited by the prospect of her English and writing classes. She was doing really well but unfortunately she couldn't justify her studies to Carl. He kept asking her why she was doing it and found the concept of learning for learning's sake impossible to comprehend. What was the point? Where would it lead to? When she explained she was hoping to get an 'O' level and possibly even an 'A' level in English he scoffed and asked again *'what for?'* She was unable to articulate her desire to learn and his increasing irritation with the time she 'wasted' on homework led to her quitting both. Her spirit was weak and she didn't have the energy or the will to fight him.

She enrolled in an advanced driving course which was quite successful in that she did actually manage to pass the test, but she hadn't enjoyed the course as it was run by an even bigger chauvinist than Carl. Liv was the only female in the class and he hated her the minute he saw her *'wheels'*. An ex traffic cop, he was mightily aggrieved by her beautiful Mini. *'It's a Cooper "S" actually!'* Liv had smiled in reply when he had asked who owned the flashed up Mini Cooper. She loathed his pathetic macho jokes. *"So lads, remember that concentration is paramount – don't let your eyes wander from the road if you spot a gorgeous pair of legs in a mini skirt. I s'pose for the lady amongst us, you'd best not turn your head to see if the sales are still on."* The only reason she stayed the course was to give him one in the eye by passing; which she did in a satisfying *'Shove that up your exhaust pipe and choke on it!'* kind of way.

As her classes fell by the wayside and with depression threatening to engulf her, she suddenly became aware of a strange new phenomenon stirring deep within. She started noticing babies everywhere and during a shopping trip to Brent Cross, she found herself wandering around the baby department of John Lewis, picking up tiny booties and sighing wistfully. She had no idea that broodiness could be such a powerful force. Her maternal urge would not be denied and after much private soul searching she decided to broach the subject with Carl. She knew her decision was completely selfish and that she would be having this baby for herself, but her biological clock had been extremely convincing. Reasoning she was already tied to Carl because of Charlie and kidding herself a new baby might bring them closer together, she went ahead. Six months later she was pregnant, and the following July, Joe was born, three weeks before Charlie's sixth birthday.

Her new baby brought Liv much happiness and just as with Charlie, she'd enjoyed a wonderful period of post natal elation; but the marriage was a farce. After his initial excitement over the birth of his second son, Carl was away as much as ever. Liv knew for sure that he was up to his old tricks but felt she couldn't really blame him this time. The physical side of their marriage, apart from the brief interlude when they had been trying for Joe, had been dispatched once more to the doldrums, regaining its previous position as the number one cause for their domestic disharmony. She turned a blind eye to Carl's extra marital activities and tried to get on with her life, but worn down by the constant rows and fretting over the knowledge that her sons were growing up in an increasingly damaging environment, she'd reached breaking point. She had hoped that Carl would share her view that they should accept their marriage was over and begin working towards an amicable divorce. She had no way of knowing, at that stage, that the words amicable and divorce did not compute in Carl's mind and that she had as much chance of reaching her objective as landing on the moon.

Liv fumbled for her bedside clock. 1am – she climbed out of bed, crept downstairs, located and pocketed the cordless phone and tip-toed back up to her room. She knew it was late, but he'd said she could always call him whatever the time, and at this late hour, she was confident he'd be alone.

"Sorry Michael," she whispered, "It's Liv, did I wake you?"

"Only from the dead," he mumbled, checking his watch. "No, it's fine," he added as she started to apologise again. "What's up? Where are you?"

"I'm in bed," she whispered, "I've got Jim and Alison's phone from downstairs. How are you?"

"I'm fine, but what's up?" he asked again. "Why are you ringing – and why am I whispering?"

Liv chuckled softly. "Sorry Michael – I just can't sleep. I'm going nuts here – I've got all this stuff going on in my head and it won't shut up."

"What kind of stuff?" he asked.

"Oh you know – Carl stuff. Different scenes keep playing in my head like a mad video you can't switch off. I've been all over the place tonight. It's exhausting."

"Well change the video then," said Michael.

"Huh?"

"Play scenes from a different video. Play a funny one."

"Oh right," she whispered. "Good idea, thanks Michael… I'll give it a go… umm… do you want to hear my favourite joke? It saved me from a panic attack earlier."

"Go on then," sighed Michael, sensing her reluctance to get off the phone.

"Right," whispered Olivia from under the duvet. "So there's Lord Farquhar and his butler Waddle."

"Lord who?"

"Farquhar."

"Oh right."

"And his butler Waddle."

"Yep, got that – come on!"

"I'm trying!" she protested. "Anyway… so Lord Farquhar tells Waddle to run him a bath. Everything is prepared just the way he likes it, with a large brandy and a copy of The Financial Times on the side. He tells Waddle to wait outside for his call. As he settles down into the bath, he lets off an enormous underwater fart! Minutes later Waddle appears carrying a hot water bottle on a silver tray. Farquhar erupts yelling *'I said to wait outside 'til I called!'*

'But you did call sir!' said Waddle. *'You said'* ... (Liv dropped her voice down to a deep monotone)... *'WADDA-BOUDA-HOD-WADDABODDLE-WADDLE!'"*

Hearing Michael's laughter down the phone set her off too and she was guffawing away under the covers until a sharp knock at her door made her jump.

"You okay Liv?"

"Er... yes, sorry Al, I'm fine. Just having trouble sleeping."

"Is someone in there?"

"No, no, I'm just on the phone. Sorry if I woke you."

"Okay, just keep it down will you – Jim's got an early start tomorrow."

"Yeah, I'm really sorry." She heard Alison go back to bed. "Oh God," she whispered to Michael, "That's me in the doghouse – again! I'd better go."

"Okay," he whispered back, "and if you can't sleep, remember what I said – play a funny video. What about when we took Elizabeth to the vets? Stick that on!"

"Thanks, I will – sorry I woke you, go back to sleep."

"I'm gone, g'night."

"Night."

She stole back downstairs and returned the phone to its cradle. Back in bed she snuggled down, made a selection from her archives and pressed... 'PLAY'...

'ELIZABETH'
THE TALE OF THE BUTCHER'S BAG TAIL

The door opened and Michael was met by an extremely flustered Liv. She was wearing large, gauntlet type gardening gloves and a look of sheer panic on her face.

"Oh Michael – it's you, thank goodness! I've got a problem with Elizabeth – we might have to go to the vet."

"What's up?" asked Michael, but then as Elizabeth came in to view, his question was answered. Protruding from the rear end of the dog was a blue and white striped plastic tail. It was hanging just beneath the real tail which, Michael noted, was not wagging. He was not particularly fond of dogs, especially thugs like Elizabeth. He found himself fixed in its squinty eyed glare. The feeling was obviously mutual. "Er – so what do you want me to... I mean, have you tried to pull it out?" The dog growled and Michael took a step back. "What the hell is it anyway?"

"It's a carrier bag," the agitated Liv informed him, "from the butcher. It popped out when we were over the fields. He'd just had a poo and suddenly, there it was – like a bloody sail flapping in the wind as he ran along!"

"How d'you know it's from the butchers?" asked Michael, trying not to laugh.

"Because when I was putting the shopping away yesterday I realised I was a bag short. It was the chicken pieces and I thought I'd left it behind, but Elizabeth must have stolen it because that's definitely a butcher's bag, and the thing is, it's got bones and chicken bones can kill a dog and—"

"Whoa, calm down, don't worry, we'll take her to the vet. It's not that bad, she'll be alright," soothed Michael.

"No, you don't understand, it's really serious. I tried pulling it, you know thinking it would just slip out, but it's well and truly stuck."

"Hmmm, well how about I stand on the bag – and you walk her off on the lead." He looked down at Elizabeth, who was growling again, and then at his ankles. "No hang on, maybe *you* stand on it and *I'll* walk—"

"We can't do that," interrupted Liv, "supposing it's all tangled up with his innards. We might pull his stomach or intestines out too!"

"Jesus Christ!" Michael shuddered, "let's just get it to the vets eh? Let them sort it out."

As they walked towards Michael's car, Elizabeth started pulling to get to the grass verge.

"Sorry Michael but I think he needs a wee." She handed him the lead. "You take him, I forgot my purse. Won't be a sec." Liv dashed back into the house as Elizabeth dragged Michael up and down the verge in a frenzy of sniffing before taking up the classic '*dog peeing up a lamp-post*' position. Michael was perplexed, he may not have known a lot about dogs but he knew that lady dogs weren't supposed to do that.

"Liv," he said on her return, "she just cocked her leg."
"What?"

"Elizabeth, she cocked her leg like a dog – you know, like a man dog."

"Well that's because he is – kind of."

"He? I'm talking about Elizabeth."

"Yeah, I know, so am I! She's a he – well actually, he's not strictly a he or a she – he's been neutered, so he's neither." They got themselves into the car, Elizabeth sitting in the front passenger seat with Liv holding him still from behind.

"But why is he called Elizabeth for God's sake?" continued Michael.

"Oh, you don't want to know," replied Liv, "it's complicated…"

"Try me," said Michael as he picked his way through the traffic. "Looking at this lot, we've got plenty of time."

Liv sighed. "Well, it came about by accident really. The boys and I had always wanted a dog. Carl flatly refused saying that animals should be kept outside—"

"He's got a point there," said Michael as Elizabeth's rear end lifted and emitted a blast of wind that had the plastic tail a-quivering and Michael asphyxiating in one. "Liv! – do something will you! I can't drive in these conditions! Just get it to sit down, oh for fucks— GET OFF ME!"

Liv managed to regain control and continued with her story. "As I said, we were desperate for a dog – especially Charlie. He'd seen Oliver Twist and fallen in love with Bulls Eye."

"Bill Sykes' dog?"

"An English Bull Terrier," nodded Liv.

"Or as Billy Connelly would say, a shark on a leash!" added Michael ruefully as Elizabeth changed position and fixed him with a particularly malevolent eye. It was the pink one. The other one, the one in the patch, was alright

– but the pink one was positively evil. He tore his gaze back to the road ahead and tried to ignore the sights and sounds emanating from the front passenger compartment.

"Anyway, Carl had been quite taken with Bulls Eye too and after months of badgering, he finally relented and said we could have one. The boys were ecstatic. I didn't rush straight in – I did the sensible thing and went to the library to check out the breed. It didn't look good. Generally speaking, they made good pets in that they liked children and usually had a good temperament, but—"

"Yeah, there was always going to be a 'but'," said Michael, "go on."

"Un-neutered males had a tendency to view small mammals as prey."

"Oh dear."

"Exactly!" said Liv. She went on to explain that not only were there lots of cats in the neighbourhood, she was afraid it could view Joe as a small mammal too. Following advice from the vet, they opted for a female and booked one with a reputable breeder. The litter was due in about two weeks. The bed was bought, the collar and lead, the brushes and toys, and of course… the name was chosen. Joe had almost mastered it. "She was to be called Whizzapuff!" chuckled Liv. She tried to catch Michael's eye in his rear-view mirror. "Michael?"

"What?"

"Wasn't that sweet?"

"Yeah, very nice," said Michael as he caught sight of the dog – catching sight of the butcher's bag for the first time. "Liv! Sort it out for Christ's sake!" he yelled as Elizabeth began spinning round and around in ever *in*creasing circles.

"LIE DOWN!" bellowed Liv. The dog laid down. Liv smiled at Michael's surprised eyes in the mirror. "You just have to be firm," she informed him. The eyes in the mirror rolled upward.

"Go on," he prompted.

"Well, unfortunately, best laid plans and all that, the mum had six boys! We were faced with either waiting for the next litter, which was unthinkable – buying from an unknown breeder, pet shop or puppy farm, equally unthinkable – or accepting a boy."

"Unthinkable?" suggested Michael.

"Not completely," grinned Liv. "The vet said that as long as we had him castrated before his hormones kicked in, we would avoid any testosterone driven aggression."

"Hmmm really," muttered Michael, as he eyed his canine passenger, unconvinced.

"Not to mention all the other undesirable male dog traits."

"Like what?"

"I said not to mention them!" laughed Liv. "You know, scent sniffing, inappropriate leg cocking and worst of all —" she shuddered, "unsolicited humping. I don't really like male dogs. I had a bad experience when I was little. Our neighbour's dog attacked me and—"

"Hang on – so you bought him, had his little balls chopped off —" he thought for a moment, "— fair enough I s'pose, you had to go with the vet's advice, but why did you still call the poor sod Elizabeth?"

"Well, I did think about changing it, but I decided calling him Elizabeth would make him less intimidating to strangers. I mean most bull terriers are called Jaws or Meathead—"

"Yeah, I know a T-Bone."

"There you go! Plus of course, I loved the way Joe said '*Whizzapuff!*'"

"Ah hah! — Now we have it! Now we have the *real* reason, don't we?" Liv's red-faced denial cut no ice. "A shameful act of cruelty," declared Michael shaking his head. "I've a good mind to report you to the R.S.P.C.A. That's a double emasculation! And all because you liked the way your little boy said '*Whizzapuff!*'"

"It wasn't just me – Charlie liked it too," said Liv defensively. "It sounded like something from his favourite book – The BFG. Do you know it?"

"Only off by heart! It's my nephew's favourite book too… in fact, his *only* book."

"Thank God for Roald Dahl, that's all I can say," laughed Liv. "My two would never read a thing if it wasn't for him."

"Same with Joel – he comes over quite a lot and I swear that book is surgically attached! So remind me – it's the farting word isn't it?"

"Whizzpopper!" laughed Liv. "And being Roald Dahl, it's a fart with launch control and lift off. No wonder the kids love him, especially boys."

"I'll wait here shall I?" suggested Michael hopefully as they pulled up outside the surgery, but his worst fears were confirmed when Liv said he might be needed. There was a tried and tested system in place whereby he was given a sedative injection upon arrival and dispatched to the waiting room until it took effect. The nurse had put Liv's mind at rest, assuring her that Elizabeth's condition was quite commonplace. She explained that once the sedative kicked in, his muscles would relax and the offending appendage would be easily removed.

The room was packed. Michael, who knew nothing about animals never having owned so much as a hamster throughout his entire life, was fascinated by the weird and wonderful sights around him. A dumpy little dog waddled in with its matching owner in tow.

"It's true what they say then," whispered Michael.

"Shhhh!" came Liv's response. The newcomers sat down opposite them. The dog was cream with a curly tail and looked like a door had been slammed in its squashed up little face. Michael's eyebrows shot up as he took in four red boots attached to a black suspender belt around its middle. It was just an optical illusion and was, in fact, red crepe bandaged paws and a black harness.

"What's that?" he mouthed.

"A pug," whispered Liv.

"I meant the outfit!" he whispered back. "Nice! – Same lingerie as Elizabeth!"

"Shhhh!" hissed Liv again but Michael knew she was having trouble keeping a straight face. The time ticked by. He looked down at Elizabeth who looked back up at him with droopy bloodshot eyes.

"He's stoned!" chuckled Michael. "Look at him."

Everyone in the room, animals included, turned to

look at Elizabeth. Liv smothered a laugh and succumbed to a coughing fit that left her red faced and gasping. They were giggling like a couple of schoolchildren. The hushed atmosphere of the waiting room and the disapproving looks of their fellow occupants was fuelling their juvenile behaviour. Resolutely avoiding Michael's eyes and ignoring his nudges, she fixed her gaze on a rabies poster and attempted to regain her composure.

With Liv refusing to play, Michael once more cast his eye around the room. He noticed a strange phenomenon. Dogs, three in all, wearing headgear resembling inverted phonographs.

"HMV," whispered Michael.

"Huh?"

"His Master's Voice."

Liv shook her head.

"The record label? Little dog – old fashioned record player – oh never mind. What's wrong with them anyway?" he added. "Have they all got the same thing?"

"I'll tell you later – just be quiet."

Michael tried, he really did and when a new patient entered the room carrying a basket containing a cat, a cat in a hat (of the HMV variety), he did really well. He held his breath and counted to ten. It was the rabbit that broke the camel's back. Michael took one look at Thumper, his head nestled inside his little white trumpet, and started shaking with suppressed laughter. He did his best but was on the verge of spontaneous combustion before his laugh broke free. He apologised to the deeply offended rabbit owner and expressed his concern to the room in general that perhaps there was some kind of affliction in the animal world that had reached epidemic proportions.

Once the ice had been broken, the occupants of the waiting room turned out to be quite a cheery bunch. They went to great lengths to explain the purpose of the head collars and proudly showed Michael their pets' war wounds and the stitches that needed protection. Liv watched with amusement as Michael '*oohed*' and '*aahed*' accordingly.

"It's their instincts you see love," explained Mrs Rabbit. "If an animal has an injury they will try to lick the wound clean."

"Got you," said Michael.

"That's right," said Mrs Pug, keen to join in. "Trouble is, they keep licking away at their stitches and the wound opens up."

At that point, Elizabeth emitted a series of drunken howls that signified his sedation had peaked; time for the anal intrusion to begin! The vet appeared and it was all hands on deck. Michael was called upon to help Liv, the vet and the nurse, shovel him up from the waiting room floor and heave him onto the examination table next door. Declining all offers to watch, Michael made his excuses and left. Half an hour later, Liv emerged triumphant with a decidedly unsteady Elizabeth, *sans* butcher's bag, staggering about on the end of his lead. They made their way to the car.

"Come on fellah," encouraged Michael as Elizabeth struggled to get up after falling over for the umpteenth time. He felt really sorry for him and even warmed to him a little, especially when he heard him muttering under his breath as he stumbled along. Between them, they managed to get him into the car – this time lying prostrate on the back seat with Liv in the front.

"You big wuss!" laughed Liv. "The way you legged it out the door!"

"I just didn't fancy seeing his guts spilling out, thanks very much," said Michael. "What took so long anyway? I thought the nurse said it would be out in no time. You were in there at least half an hour."

"Oh it didn't take that long to get the bag out," said Liv cheerfully. "They took advantage of his doped up state and gave him a quick service first. Trimmed his nails, cleaned his ears, de-scaled his teeth, emptied his anal glands—"

"Emptied his what?? Urghhh!" he shuddered. "Animals – I just don't get it!"

Liv laughed at the look of disgust on Michael's face.

"Anyway," she continued, "by the time they'd finished all his bits and bobs, Elizabeth's muscles were well and truly relaxed. So much so, the bag just oozed out all by itself! How brilliant was that?"

"Absolutely marvellous!" agreed Michael, with more than a hint of sarcasm.

"And it was empty!"

"What was?"

"The butcher's bag – completely empty!"

"Well what did you expect? It had been through his entire digestive system – did you think it would pop out totally intact with the receipt still in the bag!"

"Well yes, sort of – not the receipt obviously you idiot, but I thought the chicken pieces might still be in there, stopping me from pulling it out."

"And you're calling *me* an idiot!"

"Yeah, well, I s'pose it was a bit stupid really – but anyway, the other good news is that raw chicken bones are actually *good* for them. The vet feeds chicken wings to his German Shepherds all the time. Bones are only dangerous when they're cooked because they become brittle and can splinter."

"Well I'm buggered!" said Michael, "it just gets better and better doesn't it!" Liv looked at him sideways and he grinned back at her. "Only joking – no honestly! I'm glad it's all turned out okay."

They drove along companionably, music playing in the front, Elizabeth snoring peacefully in the back and were almost home when the relaxed vibe was interrupted by an almighty hooting of an angry horn.

"What's up with him?" muttered Michael as he sounded his horn in response.

"WHAT'S UP WITH YOU?" he yelled in the direction of the horn blower.

Liv looked round and caught sight of the red-faced driver alongside them. Her heart sank – it was like being in the car with Carl. What was it with men? Why did the slightest altercation have to turn into all-out war? She hated outbursts of aggression and hoped she was not about to get caught up in an ugly road rage incident.

"He thinks you cut him up on the roundabout—" she began.

"I didn't cut *him* up – he cut *me* up, the tosser!" snapped Michael. "Did you see that? He's giving *ME* the finger!" Gesticulating wildly, he stamped on the accelerator and set off in hot pursuit.

"Michael please!" tried Liv but Michael didn't hear. Liv didn't exist. It was just him and the other driver. Liv sank down in her seat; she'd thought Michael was different, but here he was, driving like a lunatic, hell-bent on catching his man. The speeding cars were side by side and Liv face to face with the foe. They screeched to a halt at the next red light. Michael was out of the car like a shot, so was his adversary; four foot six of fighting fury! Michael looked down at him, completely nonplussed. He lifted his arms and shrugged his shoulders; his facial expression of *'what am I supposed to do here!'* was a picture. The mighty midget was hopping around, brandishing his fists yelling 'Let's have it! – come on big boy! – D'ya want some!' Michael shook his head in disbelief as he held his would be opponent at arm's length. The little man wrenched himself free, ran up to Michael's car and gave it an almighty great kick. Breathing heavily, he looked up at Michael expectantly. Michael looked from him to the car, then back to him, took aim – and booted the car too! The pair of them started to laugh, as did the onlookers from the traffic that had built up around them. She tried to admonish him when he got back in the car but they just couldn't stop laughing.

"Put 'em up – put 'em up!"

"Fight you with one arm behind my back!"

"Seriously though, what *is* it with you lot?" said Liv. "You don't see women behaving like that."

49

"I don't know so much, some younger ones do. I've had a few run-ins with girl drivers. Some of them are just like blokes. In fact, I've heard you're a bit blokey when you get behind the wheel. Don't tell me you've never lost your rag on the road because I won't believe you."

"I s'pose I have at times. I can't stand rude impatient drivers, nearly always men I might add. They're too quick to flash their lights or blast their horns. I had one the other day – it was a black cab as it happens." She recounted the tale of her journey home after dropping the boys off to school. There had been lots of parked cars on either side of the road and she could see him in his cab way up ahead, lights full on, coming in her direction. There was plenty of room for them to have manoeuvred around each other, but no – he drove straight up, stopped right in front of her and started hooting and a-hollering for her to reverse back out of his way.

"I'm guessing you didn't?" grinned Michael.

"Too right I didn't – but I didn't hoot and holler back. You see, this is where we differ – being a woman, I didn't get involved in an ugly slanging match – I just sat there. The thing was, I had all the time in the world, whereas he was obviously in a tearing hurry."

"Yeah, probably trying to start work, poor sod."

"Poor sod my arse!" scoffed Liv. "He shouldn't have been so rude. Anyway, I locked my doors and sat tight. After about five minutes of ranting and raving, he gave up. He walked back to his cab, reversed back up to the end of the road and drove off in the other direction."

"What? Without you so much as opening your mouth?" said Michael. "Not a single word?"

"Ah – now I didn't say that did I? I did say a few things, of course I did, but I just said them quietly and pleasantly. Every time he came up to my car, I opened the window a touch and replied to the tirade of abuse he was hurling at me."

"Things like…?"

"Well, things like '*Oh dear, somebody got out of bed the wrong side this morning*', and '*Do you know… your face is actually purple! I should calm down if I were you!*'"

"Yeah, I thought as much. Now you see in my opinion that's worse, *much* worse than the way blokes deal with things. There's a certain honesty in our actions, whereas you females—" he shook his head, "you're just so – so –" he was stuck for words. "I tell you what, you were lucky he didn't smash your window and haul your sorry arse straight out of there!"

"I thought he might at one point!" laughed Liv. "I'd said, '*Just because you're an impotent little man, there's no need to take it out on me.*' I thought his head was going to explode!"

"You should be careful Liv, you might come unstuck one day," warned Michael. "There's some right nutters out there – you could end up getting hurt."

"I never get out of the car; I always keep my doors locked. How could I get hurt?"

"Hmmm… well put it this way, if I'd been that cab driver, I'd have ripped your door off with my bare hands if necessary!"

They drew up outside Liv's house.

"I'd better get him inside," said Liv looking back at

Elizabeth. "Thanks so much Michael, I don't know what I'd have done."

"That's alright mate – it was a pleasure. No really," he added, seeing her dubious expression. "I've had a great time."

"Me too," laughed Liv. "Me too!"

Michael's suggestion had worked – long before Elizabeth parted company with the butcher's bag, Liv had joined Michael in the sleepy land of nod.

Deputy Dog's Boarding Kennels

8th August 1987

Hello again! You wait months for a letter then get two in as many days! This is part of my new strategy. Instead of sending letters the size of a novel once in a blue moon, it's going to be little and often from now on. If something extraordinary happens I'm going to let you know straight away. Well, to say that something extraordinary happened tonight is putting it mildly. Are you sitting comfortably? Then I'll begin...

Actually, before I begin, I'll have to introduce you to George because he's the star of the show! As you know, I've taken on an extra job collecting and delivering cats for the new cattery that's opened up in the village. The reason it came about was because George (Sasha and Maurice's regular driver) wants to leave. He's never really been happy with the job and they'd had a hell of a time persuading him to take it on in the first place. He's a bit of a rough diamond but his credentials were top class and they were sure he was 'their man', so to speak. I should imagine that was half the trouble! I wish I'd been there at the interview when he'd first clapped eyes on Sasha and Maurice. Ex Royal Navy and latterly ex London Fire Brigade, I doubt he'd encountered anything quite like them before. To him, they were just one step away from Danny La Rue! He's not exactly homophobic or anything but let's just say he's not terribly in touch with his feminine side!

Apparently his wife had applied on his behalf and was insisting he gave it a go. He was newly retired and driving her mad at home. Initially it had all gone well. He was reliable, punctual, trustworthy and knew London like the back of his hand. After a while, George came to realise that Sasha and Maurice were a couple just like any other, and certainly posed him no threat. Much to everyone's surprise, he began to relax about the whole gay thing. I think that given his background, S & M saw him as a little triumph in their ongoing quest for acceptance. How sad then, and how ironic that the reason George wants to quit is that he cannot cope with the predominantly gay clientele. Everyone will assume it's because George has a problem with gays, but it has nothing to do with their sexual persuasion, as I said, he's not really like that. The thing that's driven him mad is the way nearly all of the clients, straight or gay, are about their cats - the way they fuss and fawn over their 'ickle babies'!

He has a point. I mean, I've been doing his job, and you wouldn't believe what some of these cat clients are like. They send postcards addressed to their cats and apparently sometimes, they ring up and ask for the phone to be put to their cat's ear so they can say hello! I can see how this would all start to wear a bit thin, especially for someone like George who's a bit of a geezer - you know, a real man's man.

In the beginning, I accompanied George on his rounds, familiarising myself with the routes and meeting many of the clients and their cats. During the first week we picked up a couple of cats from a lady who'd sent them in with individual portions of Mediterranean prawns, smoked salmon and bloody venison would you believe! When we got back into the van George went ballistic!

" Smoked Salmon? Mediterranean prawns! MEDITERRANEAN FUCKIN' PRAWNS!! - Me and the missus love a Mediterranean prawn - but do we 'ave 'em? Do we bollocks! You know why? 'Cos we can't fuckin' afford 'em - that's why! 'Scuse my French darlin' but it makes me puke!"

I tried to get him to understand that these cats are like their babies - their substitute babies - but I didn't get very far! He was off again, ranting and raving...

" Babies? But they're not babies are they? At the end of the day, they're cats! - they're just fuckin' cats! All this mamby pambying, it's doing my 'ead in – and how comes so many of 'em are gay, eh? Answer me that! It goes against the law of averages to 'ave so many." I had to agree that there were quite a lot and suggested that maybe it was because gay couples had a greater need for substitute babies. I explained that for them, it was like handing over their children and asked him to try to make allowances. He eventually calmed down and promised to do his best to hold on, at least until I was up and running, but added ominously he didn't know how much longer he could last. Prophetic words! Tonight saw poor George's patience finally snap!

After a couple of weeks shadowing George, I had progressed to driving the van myself. The jobs were shared between the two of us and we each had our designated areas. To save him driving all the way out to the cattery, we chose a convenient rendezvous spot where I would either hand over cats to be delivered or receive cats to be taken back to the cattery for boarding. He would head off to central London, leaving me to take care of clients closer to home. As you can imagine, George, an ex-serviceman, ran the show with military precision. I had to get used to his strange vernacular, which was all 'ETA's' and phonetic alphabet stuff – you know F – Foxtrot, T – Tango. I drove him to distraction with my version, which was along the lines of O for Octopus and E for Elephant! My grasp of the 24 hour clock wasn't much better either – but at least I tried! Anyway, George was much happier once he was out of the pink cat mobile and driving his own car. Things were going well – until tonight!

We met at the appointed place and the appointed time (well, a bit late obviously – my timekeeping habits have not improved!). I handed over George's baskets along with the paperwork and we went on our merry way. Half an hour later, I was in a phone box in north London, phoning the cattery.

Me: Hello Sasha? It's Liv – has George phoned in yet?

Sasha: No?

Me: (trying not to laugh) He will be! I've got the wrong cats!

Sasha: WHAT!!!

Me: I've got the wrong cats.
           I got to The Henderson's.
           We went through the normal
           drill - you know, checked our
           emergency   escape   routes,
           gently   removed   the   basket
           rod and stood well back. But
           when the lid opened - out
           strolled Mork and Mindy!

Sasha: (sounding faint) Oh dear God!
           That means George is taking
           Beelzebub to - Oh sweet
           Jesus!... Alastair!

Me: Exactly! You'd better ring and
           warn them - (sound of phone
           ringing in the background)

Sasha: (decidedly hysterical) Jesus
           Christ! Hang on - the other
           phone's ringing. It might be
           George.

It WAS George. Sasha left me hanging
on and I could hear George yelling down
the phone. It sounded like he was on
loudspeaker.

George: There's been a cock up.
              Where's FiFi and FooFoo?

Sasha: (confused) Who?

George: FiFi and fuckin' FooFoo - the
              poofter's cats.

Sasha: (his voice breaking) George
              - you haven't opened the
              basket have you?

George had! Sasha lost the will to live
and passed the phone to Maurice.

Maurice: George, it's Maurice.
               What's happened?

George: I'll tell you what's 'appened.
              A bleedin' great airball with
              teeth's come flyin' out of its
              basket, ripped into matie 'ere
              then shot up the chimney,
              that's what's fuckin' 'appened!
              I suggest you get some
              reinforcements down 'ere
              pronto.

Maurice: Is Alistair alright?

George: Take a wild guess.

There was a strange whimpering sound in the background.

Maurice: What's happening now?

George: He's 'avin' an attack of the vapours. He's got blood 'n' soot all over his shag pile and a Tasmanian Devil stuck up his flue!

So there you go - just another day's work in the employ of Mrs Slocombe's Pussies Hotel.

Will write again soon,

Love as always from dear Old Blighty
x x x

Foghorn Leghorn

Liv finished her letter to Clare and looked at her watch. It was almost time for Michael's call. She nipped downstairs and checked with Jim before taking the phone back up to her room. Right on cue, it began to ring.

"Hi – just made it!" she said breathlessly as she threw herself on the bed.

"Been out with Nosebag again?" asked Michael, "you sound knackered."

"No…" she laughed, "I was just running up the stairs with the phone when you rang. How are you?"

"Good thanks, really busy this evening – it's going well. How about you?"

"No, not so good. Major disaster tonight – George has quit!"

"Uh oh! Can't say I'm surprised though, it was only a matter of time. What happened?"

Liv explained the circumstances leading up to George's resignation. The back of her van had been stuffed full of baskets and she'd been flustered by George's huffing and puffing over her late arrival. During the rushed exchange, a mix-up had occurred between two covered baskets that were used to transport nervous or vicious cats. Liv's mistake was directly responsible for unleashing mayhem in Maida Vale as 'Boo-Boo', aka Beelzebub, was released into the open arms of the unsuspecting Alistair. Everyone had rushed to the scene of the crime. Once his precious puffballs were back in his arms, Alistair allowed himself to be comforted by his dear friends, Sasha and Maurice. This friendship turned out to be extremely fortunate; Alistair just happened to be a lawyer and he had made it abundantly clear he would have sued the pants off them otherwise. Liv and George left them to their cosseting and set about the task of retrieving an extremely pissed off 'Boo-Boo' from his bolthole. Three hours later they emerged from Alistair's previously pristine apartment looking like members of an Al Jolson chorus line.

"Christ!" said Michael, "Talk about comedy capers!"

"I know…" groaned Liv.

"You must be popular – have they sacked you?"

"They can't afford to, what with George quitting and everything. To be honest, they were quite nice about it really."

"Was it definitely your fault?"

"Afraid so," she said dismally.

"So it's a fair cop then."

"I've offered to pay for the damage to Alistair's flat. I hope I get my divorce settlement soon 'cos if they take it out of my wages, I'll be working for them until I'm about seventy-two!" came the glum reply.

"Don't worry mate, the court hearing's less than a month away now – nearly there – you'll be able to put all this behind you and get on with your life."

"I don't even know if I'm capable anymore," sighed Liv heavily. "I'm a walking disaster. No wonder Jim calls me Calamity Jane all the time. I'm worse than Calamity Jane! I'm like a cartoon character. I'm…I'm like—"

"Daffy Duck?"

"No, more like Leghorn Foghorn."

"It's Foghorn Leghorn, dummy – and no, that's me!" laughed Michael, and giving his best rooster impersonation he boomed, "AND I'M A'STANDIN HERE… LOOKING AT YOU, I SAY, LOOKING AT YOU BOY… AND SCRATCHIN MA HEAD!"

"Don't!" wailed Liv, "That makes me the little critter that causes all the grief then! It's not funny Michael – I just blunder through life lurching from one catastrophe to the next. This isn't the real me you know," she added, her voice breaking, "I wasn't always like this."

"I know that Liv, you don't have to keep telling me," said Michael gently, "stop beating yourself up. Look, you're under so much pressure and it's been like this for I don't know how long – it's bound to have taken its toll." He knew she was crying now and unable to speak. "Come on mate," he urged, "where's your Dunkirk spirit? I wouldn't want you beside me in the trenches, you big Jessie."

"Hang on—" came Liv's choked response. Michael heard the sound of some serious nose blowing going on and started to laugh. It never failed to surprise him how so much noise could come from a nose so small. It sounded like the QEII was coming in to dock.

"Christ! Thar she blows!" he laughed. "You were right."

"Huh?"

"You *are* Foghorn Leghorn!"

Flora's Story

By the time they said their goodbyes, Liv's flagging spirits had been revived. It never ceased to amaze her how Michael was able to lift her from the depths of despair and in no time at all, have her smiling again. The teacher responsible for an early school report had shown great insight when she had written "Olivia has a sunny disposition." Her default position was most definitely sunny side up but recent years had seen her engaged in an epic struggle to keep that sunny disposition, when all about her were losing theirs.

Her attempt in 1981 to persuade Carl to at least consider the possibility of divorce had been an abject failure. History had indeed repeated itself and faced with Carl's emotional collapse, his pleas for forgiveness and promises of yet another fresh start, Liv had reluctantly agreed to try again. As in 1975, Carl had decided the fresh start should take place in a fresh environment and with this in mind he had taken her to see a house he had decided to buy. Fortunes had been spent renovating and extending the property before they took up residence later that year.

It was during their move that Carl had discovered a box of personal effects belonging to his late mother Flora. The box had been gathering dust in their attic and unbeknown to Carl, contained a ticking time bomb – a bundle of papers relating to Joseph, his estranged father. Carl rarely spoke of his past and the little that Liv knew of his family history had come directly from Flora. Had this not been the case, given Carl's tendency to embellish the truth, Liv may well have dismissed the whole bizarre story.

She had been about sixteen when she first heard snippets of information relating to Carl's father; how his brutality towards both his wife and child had driven Flora to flee her native Austria with just her son and a bag of jewellery to her name. It had been difficult for Liv to piece together the story mainly because of Carl's refusal to talk about it and his reluctance to spend much time at home. He and his mother were living in an enormous old house that belonged to a middle aged widower and his invalid mother. Flora was their cook/housekeeper and she and Carl had their own rooms within the house. They had lived there for about ten years and the arrangement had suited both parties well, apart from the fact that Carl hated it there. His description of Mr Warwick and the mad old lady upstairs sounded like something straight out of a Brontë novel.

Liv had been extremely nervous the first time Carl had taken her there to meet his mother. The atmosphere in the gloomy old house had been dark and foreboding. Heeding Carl's warning not to make a sound, she had tip-toed along behind him, casting fearful looks over her shoulder as they made their way down the dark oak panelled corridor towards what he mockingly referred to as the servant quarters. Liv would never forget her first sighting of Flora and whenever she thought of her, this was the image that came to mind, warming her heart and making her smile. She had come bustling out of her kitchen and it was like the shutters had opened letting the sunshine in. Short and wide with rosy cheeks and a beaming smile, her dark hair drawn up into a dishevelled bun, she was wearing a crisp white pinafore over her floral dress and a liberal dusting of flour. She reminded Liv of a Russian nesting doll. Radiating warmth, she had welcomed Liv immediately, her plump arms drawing her into her ample bosom that would shake up and down as she laughed. Liv soon learned that Flora laughed a lot!

Carl spent many hours in the garage to the side of the house tinkering with the engine of his beloved MG. It was during these times that Liv would sit with Flora in her wonderful kitchen, the hub of the house from where mouth-watering smells would emanate, wafting through the rooms and stimulating the senses in the most delightful way. According to Flora, Liv was painfully thin; something that Flora had been determined to remedy. She would present Liv with all kinds of continental delights both sweet and savoury, from schnitzels and goulashes to delicious pastries and cakes that were truly to die for. Each plate was laid in front of her with an enthusiastic

"Essen essen!" … EAT EAT! *"Du hast kein fett!"* … YOU HAVE NO FAT! Flora's sense of fun had come to the fore during these little tastings. She would set a dish down in front of Liv and get her to guess what she was eating. Liv soon learnt to be suspicious of anything cooked in breadcrumbs. Flora would shake with laughter, tears streaming down her face at Liv's horrified reaction when she revealed the tasty little morsels she had just eaten were sweetbreads or calves' brains.

In the beginning, their conversation had been somewhat limited due to the fact that neither could speak the other's language. Liv had only a little schoolgirl French and absolutely no German and although Flora had been living in the UK for years, her English had not really progressed much further than the basics. She spoke German at home with Carl, there was very little conversation between herself and her employer and no one could understand mad old Mrs Warwick whatever their language. She had no friends in England and only visited her sister, where naturally, they spoke in their native tongue. She had been able to make herself understood whilst shopping and that was all that was needed to get by.

As time went on their friendship had blossomed and as Flora's English improved, so did their conversation. Gradually Flora began to open up a little, with revelations here and there from her past. Liv had looked forward to her time spent in the kitchen where she would beg Flora to tell her more. It had been hard work getting her to talk, especially about the war. Liv had always been fascinated by the Second World War; her father had served in the Royal Navy, her mother the Land Army, and as a child, Liv would question them endlessly about their wartime experiences. When she realised Flora had been living in Austria when Hitler invaded she was enthralled. She was to be sorely disappointed however, as Flora would not be drawn on the matter. All she would say was she should have left Austria with her sister in 1935, and that as bad as the Nazis were, they were nothing compared to the Russians.

Liv had more luck persuading her to talk about when Carl was a little boy. She learned that when he was born, his father Joseph had been insanely jealous of her precious *liebchen* and resented her profound love for him. She had met Carl's father during the aftermath of the war. Following Yugoslavia's surrender in 1941 Joseph had joined the Yugoslav Resistance Movement. Just before the war ended he had been captured and sent to a concentration camp situated in Austria. Liberated by the Americans in 1945 Joseph joined the legions of displaced people in Vienna. Flora took pity on him when he collapsed beside her whilst queuing for bread; he was in a bad way. She helped prop him up against a wall and rejoined the queue; she returned with bread and water and stayed with him until he had regained enough strength to make it to her apartment. She nursed him back to health and by 1946 they were married. Joseph had nothing to go back to in Yugoslavia; his family had been wiped out and he had lost everything during the bombing of Belgrade by the Luftwaffe.

Flora had been 45 years old when she discovered she was pregnant; she had assumed she would never have children and felt Carl was a miracle – a gift from God. Already a heavy drinker, following the birth of their son, Joseph spent more and more time in the local bars. He became violent and abusive and for the next five years Flora did her best to protect her child from his alcohol fuelled rages. He regularly smashed up their home and she would be forced to lock herself and Carl in a bedroom until he either passed out or went back into town. His violence was escalating. Irritated by Carl's pet canary's singing, his hair-trigger temper erupted; he hurled the cage against the wall, reached in and crushed the tiny bird, then threw it at Carl's feet.

The final straw came when he staggered in drunk one day, dragged the five year old Carl from the apartment and sat him on the handlebars of his bike. Ignoring Flora's pleas he rode off veering all over the road that led into town. Careering down a steep hill the bike gained momentum and Joseph lost control, crashing into a fountain in the town square. Tending her son's injuries that day, she knew that for his sake, they had to leave.

Liv had sat spellbound as Flora explained the carefully constructed plan that led to their escape from Austria. Without the drunken Joseph suspecting a thing, she had managed to negotiate a deal, selling her apartment and its entire contents to a wealthy jeweller, the brother-in-law of a sympathetic neighbour who knew of their plight. Accepting payment in kind, she had signed everything over to him on the proviso he would delay taking ownership until she was safely out of the country.

In the weeks leading up to their departure, Flora had

suffered many a sleepless night as she imagined the scene when Joseph finally discovered what she had done. As she boarded the train she had been terrified that he would suddenly appear and drag them from the carriage. Her heart had been in her mouth as she sat waiting for the train to leave, expecting at any moment to see his face appear at the window. This same fear had gripped her each time they pulled into a station and Liv could picture her, the young Carl in her arms, cowering down out of sight lest Joseph should be there waiting for them, ready to force them from the train. Flora told of her sense of relief at the growing distance between them, as hour by hour the train chugged its way across Europe. She described her elation as they crossed the English Channel. Hitler had not managed to cross that channel – and neither would he.

They moved in with Flora's sister who had fled to England before the outbreak of war. Their mother was Jewish and when Hitler came to power in 1933 the family had become increasingly concerned about the growing Nazi movement in Germany. By 1935 the writing was on the wall and amid terrifying rumours of widespread anti-Semitism raging across the border, the family made plans to leave. When Liv asked why Flora had risked her life by staying – there had been more shocks in store.

Joseph was Flora's second husband. In 1923, when she was just seventeen, Flora had married Hugo, a young officer in the Austrian Army. Although childless, it had been a good marriage and remained so until the day in 1938 when Hitler marched his storm troopers across the border and The Anschluss was declared. Flora told of the quiet invasion that had torn their lives apart. The Austrian Army was absorbed into the Wehrmacht and Hugo found himself a reluctant member of The Third Reich. Flora had shown Liv a photograph of the handsome Hugo in his SS uniform. Sadly, his reluctance had been short-lived and embracing his superior Aryan heritage, he took steps to avoid the ignominy of a half Jewish wife. He declared their union untenable and filed for divorce. By this time it was impossible to leave the country and Flora was left to survive the war years alone. In recognition of their long marriage, Hugo had provided her with a small apartment on the outskirts of Vienna and a set of false papers hiding her Jewish heritage. She never saw him again.

It was an amazing story, made more so by Flora's refusal to allow her traumatic past to affect her natural *joie de vivre*. After she died, Liv wept over the loss of her. She was an incredibly strong woman, with a wonderful sense of fun and a huge capacity for love; Liv felt privileged to have known her. The boys would have adored her and Liv could only begin to imagine how much she would have loved them. How sad she had been denied that, dying before her time from a disease that had taken her in the most distressing way. Her life had been one of disillusionment, suffering and pain; but not according to Flora. She had never moaned about her lot and had managed to keep smiling no matter what life had thrown at her along the way.

Liv's favourite memory of Flora was the day she had invited Liv to choose a piece from what remained of the collection of jewellery from Austria. Flora had chuckled when Liv picked out a delicate gold pendant and chain. The pendant was a disc in two halves engraved with seemingly random lines and squiggles that when the discs were spinning came together to form letters. Liv had seen a similar pendant that spelt out 'I LOVE YOU'.

Flora's mirth was building as Liv blew on the discs and puzzled over the German words.

"It doesn't say 'I love you' does it?"

Flora snorted from behind the hanky she held to her face, mopping up the tears of laughter rolling down her chubby cheeks.

"Nein!" she gasped, shoulders shaking, bosom heaving. Liv spun the discs with her finger.

"Is it an old German proverb?" she asked, wondering what on earth Flora had found so amusing. By now Flora couldn't speak. She was shaking her head, holding her sides and flapping the hanky about. Liv blew on the discs again and began spelling out the letters.

"L… E… C… K… M… E…"… then as she hesitantly read the words out loud, Flora almost fell off her chair laughing. "Leck mein arsch… LECK MEIN ARSCH???" The penny began to drop. She looked incredulously into Flora's squinty little eyes – surely not!! "Is it… does it…??" Flora's chair clattered to the floor as she fled the room lifting her skirts and pulling down her bloomers as she ran for the loo. Another second or so and she would have been mopping up more than just tears!

Although Liv understood Carl's natural curiosity about his father, she was concerned by his desire to find out if he was still alive and utterly appalled by his decision to try and track him down. She begged him to reconsider, pointing out that the circumstances surrounding their separation some twenty-five years before did not augur well for a happy outcome. She implored him to think of his poor mother who would be turning in her grave if she had known of his intention to trace the man she had fled her homeland to escape.

Kylie

Mindful of the necessity to keep his relationship with Liv on an even keel, Carl had agreed to give up his quest. He'd admitted, somewhat ruefully, that if he'd been successful, he didn't know whether he'd have embraced his long lost father or knocked him out. Liv had been delighted by Carl's change of heart but she should have known better. Once Carl made his mind up about something, nothing would stand in his way. He had merely been paying her lip-service; far from abandoning his mission, he had simply gone underground. He'd launched a covert operation, vowing that if Joseph was still out there, he was going to hunt him down. He'd tried imagining coming face to face with his father and had realised that at least one part of his declaration to Liv had been true; he had absolutely no idea what his reaction would be, but he was determined to see it through.

Blissfully unaware of Carl's ongoing search for his father, Liv had thrown herself into the business of getting their new home just as she wanted it and things had been going well. Charlie had settled happily into his new school and Joe was attending the attached nursery three mornings a week. They'd celebrated his fourth birthday by inviting everyone over for a huge garden and pool party complete with bouncy castles, an enormous paddling pool and carousel rides for the little ones. Carl had been in his element behind the barbeque and the day had been a resounding success. Liv's friends and family had been relieved to see her looking so happy. It seemed that the trials and tribulations of the past were finally behind them.

Unfortunately, Joe starting school in September had threatened to undermine this happy state of affairs. He had been looking forward to joining his brother at 'big school' and took the step up from nursery to primary school in his stride. The same could not be said for Liv however, and reminiscent of when Charlie had started school, she was lost. In a bid to keep her demons at bay she had joined the legion of volunteer mums helping out at the school. Unfortunately listening to the children read a couple of times a week and the occasional spot of fundraising had not been enough to keep her mind occupied and before long, Liv had been battling a new wave of melancholy. All-pervading, it had threatened to suck the life right out of her. Since moving to the new house, Carl had insisted they kept up with the Joneses and had employed a cleaner and a gardener. Once she had dropped the boys off to school, the days stretched endlessly and pointlessly ahead; she had absolutely nothing to do. Her suggestion of looking for a part-time job had been dismissed out of hand by Carl, who was of the opinion that working wives were an indication that the husband was incapable of providing for his family.

Aware of the need to keep herself busy she had made various attempts to fill her days with some of the distractions open to 'women of leisure' at that time. She frequented various hairdressing, nail, and beauty salons, held coffee mornings, did lunch and shopped with the best of them, accompanied as always by her depression; it had padded along beside her like Winston Churchill's black dog and worryingly, there had been a new dimension to it; a running commentary inside her head, a persistent voice exhorting her to '*snap out of it*', '*count your blessings*', '*look at your wonderful sons – your beautiful home*'. She had feared for her sanity. '*I should be so lucky: lucky, lucky, lucky*', the voice would sing, like a demented Kylie. On and on it would go apart from a brief respite now and then when Carl's voice would fill her head singing a different song; that bloody tune he found so funny but she had found so hurtful; '*Busy doing nothing, working the whole day through, trying to find lots of things not to do!*' Ever since hearing it on one of the boys' videos, Carl had decided it was her signature tune.

Realising she needed something less frivolous to occupy her time, she had decided to join a new gym that had opened in town. She'd really enjoyed it and had felt herself getting stronger both physically and mentally. It was around this time she had been contacted by The Paddington Women's Workshop, a lady called George (?) offering her a place in a bongos class that was due to start shortly. She had been on their waiting list for so long, she had forgotten all about it. She had seen their flyer on the notice board of her local library and in a moment of madness, had called, only to find the classes were full. Thrilled at this unexpected turn of events, she had accepted the offer and assured George she would be there the following week. Luckily she had decided from the outset not to mention it to anyone – just as well because the whole thing crashed on take-off.

She arrived late and found the reception area empty. There was a lot of noise coming from the hall to the right, so she nervously followed the sound and peeked through a small porthole window in the door. 'Oh my God!' she mouthed silently as her eyes scanned the room, taking in a sight that truly was one to behold. There were at least a dozen women sitting cross legged in a circle with a great behemoth of a woman in the middle, thumping a pair of what looked like toy bongos wedged between her ample thighs. There was so much noise – and not only from George (Liv decided she had to be George!) but from the rest of the group too, who obviously knew each other well, judging by the uproarious laughter, good natured shoves and slapping of thighs that was going on. Some were brightly coloured, with psychedelic leggings and matching turbans, lots had spiky hair, improbable shades of orange and maroon, whilst others were clad in flowing skirts or dungarees.

To Liv's horror, George, who was of the dungaree variety, suddenly turned and spotted her at the window. Liv backed away from the door just in time as George came crashing through, the 'toy' bongos peeping out from under her impressive arm. She grabbed Liv's hand and gave it a hearty shake, booming "You must be Olivia – wondered where you'd got to – had to start without you I'm afraid – not too late though – in you come!" As Liv took in

*the short back and sides, the whiff of Brut 'Splash it all Over',
the tache and the hair on her chinny chin chin, she knew this was
another fine mess she had gotten herself into. So she lied, lied her
head off, denying any knowledge of Olivia, workshops, with or
without bongos, and babbling something about being lost, wrenched
her arm free and fled!*

She had driven home, cursing her stupidity. The
clue had been there all along; The Paddington Women's
Workshop for God's sake! Still, at least no one, especially
Carl, knew anything of this latest fiasco. With her radio
blaring she'd driven through the streets of London in a
highly agitated state. "Oh fuck off Kylie!" she'd snarled,
hitting the off button and halting '*I Should Be So Lucky*' in
its tracks. The ferocity of her outburst towards the tiny
antipodean made her laugh, and as the memory of the
evening's events had washed over her, she'd found herself
laughing so much, she had been forced to pull over,
completely unable to drive.

Undeterred by this minor setback, she had thrown
herself into her training regime at the gym. She'd made
friends with quite a few of the regulars and had been
intrigued to discover that one of their group was a
marriage guidance counsellor. Something of an agony
aunt herself, she'd found herself drawn towards this
quiet, unassuming lady, shadowing her around the gym
and asking as many questions as gym etiquette would
allow. Unfortunately, Liv's quest for knowledge had
taken over and as she bore down on her quarry for the
fourth time that morning, the ever patient Catherine had
suggested they met up in the bar later where Liv could

question away to her heart's content. Liv had taken her up on this kind offer and as she left the gym that afternoon her destiny had been clear. She was going to become a Marriage Guidance Counsellor!

1986…

Grumpy Harpo

Nearly two years had passed since their first, somewhat inauspicious encounter, and when he saw Olivia's car parked on the driveway, Michael found he was looking forward to meeting her properly at last. She had been dressed up as Harpo Marx the last time he had seen her, totally trollied and dancing around honking her horn merrily in time to the music.

"Olivia isn't it?" He was a bit disappointed. *'Not all that really – pretty girl but nothing special'*. He couldn't see what all the fuss was about. Since becoming embroiled in the Carl/Olivia situation it seemed that all he'd heard for months on end was Liv, Liv, Liv. He'd heard through the grapevine she was back and sure enough here she was; looking decidedly unfriendly and a bit pissed off.

"Sorry, do I know you?"

Michael grinned apologetically. "Er no, I s'pose not really – but we have met." He stuck out his hand, "I'm Michael, Carl's trainer."

Slightly taken aback, Liv found herself accepting Michael's friendly handshake. "Oh right, well, I'm sorry but Carl's not here so…"

"I was supposed to meet him here at two?"

"Really?" she hesitated for a moment, clearly puzzled. She and Carl were separated now, so why were they meeting here? He hadn't even had the decency to let her know. "Well… I suppose you'd better come in." He followed her into the hall and placed his training bag down by the front door. There was an uncomfortable silence. She checked her watch, it was quarter to two. She was starting to fizz; on top of everything else, he was fifteen minutes early! She couldn't stand people being early; it clashed with her tendency to be late. "I'll ring the office – he didn't mention anything."

"Oh right… er… I haven't actually seen him for a while," said Michael, looking a little uncertain. "He stopped training just before Christmas…"

"Yes, he moved out."

"Oh right. Well, he's definitely in the diary for today – he booked it last week. He's probably forgotten what with everything…" His words petered out as he caught her expression. It was so weird, he felt like he knew her but obviously, as far as she was concerned, he was a complete stranger. He was about to say as much, but not wishing to freak her out any further, he thought better of it. "We have met," he said again, trying to get on more friendly terms.

"Have we? Sorry, I don't remember."

He reached out and honked an imaginary horn down by her side. "Whah! Whah!"

She jumped back in alarm.

"Oh no, sorry! It's alright – I'm just honking a horn! You know, like Harpo?"

"Oh! The party!" Her smile, when it came, instantly transformed her face and took him by surprise. He grinned back at her. "What were you?" she asked.

"Huh?"

"Fancy dress?"

He suddenly realised he had been grinning away like a complete idiot and quickly snapped out of it. "Oh!… Er, no. I didn't."

"You didn't what?"

"Come as anything."

"You didn't bother with the fancy dress?" Her smile faded.

"Well no, I don't usually like them… didn't plan on coming." Once again, he dried up – the smile was gone. "Anyway – I wish I had! Great party, you know, the fancy dress and everything – loved it!" He followed her into the kitchen and waited as she made the call.

"He's on his way – he'll be about fifteen minutes."

"Right." They stood in awkward silence for a moment before she reluctantly offered him a coffee.

"Coffee would be great, one sugar, white – thanks."

He sat down at the kitchen table feeling decidedly ill at ease. She brought the coffee over and excused herself, saying she had to get on. '*So that's the lovely Olivia is it?*' thought Michael as he watched her retreating back. Surprised and somewhat miffed by her hostile behaviour, he sat morosely looking into his coffee cup and awaited Carl's arrival.

Twenty minutes later and still no Carl. He walked back into the hall. "Hello?... Olivia??" Nothing. *How fuckin' rude!* "Olivia, I'm off. I'll leave Carl's schedule on the table." Still nothing. "I'll just let myself out then..." called Michael, picking up his bag and opening the front door. "Bye..."

Hearing him call out to her, Liv had tip-toed out onto the landing and was waiting for him to leave. *Just go will you!!* Thinking she'd heard the door close she peered over the banisters.

"Oh! I was just going..."

"Yes."

"I've left his schedule on—"

"I heard. I'll tell Carl."

"Bye then."

"Bye." She looked a bit upset.

"You okay?"

"I'm fine. Bye," she repeated and withdrew. This time he did leave. She sat down at the top of the stairs with her head in her hands and sighed with relief. She'd been stuck in her bedroom for ages. Familiar feelings of being a prisoner in her own home had overwhelmed her bringing tears of frustration and a tension headache that felt like a tight band around her head. She'd soaked a flannel in cold water and had been lying on her bed with the cloth over her eyes waiting for Carl to arrive and bugger off with trainer guy downstairs.

She went back down, made some tea and glanced at the training schedule Michael had left on the kitchen table. She recognised the writing; not long after she had moved back, she had come across handwritten diet and nutrition sheets and had wondered where they had come from. She heard the front door bang again and voices in the hall. It was Carl – with Action Man! She had suddenly clicked and remembered him from the party. He was the poser in the suit, worse than a suit actually, he had been wearing a suit jacket, but with jeans and a white vest. *How posey can you get!* she'd thought at the time, and again now.

Action Man

Miss Clare Page
1737 Shadybrook Drive
Beverly Hills
CA 90210
U.S.A.

25th February, 1986

Hello Briany!

Thanks for your letter and the amazing photos. Wow! The great big U.S. of A.

I still can't believe you did it. I'm so envious but I know I could never have done anything like that. To just up sticks and fly off into the unknown - all alone. How brave! God knows how you managed to land that job though you jammy bugger. Let's face it – you're not exactly the archetypal British Nanny are you?

I'm glad it's all going so well for you out there. The family sound great, the little boy looks adorable – your car – the house! The whole thing is just like something out of a movie – but then you are in 'Movie Town' after all! You did make me laugh about all the bandaged noses on Rodeo Drive. I'd have thought the same and been terrified of getting mugged too – but nose jobs! Are you sure? Bizarre! You'll probably get 'discovered' by some casting agent because you're so different with all your little imperfections (ha-ha!).

It's all quiet ('ish) on The Western Front. I'm still having trouble with Charlie and Joe – it's like they are testing me to see how far they can go. We are still trying to find our feet after the upheaval of the last few months. I feel so sad for them – their lives have been turned upside down. One minute their mum's gone, then she's back, then she's gone again – and now she's back

91

and their dad's gone. No wonder they're
playing up. Hopefully things will get
better once we're back on an even keel.
Not much else to report from here -
how can I compete with Hollywood
for Christ's sake! Actually - thinking
about it, I do have some news! I think
Carl is trying to set me up - either
that or I've got a stalker! How Beverley
Hills is that? There's this guy that
keeps coming round, Carl's personal
trainer, and the thing is, he's absolutely
gorgeous! If I didn't know better I'd
feel really flattered but honestly Clare,
you should see him - there's no way!
You might remember him actually. He
was at our fancy dress party - the
good looking poser in a suit. He looks
like Action Man, you know, all jutting
jaw and bulging biceps. I've heard he
was in The Royal Marines. It wouldn't
surprise me - I can just imagine him in
his Commando uniform!

Carl used to meet him here for his
training sessions. Parking's a problem
at the gym apparently, so Carl would
leave his car here and the guy would
pick him up on his way through. Carl
kept turning up late or not at all and

then eventually he quit. I thought that would be the end of it but the thing is, he's still coming round! He just turns up out of the blue, tells me to stick the kettle on and then stays for an hour or so chatting! He's nice enough, really easy to talk to, although sometimes it's more like an interrogation! I don't know what to make of it - is he a plant, spying on me for Carl or is he going to make a pass at me and report back to Carl if I respond. All very intriguing! I have to confess though, I quite enjoy his company. He makes me laugh and I find myself looking forward to his visits - they are certainly making life more bearable.

I shall keep you posted!

Lots of love,
Brian
x x x

Clare

Liv's face had lit up when she'd spotted the blue airmail letter in the post that morning. Her first letter from Clare! It had been a month since their tearful farewells and it was great to be in contact again; she'd penned her reply straight away. Clare's letter had been bursting with news of her 'big adventure' and much to Liv's relief, she sounded really happy. She'd had a tough time of it these past few years and Liv could completely understand her need to get away, she just wished her plans hadn't been quite so drastic; but then Clare was never one to do things by halves.

They'd known each other since they were five years old but hadn't become friends until their first day at secondary school. Liv still remembered the feeling of dread as she'd set off from home that morning wondering what fresh hell this new school would bring. Her worst fears were soon realised when the teacher called out her name and placed her next to Clare Page, the most popular and, in Liv's mind, scariest girl from

Merryfields Primary. Clare had been equally unimpressed with her new classmate but had been grateful, at least, for a familiar face. Like Olivia, she'd lost all her friends to other schools and was feeling just as vulnerable. She'd decided that as they were the only two from Merryfields in the whole class, they'd have to make the best of it. Polar opposites; it was a mismatch made in heaven.

Their paths had rarely crossed during their seven years at primary school; Clare was almost a year older and they'd moved in very different circles. Their only contact had come through their mutual friend, Donald Little; School Sports Captain, Clare's hero and Liv's guardian angel. Clare was the girls' netball and rounders team captain and trained regularly with the boys' all conquering football team. They were flying high, top of their league and it was her greatest wish to be their goal-keeper. Donald had done his best to get her in but it was hopeless; he'd been sent off with a flea in his ear, "You'd think I'd asked to put my granny in goal!" he'd reported back dejectedly. The PE teacher knew how good she was; strong, agile and utterly fearless, but his hands were tied. She was a girl for Christ's sake!! His one concession had been to allow Clare to play during their training sessions; the thought being if they could get one past 'Pagey' they could score against anyone.

Clare was bemused by Donald's loyalty to Olivia. She knew her as the skinny little kid you didn't *ever* want in your team, but sometimes ended up with by default. A complete lightweight and without a competitive bone in her body, she was worse than useless. She couldn't understand why he bothered with her, but recognising her as a loyal supporter of the school football team, who like Clare, went to every game, she'd respected their friendship. Olivia and her sisters were part of a small group of girls who ran their own pony club and clip-clopped around the playground at a steady canter, with much whinnying and neighing along the way. Clare thought they were nuts, especially when she heard the 'ponies' they supposedly owned were actually hobby horses they'd made themselves at home. Donald was going to watch a gymkhana they were holding in Liv's nan's back garden and she'd gone along, fully prepared to heap scorn upon the proceedings; but to her surprise, she'd had the time of her life and was the proud recipient of a red rosette for jumping the only clear round of the day!

During their final year at Merryfields their year group had been shepherded into the school hall and placed under exam conditions for the all important 11+. Both girls were bright and had been expected to win places at the county grammar, but much to the surprise and disappointment of their families, they'd failed the exam and were consigned to the girls' secondary modern that together with the boys' counterpart, occupied a huge site on the outskirts of town. Liv liked to say that Clare had rescued her; taken her under her wing and helped her cope with the transition from tiny primary to the sprawling great complex that provided secondary education for up to 1000 pupils. Liv's mum, however, had seen it quite differently. She saw Clare not as a saviour, but as a bad influence, solely responsible for changing her innocent little girl into a rebellious teenager, seemingly overnight!

Although the two schools shared the same site, they were completely separate entities with little or no contact between their pupils. Any form of fraternisation was frowned upon and they were not allowed to loiter on school grounds at the end of the day. Over time, this enforced separation caused them to be awkward with each other and as their hormones kicked in, led to some disagreeable behaviour from the boys. With a surprising lack of foresight, the shared gymnasium was situated deep within the boys' school which meant that twice a week the girls had to run the gauntlet of wolf-whistles and catcalls as they trooped single file down the testosterone filled corridors clad only in aertex vests and gym skirts. Clare had her bra-strap pinged once too often during such an excursion and upon realising the culprit was from the old Merryfields Football Team, she slammed him up against the wall and administered an eye watering wedgie he wouldn't forget in a hurry. The girls agreed this sort of thing wouldn't be happening if Donald was there; to their mutual dismay, he and his family had moved to Buxton at the end of term and his presence was sorely missed.

Their home lives could not have been more different. Clare's house was the last word in elegance and her beautifully furnished bedroom was Liv's idea of heaven, whereas Clare found the rough and tumble of Liv's funny and chaotic household equally irresistible. There were kids and animals everywhere! Apart from Liv and her four siblings, the Johnsons had managed to collect just about every species of family pet known to mankind. Clare's mouth had literally dropped open as she was introduced to the dog, the cat, various rabbits, guinea pigs, hamsters, mice and gerbils, birds, fish, terrapins, a tortoise and a colony of stick insects that with their chameleon-like qualities, caused havoc whenever they escaped. There was just the one pet in the Page household; Tina, a chocolate poodle in a long line of chocolate poodles; all called Tina. Coming from a family who took the naming of all their pets, even the stick insects, very seriously, Liv couldn't fathom the thinking behind such a thing!

Clare's parents were more than twenty years older than Liv's and on first meeting, she'd found them quite terrifying! Edna Page was a force to be reckoned with; she owned her own car, unheard of in those days, and trundled around in an enormous old Rover that with its khaki paintwork looked more like an armoured tank. She was involved in all kinds of clubs and committees and ran a successful hairdressing business from home. She referred to Clare as her 'change of life' baby. The girls had discussed this and Liv suggested optimistically it meant having Clare had changed her mum's life. Clare agreed but suspected it hadn't been for the better! Liv had always assumed Clare was an only child and was surprised to discover she had a sister; eighteen years older, an ex Jaeger model, married to a film producer with homes in Chelsea and the South of France. Weighing up the unfair distribution of her parents' genes, Clare had decided at an early age it was pointless trying to follow in her glamorous sister's footsteps. Susan was a tall willowy blonde with their mother's smoky blue eyes and effortless grace, whereas Clare favoured their father; also tall but with his muscular build, fiery red hair and accompanying temperament. A natural athlete, she excelled in all sports, track, field and court, and was an unabashed tomboy. She became the apple of her father's eye and the son he never had.

Liv soon realised that Mr Page's bark was far worse than his bite and he'd won her undying affection on the night of her first sleepover. The girls had gone into town to spend their pocket money and as always, had blown the lot in Woolworths. Liv's had been spent on sweets, cake and fizzy drinks for the midnight feast they had planned for later and Clare's on a selection of jokes and party tricks including a whoopee cushion, some pretty convincing fake dog poo and a pack of exploding cigars. Clare had emptied the explosives from the cigars into her father's pipe and placed it, fully loaded, in the ashtray by the side of his favourite armchair. Mr Page's head had been buried inside his evening paper when it blew! The two girls had watched in horror as he slowly lowered the paper to reveal shell-shocked eyes in a blackened face, tendrils of smoke curling through scorched eyebrows, and his pipe, still smouldering, clamped rigidly between his teeth. They were already in the doghouse following Mrs Page's discovery of the pretend doggie poo in her 'salon', the conservatory at the back of the house from where she conducted her hairdressing business. One of her ladies had spotted it, and bellowing from her deafened state under the hairdryer, had alerted the rest of the street to its presence. Tina had been launched through the back door, crash landing in the middle of Mr Page's prize dahlias, before their cruel trick had been laid bare. Being packed off to bed early without any tea had done nothing to dampen their spirits and after devouring their 'midnight feast', they had embarked upon a boisterous farting competition with the newly acquired whoopee cushion. Their raucous laughter had been interrupted by Mr Page hammering on Clare's bedroom door and bellowing "WHAT'S ALL THIS NOISE?" and then somewhat incredulously, "ARE YOU GIRLS TRUMPING IN THERE???" Utterly destroyed, Liv fell back onto the whoopee cushion and produced an explosive ripsnorter that answered his question beautifully. She held her breath, expecting the worst, but the sound of Mr Page laughing as he went back downstairs won him a place in her heart for ever.

In the early days of their friendship they usually played round at Liv's house for much as she admired Clare's beautiful home, Liv had to admit there wasn't much fun to be had there. Following their sleepover shenanigans, all manner of jokes and trickery had been banned and subsequent sleepovers were strictly monitored. Clare's mum insisted they 'should be seen and not heard' if they played in the house, the garden was off limits because of the dahlias and whatnot, and they weren't allowed to play in the street because Mrs P said it was common. This, of course, was in complete contrast to Liv's where hurling water bombs from upstairs windows, sliding down the stairs on tea-trays and having ferocious water fights with her brothers and sisters in their rambling, overgrown back garden, was more the order of the day.

By the time they entered their second year at school

however, everything changed and Clare's house was favoured by the fledgling teens. Clare's parents had decided she was old enough to be left alone and spent many an evening down at The Conservative Club… which was extremely convenient for Clare as it meant she and Liv could learn how to drink, smoke and experiment with their hair all in the privacy of her own home! They still shopped at Woolworths but now their money was spent at the hair and beauty counter and the all important tobacco kiosk where Clare had bluffed them into believing she was over sixteen. Their Girl Guide group met up with the Sea Scouts once a week and they'd all hang around outside the local chippy drinking Pepsi and smoking, or in Liv and Clare's case, coughing and spluttering, so learning to smoke was a must. Determined to master the art, they'd sat round Clare's mum's fireside and with a few slugs of her finest sherry inside them, they'd puffed away on their menthol cigarettes until Liv threw up in the coal scuttle and Clare passed out cold on the floor. The hair products hadn't gone too well either. Clare had tried everything in her quest to become a strawberry blonde, but had succeeded only in turning her flaming locks ever more carroty as the weeks went by. One day, in a fit of pique, she'd grabbed a box of semi-permanent from her mother's salon and dyed it raven black! No thought had been given to her ginger complexion and with her black Twiggy hairdo and deathly white face; she looked like the ghost of Hitler's daughter! Liv had been using similar products along the way and had seen her own hair take on the colour and texture of straw. Surveying the damage they'd wreaked upon their respective crowning glories, Mrs Page decided there was nothing else for it and chopped the lot off. Lucky for them, short spiky crops were quite the thing and with a little adjustment here and there, they'd got the haircuts of their dreams.

At some point during the summer term, Clare had, as Mrs P put it, 'become a lady' which sent Liv into a tailspin about becoming a lady too! She looked on in awe at Clare's shapely curves and despaired that all her own body had managed was a spectacular prepubescent growth spurt that had taken her from half a head shorter to a full head taller than Clare in less than a year. This elongation of her already slender frame had thrust her into the spotlight and scuppered all hopes of remaining hidden in Clare's shadow. She tried lessening her height by stooping her shoulders and keeping her knees almost permanently bent, but abandoned this strategy when her dad pointed out she'd taken on the posture of a praying mantis. For Liv, this was a time of recurring nightmares about walking to school and suddenly realising all you had on was a vest! Completely out of her depth, she'd grabbed hold of her friend's shirt-tails and clung on tightly as Clare navigated their way through the bumpy ride of adolescence.

Clare had started to change in her attitude towards boys and when she started practising her feminine wiles on Liv's older brother and his friends, Liv found her newfound coquettishness quite unnerving! Much to Liv's relief, Clare turned her attention to one of the sea-scouts and pretty soon they were dating. Meanwhile, Liv had caught the eye of a certain new boy who'd been expelled from his last school, rumour had it for fighting, but no one knew for sure. He was in their year but he looked older and tended to hang round with the year above. The girls had noticed him lounging against the fence in the boys' playground and had decided he was tall, dark and with his bad boy image, definitely interesting. Quite often, Liv felt him looking at her and once, at Clare's insistence, she had looked straight back. Clare said he'd be embarrassed and look away, but he hadn't! He'd just raised his eyebrows and held her gaze. At the annual school disco as the DJ urged them to take their partners for the last dance, Liv was about to head off to the cloakroom when he'd appeared at her shoulder and asked her to dance. As she'd reported to Clare later, her legs had gone to jelly as he led her onto the floor but he was really nice, his name was Carl and he was taking her to the pictures on Saturday! Many years later Liv remembered being asked why she had chosen Carl – and the truth of it was she hadn't. He had chosen her.

Dictionaries

Liv watched through her kitchen window as Michael's car pulled into the drive. She felt her stomach knot with apprehension; she'd promised herself that next time he came, she was going to have it out with him and find out what he was up to; because as she'd said to Clare, his motives were far from clear. He breezed in, bright and cheerful as ever, "Ah Frau Vogel, guten morgen!" She found herself grinning in spite of herself as she followed him through to the kitchen. "Coffee, white, one sugar, stirred *anti* clockwise please" he continued, taking up his usual position at the table. He looked up at her. "Why the long face?" Her smile had gone as she readied herself for the conversation that was to come. She took a seat opposite him and drew a deep breath.

"I need to talk to you Michael."

"Sounds ominous – what's up?"

"It's about you coming round so much."

"Oh right!" he laughed. "That's what I like about you Liv – you don't hold back!"

"Oh look, sorry to be blunt, but I don't know how else to say it. It's nice to see you and everything, but you've been here twice already this week, two or three times last week and probably the week before too."

"Really?" said Michael, taken aback, "No it can't be that much!"

"It is – and I'm just… you know, I'm wondering why?"

"Well this is all a bit embarrassing isn't it? It can't be that often – are you sure?" She nodded.

"I'm seeing more of you than my own family!"

"Okay… right… point taken. Sorry mate, I didn't realise. You're just round the corner from the gym and I s'pose I've got used to dropping in for a cuppa on my way home."

"So it has nothing to do with Carl?"

"Carl? No, he's not training now is he?"

"No, I meant has Carl put you up to this?"

"Put me up to what? What are you talking about?"

"Look, if Carl has asked you to come round here, either to keep an eye on me, or to… to… you know, chat me up or something—" Michael's laughter eased her embarrassment.

"No mate, hand on heart, I can promise you he hasn't. Far from it in fact!"

"What d'you mean?"

"Well it's funny you should ask that because going back awhile, I offered to… well, I offered to pull you."

"Pull me?" she said, aghast. "So I was right!"

"No, not now! This was ages ago when you were living with your parents. I knew him from the gym –

that's how I came to be at your party that time, but he quit and we lost touch. He turned up one day and he looked terrible – told me about you walking out on him and the kids and I—"

"It wasn't like that, I had no choice—"

"I know that now, but at the time all I knew was what he told me. I thought you were a right bitch to be honest, but if ever I voiced that, everyone without exception defended you."

"That's nice to know."

"Yeah... I didn't know what to make of it all really. Anyway, he was in a right state, really cut up about it and I felt sorry for him. I took him on as a client and he started to get his shit together. We'd go for a drink sometimes, or I'd come back here and he'd talk and talk – I tell you, that bloke could talk – mainly about you and how he had to get you back. One night he drove over to your mum and dad's in a big looping detour from the gym. He checked your car was there, parked up round the back and waited to see your bedroom light go off."

"God, that's creepy. I had no idea!"

"Yeah well I thought so too to be honest. I wasn't comfortable with it. He went to your mate's place too."

"Clare's?"

"I don't know."

"Must have been Clare's. I used to stay over sometimes."

"Well anyway, like I say, he was obsessed with finding out what you were up to so that's when I offered to pull you... but when I suggested it, you should have seen his reaction!"

"Yeah, I can imagine!" she laughed. They sat drinking their coffee for a while. She looked across at him. "Offered to *pull me*?"

"Sorry, but I didn't know you then did I? I just thought it would be good for him to find out if you were... you know..."

"Up for it?" she finished for him, eyebrows raised.

"Yeah... but like I said, I didn't know you, hadn't even met you and to be honest, I just saw it as a process of elimination – if you blanked me, at least Carl would know you weren't shagging around." She sat quietly for a moment, digesting what Michael had just said.

"Do you know how arrogant that sounds? That's like saying if you couldn't pull me, nobody could!"

"I didn't mean it like that!"

"Really?"

"Of course not! But I s'pose looking at it that way..."

"How else can you look at it?" He considered her statement and sighed.

"Yep – complete tosser! I'll get my coat."

"Okay," she laughed, "as long as I know you're not part of a set up from Carl."

"I can promise you that, and look, I am sorry. I don't think I even meant it really, probably just one of those stupid throwaway remarks that blokes come out with."

"That dickheads come out with!"

"Okay yes, I am that dickhead," said Michael with his hands up, "but can we drop it now? I feel like a right prat!"

"Okay, forgotten," laughed Liv, "more coffee?"

"Smashing, thanks. So has Carl always been jealous?"

"He's always been possessive, but it got much worse after I found out about his affairs. I think he was worried I was going to have one myself out of revenge."

"And did you?"

"Now see, there you go again, that's one of the reasons I thought you might have been planted by Carl! You turn a conversation into an interrogation… you're so bloody nosey!"

"No I was just wondering if—"

"Well don't! If I want to tell you something I'll do it in my own way, so don't be jumping in with questions every five minutes!" There was an uncomfortable silence. "Erm, sorry about that… bit of an overreaction," said Liv, "it's just I get it from Carl all the time so I'm a bit over sensitive—"

"And defensive?"

"Yeah probably, but anyway… after that initial knee jerk reaction, his jealousy and lack of trust gradually settled back down, but then something happened that sent it shooting through the roof again. Hang on, let's just get this coffee sorted – help yourself to a cigarette." Michael smiled as he lit up. She poured the coffee and lit her own. "So my best friend Clare had left her husband and come to stay with us while her divorce was going through. It had an unsettling effect on Carl – I think he was worried I might decide to join Clare in her new found single life. We used to go out sometimes and he absolutely hated it."

"Well that's pretty standard I reckon. Loads of blokes are wary of their wives going on girls' nights out."

"Yeah, only because they know what *they* get up to on boys' nights out!" replied Liv hotly, "So anyway, this one particular night, known forever after as '*The Night of the Blue Dressing Gown*', Clare and I had gone out with some other friends for a drink and then on to a club. It had been a great night, really good fun. We got home about two in the morning and Clare wanted to carry on drinking. She had really let her hair down and I don't think she wanted the night to end. We found a joint in Carl's puff box, cracked open a bottle of wine and laughed and chatted away 'til almost dawn. I remember staggering through the kitchen on our way to bed and Clare saying, '*Oh Livvie, wouldn't it be great if you were single too!*' to which I replied something like, '*Well if Carl's heard our conversation tonight, I soon will be!*'

"What had you been saying then?"

"Oh just hypothetical stuff about what life would have been like if we hadn't got married so young – you know, if we had shared a flat together, that kind of thing. We'd been laughing about what had happened that night. We'd been chatted up quite a bit and I think it had gone to our heads – we didn't get out much so I s'pose we were flattered by all the attention. Clare was saying, '*if we had our own place, who would you have brought back tonight?*' and I was laughing and saying stuff like '*well I wouldn't mind waking up next to the one who'd said he was an airline pilot!*' It was all total bollocks, you know, just messing about, having a laugh."

"So what happened?"

"Well like I say, there we were, staggering out of the

kitchen and into the hall. Clare's saying her thing about wishing we were both single and I'm saying '*if Carl's overheard this lot, I soon will be*' – then suddenly – there he was, right there in front of us in his blue dressing gown. He'd been sitting on the stairs listening to our every word!"

"Jesus!" laughed Michael.

"It wasn't funny I can tell you, the shock of coming face to face with him like that, I swear we nearly jumped out of our skins! He was a terrible sight – bright red face all mottled and blotchy with snarly lips and his eyes bulging out of his head. I still have nightmares about him in that blue dressing gown!"

"Bloody hell – I bet your sphincter was quivering."

"My what?"

"Your sphincter," laughed Michael, "you know, like Luca Brasi's in The Godfather."

"I know the film," she said shaking her head, "but—"

"Did you read the book?" She nodded. "Well it's the bit where Luca Brasi, the huge guy with no neck, gets it. He's garrotted in a bar, remember? – and as he's choking to death, the book says something about his sphincter letting go."

"I did read it, but I don't remember the word sphincter leaping out at me."

"Just as well!" laughed Michael, "Anyway, I must have been about fourteen or so, and I had no idea what a sphincter was. For some bizarre reason I decided to look it up. D'you know what it is?"

"No, not really. Is it something to do with the spleen?

No, hang on, spleens don't 'let go', they get 'vented' don't they," she shrugged, "Dunno, give up. What is it?"

"Have you got a dictionary?"

"Of course!" she laughed and went to find one. Heads together, they looked it up.

'Sphincter (n) A circular muscle that constricts a passage or closes a natural orifice. When relaxed it allows materials to pass through the opening.'

"So he—"

"Yep, poor old Luca dropped the lot – and who can blame him!" laughed Michael.

"Oh I love looking things up, don't you?" said Liv, wiping her eyes.

"Yeah…" nodded Michael, but then added, somewhat perplexed, "well, no not really. I mean it's useful to find things out but it's not exactly—"

"Oh no course not," she added hastily, "but I loved it as a kid and I suppose I still find it quite…" she stopped before making herself look even more of an idiot. Also, she had started remembering one dictionary moment she would far sooner forget.

It was her first day at a new job. She was just seventeen and had been under constant pressure from Carl to quit her job in London and find something closer to home – closer to him. He was incredibly possessive even then, and liked to keep her under his watchful eye. Liv had smiled at this, thinking it was sweet. No warning bells had sounded at his controlling behaviour – she just felt it showed how much he loved her. Although she had been quite happy where she was, when he showed her the local paper stuffed full with suitable positions, she had agreed to leave.

Back in those days, employment was never a problem. You could book yourself in for two or three interviews a day, then meet the resulting job offers with a cheery 'Thank you, I'll let you know.' She soon found a job as a secretary to a local building contractor, earning not much less than she had been in town. The fact that she would be situated just down the road from where Carl was serving his apprenticeship made it, literally, just the job.

"Perfect!" he'd said, "I can give you a lift in every morning and pick you up on the way home." Why had those alarm bells not been ringing? Her one misgiving was that she would be the only female in an all male office of about ten, plus a further twenty or so men working in the various workshops situated behind the main office. The atmosphere was very relaxed and as her first day progressed, she felt optimistic that this new job was going to work out fine. She familiarised herself with the switchboard, made friends with her typewriter and had just found the kettle when her new boss brought in a quotation for her to type. It had been handwritten and she was having trouble with some of the technical terminology. Things started to go wrong when she came across the word 'nipples'. Nipples? – how could that possibly be in a quote for central heating? She couldn't work out the preceding word, but with a sinking feeling, she acknowledged there was no doubt about the nipples! She knew she had to ask, but to make matters worse, although her boss had his own office, he spent most of his time in the large room that Liv occupied along with several contract supervisors.

"Um Frank," she began, red faced, "I can't quite make this word out," she said, pointing to the word before the 'N' word.

"Grease," he informed her.

"Ah right, so it says – Supply and fit 20 no. grease um… grease…?"

"Grease nipples."

"Right." She walked back to her desk, trying to ignore the buzz of amusement in the air and carried on typing. Page two brought further problems. A strange squiggle kept appearing. She thought it was M&S but could not be sure. It usually prefixed 'couplings'. Marks and Spencers couplings?

"No luv," said Frank, "it's M & F – male and female couplings. You know – the male connector fits into the female." Without realising, he had been demonstrating the concept of male and female couplings by poking the index finger of his right hand into the loose fist of his left. Liv stood transfixed, watching him perform his little mime, and as he followed her gaze, his hands dropped immediately and guiltily to his sides. Both were acutely aware of the suppressed laughter building up in the office.

Eventually, the finished article was presented to, and approved by, Frank. A few more letters and quotations followed without incident and once again, Liv's confidence began to grow. Right on cue, the 'coup de grace' arrived in the form of a notice that Frank wanted typed and displayed in the shared cloakroom facility. It was a health warning for individuals exposed to certain hazardous oils and chemicals stored within the workplace. It explained the necessity for the careful washing of hands and warned that special care should be taken to ensure the oil did not come into contact with the eyes, mouth or scrotum.

"Frank," she called – had she learned nothing from her earlier embarrassment? – evidently not. She should have just typed the notice, stuck it on the wall and not given it another thought. Of course she should, but instead…

"What's a scrotum?"

The whole place erupted. They fell about laughing and every time one of them tried to speak, it set them off again. Eventually, Frank managed to hand her the office dictionary.

"Look it up!" he croaked. She did...

'Scrotum (n) The scrotum is a soft muscular pouch, underneath the penis, containing two compartments to hold the testicles.'

Oh my God! I'm going to have to leave!

"Oi! Looby Loo! – where have you gone?" called Michael.

"Sorry, miles away – my dad calls me that!" she added with a smile.

"Looby Loo?"

"And Dolly Daydream," she laughed, "still... better than the stuff I got at school."

"So what did you get at school?" he grinned.

"Oh, 'Pinocchio' because of this," she said pointing to her turned up nose. "The boys used to stand behind me and pretend to work my strings! 'Olive Oyl', a double whammy there, not only the name but I was built like a bean pole too! 'Porky', the nose again, as well as being the furthest thing from a porker. Oh there were loads – how about you?"

"Well no nicknames as such, but there was a chant..."

"Go on?"

"Michael Brookin – thinks he's so good looking..." he mumbled with a pained expression.

"Aw, poor Michael, I can't think why!"

114

"Hey I thought we'd dropped that!" he said with an air of indignation. "Anyway, back to Carl and the infamous blue dressing gown. What did he—"

"Nothing thank God! He just stormed off back to bed. I slept with Clare that night – we were both terrified! I tried talking to him about it the next day, you know… tried to explain it was just drunken burbling and didn't mean anything, but he just wouldn't listen. He most definitely changed after that night. I'd catch him looking at me like I was a fallen angel or something – he was acting like he'd actually caught me cheating, which was ridiculous because it was all just hypothetical. Nothing had happened, nothing at all, but he couldn't get over it."

As he drove home that night, although he had not admitted as much to Liv, Michael felt some sympathy for Carl and up to a point, understood his reaction; especially the 'fallen angel' bit. He'd heard it said by others, and had to agree, that when in Olivia's company, you felt you should be on your best behaviour because she had an almost schoolmarm air about her. It was strange because she was far from angelic; she drank, smoked, enjoyed a puff and swore like a trooper, but there was definitely something a bit different about her, a line you couldn't cross. He soon learnt, for instance, that any hint of flirtatious banter would be met with a look of such distain he'd be left feeling like Finbarr Saunders and his Double Entendres, the 'fnarr fnarring' character from Viz! She was certainly a bit of an enigma, but one thing was for sure, he could understand Carl's shock at overhearing that conversation with her mate – *you'd think she'd be a bit above that kind of thing* – the truth of it was, he was slightly perturbed by it himself.

Grasshopper

"Hi, it's me, Michael."

"Oh!" said Liv, somewhat surprised.

"I had the number there already... you know, from Carl."

"Oh yeah, that's fine."

"I'm just phoning to see if I left my locker key there the other day. It's like a little padlock key?"

"No... I don't think so. I haven't seen it."

"Damn! That's the second one this month."

"Don't you have a spare?"

"That *was* the spare!" he groaned, "I'm gonna look a right twat now. I've been bollocking the kids at the boxing academy about losing their gear all the time – you know, boots, gloves, trainers—"

"Can't you just get another padlock on the quiet?"

"Yeah, but the maintenance bloke will have to come stomping through the gym with a bloody great pair of bolt-cutters to get the old one off. Bit hard to keep that quiet!"

"Oh right," she chuckled, "well don't do anything yet. Bridey's coming tomorrow – I'll ask her if she's seen it. Sometimes she presents me with a little pot of odds and sods she's picked up on her travels – ring me tomorrow afternoon."

"Okay, thanks."

"How are you anyway?"

"Good, you?"

"Yeah I'm fine thanks. I think I saw you earlier. Were you in town?"

"When?"

"About elevenish, in the High Road?"

"Oh yeah, I went to the bank."

"It was you then! With the orange crash helmet?"

"Yep."

"And you got on…" she started to giggle, "you got on a… a pop-pop?"

"A pop-pop?"

Liv was really laughing now and was unable to answer.

"It's not a bloody pop-pop!"

"It is! My dad had one. He had to pedal away like the clappers to get it going – his little legs going ten to the dozen – we used to line up to wave him off and nearly wet ourselves laughing."

"Yeah well mine hasn't got pedals, alright? It starts with an ignition key."

"Woooo! Okay so it's a top of the range pop-pop, but it's still—"

"It's not a fucking pop-pop! Anyway, I need it for The Knowledge."

"Huh?"

"I'm learning The Knowledge."

"Oh are you? I didn't know that."

"Yeah… well I am… and you have to have a moped."

"What? You need a moped to study The Knowledge?"

"Yes."

"A MOPED?"

"How many more times! Look – I have to practise everything I learn from the Blue Book, and the best way of doing that is on a moped."

"So this blue book, is that like your bible?"

"Yeah, exactly."

"Okay… but I still don't get the moped."

"Oh look, don't worry about it, I'll explain next time I see you – this card's nearly run out."

"Actually, a friend of mine's studying it too. You might know him – he lives out your way."

"I doubt it."

"Little Pete – you met him at the party. No prizes for guessing who he was."

"Huh?"

"Gandhi!"

"Zero credit – gotta go, I'll ring tomorrow."

"Okay, bye Grasshopper!"

"What?"

"Patience young Grasshopper…" she called, but the pips had sounded and Michael had gone.

Five minutes later he rang back.

"It's me again. What were you saying when the pips went?"

"Patience young Grasshopper!"

"Yeah, that's what I thought. Olivia, what do you think The Knowledge is exactly?"

"Um, Buddhism?" she could hear him laughing down the phone.

"No Liv, that's The Enlightenment! I'm hoping to become a London taxi driver, not a bloody monk!" She joined in his laughter.

"Oh right! I thought it was funny, you know, the moped and everything. I was imagining you riding around in your orange crash helmet, with your matching orange robes billowing all around you!"

"And an A to Z stuffed down my underpants. Tell you what, I wish I just had to snatch a pebble from the examiner's hand to pass the final test!"

You're So Vain

7th April, 1986

Dear Clare,

Thanks for your letter. Hmmm, it all sounds a bit worrying to be honest. I think you're right, she is definitely showing all the signs of being a coke head - the mood swings, the weight loss, the nervous energy and her bizarre behaviour towards you. Don't speak to the husband about it - for all you know, he could be doing it too! I think you should speak to your agency and ask them to find you another position. I saw a programme on tele the other night and apparently having an English nanny is a bit of a status thing out there at the moment so you shouldn't have any trouble getting another job. Maybe ask for somewhere less glitzy. From what I can make out, Tinsel Town is rife with coke and you don't want to risk jumping out of the frying pan and into the fire!

Don't fret about the little boy, he has both sets of grandparents living nearby and it sounds like they're very hands on. The thing is Clare, this isn't your responsibility and if you stick your neck out and speak to either the husband or the grandparents you could end up getting kicked out without a reference - paddles and creeks come to mind!

Not a lot to report this end. The separation is holding but Carl is taking liberties with the visiting arrangements. We'd agreed he should visit at the weekends and to begin with it was fine, everyone knew where they were, but just lately he's been turning up whenever he likes and it's really unsettling for the boys. They keep asking him when he's coming back and he looks sorrowful and says " Ask your mum." 'Tis total shite but what can you do?

I'm looking into getting an au pair so that I can go back to work. Do you fancy the job? Lousy pay and no job security, but the working conditions are great and you couldn't find a nicer boss! Seriously though, I need to be financially independent. Obviously Carl is paying the bills and supporting the boys but there's no way I am going to be beholden to him for anything. By the time I pay for the au pair I won't have a lot but at least I won't have to go cap in hand to him every time I need to buy some tampons for Christ's sake!

No other news other than a quick update on my stalker! Well, I had it out with him and he's definitely not been planted by Carl so that's a relief! According to Carl, he's a terrible womaniser, but he doesn't come across that way to me - talking to him he seems like a genuinely nice guy. He told me he had recently split up with his fiancée because he knew he wasn't ready for marriage. I mentioned I'd heard he had a bit of a reputation and he admitted that sometimes, it was hard to turn the offers down. It was quite refreshing in that he didn't insult my intelligence with a display of false modesty but said that most of the time his looks were a huge pain in the arse. Most people disliked him on sight, assuming he thought he was God's gift to women - I had to confess to thinking the same! He reckons the way he looks only seems to attract old slappers, horny housewives or little old biddies who say 'Oooh! If only I was forty years younger!' He was in the Marines by the way. We went to his nan's the other week (don't ask!) and there were photos of him in his uniform everywhere. Since leaving he's had loads of jobs, mainly security work, but now he's trying to build up his business as a personal trainer. He's also learning The Knowledge to become a black cab driver and in his spare time he helps out at his local boxing gym, mentoring some of the young tearaways they have down there.

Anyway me old mucker, it's time to go. Hope to hear from you soon but from a different address! You have got to get outta there!!

Love you muchness,
Brian xxx

John Wayne

Mindful of their last conversation, Michael left it a few days before going round to collect his padlock key. Liv looked pleased to see him and invited him in straight away. He was delighted to hear that her cleaning lady had found not one, but two of his locker keys; no mention was made of their previous encounter and before long they were chatting away as if nothing had happened.

"They bring back memories," he said, nodding towards the blue airmail letters on the kitchen table. "We used them all the time in the services." He moved as if to take one but Liv, painfully aware that his name featured in all of them, snatched them up and shoved them into the cutlery drawer.

Jesus! thought Michael, *Does she think I was going to read them!* "Steady Liv! I was just seeing how flimsy they were!"

"Sorry... I just... you know..." She sat there with guilt writ large across her face. Michael had no idea what had prompted her bizarre reaction, but keen to restore the status quo, he decided to let it go.

"Pen-pal?" he asked with a smile.

"Er, not exactly. It's my friend, Clare. She's in America... you know, working out there."

"Was she married to Carl's mate?"

"Mark," nodded Liv. "Do you know him?"

"I've met him a few times. Seems alright?"

"He is really. It's a shame how it all... oh well... never mind."

"Sometimes people get forced into taking sides Liv."

"Yeah I know... and doubly so in our case. When our marriage hit the rocks, theirs went too. They split up before we did."

"Yeah, Carl told me. You were all quite close weren't you?"

Liv nodded. "Clare and I grew up together and I met Carl at secondary school. We started going out from then really and Clare and Mark got together a bit later. We introduced them."

"So Mark was already Carl's mate?"

"Yes... my best friend married Carl's. Perfect!"

"You'd think so."

"Well it was... but like I say, they got dragged into our mess and nothing was ever the same."

"So when did they get divorced?"

"Four, maybe five years ago I think. She was happily single for a while – great job and a gorgeous little flat, or *bijou apartment* as she called it," laughed Liv. "She had a few relationships along the way and then bang! She met

Grant – the love of her life! They sold up, bought a house together and decided to start a family straight away."

"They didn't hang about then!"

"Well no, Clare was into her thirties by then and Grant was nearly forty, so they didn't want to wait," explained Liv. "They tried for two years and then went the IVF route. Nine failed rounds left them broken, emotionally and financially. It cost them their relationship in the end too."

"Is that why—"

"Yeah... she had to get away." They sat quietly for a few moments and then Liv broke into a smile. "I've had some of the best times of my life with Clare. She's great! When we worked together—"

"You worked together?"

"In Piccadilly..." nodded Liv, "running an airline reservations office! Clare was brilliant but I was absolutely—"

"I didn't realise you'd worked!" butted in Michael.

"Of course I've worked!"

"Sorry it's just that Carl said—"

"Oh I'm sure he did!" interrupted Liv, her eyes reflecting the anger she felt at Carl's frequent references to her as a kept woman. "He seems to have forgotten that when we first got married, I was earning more than him and it was *my* salary that paid the mortgage on our first flat."

"Oh right!" said Michael. "I stand corrected." He'd heard so much about her from Carl it was good to hear things from her perspective. It would appear his doubts over Carl's version of events hadn't been unfounded. "Then I s'pose when Charlie came along?"

"Yes, I gave up work then. I was happy to stay at home, completely besotted with Charlie and I loved being a mum."

"And Carl? How did he take to being a dad?"

"Well, you know Carl," she shrugged, "he was over the moon at first. He had his son and heir to carry on the family name and all that, but once he'd shown him off to everyone and all the hoo-hah had died down, it was business as usual."

"For him."

"Yes, but not for me. I mean, it was still the same old thing. He was never there, always working or whatever, but it didn't matter so much," her voice softened, "I had Charlie." She was smiling now, remembering how complete she had felt. She always said to new mums-to-be *'Nothing can prepare you for how hard it is, but then nothing prepares you for the love you feel for them either – it's all consuming, like nothing you've ever felt before.'* After Charlie's birth, she understood why the process was called labour, because that's exactly what it was, bloody hard work! She also shared a valuable piece of information she wished she'd been privy to at the time. *'Towards the end, the strangest thing happens. The pain changes and you get this unbelievable urge to push. It's called "bearing down". The midwife will probably tell you to push, as hard as you can, right through to your bottom. I didn't know what she meant and although I was well into the throes of "bearing down" I didn't dare! I thought I needed the loo! I was pleading with them to let me get up, but they just shoved me back down and told me to push as the baby*

128

was coming. Everyone was gathered round the foot of the bed and I was convinced, utterly convinced that what I was about to deliver was not the bouncing baby they were expecting! Eventually, nature took its course and I pushed in spite of myself. When the cry went up, "It's a boy!" I couldn't have cared less – I was just so relieved it was a baby!'

She remembered, after he was born, being wheeled onto the ward with him cradled in her arms. She'd wanted to shout out *'I've just had a baby! A baby boy! He has finger nails and eyelashes and everything!'* She had been stunned. So full of love for this precious little baby with hair so long the nurses laughed and with tiny fingers and toes all present and correct. Gazing in wonderment at his long lashes and stroking the soft down covering his little body she'd laid on her hospital bed for hours, mesmerised, just looking at him through the side of his Perspex crib.

Her thoughts drifted back to Michael. "Anyway, like I say, things were fine to begin with. My whole life revolved around Charlie – but when he started school, I didn't know what to do with myself."

"Did you go back to work in between having the boys?"

"Well, sort of… from time to time."

"There's quite a gap between them isn't there? What is it, six, seven years?"

"Almost six," she confirmed, "I didn't think I would have any more after Charlie."

"Oh right…" said Michael, "so what, you thought you couldn't or…" his voice trailed off. "Sorry Liv, I didn't mean to—"

"No, it's okay… just a bit of a long story really. More coffee?" she offered, busying herself with the cafetière. She returned with the fresh pot of coffee, accepted his offer of a cigarette and settled back down.

"So you were saying…" prompted Michael, "about work?"

"Oh, was I?" She drew on her cigarette and exhaled with a long sigh. She was reluctant to continue with this. She could see where it was going but felt she couldn't just change the subject without seeming rude. "Right… well," she sighed again, "I knew I had to do something after Charlie started school. I was feeling pretty lost. I tried all sorts of things, a bit of voluntary work here and there, and I took some classes."

"Any good?"

"Yeah, it was okay. I even passed my advance driving test!"

"Excellent!" said Michael, suitably impressed.

"Yes," she grinned, "It was!"

"And the other classes?"

"Oh, I gave them up… Carl wasn't very supportive, putting it mildly, so eventually I quit."

"Shame…" commented Michael sympathetically.

"Yeah well, never mind – anyway, enough of me," she said, eager to move on.

"But what happened then?"

"Well then Joe came along," she replied with a shrug. "So there you go, end of story."

'*Nicely done*', she congratulated herself on her smooth manoeuvre but Michael was not so easily sidetracked.

"But what about the charity work?" he persisted, "you didn't say what it was."

"It wasn't charity work… it was more like voluntary work."

"Voluntary work? – Like what?"

"Well, I helped out at the boys' schools," she said vaguely.

"How did that go then, must have been nice?" '*God*', thought Michael, '*this was like pulling teeth!*'

"Hmmm… yes, it was…" *Well it was nice in Joe's class but Charlie's had been a bit of a disaster!* thought Liv, remembering the time she'd been told to go and stand in the corner by his teacher…

What a bitch! Mrs Hogbin. Hogbin? What kind of name was that? She didn't want to entrust the care of her little boy to someone whose name sounded like a pigs' trough! She was more suited to an army boot camp than the nursery class of a primary school; a point she raised in the letter of complaint she wrote at the end of this sorry tale. Charlie was an August baby, and was just 4 years and 8 days old when he started school. Liv had been out of her mind with worry, knowing he was far too young. She decided to speak to the Headmistress, who was a kindly soul and gave Liv permission to help him settle in. Mrs Hogroast was furious; she felt her authority had been usurped and threatened resignation. After assurances that this was strictly a one off, temporary measure, she relented and Liv was allowed to stay.

It was a hollow victory however, because Mrs Hogsbreath went out of her way to be unpleasant, not only to Liv and Charlie, but to the whole class. Before long, nearly all the children were hanging on to or hiding behind Liv's skirts. They climbed onto her lap and called her 'teacher' and she loved them! This, of course, went down awfully well with Mrs Hogwash and the situation went from bad to worse. At one point, during a wet playtime, when the little darlings were releasing some pent up energy, she'd actually screamed, "STOP ACTING LIKE A BUNCH OF FOUR YEAR OLDS!" Liv had started to laugh, but quickly smothered it when she realised it wasn't a joke!

The final straw came when they went to the hall for P.E. The equipment had been set out like a mini assault course. The kids were incredibly excited and started charging around the hall, jumping, rolling, climbing, balancing until The Hogbin bellowed "STAND STILL THIS INSTANT!" She had yelled in such a rage, the poor little mites did exactly that; every last one of them stopped in mid flight! The stupid woman then instructed them to jump, roll, climb and balance – but on her terms. They just stood there, frozen to the spot. Liv had tried to coax them along, but was shot a venomous look and told in no uncertain terms, she was not to interfere. Eventually, they started working their way round the mats, beams and climbing equipment in a solemn little line. All was going well until a straggler, way behind the rest of them, was having difficulty executing a forward roll. Liv bent down to help him and the next thing she knew, she was being frog marched to the corner, where she was told to stand and think about what she had done! She thought about it alright and that night penned a letter of complaint to the Head. It was an excellent letter, supported by the other parents and suffice to say, by next term, Mrs Hogbin was teaching in the junior school and had been replaced by Mrs Benson, a kindly mother hen like figure, not unlike the Head.

"Liv?" Michael's voice broke into her reverie. "So apart from helping out at Charlie's school, you haven't really—"

"And Joe's," she cut in, "I helped out in Joe's class too."

"Yeah, but—"

"And I got a job!" '*SHIT! What did I go and say that for!*' She could have kicked herself. '*Well done Olivia*', she fumed, '*you've just talked yourself straight back in there!*'

"A job? When?"

"Christ! What is this? The Spanish Inquisition?"

"Alright, get back in your pram!" laughed Michael, "I just wanted to know what you did."

"I've already told you – voluntary work!"

"Oh not the bloody voluntary work again! Come on Liv, stop being so mysterious. WHAT DID YOU DO?"

"MARRIAGE GUIDANCE!" she yelled back.

"Marriage guidance?" he repeated, clearly puzzled. "What, you went for marriage guidance?"

"No – I worked there."

"Huh?"

"I was a Marriage Guidance Counsellor!"

His ears had obviously deceived him. "Sorry? What did you say? I thought for a minute you said you were—"

"I did!"

He howled with laughter, his eyes incredulous, speechless apart from the occasional "YOU! –YOU???"

"Oh shut up Michael, it's not that funny!" But she knew that it was.

"Olivia Vogel, Marriage Guidance Counsellor! That's like trying to imagine Maggie Thatcher as Mother Teresa!"

"Yeah, yeah, I know," agreed Liv with a reluctant smile.

"Or Nelson Mandela as Idi Amin!"

"Yes, alright Michael, I get your point!"

"Sorry Liv, don't get arsey. It's just miscasting in general – it makes me laugh!"

"Mmmm…"

"No really! For instance, off the top of your head, what's the worst, or should I say the best, piece of miscasting you can think of?" A lively debate followed, each of them coming up with ever more funny and outrageous examples. Dick Van Dyke's cockney chimney sweep from Mary Poppins was a strong contender for a while, but Michael was sure there was one better.

"It's definitely John Wayne, but I can't think of the film. Can I borrow your phone? I'll give my nan a ring, she'll know for sure." Liv passed it over. "She loves John Wayne, knows every film he's ever made. It's ringing… Hello Nan, it's me. You okay? Yep, I'm fine – right… now, get your thinking cap on. I'm trying to think of a John Wayne film where he's all done up in a ridiculous costume with loads of make-up, slanty eyes…" a short pause, "That's it!" He gave Liv the thumbs up, a big grin on his face. "Excellent, thanks Nan… oh do they?… did he?… Blimey, I didn't realise that… okay, thanks again, gotta go!" he grinned at Liv, with a shrug that said *'what can you do?'* "No it's not a pub quiz, I'm just here with a friend… Olivia… yes, she *is* a lovely girl," he rolled his eyes and mouthed *'sorry'* to Liv who was finding the whole thing highly amusing. "Bad nerves? No I don't think so… she seemed a bit uncomfortable did she?" He started to laugh as Liv covered her face with her hands. "No, she was probably just a bit shy… yeah, anyway Nan, I've really got to go… yes I will… bye then, love you too." He replaced the receiver. "Sends her love – Genghis Khan!!!" he added triumphantly, "in '*The Conqueror*'."

"Oh God, yes!" laughed Liv, "I think I've seen it! Black and white, really old? Did he have a Fu-Manchu moustache?"

"He did – hilarious!"

"My dad loves the old John Wayne films too – we watched them all the time when we were kids."

"Nan was saying, making that film led to his death."

"What, of his career?"

"No – the death of him! Loads of the cast and film crew got cancer years later and they reckon it's because it was filmed near an atom bomb testing site in Nevada."

"God! I didn't know that. Ah, poor old Duke, bless him. The consummate cowboy."

"Yeah," agreed Michael, "but every time he stepped out of that role, it all fell to bits for me! Did you see '*The Greatest Story Ever Told*'?"

"Probably!"

"It's the Jesus one that gets shown every Easter."

"I thought that was *Ben Hur*?"

"No, this is the one where loads of Hollywood stars popped up in cameo roles."

"Oh yeah, I remember, he was the Roman Centurion wasn't he?"

"That's right – he had just the one line. He had to look up at Jesus on the cross and say, 'Truly, He was the Son of God.' But of course, he said it in his usual cowboy drawl! Apparently the director was pulling his hair out. After several takes he said tactfully, '*Duke, what we need in this line is something more. Look up at Him and give us… give us some awe!*' The Duke nodded and the cameras began to roll, he looked up at Jesus and solemnly intoned… '*Awwww!… Truly, He was the Son of God!*'"

"Priceless!" she laughed. Michael looked at her and shook his head. "I still can't get my head around you being a marriage guidance counsellor! Mind you, thinking about it, I suppose you are pretty experienced in the field of marital misery. You could certainly empathise with your clients."

"Yeah smart arse, which was exactly why they wanted me!"

Michael settled himself down for what he felt sure was going to be an extremely enjoyable interlude, as the story of her meteoric rise, and subsequent fall from grace unfurled.

"So, are you still…?"

"No," she interrupted.

"How long did—"

"About a year… including the training."

"How long was the training?"

"Well, officially I was still a trainee."

"So you didn't actually qualify?"

"No, but I had been seeing my own clients for ages."

"How long?"

"About three months," she answered miserably, wondering how on earth she was going to explain the idiotic chain of events that had led to her humiliating dismissal from the hallowed halls of the Marriage Guidance Council.

"So…?"

"Oh bloody hell Michael! I really don't want to—"

"Oh come on Liv, what happened? How the hell did you get into it for starters?"

"Well…" she gave a huge sigh of resignation, "… it all started when I met this lady down at the gym…"

Back To The Future

She had struck gold in Catherine. Not only was she intelligent, well educated, and incredibly knowledgeable, she was also one of the nicest people Liv had ever met and had been more than happy to help in any way she could. She had passed on a wealth of information covering every aspect of counselling and paved the way for Liv to enrol as a trainee. The only blot on the landscape had been Carl. She had decided the best way to pre-empt his objections would be to casually mention the fees a fully fledged counsellor could command in the private sector. When he'd heard the training was sponsored by the Marriage Guidance Council, he'd agreed quite happily; in fact, he'd been over the moon. One of the many things that drove him mad about Liv was the time she wasted listening to and dealing with other people's problems. This had sounded just the thing; getting paid shed loads of money to do something she was already doing for nothing. Marvellous!

Liv, however, had no intention of going into private practice. Once qualified, she intended to stay loyal to the Marriage Guidance Council. She felt that to benefit from their training only to set herself up as a private practitioner would be tantamount to selling her soul. She knew she was storing up trouble for the future but decided to worry about that when she got there. The main thing had been getting him to agree in the first place.

She had breezed through the training, her self-esteem growing as she discovered she really did have a flair for this kind of thing. Within a year she was ready to start seeing clients of her own. She soon realised that initially, cases fell into two main groups. The couples in the first group had not really come for guidance; it was too late for that, both parties had made their minds up long ago. They were there for official confirmation their marriage was over, thus handing over the decision to start divorce proceedings to someone else. This, of course, was not the way of The Marriage Guidance Council; as with defence lawyers defending old lags as guilty as the day is long, she had to accept that everyone and every marriage was entitled to a fair defence. When faced with a marriage as dead as Monty Python's parrot, she would have to sit there murmuring 'It's not my view that matters here, it's yours.' She had found this particularly difficult at first, as her style as an amateur had always been extremely candid. In her opinion, a simple 'You're absolutely right – this marriage is over.' would have been far more appropriate. Her light-hearted suggestion that a rubberstamped D.O.A. would save a lot of time and effort was met with stony disapproval.

Aggrieved by this waste of time and resources, she soon learnt to put such cases on the back burner. It usually only took a couple of sessions for them to understand that it was not within her remit to sign marital death warrants and the case would invariably be closed. If, however, there were children, she would do her utmost to see if there was any way back, but sadly the mere thought of trying again was often beyond them; their minds were closed. If all else failed, she would refer them to the Family Conciliation Service, which had been set up specifically to help children, and the family as a whole, through the painful process of divorce. Damage limitation; sometimes there was nothing more she could do.

Liv was far happier working with the second group; couples who genuinely wanted to work things out. She felt comfortable talking to them about their relationships, probably because she was on familiar ground. It was all a matter of communication; somewhere along the line, they had stopped talking to each other. Resentment built up and festered away until eventually the relationship broke down. Usually, once she managed to get them talking, they were already on the road to recovery.

Things were going along nicely when a case was passed on to her by one of her colleagues. She discovered she was to become the third counsellor to work with this particular couple. Reading through the case notes of Nick and Sarah Evans, she soon formed a picture of young love gone tragically wrong. Not much progress had been made, due mainly to the refusal of the husband to accompany his wife on her fortnightly trips 'to the shrink' as he put it. *Therein lies the problem*, she thought. Before she could even begin to tackle their marital problems, she had to deal with the husband's deep-rooted mistrust of all things he considered 'psycho'. To his mind everything from psychotherapy at one end of the scale, to psychopath at the other, meant bad news. He could think of only two exceptions to this rule. Hitchcock's '*Psycho*' and '*Psycho Killer*', a track by his favourite band. Even those, he had pointed out, had to be viewed with caution given their grisly content!

She decided to write to him, briefly explaining what counselling was all about. She told him how much his wife still loved him and how desperate she was to get back to the way they once were. She assured him it was most definitely possible for this to happen and suggested he had nothing to lose and everything to gain by coming in. None of this, of course, was in the training manual, but she was on a mission now. Nick and Sarah had become personal, another cardinal sin, but by now she was back into her old agony aunt ways. All her training, especially the section on not becoming personally involved, went by the board. Caution met with a similar fate and was thrown recklessly to the wind. She knew instinctively what she was doing; she was on auto pilot, firing on all cylinders and felt better than she had for ages. There had been a certain amount of frustration dealing with the constraints of professional counselling. It was fine doing things by the book, she had nothing against the book, but sometimes you just had to follow your instincts. Her predecessors had tried and failed to get Nick to come in with Sarah; she was getting nowhere too and without his involvement they were doomed.

He turned up at Sarah's next appointment; grim faced, decidedly uncomfortable but at least he was there. Liv's high hopes were soon dashed; instead of Nick opening up, all that happened was Sarah clammed up too. Liv suggested seeing them both individually for a while. There was a collective sigh of relief as they settled into this new arrangement. Pretty soon, she found she was able to talk as freely with Nick as she did Sarah.

It was clear they still loved each other, but they'd managed to alienate themselves to such a degree, there seemed no way back. They'd been together since the age of sixteen and although no definitive plans had been made, they'd always known that one day they would marry, have kids and live happily ever after. Sadly, their birth control failed and they found themselves pregnant. Both came from families where 'doing the right thing' still mattered, so long before the blue line of the pregnancy test had faded, dates were set, wedding cars booked, invitations posted and their whole lives were turned upside down. Four months into frantic preparations for both the wedding and their new lives together, Sarah suddenly and inexplicably miscarried; their baby was gone. Still in shock, they broke the news to Sarah's parents. Equally shocked, her parents asked if they intended to go ahead with the wedding. The question hung in the air. That momentary hesitation was all it took; by the time they'd stuttered the words '*we do*', the seeds of doubt and uncertainty had been sewn.

During their individual counselling sessions, Liv discovered that although neither had known how to answer, both had been shocked by the other's silence.

They'd taken it to mean they didn't really want to get married and had only gone along with it for the sake of the baby. The wedding, however, went full steam ahead; the fact that the invitations had gone out seemed to matter more than the state of everyone's emotions. The wedding was understandably a rather subdued affair and after a chilly week in sunny Corfu, the young Mr and Mrs Evans started married life together as total strangers, grieving not only the loss of their baby, but of their carefree love for each other too.

Liv could have wept in frustration at her inability to heal the rift between them. She searched for a way of getting them to open up to each other but it was hopeless. She had tried to get them to go back to that pivotal point where their love was lost and to work forward from there. There was no point in picking over the bones of their failed marriage, no point in her listening to their petty niggles over current issues; this was not about what they had become; this was about what they should, and could, still be.

"So you wanted to rewrite their history," commented Michael. "You know what you needed don't you?" She shook her head. "You needed Marty to whisk you back to the future in his DeLorean!"

"Ah yes!" laughed Liv, "wouldn't that have been just the thing. Trouble was – this was 1984. The Flux Capacitor hadn't been invented yet!"

Liv's attempts to get them to talk about that time were met with stubborn refusal. The misunderstandings born out of that moment had been set in stone; their pain had been buried away for the last three years and as far as they were concerned, that's where it was going to stay. The trouble with buried emotions, as Liv knew full well, was that they had a nasty habit of festering away, effectively sabotaging any hope of reconciliation.

The thing that was driving her nuts, and keeping her awake at night, was the feeling that somewhere, scratching away at the back of her mind, was the solution she was so desperate to find; some distant memory she couldn't quite put her finger on. She went through the training manual from cover to cover; she was sure it was there somewhere, something she had read and filed away for future reference. She dug out the box file containing everything she had ever read or written during her training and suddenly, there it was – in a file marked 'CATHERINE' – papers outlining the work of a certain Doctor Alexander Shulgin.

Alexander Shulgin

Liv had come across the file way back when she was taking her first steps towards becoming a marriage guidance counsellor; she'd found it really interesting but soon realised it had been mistakenly included in the bundle of information passed on to her by Catherine. She had mentioned it to her at the time and Catherine had explained it was part of a study led by her husband, an eminent psychologist, to evaluate the success, or otherwise, of using certain drugs during psychotherapy.

As she re-read the article, what had seemed totally irrelevant back then was suddenly absolutely pertinent to her situation now. A tool that could, as Dr Shulgin put it, "*open up a person, both to other people and inner thoughts.*" Other quotes jumped out at her; '*that by lowering patients' defences, MDMA allows them to face troubling, even repressed memories.*' Others focussed more on '*the empathic rapport catalysed by MDMA.*' "*I don't know of any other compound that can achieve this to the degree that MDMA can.*"

"Hang on…" interrupted Michael, "hang on a minute." He had managed to keep quiet throughout the telling of her story, not wanting to interrupt her flow, but – MDMA? "What, as in ecstasy MDMA?"

"Yes, but—"

"Yes but what for Christ's sake?" interrupted Michael. "Are you honestly telling me you gave this couple Ecstasy?"

"No! No, of course not! Ecstasy as we know it hadn't been invented yet either. This was the precursor to Ecstasy… a pill made from pure MDMA."

For the second time that day, he was completely lost for words. He had thought at first she was winding him up, but the look on her face told him otherwise. His face was working, struggling to arrange his features into something other than jaw dropping surprise. Liv smiled at the range of expressions being played out on Michael's face. She shook her head, "It's not as bad as—" she started, but then the phone rang, shattering the silence and the moment in one. Michael almost snatched it up and yelled 'PISS OFF!' to the unsuspecting caller. He refrained but caught her arm as she reached for the handset lying on the table between them. He wasn't about to be left hanging like Wile E. Coyote, dangling over the edge of the Grand Canyon, watching the Road Runner flash past with the rest of the story and a cheery '*meep-meep!*'

"Let the machine pick it up!" he insisted.

Luckily, it was just a marketing call. "It's not as bad as you think," she repeated once the caller had finished his pitch. "It's not like I was handing out pills willy-nilly or anything. It was just the once – a tiny little smidgeon of—"

"Pure MDMA!" he finished for her. *'Wasn't as bad as he thought?'* He wasn't entirely sure *what* he thought, other than it was far worse, or far better, than he could ever have imagined.

Liv took Michael back to the early 1980's when she, along with the rest of the general public, had never heard of MDMA. Maybe it was the fact that initially it was referred to as *'an aid to therapy'*, *'a tool'*, *'a compound'* and not as a drug, that led Liv down a path she should never have ventured. Perhaps she was just so desperate to help Nick and Sarah, her judgement was askew. Probably a bit of both, but for whatever reason, this was the path she found herself on and before long, she was hurtling down it at breakneck speed.

As she re-read the article she came to realise that the good doctor was extremely well versed on the subject of psychedelic drugs. She was more than a little concerned at this because although like many of her generation, Liv had experimented occasionally and had enjoyed the odd magic mushroom along the way, she hadn't enjoyed the full on LSD experience one little bit. In fact, it had been such a disaster she, and the group of friends that had shared the experience, vowed never to go anywhere near the stuff again and had stuck to the relative safety of marijuana ever since. As she read on however, it became clear that MDMA was completely different to LSD or any other hallucinogenic drug.

"*It didn't have the other visual and auditory imaginative things that you often get from psychedelics,*" wrote Dr Shulgin. "*MDMA didn't necessarily colour the experience with pretty colours and strange noises.*"

'*Well thank God for that!*' she thought, as the old flashbacks, albeit only feint shadows of the original horrors, flickered into life once more. Faded memories of that summer's afternoon she and her friends had embarked upon the trip of a lifetime, a trip they would never forget.

They had decided their local park would be the ideal place to experience the dubious delights of LSD. Well away from the picnickers and children's playground area, they had sat in a circle beneath a willow tree examining the innocuous looking piece of card, laughing at the pictures of The Joker and his *Ho Ho Ho's* and *Ha Ha Ha's* printed on the back. The card was carefully torn into tiny squares, distributed amongst the group and chewed methodically for the prescribed amount of time. Sheltered by the gently swaying fronds of the weeping willow, they lay back in the dappled sunshine and waited for their magical mystery tour to begin.

True to his word, The Joker had kicked off proceedings with a prolonged bout of uncontrollable laughter. This was followed by a state of euphoria which found them floating in and out of reality, full of joy and wonderment at the breathtaking splendour all around them. Sadly this spell of 'all things bright and beautiful' soon went 'tits up dark and deplorable' when the flower Liv had been studying, taking in every aspect of its exquisite beauty, suddenly started to breathe! Even now, a lifetime later, her stomach churned as she recalled that awful moment when the buttercup sprang to life. The breathing had got louder and louder, the petals changing from creamy yellow to a hideous pulsating purple. It had started growing too; into an enormous Venus flytrap intent on swallowing her whole!

Unfortunately, being complete novices, they had unwittingly broken a golden rule from the *'Druggies' Guide to Substance Abuse'*. They had failed to ensure that at least one member of their party was experienced and reasonably straight in case things went wrong. Not only were her friends powerless to help, pretty soon, spun out by her alarming behaviour, they had their own horrific hallucinations to deal with. *Poor Howard*, she thought, remembering how he'd been rolling around trying to grab hold of his tongue, convinced it was a slug. *But this is nothing like that*, she reassured herself.

She discovered that Dr Shulgin had first synthesised MDMA in 1977 and had contacted an old friend, Leo Zeff, who was about to retire from his career in psychotherapy. After trying the drug, Zeff abandoned his plans for a quiet retirement and travelled across the country introducing MDMA to other therapists and teaching them how to use it in their own practice. By the early 1980's, over a thousand private psychotherapists in the USA were using MDMA in their clinical practice. It was commonly known as *'Adam'*, not an anagram, but an allusion to *'being returned to the natural state of innocence before guilt, shame and unworthiness arose.'* Some of the most dynamic people in the field claimed that a five hour session with *'Adam'* was more beneficial than five months of normal therapy. The report made fascinating reading and Liv found herself utterly seduced by the glowing testimonies in front of her. These distinguished psychologists and psychotherapists had used

MDMA to such good effect – this was the breakthrough she had been hoping for! The only problem was – how was she going to get some?

She sat at her desk deep in thought. She couldn't contact Catherine because she and her husband were away, enjoying a long overdue visit to their daughter in Australia. They would not be back for at least two months. *Far too long* she thought as she doodled on her blotter. She crossed out *CATHERINE* and began playing with the letters M D M A realising as she wrote them, you couldn't make the word ADAM out of MDMA. She carried on doodling… MD MA… M DMA… MDM A. She stopped abruptly and stared down at what she had just written. She wrote it again – but this time as Mdm A. *'Oh my God'*, she whispered, *'Madam "A"! Carl's infamous Madam "A".'* Everything came flooding back – the spectacular row with Carl over what she thought was evidence of him frequenting a house of ill repute! *'So he had been telling the truth! There was no Madam "A"!'* She struggled to contain the maelstrom of thoughts whirling around inside her head, eventually managing to stack them up in some kind of order. It had been a couple of months ago; she had returned home early from the gym in urgent need of an icepack after pulling a muscle in the first ten minutes. She had let herself in, noticing with some surprise that Carl's Mercedes was in the drive. The door to his study was open and she could hear him playing back messages left on his answer machine. As she applied the icepack, she overheard the tail end of a message from The Grocer, Carl's contact for all things herbal and chemical, which made her blood run cold.

'Oh yeah, and I got a little surprise for you from Texas – give me a call and I'll introduce you to Madam "A" – Trust me Carl, this little honey's gonna blow your mind!…'

His raucous laugh had been cut short by the beep. She stood rooted to the spot. The bastard had gone too far this time! With the red mist descending, she marched into the room and found him phone in hand, tilted back in his chair, legs stretched out, feet resting on his desk. She grabbed the phone from his grasp and slammed it down.

'So he's expanded into the hooker market now has he?'

'Whaa—?'

'Who are you ringing? Madam "A"?… you horrible… disgusting…'

Carl had burst out laughing.

Liv paused – Michael was laughing too!

"So you thought Madam 'A' was—"

"Yep! – some leather clad dominatrix from Texas!"

Carl's mirth, of course, had been a huge mistake and was rewarded by an almighty shove that tipped him over backwards and clean out of his chair. She had stormed off – flatly refusing to listen to his explanation.

"So Carl had actually been offered MDMA?"

"Christened Madam 'A' by The Grocer."

"And you'd blown it."

"Clean out of the water!" she agreed. "I was beside myself. So near and yet so far!"

"So what did you do?"

"Well there was nothing else for it – I had to eat humble pie. That evening I told him I'd read an article on

MDMA that listed the drug's street names – and realised I owed him a huge apology."

"And he accepted?"

"He did!" she laughed. "Occupying the moral high ground was a unique experience for him and luckily, he still found the whole thing highly amusing."

Carl confirmed that the message on his answer machine had come from The Grocer. He had just got back from a trip to Fort Worth, Texas, where there was a new buzz on the block. Dr Shulgin and his chums had been keenly aware they had found a valuable new tool, but were equally aware that if MDMA became a street drug, it could follow in the footsteps of LSD and be criminalised by the government. They agreed to do as much informal research as possible without bringing the drug to public attention, and did pretty well – MDMA only gradually became known as a fun drug and it was not until 1984 that the bubble burst. With perfect timing, Carl's Grocer arrived in the States just as MDMA was about to make its debut. Still legal, the pills were easily available.

"They were even on sale in bars," she told Michael, "you could pay by credit card!"

"You're joking! So when did it become Ecstasy?"

"Late '84 – '85, not exactly sure. Apparently, the original pills were called '*Empathy*', which was actually more appropriate, but they found that '*Ecstasy*' had more sales appeal," she shrugged, "and they didn't just re-brand it, they reformulated it too."

"Right, yeah, I remember reading an article about

the whole Acid House thing. It was saying the drug was designed specifically for clubbing."

"That's right. Dr Shulgin didn't comment on MDMA as a dance drug though – or at least there was no mention of him and his merry band of professors dancing up a storm in his laboratory!"

"No day-glow lab coats then?"

"Sadly not," laughed Liv, "shame really 'cos I've seen photos and he looks just like the Marquess of Bath – long white hair, white beard, psychedelic shirts, a real old hippy – I think he'd have loved a rave! Anyway, so the drug barons, or whatever they're called, tweaked the MDMA formula, adding other drugs to create the first 'designer drug' for the club scene."

"What came first then – the music or the drug?"

"Dunno to be honest. It's a bit of a chicken and egg thing. Was the drug designed around the music or did the music come *from* the drug? Anyway, you can see my dilemma. I was so close. I knew where to get it, but I could hardly ask Carl. I could imagine his reaction after all the stick I had given him about The Grocer."

"Did you know him?"

"No, I'd always refused to have anything to do with him. I was at a dead end. The Grocer was the key but how was I going to approach him without involving Carl."

"Hmmm, tricky!"

"It was – but d'you know what?"

"Go on…"

"The answer was there all along, practically staring me

in the face. Well not just in *the* face, but in Karen's face, staring at me from across the kitchen table!"

"What – Karen Karen?"

"Of course!"

Karen was Liv's old neighbour from their previous house and they'd known each other for years. Michael had met her recently round at Liv's and they'd hit it off straight away. "Well you know Karen, she's up for anything so I thought there was a chance she might know The Grocer."

"I'm guessing she did?"

"She did!" confirmed Liv with a grin. "They go way back – and not just for drugs! Karen and her friends do a bit of bar work in the evenings and The Grocer, with all his contacts, gets them work in the clubs."

"Right so…"

"So everything was sorted in one go! I not only had my source, I had my partner too."

"Your partner?" queried Michael.

"Yes, Dr Shulgin had been emphatic. He said no one has the right to give MDMA to another person unless, and until, they were thoroughly familiar with its effects on their own mind. It stands to reason really, doesn't it… so of course I had to experience MDMA myself first. Not only that, I needed to share the experience with another person to fully understand the '*empathic rapport*'. Karen was just perfect. Not only could she get the MDMA, she was more than happy to give it a go and crucially, she was a trusted friend." Beyond surprise, Michael just sat back and smiled as she continued her story. "There was a lot of forward planning – arrangements had to be made on both sides but eventually, it all came together. Carl was away on a rugby tour, the boys went to my sister's for the weekend and Karen's daughter stayed at her mum's, so it was game on, easy as that! After all my fretting, it had just landed in my lap."

"Yeah but surely you must have had *some* reservations about what you were planning to do?"

"Well no, not really," she replied, "in fact, the way it had all clicked into place like that kind of confirmed I was on the right track. It felt like I'd been given a green light if you know what I mean."

"Hmmm, but even so – talk about drastic measures," said Michael doubtfully.

"I know," she conceded, "not quite the '*share a romantic, candlelit dinner*' kind of advice usually dished out by the Marriage Guidance Council, but I'd tried all that. I'd tried absolutely everything and I promise you – I did think it through. From what I had read, MDMA appeared to be completely safe. It was non toxic, non addictive, non hallucinogenic and without any reported side effects. I was sure I wasn't putting them at risk in any way. To me, it was a clear cut case of the end justifies the means. After taking it myself, I knew what it could do for Nick and Sarah – so no, I didn't have any doubts – I knew it would be okay."

"Come on then," he grinned, "how was it?"

"Brilliant…" she laughed, "absolutely brilliant!"

The Experiment

She remembered it all so clearly. She had been incredibly nervous but Karen's devil-may-care attitude soon rubbed off and as they sat at the kitchen table, a tiny half of a tiny pill in their hands, she remembered laughing at Karen's "Down the hatch!" as they popped them into their mouths. Karen had been a bit disappointed at the 'no alcohol' part of the deal, but had agreed after Liv explained that alcohol could have a nullifying effect on the MDMA. So with nothing but a jug of iced water and Liv's notebook beside them, they had settled down to see what would happen.

"It was all very gradual and sort of… gentle. All I can remember about the beginning was the smiling! We sat there for what seemed like hours, just smiling away at each other. I made a note of it – I wrote *'Very Smiley!'* in my notebook."

"Okay," said Michael, "so you really were treating this as a proper experiment then."

"Yes, of course I was – but…" she looked a little sheepish.

"Don't tell me – it didn't quite turn out that way?" suggested Michael.

"Well no," she admitted, "put it this way, apart from recording the time we took the pill, '*Very Smiley*' was the only thing I wrote!"

She had tried making further notes, but her vision had gone. Confident she would remember everything anyway, the notebook had been tossed aside, the water too. Liv had tried sticking to the no alcohol rule but Karen had been very persuasive. She'd argued that beer, especially ale, was not in the same league as spirits and probably wouldn't have the same negating effect. It had sounded reasonable so they'd trotted off to the bar where a large selection of ice cold lager and beer was available on tap.

The ambiance of the bar, with its soft lights, squashy leather sofas and music, had far better suited their mood. Liv had selected a tape and put it on quietly in the background as they'd taken their places in undoubtedly the best seats in the house; one on each end of the comfiest sofa, with cushions over their feet in the middle. Later in the evening, during some shivery spells, the cushions had been replaced by an enormous duvet, tucked up under their chins. In total harmony, they'd allowed the MDMA to take them on a journey of discovery that would stay with them forever.

Unfortunately for Michael, who'd been expecting a blow by blow account, Liv was strangely reticent on what happened next, saying only that the details of the experiment were strictly confidential.

"Oh come on Liv, you can't claim client confidentiality for God's sake, Karen isn't a client," protested Michael, "and diplomatic immunity won't wash either!" he added with a grin.

"No, I know, but it wouldn't be right. All I can tell you is that the experiment was a complete success, so much so, I had no hesitation in moving on to the next stage of my plan."

"Nick and Sarah?"

"Nick and Sarah," she confirmed, relieved that Michael seemed to have accepted her decision not to spill any beans at this stage. She wasn't ready to share with him the cruel trick fate had chosen to play; the irony of how her attempt to save their marriage had hammered another nail into the coffin of her own.

"Okay," said Michael, gracious in defeat. He'd decided that hearing how things turned out for Nick and Sarah, plus the added appeal of discovering what happened to her promising career as a marriage guidance counsellor, was an equally tempting prospect. The spillage of beans would have to wait. "So how did you tackle it?"

"I told them I had an important proposition to put before them and persuaded them to attend their next appointment together – thankfully, they both agreed."

"Weren't you worried about their reaction? They could have been horrified at what you were suggesting."

"True, but don't forget, I knew them pretty well by this stage. I was fairly sure they wouldn't be freaked out by the thought of taking something that would open up their minds, so to speak. If you'd met them, you'd understand why I was confident I'd get the right reaction."

"But what did you say?"

"I was completely straight with them," she assured him, "I laid everything on the line, told them about Dr Shulgin and his work and showed them the reports on MDMA. I explained that after trying it myself, I was convinced it would help them."

"How did they react?" asked Michael, still trying to get his head around the enormity of what she had done.

"Fine – honestly!" she added seeing his dubious expression, "I mean, obviously, they had loads of questions, but we talked it all through properly and they were absolutely fine with it."

"Carry on…" said Michael shaking his head.

"So that was it really. I gave them the MDMA and—"

"What?" interrupted Michael, "you gave it to them there and then – in your office?"

"They didn't actually take it there, obviously, I just gave them the—"

"In your office, in your official capacity—"

"Um, yes. I have to admit, that was probably a mistake."

"PROBABLY?" yelled Michael, his voice rising in tandem with his astonishment.

"Oh alright then definitely – it was definitely a mistake," she conceded. "I shouldn't have given it to them there. I had thought about inviting them round to my house, but that seemed a bit unethical."

"UNETHICAL? – UN-FUCKIN-ETHICAL!"

"But…"

"But what? Handing out ecstasy tablets, from your office – your office in the Marriage Guidance Council – that was ethical was it? That was totally tickety-boo! What did you do, pack them in a little box with a smiley face on the lid! Jesus Christ Liv, I worry about you sometimes, I really do!"

"Oh shut up will you, and it *wasn't* Ecstasy – how many more times! This was a million miles away from the stuff that's out there now." She stood up from the table, "I'm not telling you any more, I didn't want to tell you anyway. It's none of your bloody business – and don't you be worrying about me – I'm none of your business either! I don't want… I don't… I…"

To her utter dismay, her voice quivered and she started to cry. Michael's face fell and he went immediately as if to comfort her.

"Go away!" she managed. She was crying in anger, nothing but sheer anger. She stomped over to the counter, grabbed some kitchen roll, dried her eyes and blew her nose furiously.

"Jesus Christ!" said Michael, pretending to duck. He saw the rigidity of her back soften and her shoulders relax as she smiled in spite of herself. "Look, I really am sorry," he continued, "I had no right to yell like that – and no right to sit in judgement like some sanctimonious arsehole."

"You said it," she muttered in reply.

"Huh?"

"I said… you said it!" she repeated, turning towards

him with the hint of a smile still in her eyes. "Sanctimonious arsehole!"

"I did – and I am! Oh look, I've said I'm sorry haven't I? Come and sit back down."

"Hmmm…"

"Oh come on mate – this is hilarious! What happened?" She returned to the table.

"One word and I mean it—"

"I know," said Michael, making a zipping motion across his lips. He was having a great afternoon and had no intention of messing up for a second time.

"So…" she continued, "like I say, I gave them the MDMA and went through it all with them, you know, let them know exactly what to expect, how long it lasted etc."

"I hope you told them how long it took to kick in," said Michael, "you wouldn't have wanted them taking the second half too soon."

"They didn't have a second half. I knew from my experience with Karen they'd only need one between them," she said keeping the details of what happened when she and Karen took *their* second halves to herself. "And I was right, just a little half each was enough."

"So you sent them home with it?" She nodded. "You didn't think you ought to be with them then, you know, to mediate or anything?"

"No, not at all. This had to be their own personal experience – they didn't need me there getting in the way. I gave them my home phone number and said they could call me any time, night or day, and I'd be there. They don't live far from here so it wouldn't have been a problem. Carl

161

was away and I had Karen on standby just in case, but I knew it was highly unlikely."

"And did they?" asked Michael.

"No – well at least not until the following day. They had taken it on the Friday night and they rang me Saturday afternoon. They were so sweet!" she smiled as she remembered their call, "they kept grabbing the phone from each other, both trying to talk to me at once – it was such a relief to hear how happy they were. They asked if I could come over. They were dying to tell me all about it and of course, I was dying to know, so as soon as Karen arrived – I was there!"

"It had gone well then, obviously," said Michael with a smile.

"Yes, it was wonderful. They'd had an epiphany – a simultaneous epiphany!"

"What? They both saw the baby Jesus – at the same time!" said Michael, feigning astonishment, "must have been excellent stuff that MDMA!" She threw a cigarette packet at his head.

"Not that epiphany!"

"I know, I know, only jokin', go on."

"So anyway," she continued, "we were all laughing and crying at the same time, our cups runneth over! I didn't stay long. They'd talked right through the night and hadn't had a wink of sleep, not that they seemed the least bit tired – a bit dazed maybe, and clearly besotted, but not tired."

"Yeah, well, must have been pretty heady stuff, suddenly discovering you are madly in love with the person you've been *un*happily married to for the past three years!" laughed Michael.

"I know, can you imagine!"

"So, a happy ending."

"Very… and do you see what I meant now, about the end justifying the means?"

"Yeah," he nodded with a smile, "course I do. So what happened then? I'm guessing you were a victim of your own success?"

"Kind of," she agreed, "Nick and Sarah's case certainly got me noticed. Everyone wanted to know how I'd managed it and were keen to get my opinion on other cases."

"Must have been a bit tricky," he chuckled, "you could hardly tell them…" and then realising that *anything* was possible with Liv, he added, "You didn't, did you?"

"Course not! I just waffled on about it being their love that got them through, which was completely true anyway. It had been clear from the start they still loved each other. An unplanned pregnancy has a way of letting you know if you're with the right person. It tells you in no uncertain terms that you're in it for the long haul – together forever and all that. If they hadn't loved each other, losing the baby would have been a 'get out of jail free' card."

"But neither of them took it," said Michael.

"No, the hesitation in front of Sarah's parents had nothing to do with their commitment to each other. They were still reeling from the loss of their baby. How could they contemplate a wedding and all the rigmarole that went with it?" She shook her head. "I just said I'd helped them revisit that time and address the misconceptions that had taken place."

"Which is, in a nutshell, exactly what you did," said Michael. "So what went wrong?"

"Well, obviously, Nick and Sarah understood from the outset that our little experiment was strictly off the record. They'd promised faithfully not to breathe a word to anyone, but their closest friends had been having relationship problems too. They'd noticed the miraculous change in Nick and Sarah and had demanded to know what had happened, as did Nick's sister, and Sarah's colleague at work. Before long, suspicions became aroused by the sudden wave of new clients ringing in—"

"All trying to book an appointment with you!"

She nodded, "I was in a complete panic. The whole thing was about to blow. I left work early that Friday and thanked my lucky stars I had already booked the following week out for the boys' half term. I took them to my sister's in Wales for the week hoping things would calm down while I was away – but as soon as I got back, I got a phone call demanding I came in. They'd had a bloke in reception asking to see '*the bird dishing out the pills!*' I was fired, of course, but thankfully no further action was taken. They wanted to avoid the adverse publicity. So there you go."

"Hoist by your own petard!"

"The very chap!" chuckled Liv as she stood up, making ready to leave.

"I wonder what that means," mused Michael as they left the house, "well, I know what it *means* – but what the hell's a petard?"

"It's French," said Liv, "it came up in that English course I did. Apparently William Shakespeare used it in Hamlet. '*Hoist by your own petard*' actually means – to be blown up by your own explosive device."

"Get out of here!" laughed Michael. She got in her car and started the engine. She was running late.

"No really!" she said, lowering her window. "In fact, the exact translation from the old French is even funnier."

"Go on," called Michael, as she manoeuvred her car through the gates.

"According to the French," she called back, "I was blown up by my own fart – parp parp!"

Liv pulled up outside the boys' school puzzled by the lack of cars. It was usually mayhem trying to park at this time of day but it was strangely deserted. *The school trip!* She had completely forgotten. The whole school had gone to Walton-on-the-Naze and would not be back until gone four. She checked her watch. No point in going back home; fifteen minutes and she'd have to drive straight back again, so she parked up, reclined her seat and settled down for the wait. She ran through the events of the afternoon smiling at Michael's shocked reaction to her story. *And that was only the half of it!* she thought ruefully. She and Karen had made a solemn vow that weekend. '*What went on in the experiment stayed in the experiment!*' It was a promise she intended to keep.

Instead of giving Michael a detailed account of everything that had happened that night, she had simply explained the conception and instigation of the plan and its outcome, which, in the context of the experiment, had been a complete success. The effects of the MDMA, particularly the empathic rapport, had been everything she had hoped for; she and Karen had shared something very special that night, connecting on such a deep level, the closeness they'd experienced was far beyond anything they'd ever known before. Liv closed her eyes, enjoying the warm sunshine streaming through the car window as she recalled the crazy, drug addled weekend she had shared with Karen; all in the name of science.

***

Karen had driven directly to Liv's after dropping her daughter off at her mother's for the weekend. Liv's boys were with her younger sister Helen until Sunday; she was taking them to Alton Towers with her brood and they had been literally bouncing off the walls with excitement. Carl was in Belgium on a rugby tour, also due back on Sunday. It was 7pm, Friday. They had forty-eight hours in which to make the acquaintance of Madam 'A'. They went through to the kitchen and Liv put the kettle on. She had been meticulous in her research and wanted to be as scientific as possible. She had asked Karen to skip breakfast, have a late lunch and fast from then on. They sat at the kitchen table drinking their tea.

"When do you have to collect Emily?"

"Sunday afternoon. We've got the whole weekend to ourselves Liv." She rubbed her hands together, "Shall we get started? I've got the little chaps right here so we're ready to go!"

Liv laughed at her enthusiasm and agreed they may as well start the experiment straight away. She had a notebook and pen on the table and went to get a jug of iced water and two glasses. They grinned at each other across the table. Karen took a tiny pill from a cellophane wrap and broke it in two. They swallowed their halves at precisely 7:15pm. Liv recorded the time in her notebook.

"It can take up to an hour apparently, but could take effect within thirty minutes. Depends on stomach contents, body weight—"

"Jesus Christ Liv, lighten up! You sound like Quincy ME going on about stomach contents and stuff! Let's just go with the flow!"

"Sorry Karen, but this is really important. I'm trying to conduct an experiment here."

"Yep, totally get that, but we can still have some fun with it can't we?" she looked at the kitchen table with its teapot, teacups and water, "Blimey, that's a depressing sight! A party with no booze?"

"Karen! It's not a party and there's no point in drinking alcohol, it could negate the effect of the MDMA."

"Okay, okay, point taken," she said with an air of resignation. She looked across at her friend and grinned to show there were no hard feelings. "So Mrs Fully Fledged Counsellor, how's it going? I'm guessing this kind of experiment isn't exactly normal practice?"

"Not fully fledged yet," grinned Liv, "and no... this

is what you call special measures. It's all strictly off the record of course."

"No shit Sherlock! Don't worry, I'd worked that one out!" laughed Karen.

"To be honest, I'm not really enjoying it that much. It's so frustrating not being able to go with your instincts. There are so many rules and regs about what you can and can't say and the paperwork is mind-blowing. I look back at our coffee mornings…" she sighed despondently, "it was all so simple then."

"Aw, the dear old Fucking Disorder Clinic – we've all missed you since you turned pro."

"That was your name for it, not mine!" laughed Liv. "I've missed you too – we used to have such a laugh."

"Didn't we just!" agreed Karen. "We carried on for a while at my place but it wasn't the same."

Liv and her friends used to enjoy regular coffee mornings at her house at least once a month. The conversation usually centred around their marital problems and with sex always high on the agenda, their exclusive club soon earned its unique moniker. Liv, who was nearing the end of her training, had become quite an authority on such matters and her advice to the group was well received.

"Do you remember the last one we had before Carl put a stop to it?"

"How could I ever forget!"

During the previous session, their friend Sally had told the group of her husband's suggestion to make love with the lights on. She had been complaining for months about his lack of interest so Liv had encouraged her to give it a go. This was rich coming from Liv, considering the only people ever to have seen *her* up close and personal were members of the medical profession and her mum; however the group were not to know this and as far as they were concerned she was virtually a qualified sex therapist. Liv had been keen to find out if Sally had taken her advice. It seemed she had.

"So you left the lights on?"

"I did."

"And was Mark turned on by that?" asked Karen.

"Most definitely, yes."

"So…?"

"Well all was going well… so well in fact he slid down the bed to… you know… pleasure me."

The group murmured their approval.

"And…?" they urged.

"Well, I don't know if you know this but – I'm a natural redhead."

"Huh?" the group were puzzled.

"What's that got to do with it?" asked Karen.

"Everything!" came Sally's reply. "Up 'til then I'd kept my eyes tightly shut, but following your advice to be more adventurous Olivia…" Sally shot her an accusing look, "I looked down, and there he was – Yosemite Sam – leering up at me from behind his pubic beard!"

The whole group had collapsed with laughter, and were soon warming to the theme. Captain Pugwash, ZZ Top, Catweasel, Rasputin… each one funnier than the last but for some reason, Liv's offering of Wyatt Earp brought the house down – made even funnier when the door was flung open by an irate Carl, demanding to know what they were laughing at. Needless to say, Liv had been hard pressed to convince him of the serious nature of the work carried out there so sadly, the doors of The FDC had been closed – never to open again.

"Ah, the good old days," laughed Karen. "How're you feeling? Anything happening?"

"Actually, yes…" she put her hand to her chest and took a deep breath, "I've got this flickering going on at the side of my eyes and a kind of fluttery feeling here."

"Me too! Wooooh!"

The Pill Of Two Halves

Aware of a definite heightening of their senses, a sudden rush of elation coursed through their bodies bringing about a sense of enormous wellbeing. As the effects of the MDMA kicked in, they adjourned to the comfort of the bar. Their ice cold beers were delectable and the music coming from the speakers all around them was spine-tingling but the most important aspect of all was the deep connection they felt during the conversations they shared. Wrapped in a warm cocoon of love and total empathy, they talked for hours, but even time was being kind to them, passing so slowly, they were constantly amazed to find they still had the whole night ahead of them. They talked about everything; their lives, their loves; their hopes and dreams; their families, their childhood and their beloved children.

Liv opened up about her life with Carl and told of her sadness that things hadn't worked out as she'd hoped. She admitted she didn't love him anymore and that if it wasn't for the boys, she would have left long ago. She hated that they were growing up in an unhappy marriage and wished things could be different. She was worried about the effect their constant rows were having on them and was not sure that 'staying together for the sake of the children' was the right thing to do. That was what her own parents had done and she could still remember the agony of lying in bed with her sisters, listening to their endless arguments downstairs. They would whisper to each other *'who will you live with if they get divorced?'* How can you choose between your mum and your dad?

Karen didn't remember her father and was raising her daughter alone. Her childhood and experience of motherhood were totally different to Liv's but she understood her feelings perfectly and felt her pain. She revealed to Liv how at the age of twenty-one, she had been given the news her baby daughter had Down's syndrome. Liv's heart went out to her as she described her feelings of shock and disbelief when the medical team told her she should give the baby up straight away. She was young, they said, young enough to go on and have lots of normal children. She told of her outrage that they could suggest such a thing. They were talking about her baby, her beautiful baby as if she were just a defective commodity that should be rejected without another thought. She loved her and was determined to keep her. The father had disappeared as soon as he found out she was pregnant, so it was solely her decision. Liv had come to love Emily over the years and was horrified to hear of the callous advice given to Karen when she had been born. She found herself crying, but the tears rolling down her cheeks weren't salty or stinging; in the rosy glow of MDMA, they were soft and gentle, like rain water.

Liv was starting to feel sleepy. The experiment had been a great success and she was delighted with the outcome. She was convinced it would be perfect for Nick and Sarah and couldn't wait to put the final part of her plan into action. She suggested to Karen they had a final night cap.

"WHAT? You're kidding me! Go to bed now? It's not even twelve o'clock! We've got the whole night ahead of us! Come on Liv, let your hair down. Let's take another half – live dangerously for once!"

"No Karen, really, I'm quite sleepy now. I think I could just float away if I shut my eyes. We don't have to go anywhere – we can just crash here if you like." Liv started to snuggle down into the sofa but Karen was having none of it.

"No you don't!" She took hold of Liv's hands and pulled her up into a sitting position. "Up, up, up! Come on! We've got the whole night and all day tomorrow to recover." She broke a second pill in two and immediately popped her half. "Open up! You've got to now, you can't leave me on my own – the good doctor said so!" Liv reluctantly swallowed her half too.

Twenty minutes later. "Anything?"

"Um, no, I don't think so, not really. I'm still feeling sleepy. You?"

"Nothing. I think we should take another half. It's

been ages. Something should have happened by now."

"What do you mean another half? We've taken the other half. How many halves have we got?"

"I've got another whole one – another three actually!" laughed Karen. "Don't look so shocked. I didn't ask for them, The Grocer just gave me the wrap and there happened to be five in there!"

"No Karen, stop – this is getting nuts! We should wait. How long's it been? What time did we take the other half?"

"Ages ago – an hour at least, I reckon."

"No, I don't think it's been that long. We should definitely wait. Dr Shulgin—"

"Shulgin Schmulgin!! What does he know anyway?"

"Everything there is to know you big dope! He's the one who invented it!"

"Maybe the last one wasn't that strong. Trouble is you never really know what you're getting with drugs. It's not like when you buy a drink. You order a vodka and that's what you get! Mind you, The Grocer said these were good so hopefully – what are you smiling at?"

"You! Sitting there all agitated! Just relax… it's fine. You're fine, I'm fine, and this is fine—"

"There's no quality control you see," continued Karen unabated, "with your alcohol, there it is – printed on the side of the bottle. But drugs – it's pot luck every time! Come on… if we take it now it'll catch up with the other half and we'll get the full effect!"

"Stop!" laughed Liv. "I've got this image in my head

now – half a pill with arms and legs, sprinting round our systems looking for its other half!"

"Yeah… calling out '*wait for meeeeee!*'"

They swallowed their third halves; moments later their second halves kicked in!

One Step Beyond

Their rush was simultaneous and Karen whooped with delight. "Here we go!"

Liv laughed at first but her elation was short-lived. Hot on its tail came a wave of paranoia. The surge that rushed upwards through her chest was so strong she felt like her head was going to blast off from her shoulders. It took her breath away and she could hardly speak.

"Karen!... Karen!"

"What?"

"Karen!" It seemed that all she could manage was the word 'Karen'.

"What's up Liv?" She couldn't answer. She was shaking violently and her teeth were chattering so hard she literally couldn't speak. Karen went to her immediately, wrapped a duvet around her and pulled her in close. "Shhh... shhh... shhh, it's alright Liv, I'm here, you're okay, you just got a little wobble on that's all, calm down now, calm down." Karen was rocking her gently and making soothing sounds.

After a while the shaking lessened but almost immediately she was gesturing to Karen that she was too hot and was frantically pushing the duvet away. Karen led her to the guest cloakroom where she ran cold water on her wrists and held a damp towel on the back of her neck. They stayed there for a while alternating between the duvet and cold water until eventually, Liv was able to speak.

"We've taken too much – what's going to happen when the other one… when…" she started shaking again.

"Nothing! Nothing's going to happen. Now listen to me Liv, this is just your own mind doing this." Karen took her firmly by the shoulders. "Look at me, Liv look at me – I've had exactly the same as you and I'm fine." She continued to speak gently and reassuringly as she walked her back to the comfort of the bar. "Liv, you have to relax into this, stop fighting it, that's what's going wrong." Liv nodded, lay back on the sofa and tried to relax but the ominous words of an old song kept playing in her head, causing a fresh bout of shivering. She tried to sing it out loud but with the teeth chattering accompaniment it sounded hilarious.

"There could be trouble ahead!"

Karen laughed and attempted to complete the line.

"But while there's music… and something, lah lah lah, lah lah lah, let's face the music and dance!" It gave her an idea and while she was singing, she skipped round to the back of the bar and located the sound and lighting systems. Selecting one of the tapes from the summer party she cranked up the volume, dragged Liv to her feet… and the party began!

Liv was laughing, freed from her paranoia, her spirit

soared. The next minute they were bopping around like a couple of loons totally immersed in the dance music that was belting out from all around them. Every now and then the strobe lights flicked on, causing their flailing arms to leave glowing tracer trails that blew their minds. Once again, time stood still. The more they danced the higher they flew until eventually they collapsed into a laughing heap on the sofa. Liv changed the tape from dance music to something calmer, one of her brother's toe tapping compilations. They lay on the sofa in total bliss as Steve Harley's voice came over the speakers inviting them to come up and see him, make him smile. They sang along happily for a while as track after track of their all time favourites reverberated around the room. They were enjoying the breather but before long they found that once again, they were unable to resist the beat. Chuckling away on the sofa, they began seated synchronised dancing until Ian Drury arrived with his *'Reasons to be Cheerful Part 3'*. They jumped to their feet and just like Baloo in Jungle Book, they were *'gone man, solid gone!!'* They leapt about to *'Baggy Trousers'* and then *'One Step Beyond'* had them under the strobe lights doing the Madness walk all around the room. They sang and danced the night away until once again, they found themselves flaked out, head to head this time, on the L-shaped sofa. The tape had finished and as they lay there together, comfortable, contented and enjoying the silence, they drifted off for a while, floating in and out of consciousness, completely at peace. Karen rolled over and flopped an arm across Liv's back.

"Love you." Liv lifted her head and grinned.

"Me too… you too."

"You're lovely!… lovely Livvie!"

"Doh!… and you're beautiful."

"You're beautiful too."

"We're beautiful and we're lovely…"

"Shame we're not gay – we'd make a lovely couple!"

"We would!" laughed Liv in agreement.

"Have you ever… you know…"

"What?"

"You know… with a girl?"

"Nah… have you?"

"Not even a bit? – not even nearly?" persisted Karen. Liv rolled over so that they were face to face, chins resting on their hands. She tried to focus on Karen's face to gauge whether she was joking but there were at least three Karen's grinning back at her. She laughed uncertainly.

"Are you kidding with me?"

"No, no, just wondering, that's all. Have you thought about it then?"

"No! Stop it, you're making me feel weird – and you didn't answer me!"

"Calm down!" laughed Karen, "I was just remembering something you said once and it got me thinking."

"What did I say?"

"It was when we were having that debate at the Disorder Clinic about threesomes."

"Oh yeah, and you all tore into me because I said, hypothetically—"

"You'd rather two girls and a guy—"

179

"Yes – but you didn't give me a chance to explain!"

"What's to explain?" laughed Karen. "We all said we'd go for two guys and there was you, Miss Butter Wouldn't Melt, calmly announcing she'd like a threesome with another girl!"

"I didn't say that! It was all hypothetical for a start and what I meant was… what I didn't mean was… I didn't mean I wanted to, you know, actually do anything with the girl."

"Why did you say you'd want a girl then?"

"Because I knew I definitely wouldn't want two guys!"

"Well why didn't you say so?"

"You lot didn't give me the chance! I was trying to say that being with another girl was less intimidating—"

"So you weren't saying you'd get it on with the girl?"

"No!"

"What were you going to do then," laughed Karen, "just ignore the poor cow?"

"No, I was thinking that we'd both kind of, you know, make love to the guy!" They rolled back over onto their backs and settled down once more into a companionable silence. "Mind you, I did have a massive crush on the Head Girl at my school!"

"Ah ha!" laughed Karen, "Yeah well, I have to confess to a little confusion along the way too, but basically —"

"We're both straight!"

"Well I'm glad we've got that one out the way," laughed Karen, "how're you feeling?"

"Great. Are you sleepy yet?"

"Not at all," said Karen.

"No, I'm not either. What's the time?"

"Um… can't see properly… half four I think."

"Do you reckon that last half is still waiting in the wings?"

"Nah, that probably came on when we were dancing." Karen sat up as a light bulb pinged in her head. "Tell you what, why don't we take the last one!" She looked across at Liv expectantly. "We're not going to sleep now and let's face it – we'll never get another chance for a night like this – might as well make the most of it."

"We can't! We've got to save the last one for Nick and Sarah – that's the whole point of the exercise!"

"I've got two! One for us and one for them – I take it you're not going to give them more than one are you?"

"Good God no! Half each will do them just fine."

"There you go then, one last hurrah and we'll call it a night. What'd you say?"

"You've definitely got Nick and Sarah's?"

"Yep, look. Here, take theirs and put it somewhere safe." She passed it over, broke the remaining pill in two and swallowed her final half. With Nick and Sarah's pill wrapped in cellophane and safely in her pocket, Liv popped her half too.

"Cheers!"

"Cheers! Right, I think I should roll a puff, just in case, for medicinal purposes only of course. Is there any in the house?"

"Don't think so, only Portaloo Blue, and I'm not going anywhere near that stuff! Anyway, what'd you mean, '*just in case*'! What do you think is going to happen?" Karen had been about to give an impersonation of Liv's teeth

181

chattering episode of paranoia but thought better of it. She didn't want to bring on another one!

"Nothing, nothing at all!" She started rummaging around in her bag, "Don't worry Liv, I'm bound to have some, I'm like a good Girl Guide, always prepared!"

"It's *'Lend a Hand'* – *'Be Prepared'* is The Scouts."

"Nope, *'Lend a Hand'* is definitely The Brownies. I know that because Emily has just joined and she's been following me around offering to lend me a hand with just about anything and everything ever since. She's doing my head in! I've had her reciting that bloody motto and the brownie promise ad nauseam – and that's on top of the times tables and body parts she was already learning."

"Body parts?"

"Yeah, they've been doing some kind of sex education at school. The other day, we're standing in the queue for the checkout at Sainsbury's and she points to the couple in front of us and announces in a very loud whisper, *'She's got a vagina and he's got a penis!'*"

"Ah bless her!"

"I know, and then last night, we were sat watching tele when the phone rang. I went to answer it and told her to carry on watching. When I got back I asked what was going on and she said *"Well... you see that lady... she dropped a cup of tea in her lap and burnt her vulva!"* Liv rolled off the sofa she was laughing so much. "Anyway," continued Karen, "being prepared or lending a hand is a moot point because I was never in The Guides, The Brownies, or The Scouts for that matter! I've got my own little twist to that motto anyway. Forget the Swiss Army knife and a needle and thread… to my mind, '*be prepared*' means keeping a little puff about your person – you never know when you might need it!" She found what she was looking for and proceeded to roll a couple a joints. "These will make sure we come down gently."

"Lovely…" agreed Liv, lounging comfortably on the sofa observing Karen's expert spliff rolling technique.

"So, where were we? Ah yes," said Karen, answering her own question, "hypothetical threesomes! So none of that malarkey for you then?"

"Nope."

"Affairs?" She shook her head. "So Carl's your only one?" No reply. She looked up from the task in hand. "Liv?"

Olivia's teeth started chattering again.

"One other."

"Hang on – I thought you were a virgin when you met Carl!"

"I was!" replied Liv trying to relax her jaw. "Okay," she continued desperately, "look I'd better just tell you. I had a brief fling with someone, not an affair – it only lasted about six weeks so that doesn't constitute an affair really does it?"

Karen sat bolt upright. "What?" She was literally agog. "Blimey, this is a turn up for the books! Why didn't you tell me before? Who? When? How come I didn't know?"

"I'm sorry Karen. It was… it was a very difficult time for me and he… well he was the one who got me through."

"Do I know him?"

"Erm… well… yes, you do actually." Liv closed her

eyes and took a deep breath. "It was Terry." She winced in expectation of the furore that was sure to follow, but there was just silence. She looked up to see Karen in a state of suspended animation, the almost completed joint held to her mouth, tongue poised, ready to lick the Rizla.

"Terry?" Liv nodded. "Terry Mitchell?" Another nod. Karen slowly and deliberately finished rolling the joint. "Well bugger me sideways!" She lit the joint and joined Liv on the sofa. Their final halves brought about a gentle rush, similar to the first, and helped them through what could have been an extremely tricky tête-à-tête. Liv knew that Karen, along with other members of the Disorder Clinic, had fallen victim at some point to Terry's dubious charms. "Well," said Karen as Liv came to the end of her tale of damsel in distress and knight in shining armour. "All I can say is, I'd love to believe that Terry was being that honourable, but honestly hun, I think you're deluding yourself. There would always have been the ulterior motive with Terry – he just can't help himself. Mind you," she added, "great shag!"

"Honestly it wasn't like that. It wasn't about the sex, he was so kind to me – he's a good man. I genuinely believe he loved me."

Karen cocked a quizzical brow. "Hmmm okay, well you believe what you want to believe, but I still think he took advantage of the situation. I've seen him in action at the clubs Liv. He should have a government health warning on his back."

"Hazardous to the heart?"

"No, Horny Old Goat!"

The Exorcist

"Anyway, enough of Terry, what about you! You are *such* a dark horse Olivia Vogel!" She shook her head, "It's just one thing after another."

"What do you mean?"

"Well, there was the threesome thing—"

"I've explained that!"

"The kinky mirror and now Terry bloody Mitchell! What's next I ask myself?"

"Kinky mirror?"

"Oh come on Liv, don't play the innocent. The kinky mirror in your bedroom."

"They're not kinky! They're nowhere near the bed."

"What are you talking about?"

"The mirrored wardrobes – what are *you* talking about?"

"The one in your en-suite."

"Huh? Karen, I honestly don't know what you're on about."

"Why were you laughing then?"

"When?"

"When I was doing the '*nudge nudge, wink wink, say no more*' thing!"

"Eh?"

"When we were dancing to '*Mirror in the Bathroom*'" laughed Karen. "I was doing this!"

She jumped up and starting dancing about, flapping one elbow and winking her eye.

"I thought you were cockney dancing or doing the funky chicken or something!"

"What – a funky cockney chicken with a dodgy eye?"

"Oh I don't know!" laughed Liv. "What *were* you doing?"

"This!" said Karen, tapping her nose and demonstrating once more with the elbow and the eye. "You know, '*wink wink, nudge nudge, know what I mean!*'"

"But I don't know what you mean!"

"The dodgy mirror in your bathroom!"

"What dodgy mirror? – I DON'T KNOW WHAT YOU'RE TALKING ABOUT!"

Karen studied Liv's face for a moment. "God, you actually don't, do you?" She got up and took her by the hand. "You'd better come with me." She led her upstairs to the master bedroom and through to the en-suite shower room. She stood by the side of the hand-basin and took up the pose of a magician's assistant. She presented the mirror that was fixed flush against the wall above the basin, pointed to the hinges at the top, and with a theatrical flourish and a jaunty '*Ta-dah!*' she lifted it up. Liv was astonished. She walked up to it and inspected the hinges she was seeing for the very first time. She swung the mirror up and down and looked at the bare brickwork that edged a black hole, previously hidden by the mirror. She thought at first it was some kind of wall safe, and felt around inside. There was nothing there apart from a neatly folded length of thick black material. She looked questioningly at Karen.

"Put your head in."

"My head? Why, what is it? What's in there?" Liv was feeling increasingly uneasy and certainly didn't fancy sticking her head inside the dark cavity.

"Nothing's in there Liv, trust me, just put your head in and wait." She gently guided Liv's head towards the opening. "Go on, it's okay." Finally she got Liv to comply. "Right, don't move – stay exactly where you are – I'll see you in two ticks!" She promptly disappeared. Liv pulled her head back out and called after her. She was about to leave when suddenly – the hole lit up! She gingerly placed her head back inside – and saw Karen dancing around in the family bathroom, laughing and waving at her! "Coo-eee! Olivi-ahhh!"

Her befuddled brain was trying to make sense of what she was seeing but it was unfathomable. *I'm standing here with my head in the wall and I'm looking through a… what?… what is this?* She was losing touch with reality. Karen was now a performer in a bawdy burlesque. Lying in the sunken bath, one leg in the air and pouting in Liv's direction, she was enacting a striptease. Liv could just hear her singing the strippers' tune… "Da, Da, Dah… DaDa, Da, Dah!" She was calling out, beckoning for Liv to join her, but she was rooted to the spot. Karen blew a final kiss, hopped out of the bath and then disappeared from view. The next minute Liv felt herself being pulled back from the abyss. She was as stiff as a board, her eyes were blank and unseeing and she was as white as a sheet. Suddenly and without any warning, she vomited spectacularly.

"What the fuck!" yelped Karen as the jet of liquid quite literally shot out of Liv's mouth with the velocity of a fire hose. It arced across the room, narrowly missing Karen as she jumped back out of harm's way. "Woooh! Great shot!" she added as the contents of Liv's stomach hit the far wall of the shower, an impressive ten feet away.

"Sorry!" gasped Liv, "Didn't know it was coming – just happened!" No sooner were the words out of her mouth than another blast followed with the same explosive force as the last.

"Jesus Christ Liv! Talk about The Exorcist!" She held her over the sink in case there was more to come. Thankfully, it was over as quickly as it had begun and although horrific, the projectile vomiting had snapped Liv out of her stupor. Karen was relieved to see the colour returning to her face. "Right matie, let's get you sorted." She lowered her onto the bidet and sat beside her on the loo. She took her hands and rubbed them vigorously. "How you doing?" Liv's eyes stayed shut but she managed a nod. "Lucky for you, Aunty Karen has just what you need." She shot back downstairs to the bar and returned moments later. "Here, have this!" She stuffed a joint into Liv's mouth and lit it. Liv drew the smoke deeply into her lungs and after a few tugs, she visibly relaxed. "See what I mean about being prepared? Better than a piece of string or a safety pin!" Liv nodded and continued puffing away. "Tell you what, you crack on, I'll get another one." Ten minutes later, lying slumped on the toilet, she looked across at Liv through half closed lids as she lay sprawled beside her in the bidet. "Alright Liv?" Liv gave her a thumbs up. "Glad you've stopped with the Regan impersonations – fuckin' hell! I thought your head was gonna start spinning round!" She heard a gurgling sound and ducked expecting the worst. Happily it was just the beginnings of a deep belly laugh and moments later the pair of them were swallowed up in a paroxysm of uncontrollable laughter.

Mirror In The Bathroom

As soon as Liv felt able, she wanted to examine the mirror from the other side. She had started to work out what she had seen but still couldn't quite believe it. Karen helped her to her feet and followed her into the family bathroom. They stood in front of the large mirror that was fixed to the adjoining wall of Liv's en-suite. "But you can see it quite easily from here!" said Liv, totally perplexed. "Why didn't I—"

"It's because the light's on in your bathroom," explained Karen. "Hang on – I'll turn it off."

Liv, meanwhile, stood with her back to the mirror and looked at the bathroom with different eyes. She was seeing it through the eyes of a Peeping Tom. The bath was centre stage, the glass shower enclosure to the right, the bidet and toilet to the left. All could be seen perfectly from the mirror on the wall. She crossed the room and looked back at the mirror from the edge of the bath. It looked absolutely normal. She wondered if Karen was looking at her. It was the creepiest thing she'd ever experienced. She walked back up to the mirror, right up close to it, but all she could see was her reflection. Bizarre thoughts went through her mind. *'I've plucked my eyebrows in front of this mirror – I've picked my spots – and he could have been inches away from my face!'* Other embarrassing rituals carried out in the 'privacy' of this bathroom came to mind and she cringed picturing the positions she had taken up when waxing her bikini line. She suddenly thought of her sister and Clare and her stomach turned over. They had both lived here and had used this bathroom.

"You can't tell can you?" said Karen as she came back into the room. Liv shook her head.

"It's unbelievable! So he could stand there, completely undetected, as long as there was no light on his side."

"Yes – that's why the black cloth's in there. He'd pull it up over his head, you know, like an old fashioned photographer, to block out all the light." Liv found the mental image of Carl hunched under the black cloth peering through the hole so repugnant, she rushed to the toilet and threw up. Not projectile this time, but a deep dry retching that came up from her boots. Karen knelt beside her, rubbing her back. "What we need is a nice cup of tea. Come on mate, let's get out of here." They went back downstairs to the kitchen. Liv was absolutely exhausted, but the tea and a cigarette soon hit the spot. She began firing questions.

"Where did it come from… who fitted it…?"

"The builder put it in when all the work was done on the house before you moved in. He'd foraged it from a demolition job in London somewhere and was bragging about it down the pub. Carl made him an offer he couldn't refuse."

"So it's been here all along!"

"Yep, from day one."

"How did you know about it? Who told you?"

"Jonty, but Liv—"

"Oh God! So the rugby lot know?"

"Liv hun, everyone knows. It's the worst kept secret in North London."

"Why didn't anyone tell me?"

"We thought you knew!"

Liv was aghast. Out of all the information she had needed to process, this was perhaps the hardest to accept.

"You thought I knew about that disgusting thing in my house? You all thought I knew?"

"Sorry Liv… we just assumed… I mean, you wouldn't think he'd have the front to…" Liv raised her eyebrows. "Yeah… thinking about it," conceded Karen, "this is Carl we're talking about."

"Exactly," said Liv wearily, "so the usual rules don't apply. Oh God Karen, so tell me – who exactly knows?"

"Well… the rugby crowd obviously and I suppose everyone else who came to the pool parties. The blokes warned their wives and girlfriends about it, for obvious reasons, and that's how the news spread. Didn't you notice how they would queue up for the other bathrooms and toilets rather than use that one?"

"No! Not at all… but thinking back, I was surprised when girls used the outside changing rooms, you know, because of the louvered doors. I always thought they'd have preferred somewhere more private. How ironic!" She laid her head down on the kitchen table. "Oh God, what am I going to do? I'm married to a Peeping Tom!"

"Will you tell him you know?"

"I'll have to," shrugged Liv, "but it's okay, I won't tell him you told me."

"Tell him – I don't care!"

"No, I'll just say I noticed the hinges and found it myself. No need to drag you into it."

"Okay mate, you deal with it your way."

"I keep wondering when he'd have used it, you know, who he's peeped on."

"Well... the pool parties..."

"Yeah, I get that. It would've been easy with all that going on. You remember those parties – they were mayhem! All those people traipsing in and out – I didn't even know half of them! But Clare and my sister? It's in my en-suite! Surely he couldn't have risked it with me being there?"

"That's true."

"But what if I wasn't there?"

"Liv you can't—"

"But that'll be their first thought – it was *my* first thought! *Did he spy on me?*"

"Yeah of course."

"You feel so..."

"Violated."

"Exactly that! And it's horrible not knowing."

"You'll probably never know – he'll never admit it."

"Yeah but I need to know – I have to find out." Liv sipped at her tea, smoking cigarette after cigarette, deep in thought. Karen just sat quietly, not intruding in any way but just being there. Eventually, she saw a smile begin to form on Liv's face. "Got it!"

"Hold that thought!" said Karen, "I've got a feeling this will go down better with some alcohol and a spliff!" Liv laughed. The mood had lightened immeasurably and five minutes later, '*Horses for Courses!*' was the toast, as they enjoyed a ramped up version of the tea and cigarettes they'd partaken earlier.

"Right…" said Olivia, "I've been thinking. Most nights I just have a shower in my en-suite, but sometimes I fancy a nice long soak in the bath. Now looking back, it seems that whenever I've done that, Carl would follow me up, saying he was going to watch tele or read for a bit. I reckon that on those nights he peeped on me because he was always, you know… aroused when I got into bed."

"Oh God!"

"Don't!" Liv shuddered. "Anyway, here's my plan. I'm going to place some strands of hair behind the mirror in the en-suite. Next time he follows me up, I'll have my bath as normal and then afterwards, I'll check if the hair is still there. If it's gone – voilà! – I'll know he's been peeping!" Karen snorted with laughter. "What?" demanded Liv, "why are you laughing, it's a brilliant idea!"

"Sorry Liv, it's the word 'peeping' – it's cracking me up!"

Liv began to laugh in spite of herself, "Yeah I s'pose

it *is* a funny word – but that's what he's doing isn't it – creeping and peeping! Urghhhh!" she shuddered again. "So, you weren't laughing at my plan then?"

"No, not really. Well yeah, a bit! I mean it *is* good, and it *could* work, but it just sounds a bit, you know, Inspector Clouseau!" They laughed as she '*da dum, da dummed*' the Pink Panther theme tune. "That'll be so weird Liv… lying there… having your bath, not knowing if he's next door with his head stuck in that hole, peeping at you! You could give him a little show like I did earlier."

"Yeah and half way through I'll leap out and rush at the mirror screaming 'PERVERT'!"

Karen roared with laughter. "He'd absolutely shit himself!"

"I'll stick a note on it – Mirror Mirror, on the wall, who's the biggest perv of all!"

"You know what else you could do – you could leave something inside the hole."

"What, sexy underwear?"

"I was thinking more like a gimp mask!"

Liv laughed, "Yeah – *wear this while you're perving!*"

"You fuckin freak! – You could write that on the mask."

"What – *wear this while you're perving?*"

"No! – *FUCKIN FREAK!*"

They finally crashed out late Saturday afternoon and slept right through until the following day. They enjoyed a fry up together before Karen left at about twelve. She had been reluctant to leave, but Liv assured her she was perfectly okay. The boys would be back soon and Carl's flight was due in early that evening. She needed a little time on her own, she'd said, to clear her head.

She was feeling comfortably numb, completely devoid of any emotion. She hadn't come to any decision about the future but one thing was for sure, she would be putting her plan into action as soon as possible, hopefully that very night. She went upstairs to her bedroom and through to the en-suite. She pulled six strands of hair from her head, carefully placed them around the inside of the mirror and closed it down on them. She held her breath as she pulled it open, and watched as the hair fell into the hand-basin below. It had worked, but there was too much hair. It was too long and too visible. She tried again but with just three shorter strands. This time when she pulled it open, two strands fell either side and the third dropped into the basin. She found them easily enough but was confident Carl wouldn't notice a thing. She repeated the procedure twice more and then opened and closed the en-suite and bathroom doors a few times to make sure the hair stayed in place. After one last look around she turned off the lights, went back downstairs and rang Karen to let her know the trap had been set. Karen was worried about Liv's state of mind. She sounded strange, monosyllabic, detached.

"Liv, why don't you wait a bit – you don't have to do this straight away. You're exhausted, both mentally and physically. I don't think you could cope with a huge showdown right now."

"I'm not going to have a showdown. I just want to find out. I need all the facts before I confront him with it."

"So what will you do if—"

"Nothing! I'll just file it away with everything else and work out what I'm going to do."

Cymru

As is often the case with best laid plans, Liv's went awry. Her sister dropped the boys home mid afternoon and Carl arrived just after they finished dinner. He looked terrible and refused all offers of food. After she had finally got the boys to bed, happy but exhausted from their weekend at Alton Towers, she told Carl she was going to have a bath and an early night. As expected, he said he fancied an early night too and would be up shortly.

Words could not describe her feelings that night; surreal did not begin to capture the level of weirdness as she undressed and stepped into the bath. She kept her head down, forcing herself not to look up at the mirror. Her skin crawled and she felt a terrible panic rising in her chest. She had to push the image of Carl right out of her head for fear of throwing up. She got it over with as quickly as possible and wrapped herself up in a towel; she turned off the lights and walked through to the bedroom. To her utter amazement, the room was in darkness, there was nobody there.

She ventured downstairs and found him sprawled in front of the television, fast asleep. He was clearly wiped out from his rugby tour and Liv knew there would be no waking him. She felt the bile rising in her throat as she looked down at him and overcame the urge to kick him while he slept. She lay in bed tossing and turning for hours, adrenaline and unspent anger festering as she waited for sleep to come. She told herself it was probably for the best that her confrontation with Carl had been put on hold. Karen had been right; she was exhausted and needed time to regroup. She had decided to leave the hair in place behind the mirror knowing the right time would come, but for now she had to let the whole thing go. Eventually turning her thoughts to Nick and Sarah helped eased her mental anguish. Feelings of hope and optimism lifted her spirits and the belief she had found a way to heal their misery became a perfect panacea for her own.

The next few weeks of her life flew by; the appointment with Nick and Sarah, their favourable reaction to her proposition, the joyous outcome; swiftly followed by her unexpected and terrifying popularity at the MGC. Everything was spiralling out of control but she clung on, knowing she only had to make it to the end of the week. She had booked herself out for the October half term and now planned to head for the hills; the Welsh hills where Liv's sister had made her home. She and the boys loved it there and over the years it had become her precious bolt hole. Whenever life got crazy she would head to the safe haven of St. Davids on the Pembrokeshire peninsular, leaving the ills of the world behind her as she crossed the Severn Bridge. She was desperate for some breathing space and fervently hoped that in her absence, the dust would begin to settle.

Her sister Yvonne and her husband Ed had moved to Wales to look after Ed's elderly parents some years ago. They had taken over their rundown small holding and turned it into a successful children's farm and tea shop. With no children of their own they loved having their nephews to stay and always gave Liv and her boys a huge welcome. Joe loved life on the farm and pottered around with Yvonne helping her feed and muck out the livestock. He was in seventh heaven bottle feeding the lambs and kids and was learning how to milk the cows. Ed delighted in taking Charlie off to do 'big boys' stuff'; fishing, sailing, tractor driving and the like, which gave Liv some much needed time out. She went for long walks with the dogs along the coastal path and before long, the clean fresh air worked its magic, clearing her head and calming her mind. She arrived back at the farm from her early morning walk just in time to wave the boys off as they bounced down the lane in Ed's old open topped jeep. He was taking them on a rigid inflatable boat trip to Ramsey Island. They had pored over the brochures the night before and the boys were in a high state of excitement at the prospect of riding on '*a giant lilo with jet engines!*'

As was always the way in their family, Yvonne had given Liv her space and had not pried into her affairs. She knew she would talk when she was ready and as they sat at the kitchen table tucking into one of Yvonne's legendary full English/Welsh breakfasts it all came spilling out –

Nick and Sarah, her weekend with Karen and the debacle at the Marriage Guidance Council that was set to blow. The normally unflappable Yvonne had sat quietly eating her breakfast with just the occasional nod here and there as the story unfurled. She thought she was used to the mayhem of Liv's life, but this was on a different level. She found it difficult to relate to the whole drug thing with Karen because it was so alien to the life she shared with Ed, but she accepted the madcap experiment had been undertaken with the best of intentions and that Liv had achieved, albeit in a wildly unorthodox way, exactly what she'd hoped to achieve. Her mind was still processing this information when Liv dropped the bombshell of the two-way mirror. The forkful of black pudding on its way to her mouth didn't make its destination but clattered down onto her plate. It took a few moments to sink in but eventually shock and horror registered on her face. "A two-way mirror?" Liv nodded miserably. "In the bathroom?"

"In the en-suite, looking into the main bathroom."

"In your house?" Liv nodded again. "In Cedar Avenue?"

"Yes."

"Jesus Christ!" With a sudden loss of appetite, Yvonne pushed her plate aside and reached for Liv's cigarettes on the kitchen table. "You've given up!" protested Liv but to no avail. Yvonne lit her first cigarette in ten years, drew the smoke deep into her lungs and had a spectacular coughing fit. Liv took the cigarette from her and stubbed it out. "I'm so sorry... I don't know if he spied on you, I don't even know if he spied on me!" When she told her about the trap she had set, Yvonne started to laugh and Liv found herself laughing too, probably from sheer relief that the tension had been broken. "Why does everyone think it's so funny?"

"Because it's bloody hilarious! Honestly Liv, you've been watching too many films. It's like something out of an old detective movie."

"Yeah I know, pretty much what Karen said." The Inspector Clouseau reference brought about more laughter before the seriousness of the situation kicked back in. They decided Ed could never know. Yvonne had stayed with Liv and Carl for a few months while Ed organised their move to Wales and they both knew that if he got wind of this he would head straight to London to avenge his beloved wife's honour.

"Clare lived with you for a while too didn't she?"

"Yes – I've told her. She didn't know about it obviously."

"How did she take it?"

"Same as you — shocked, horrified, disgusted. Feels sick that he probably used it to spy on her. Oh God, I'm so sorry."

"Bloody hell Liv, it's not your fault!"

"But it happened in my house and I—"

"Listen to me Liv, what he's done is reprehensible, absolutely outrageous, but you are not responsible for his disgusting behaviour. Anyway, by the sounds of it, you're as much a victim as we are!" She stood up and pulled Liv into a hug. "Come on, let's go and muck out the pigs. They're more clean living than certain humans we know and there's nothing like a spot of good honest toil to take your mind off things." She had been right and by the time they broke for lunch, Liv was feeling a whole lot better. Yvonne suggested taking the horses out for a gentle hack in the afternoon. The Welsh schools had already had their half term so the tea shop and farm were particularly quiet. Yvonne's young assistant assured them she could cope on her own so they saddled up and headed off into the open countryside.

Liv used to love riding but it had become extremely hazardous back home and she had forgotten the freedom and exhilaration of riding a horse at full gallop. She looked across at her sister's grinning face as they thundered along and childhood memories of playing Cowboys and Indians, riding side by side on the arms of the sofa, came flooding back. She caught her eye and started whipping her reins from side to side with an exuberant "Yee Hah!" Yvonne nearly fell off laughing as she put her hand to her mouth and gave one of her legendary Red Indian war cries... then taking aim, she fired an arrow from her imaginary bow and dodged the bullets from Liv's imaginary gun.

The aroma of a delicious lamb hotpot was wafting from the Aga when they arrived home a few hours later and suddenly ravenous, they decided they couldn't possibly wait for the boys.

Pleasantly stuffed, they were halfway through a fine bottle of red purloined from Ed's cellar when they heard the Land Rover pulling up outside. Charlie and Joe came bursting through the door full of tales of white-water rafting, dolphins, sea lions and baby penguins. They would have none of Ed's version of porpoise, seals and puffins and refused to let anything dampen their enthusiasm. While the boys were getting washed and changed for supper Ed complimented Liv on their behaviour. "They were great – impeccable manners. No really!" he insisted as Liv voiced her surprise. "They're a credit to you. Mind you, it was funny on the way home. There was a funeral cortège crawling along with a long procession of mourners walking along behind. The traffic was backed up for miles because you had to wait for the hearse to pull into one of the passing places to get by. So finally it was our turn! Following my lead they removed their caps, bowed their heads and thanked the mourners for letting us by. As we passed the hearse, Charlie obviously felt he should say something more because he nodded towards the coffin and called back to the bereaved 'SORRY ABOUT YOUR DEAD PERSON!' I nearly bust a gut trying not to laugh!"

Carl rang just as they finished supper. The boys fought to get to the phone, eager to tell him all about their adventures. Eventually the phone was passed to Liv and she was informed he was going on a business trip to Austria and would be away for at least a week. He had taken Elizabeth to the kennels and instructed the gardener to keep an eye on the house while they were all away. While Liv was supervising the boys' bath and bedtime, Yvonne gave Ed a pared down version of Liv's earlier revelations and changed the timeline, thus ruling herself out as a possible 'peep-ee'. That evening the three of them polished off two more bottles of Châteauneuf as they discussed Liv's dilemmas. Ed's advice was typically blunt;

she should resign from the Marriage Guidance Council and file for divorce.

"Sounds like you've never really been happy in that job and if you think there's a chance they might give you the boot, jump before you're pushed!"

"Hmmmm, you're probably right."

"Of course I'm right! And as for your marriage, well what can I say that hasn't been said a thousand times before? It's over Liv, has been for years. You've just got to find the courage to walk away." He and Yvonne agreed it would be difficult but assured her that divorce from Carl was achievable. They were keen for her to look into the possibility of moving to Wales and when she saw the price of property in their area, she could certainly see the appeal. Five year old Joe would probably be fine, but Charlie was eleven and, at that age, would not appreciate being uprooted and wrenched away from his friends and everything he knew. Carl of course would do everything in his power to block such a move so although it was nice to daydream about ivy clad cottages in the beautiful Welsh countryside, she knew it could never happen.

She left Wales feeling strong and invigorated. They picked up a jubilant Elizabeth from the kennels on their way back home on Sunday afternoon. The first thing she noticed as she walked through the door was the answer machine beeping telling her the message box was full. As she played them back she discovered that most of them were from the offices of The Marriage Guidance Council. It would appear that a cow pat of enormous proportions had hit the fan. The messages began with a straight forward '*Hi Liv, it's Carol from the office, I wonder if you could give me a call when you get this message*', and became ever more urgent as the week progressed. The final one, left on Friday afternoon, sounded positively frantic! '*Hello? Hello is anyone there? Liv, if you're there, pick up the bloody phone! It's Bob. I don't know what the hell's going on but it's been mayhem here all week and now there's a bloke in reception and...*' there was a pause and then a sigh of exasperation. "*Oh look, for Christ's sake Liv, just ring me!*" Liv's heart was in her boots as the answer machine continued to play. There was just one further message. It was Carl informing her he would be arriving back that night. Hearing his voice prompted her to fly upstairs to check the mirror; it was a ritual she had been carrying out religiously ever since the MDMA weekend. The three strands of hair were still there, all present and correct.

After packing the boys off early to bed Liv made sure their uniforms and games kits were ready for the return to school in the morning and prepared their packed lunches. She poured herself a large glass of wine and relaxed with the Sunday papers for a while before heading upstairs to the bathroom. With Carl's flight not due in for another couple of hours she decided to treat herself to the full pampered bath time experience while the coast was clear. She lit perfumed candles, dropped a couple of expensive bath bombs into the running water and went back down to replenish her glass. As she lay deep in the water luxuriating in the silken bubbles as they popped under her nose, she felt the tension of the drive and all thoughts of the Marriage Guidance Council melt away. She could have easily drifted off but was suddenly aware of Elizabeth barking downstairs and then Carl's voice quietening him down!

She leapt out of the bath like a scalded cat and covered herself with a towel. He was calling out to her, asking where she was. She rushed about in a complete panic for a moment before managing to get a grip. She was angry with herself for her pathetic behaviour. This was the perfect opportunity if she had the guts to go through with it. Her decision made, she called out to him, telling him she was about to have a bath and had planned an early night after her drive back from Wales. She knocked back the wine and stepped down into the bath. She topped it up with hot water and forced herself to stay there for a full twenty minutes. Eventually she climbed out, dried herself and pulled on her robe. She emptied and cleaned the bath and snuffed out the candles. Taking a huge breath, she opened the bathroom door and walked out onto the galleried landing. Downstairs was in darkness and she could hear the television was on in their bedroom. She collected herself and with her heart in her mouth she walked through.

Carl was sat on the bed innocently flicking through the Sunday papers, a glass of wine in his hand, the bottle on the bedside table. He looked up and said something about catching an earlier flight as she walked through to the en-suite. She saw his lips move but heard nothing because, bizarrely, an old counting song from her schooldays was playing in her head. Whenever Julie Andrews was afraid, she whistled a happy tune; Liv counted potatoes... *One potato, two potato, three potato four...* she walked up to the mirror, her heart was hammering. She held on to the basin and looked at her reflection in the mirror... *five potato, six potato, seven potato more.* Gripping tightly she looked down. A single blonde hair lay in the basin and another on the side; the third was on the floor. She sank down onto the bidet with her head in her hands. Her plan had worked, she had her proof; but faced with the reality, she felt utterly alone and her fragile bravado collapsed.

When Karen had asked what she'd do if this happened she hadn't really given it much thought. Uppermost in her mind had been the need to find out – what came later was almost irrelevant. Her glib answer of *'I'll file it away'* was laughable now. As if something like this could just be filed away and dealt with at some future point. How could she function normally, how could she look at Carl without screaming, how could she not rip the mirror from the wall and smash him over the head with it? He was calling out to her, asking what the hell she was doing in there, telling her to get a move on. The irritation in his voice was just what she needed. Her anger flared, galvanising her into action. She took some deep breaths and stood up in front of the mirror. She splashed cold water on her face, and examined her reflection; her eyes looked back at her with steely resolve. No longer the victim, she squared her shoulders and walked calmly into the bedroom.

She told him she had found the mirror. She informed him she wanted a divorce and that *he* would be the one to leave. She said she would not discuss it until tomorrow when the boys were at school and finally, as she left the room, she told him she would be sleeping in the guestroom until he moved out. Carl, newspaper still in hand, had not uttered a single word throughout.

***

A sudden hammering at the car window brought her back to the present with a jolt. The boys' faces were squashed up against the glass like a grotesque Francis Bacon painting. She squished her face back at them and slowly lowered the window. They tasted of salt and suntan lotion as she kissed them through the widening gap. Agreeing to their pleas for ice creams from the van parked outside the school, she stood in the queue with them, listening to their excited chatter about their day. Standing there with her boys she felt enormous relief knowing that particular nightmare was far behind her, but sadly, there had been more to come.

The Green Beret

Throughout the rest of April and the whole of May, Michael had stuck to his resolution to limit his visits to Olivia's. The World Cup had been a great distraction but following England's defeat at the hand of Diego Maradona, he was bored and finding it increasingly difficult to stay away. Occasionally he found himself questioning his motives, but such thoughts were easily brushed aside; he enjoyed her company, that's all there was to it, so where was the harm? He had always quite liked the idea of a female friend, but for some reason, it had never quite happened until now. His first ever platonic relationship; he was actually quite proud.

It was a hot, sticky morning at the end of June and thunderstorms were forecast. The kitchen windows at the front of the house were wide open and sounds of utter mayhem drifted out into the stifled air. Clearly World War Three had broken out inside. Olivia's voice was drowned out by the sound of plates smashing, furniture scraping and her boys' outraged screams. Michael's natural instinct was to run a mile. Family fracas were not his thing and his work with the kids at the gym had taught him that children's squabbles were best left to the parents. He was about to get back into his car when the desperation in Olivia's voice nudged his conscience. He walked up to the front door and rang the bell. Unsurprisingly, amidst all the hullabaloo, his ring went unanswered. He debated for a moment then went to the kitchen window and called out "Hello?" Nothing. He peered in through the window – it was worse than he thought! A ferocious food fight was in full swing. The older one had what Michael hoped was tomato ketchup running down his face as he enthusiastically rubbed baked beans into the hair of the little one, who, in turn, was ramming a chipolata up the nose of his assailant. Stuck in the middle was a grim-faced Olivia, trying with all her might to separate her warring sons.

He assumed the role of a Royal Marine and barked a single command into the mêlée. All three swung round in astonishment as they took in the sight of Michael's disembodied head framed in net curtains yelling at them from inside their kitchen window. His order to "SHUDDUP!!" had the desired effect and they all stood frozen to the spot. "FRONT DOOR – NOW!" It was opened moments later by Olivia. He strode past her with a cursory nod and entered the kitchen. The boys' giggles were silenced by the look on his face as he took stock of the situation. He noted their attire. "Going to judo?" They nodded. "Right – you," he said, pointing to Charlie. "Bathroom – now! Get yourself cleaned up." To Olivia's surprise, he did as he was told and shot upstairs without a word of protest. Michael turned his attention to Joe who was trying to hide behind his mum. "Hmmmm… I think this one needs a hand," he said, pulling him forward and removing bits of fried egg from the front of his tunic. "Off you go then," he gestured to Liv, "I'll get started in here."

Fifteen minutes later the kitchen looked reasonably shipshape and the freshly scrubbed boys in their clean judo suits passed muster too. "Where's their club? I'll take them if you like and you can finish off here. I've had a go… but it probably needs, you know, a bit of going over." Eyeing the ketchup smears on the door and feeling her feet stick to the tiles as they squeaked across the hastily mopped floor, she could only but agree.

"It's not at the club – it's a tournament at the leisure centre. I just need to make their packed lunches."

"Don't worry about that, I'll grab them something from the petrol station on the way. Stick the kettle on – see you soon."

By the time he got back, the kitchen was pristine, the coffee was percolating and there was a delicious smell of bacon in the air. "I thought we deserved a bacon sandwich."

"Marvellous!"

"God! What a morning! Thanks for… you know, everything."

"That's alright mate, no big deal. What's going on with them though? Getting a bit out of hand aren't they?"

"They are," she sighed running her fingers through

her hair, "driving me insane to be honest. But growing up in such an unhealthy atmosphere… it's bound to affect them… what can you expect?"

"Hmmmm." He felt it best not to say too much on the subject. It was okay for the parents to call their kids little bastards or whatever, but in his experience, they didn't welcome home truths from outsiders. From his perspective it was easy to see what was happening. It was par for the course; the kids were using the situation between their parents to get away with blue murder.

"Anyway," she continued checking her watch, "for the next six hours they're somebody else's problem." She put the bacon sandwiches and coffee on a tray. "Shall we have this outside? It looks quite nice out there now." The thunder clouds had passed overhead and were rumbling away in the distance; somebody else's problem now too. They settled themselves out on the veranda, overlooking the pool. "You were really good with them, especially Charlie. I can't believe how he reacted."

"He probably picked up on something in my voice."

"Zero tolerance!"

"Years of practice," laughed Michael, "first in the Marines, then training my clients and the kids down at the boxing academy."

"How long were you in the Marines?"

"Eleven years in all. I went straight in from school at sixteen as a junior marine—"

"Sixteen? God, that was young!"

"Yeah… my parents wanted me to stay on at school and get my GCEs so that I could go in as an officer –

213

me an officer! Can you imagine?" he laughed. "Anyway, I couldn't wait – I was desperate to join up."

"Why? Was your dad in the marines or something?"

"No, it was my mate Malcolm's older brother. Whenever he came home on leave I'd go round there and hear all these great stories about life 'in the corps'. Me, Malcolm Dobson and Piggy Pilkington – we were all going to join up together, but for some reason, I was the only one that got in!"

"God, that's so young though," said Liv smiling inwardly at Michael's automatic inclusion of his school friends' surnames. "How was it – the training and everything?"

"Fuckin' awful to be honest! The first thing the drill sergeant yelled at us was '*Who's here to learn how to kill people?*'

"Oh dear."

"Exactly! Not what I was expecting at all. I thought it was going to be all 'ging-gang-goolie' round the campfire with Malcolm and Piggy but the reality of it was freezing my bollocks off on Dartmoor in the middle of the night with the worst case of homesickness ever! A few weeks in I remember ringing my mum, crying my eyes out saying I hated it and wanted to come home."

"Awww! Poor you – and your mum! That must have been horrible for her."

"Yeah probably, but she wasn't having any of it. She was really good actually – gave me a swift kick up the arse and told me I had to get on with it."

"So you stuck it out."

Michael nodded. "I passed out when I was seventeen.

I was going to come out after the statutory three years but they persuaded me to stay in, get my corporal stripes and train as a PTI."

"What's that?"

"Physical Training Instructor – based back at the Commando Training Centre in Devon. We were part of the team that trained the new recruits."

"So you didn't travel the world?"

"Not really… well, a bit. Malta, Cyprus – we went on exercise with the U.S. Marines in Fort Lauderdale – did some Arctic warfare training in Norway."

"Did you, you know…"

"See any action? No. Initially I was posted to 42 Commando who were about to do a tour of duty in Northern Ireland but at seventeen, I was too young to go."

"Lucky you!"

"I didn't think so at the time, in fact I was completely gutted. I wanted to go with them and do some real soldiering because basically, that's what I had been trained to do. I was ready to go – but looking back, maybe I was lucky. A couple of years later, one of the men from my old unit, smashing bloke, Dusty Miller… he was—"

"Dusty Miller?"

"Yeah?"

"A mate of Barney McGrew?"

"Erm… no I don't think so… rings a bell though—"

"Pugh, Pugh, Barney McGrew, Cuthbert, Dibble and Grubb!"

"Huh?"

"From Camberwick Green… you know, Trumpton?"

"Liv – that's Windy Miller."

"Oh right, yeah. Anyway, sorry for interrupting," said Olivia, realising her joke had fallen a bit flat, "you were saying about Dusty – what did he do?"

"He was killed. Poor sod got blown up in Northern Ireland."

"Oh God! Michael I'm so sorry!"

"S'alright. You weren't to know."

"No but there's me laughing and making jokes about his name and the poor—"

"Liv, stop, it's okay. Like I said, you weren't to know. Anyway, so there you go, maybe I was lucky I didn't get to see any action. It all sounds great and exciting, but the reality of it is, a young guy, he was twenty-two by the way, killed on foot patrol by a remote controlled bomb hidden in a parked car." They sat in silence for a while before Michael continued. "So yeah, I missed Northern Ireland and then because I came out in early '82, I missed the Falklands as well. So that was it – my illustrious career in the Royal Marines! I came out at the age of twenty-seven with no trade and no skills for life on Civvy Street."

"Do you regret going in?"

"Nah, not really – I've come to realise it's a big part of who I am now. The training, the discipline, it's all good I s'pose – a stronger person and all that."

"So what did you do when you came out?"

"Well… I did a bit of security work but the money was crap. Quite a few ex-marines go into the Old Bill, or become close protection officers, you know, body guards," he added seeing Liv's puzzled expression, "but I couldn't see myself in that. I did some door work for a guy who covers some clubs in London but I hated it—"

"What, like a bouncer?" laughed Liv. "With a dicky-bow and the thing in your ear?"

"Yeah…" said Michael rolling his eyes. "No sunglasses though, alright? I just want to make that clear! Anyway, like I say, I hated it so when my uncle suggested doing The Knowledge, I thought I'd give it a go. He's done alright out of it and both his sons, my cousins, have got their own cabs now. Anyway, that's my plan. Once I get my licence I'll be able to earn enough to pay the mortgage and keep the wolves at bay but still have enough time for the other stuff, you know, working with the kids at the academy and getting the personal training off the ground. It's really big in America so I'm hoping it'll catch on here too."

"Most things do."

"Yeah true… we'll see."

"Fingers crossed eh?" They lifted their crossed fingers in the air. "How's things with Hannah by the way?"

"Not so good."

"How is she?"

"Terrible. I didn't think she'd react like this – she's all over the place. One minute she's glad it's over, better off without me and the next I've ruined her life!"

"Well she's bound to be—"

"It's like the first conversation we had about it – at first she was agreeing with me, you know, saying she wasn't happy either and all that, and I'm thinking *this is going to be okay*, and the next thing you know, she bursts into tears, the ring's off, and I'm saying *'no, it's yours, you keep it'* and she's crying and saying it would just be a cruel reminder of how I'd broken her heart – and blah, blah blah – then she slams the ring down on the table, tells me she hates me and storms off."

"You didn't think that would be it, surely?"

"No I didn't, and I've told you before, don't call me Shirley!"

"Michael, this is serious!"

"Yeah, I know, but what am I supposed to do? Obviously I knew that after four years together, it wasn't going to be over just like that, but things hadn't been right for ages and I honestly didn't think she'd be this upset about it. She's gone to pieces – lost loads of weight, her hair's falling out, her teeth are falling out—"

"Her teeth????"

"Oh no, hang on, she's *dreaming* that her teeth are falling out – sorry!"

"A common anxiety dream," said Liv knowingly, "usually associated with loss and big life changes—"

"Yeah thanks Liv, I know, Hannah's already told me. Anyway, it's pretty gut wrenching seeing the state she's in and knowing it's all my fault."

"Not *all* your fault, sure—" she stopped herself in time.

"It is! And she's right, we should never have got engaged in the first place. To be honest I only did it to keep her happy and buy myself a bit of time."

"Bloody hell Michael!"

"Well that's the truth of it. All her mates were getting

engaged or married and suddenly she's demanding a ring on her finger too. Anyway, like I said, I thought once we got engaged, she'd be off my case for a while, but if anything, it made it worse – it stoked the fire! Next thing I know she's pinning me down to a definitive date, going to wedding fairs, looking at venues…"

"That's all quite normal isn't it? Marriage *is* the next step."

"Yeah, but I thought that would be years off, not the minute the ring went on!"

"So you wanted more time?"

"I did."

"Time for what?"

"Well, a bit more time before settling down I s'pose. I didn't feel ready, I wanted to be sure."

"About Hannah?"

"No, I was sure that if I *did* want to get married, it would be to Hannah, but just… not yet."

"So is the engagement still off?"

"Yeah… but I think she wants to try again." Michael sighed, a long heavy sigh with more than a hint of resignation about it.

"And you?"

"I said we needed some time to think. Like a trial thing."

"A trial separation?"

"Yeah, that old chestnut. Look, let's drop it now okay? I don't know what I'm doing yet. I feel really sorry for her. Anyway… enough of that… how about you? What are you looking for?" Liv's shake of the head and shrugged shoulders gave him his answer. "Hopes, dreams… you have to have some surely."

"You wouldn't understand… and now who's calling *who* Shirley!"

"Touché," laughed Michael, "So why wouldn't I understand?"

"You just wouldn't."

"What – too complicated?"

"No – I could sum it up in one word actually, but you wouldn't get it."

"Try me."

"Atticus."

"That's it?"

"Yep."

"That's what you're looking for?"

"Told you you wouldn't get it."

"Atticus Finch?" Olivia's heart thumped as her mouth dropped open.

Atticus

"How did you know?"

"How did I know what?"

"That it was Atticus Finch."

"I didn't – but there can't be too many of them about and he's the only one I know! Good man Atticus," he continued, "the world would be a better place if—" he stopped abruptly. "Hey, what's up mate? You okay?" Liv was struggling to control her emotions. She managed a choked "Sorry…" before grabbing a serviette and blowing her nose. "Take no notice, it's just that Atticus, you know, Atticus…" she couldn't go on.

Christ! What's this all about, thought Michael. He had studied To Kill a Mockingbird at school, which was why he'd guessed it was Atticus Finch, but he couldn't for the life of him work out why the story of a white lawyer's stand against prejudice and racism in the Deep South had caused all this. Liv was still struggling to get a grip.

"So you've read the book?" she asked shakily.

"Yeah, we did it at school. I remember the film better though, Gregory Peck wasn't it?"

"It was... he was perfect as Atticus, don't you think?"

"He was," agreed Michael. "So... what's this thing with Atticus Liv... why are you getting so upset?"

She had started the book years ago when she was going to evening classes, but had abandoned it when she quit the course. She had picked it up again recently when looking for something to tide her over until she could get to the library; she read it in a day and a night and it had struck enough chords to write a symphony. Atticus stood for everything she believed in. Michael sat quietly as she opened her heart and unwittingly bared her soul in her attempt to define Atticus. She asked if he would mind if she fetched the book, and as she read little snippets and shared her favourite quotations, he found he didn't mind at all.

"You know sometimes, when you feel like giving up – there's no one to trust, nothing left to believe in? Well that's how it was – and then suddenly I'm reading this wonderful book and..." she was welling up again.

"You found Atticus!" Michael finished for her.

"I did," she smiled.

"So you're hoping for a real-life Atticus to come along and put the world to rights?"

"No, it's more than that... it's like... it's like I'm looking for Atticus within."

"Within who?"

"Everyone, especially me."

"The essence of Atticus."

"Yes," laughed Liv, "or is it ethos? Essence sounds like a recipe ingredient."

"The spirit of Atticus then – no, maybe not, sounds like a boat! I know what you mean though, it's what he represents."

"It is. It's his values – his integrity. His courage and determination to do the right thing."

"Hmmmm, okay, so he's your role model?"

They were interrupted by Elizabeth running round their table, tearing through the house and barking at the front door.

"He wants his walk," explained Liv, "I usually take him about this time."

Against his better judgement, Michael was persuaded to join them. He was still not comfortable with dogs and was puzzled by Elizabeth's canine behaviour. It seemed his life's mission was to sniff and wee on everything in his path. Liv's estimation of a thirty minute walk would take hours at this rate. *Now what's he doing?* Elizabeth had stopped up ahead and was now skidding slowly towards them on his bottom, his eyes half closed and a euphoric smile stretching from ear to ear.

"What's he—"

"Oh it's alright – he does that when he's got an itchy bum. He did it once when I was showing some people round the house." She stopped dead and clutched his arm. "THE ESTATE AGENT!"

"What?"

"The estate agent sent some people to view the house! Sorry Michael, that's really significant. I must ring my solicitor when we get back – don't let me forget."

"I won't… but what—"

"Oh don't worry, I'll explain later. So what was I saying?"

"Elizabeth. You were showing some people round the house."

"Oh God yeah, I was absolutely mortified! They had just asked if the price included the carpets when he slid past us and did a little twirl right in front of them!"

They walked on for bit and Michael spotted a pub on the horizon.

"Fancy a drink – pub lunch?"

"Ermmm… no, better not. It'll be full of nosy neighbours and I think Elizabeth is still banned anyway."

"Banned?"

"Yes, he's banned from most of the pubs around here – he tries to mug people for their crisps. Actually do you mind if we head back? I really should make that call."

Michael didn't mind in the least; however Elizabeth, furious at having his walk cut short, had to be dragged all the way home.

"Grab a beer," said Liv, pointing towards the bar. "Snacks are in the top cupboard on the right. I won't be long." He walked through to the bar and helped himself to a bottle of lager and a packet of crisps. Elizabeth appeared out of nowhere and looked up at him menacingly. Michael made a big show of returning the crisps to the cupboard and carefully sidestepped his way back to the kitchen. He could hear Olivia's animated voice coming from the study; he couldn't hear what she was saying but it sounded like good news. He picked up her copy of To Kill a

Mockingbird and flicked through it absentmindedly. It was well thumbed and full of post-it notes flagging up areas of highlighted text. He smiled at the notes she had pencilled into the margins with arrows pointing to the relevant text. Some of them had been written so small he could hardly read them, others just said '*lovely!*'

Starting with the first post-it note, he skimmed his way through the book and gained a deeper understanding of both Olivia and the novel. She had highlighted the weighty issues of prejudice, justice, courage and bravery and he recognised many of the quotes from their conversation earlier. '*The one thing that doesn't abide by majority rule is a person's conscience.*' Michael was enjoying Liv's choices. They jogged his memory; he liked this book. Some of them illustrated the lessons of tolerance and respect that Atticus had tried to teach his children. He particularly liked the one for Scout about never really understanding a person until you consider things from their point of view, '*until you climb into their skin and walk around in it.*' There was a nice lesson for Jem too, when Atticus was called upon to save the town from a rabid dog. He discovered that their father, who didn't hunt, fish, play poker, drink or smoke, was actually '*One-Shot Finch*', the best shot in the county. Atticus had never felt the need to tell them.

Some of them were sad because they highlighted Liv's vulnerability. They were dotted throughout the book and described how Scout felt when she went to Atticus for comfort.

'*Soon I was hiding in his lap and his arms were around me.*'

'I listened to the small internal noises that went on behind the light blue cloth: his watch ticking, the faint crackle of his starched shirt, the soft sound of his breathing.'

'I felt his hand on the back of my head. "Don't you worry about anything," he said. "It's not time to worry yet."

"So sorry!" said Olivia as she came back into the kitchen. "I didn't think it would take that long." Michael jumped guiltily; as if he'd been caught reading her diary. She joined him at the kitchen table.

"Hope you don't mind," he said, pushing the book towards her, "I was just refreshing my memory. I might read it again, you know, as an adult." Her hand went out instinctively and claimed the book.

"It's just it's a bit old and messy," she said in an embarrassed attempt to explain herself. She pushed it back to him. "You should definitely re-read it."

It was abundantly clear she had found something to hang on to and she was clinging on for dear life. *Nothing wrong with that*, thought Michael, *we all need something to believe in*. But this was pretty intense and slightly worrying because if she was trying to live up to his ideals, she was setting herself up for a fall. He decided to test the water.

"Liv… Atticus's character – is he believable?"

"What do you mean?"

"Isn't he a bit too good to be true?"

"No – he's believable."

"But the person who wrote this—"

"Harper Lee."

"Yeah, Harper Lee… he gave Atticus almost super-human—"

"She."

"Huh?"

"She's a woman."

"Oh right… look, I'm trying to say something important here—"

"Atticus represents justice, tolerance… and you always know that whatever happens, he'll do the right thing."

"Yeah I know Liv, but what I'm trying to say is – no one can be that perfect. She's made him larger than life. She's exaggerated his qualities so that he can voice her beliefs – her moral philosophy if you like." Liv was still. She was weighing up what Michael had said. "Do you see what I mean? She uses him to—"

"Atticus is real," said Liv firmly.

"Do you really think so?"

"That's what Scout and Jem called his dangerous question."

"What?"

"Atticus always said '*do you really think so*' if he wanted them to think again."

"Liv, he's not real."

"What he stands for is real."

It was Michael's turn to reflect.

"Look, like I said earlier, Atticus is a good man. His character is a great role model and the world would be a better place if we tried to live by his example."

"Well that's what I'm trying to do! Atticus taught

by example, which in my book is the only way. He was a wonderful parent – kind, protective, firm but fair and always looking for ways to help his children grow up to be good people. I'm trying to follow his example in the hope it will make me a better parent – better able to pass his values on to my children too."

"And that's admirable, I'm just saying – it's a bit of a tall order that's all."

Liv was tempted to quote Atticus again – there was a good one in there about knowing you're licked, but having a go anyway and seeing it through no matter what – but she thought better of it and decided to quit while they were ahead.

"So I'm alright to borrow this?"

"Definitely."

"Cheers," said Michael picking up the book. "How did it get its title again? I can't remember."

"It's symbolism. Remember when Atticus buys them air-rifles for Christmas? Sounds funny doesn't it? Imagine giving Charlie and Joe air-rifles!"

"Imagine giving my little cousin one! Different times though… different world."

"Yeah… so anyway, he gives them the air-rifles and warns them not to shoot mockingbirds."

"Doesn't he say they can shoot anything else they like?"

"No, not exactly!" laughed Liv. "He'd rather they shot at tin cans, but he knows they'll go after birds. Can I borrow the book a minute?" She flicked through it expertly and found the relevant page. "There you go! He says they can shoot all the blue-jays they like, if they can hit them, but reminds them it's a sin to kill a mockingbird."

"Why?"

"Because they are innocent, they do no harm. They just sing pretty songs for us to enjoy. The two mockingbird characters in the book were kind, they tried to help, they did the right thing and Atticus is saying—"

"Harper Lee is saying…"

Liv smiled. "*They* are saying… we shouldn't harm innocents. It's a sin to kill a mockingbird."

"So there were two mockingbirds?"

"Yes, Tom Robinson and Boo Radley."

"Life's innocents eh?"

"That's it," smiled Liv.

'*Yes…*' thought Michael, nodding slowly as he smiled back at her across the table, '*… and I think I've just spotted another.*'

Liv checked her watch. It was almost two. "I might just nip down and see the boys. I usually go to watch them when they're in a tournament."

"What happened to firm but fair?"

"But they might be looking for me."

"You told them you weren't coming."

"Yes but—"

"You said you weren't coming as a punishment for their bad behaviour, so stick to it – otherwise they've learnt nothing."

"Maybe just the last hour?"

He shook his head. "Empty threats."

She sighed, "Yep, you're right, okay. I'll stick to what I said and collect them at four."

Michael nodded. "Consistency, that's the thing. Anyway mate, I'm absolutely starving so I'm going to have to shoot. Sure you don't want to nip out for something to eat?"

"No thanks… um… I could make something here if you like?"

"Well, I don't want to hold you up or anything…"

"You're not. I'm not going anywhere, well apart from taking Elizabeth out again later. But what about you, have you—"

"Nope."

"Okay, so what's it to be? Sandwich or Pizza?"

"Both!"

They ate their lunch outside.

"So what's the situation with you and Carl now?"

"We're separated."

"I know, but is it official?"

"Yes. I've started divorce proceedings. We agreed he should see the boys at the weekends, but just lately, he's been turning up whenever he likes – it's so unsettling."

"For who?"

"Well, all of us really. He undoes everything I try to do. I'm trying to help the boys come to terms with the fact that we are getting divorced, you know, trying to reassure them that it will all be okay. I'm making sure they know that we both still love them and that none of this is their fault. I'm telling them that whatever happens, we will always be their mum and dad and that families can be happy after divorce – but Carl keeps saying things like '*I still love your mum*' and '*I don't want a divorce*', which not only gives them false hope, it makes them hate me for taking that hope away."

"Have you spoken to Carl about it?"

"Of course I have but he doesn't want to listen. It's like he's still in denial about the whole thing. I've tried reminding him he was only supposed to visit at the weekends but he says no one can stop him seeing his own kids. He said his brief told him the courts would back him up." She shook her head despondently. "They wouldn't if they could see the reality of what it's like for them living in this environment. How can they possibly thrive in something so… so completely wrong? You've seen how they are."

"Yeah, I have mate, I have." She looked close to tears again and he didn't know what to say in the face of such despair. He knew what he *wanted* to say – something wise and noble – something profound. He tried summonsing Atticus from within, but nothing happened – so he swiftly changed the subject instead.

"So where is The Fuhrer these days?" he said cheerfully, "and that other twat, Herr Prick?"

Liv cracked up. Michael was delighted!

"Herr Prick!!" she guffawed, "You mean Herr Flick!"

"No I don't!" laughed Michael.

"And who's The Fuhr… oh!…" she cracked up again.

"So where are they?" said Michael once they'd stopped laughing. "The Fuhrer and his merry band of arseholes – where've they gone?"

"Oh God Michael, it's such a long story…"

"S'alright – like you said earlier, we've got all day!"

"I don't know where to start!"

"Well… how about… how about where you left off last time," suggested Michael, "The Marriage Guidance Council? – you'd just got fired."

"Oh yeah, thanks for that! Okay… shall we go back inside though, I think it might rain." They took up their usual positions around the kitchen table. "It was a difficult time really," began Liv, "there was other stuff going on too and to be honest, I lost the plot for a while."

"What other stuff?"

"Oh you know, last straw type stuff – I'd had it, just completely had it – I had to get away. I went to stay at my mum and dad's for a while."

"With the kids?"

"No, I knew he'd come after me if I took the boys and I didn't want to put them, or my parents, through that."

"Must've been pretty heavy then – this other stuff."

"It was."

"So?…" he looked across at her questioningly.

"I went back every day and took care of everything but I couldn't keep it up," she continued leaving his question hanging in the air, "I had no money to pay for my keep, not that Mum and Dad asked for any, but I couldn't just live off them indefinitely, plus I was borrowing money for petrol, cigarettes – I literally didn't have a bean."

"Couldn't you have asked for some kind of allowance?"

"From Carl?" Michael nodded. "Tried that but let's just say he declined."

"But Liv, I still don't understand. You say you'd had enough and had to get away – but why? It wasn't just losing your job was it, so what else had happened?" She picked up the cigarette packet and played around with his Zippo lighter, flicking it on and off, again and again as she decided whether to tell him. He put his hand over hers and silenced the lighter. She took a deep breath.

"I found out he was a Peeping Tom."

Mr Voyeur

"A Peeping Tom!!" He started to laugh, "Carl's a voyeur?"

"Seriously Michael, I'm not joking. You remember the night of the MDMA experiment?"

"I do."

"Well, there's quite a lot I didn't tell you about that night."

"Really?" said Michael enjoying the moment. He knew it would come back one day. '*Ahhh! I love the smell of spilt beans in the morning!*' He sat back quietly as she presented him with the unabridged version of what had taken place that fateful weekend.

"Bloody Hell!" he said as her shocking revelations came to a close. "I don't know what to say... I'm just..."

"I know. It's hard to get your head around. I felt... well... shock mainly. Karen said everyone thought I knew! I think that was the hardest thing to deal with. Then I thought about my sister and Clare because they had both lived with us here. He probably spied on them and everyone else who used that bathroom."

"So who else used it?"

"Mainly the rugby crowd, you know – the players, their wives and girlfriends, the team groupies and the hangers on. When we first moved in we had loads of pool parties and everyone used to shower and get changed up there so he and his mates must have had a field day – he actually admitted it! He said it was just a laugh with the lads, but swore he hadn't used it to spy on my family or friends and certainly not on me. But I knew he had. I'd set a trap… and well, to cut a long story short, I caught him bang to rights."

"A trap?"

As she explained, her words *'pause for laughter'* were lost in Michael's laughter.

"You've been watching too many movies."

"Yeah, yeah, Inspector Clouseau, I've heard it all before."

"So what did you do?"

"I told him I wanted a divorce and that this time, he was going to be the one to go.

"Brave words!"

"Yeah, but needless to say, that's not what happened. When I came down the following morning, Carl had already got the boys up and ready for school. They were all eating breakfast together around the kitchen table. Carl was acting as if nothing had happened and invited me to join them."

"Happy families."

"Bizarre! I just joined his little charade and accepted a cup of tea. He announced he was doing the school run and the boys kissed me goodbye. I remember sitting there chain-smoking 'til he got back."

"Had you worked out what you were going to say?"

"Not really! It didn't matter anyway because he'd obviously decided that attack was the best form of defence. He weighed straight in with *'What bastard stitched me up?'* And then something sarcastic like, *'Oh wait, don't tell me, the phantom letter writer's struck again!'* He didn't believe I'd found the mirror myself and said *'the slag'* who told me about it was just making trouble. I stuck to my story of stumbling across the hinges when I was cleaning, but he wasn't having any of it. He said it was obvious someone had shown me and demanded to know who it was."

"He gave *you* the third degree?"

"Yeah, like I was the guilty one! Cheeky bastard! So anyway, I've hit back with a barrage of questions of my own – Karen had already told me everything, but obviously, he didn't know that. He blamed it all on a bloke at the rugby club saying *he* was the one who'd got hold of the mirror and had talked him into having it installed."

"No names obviously."

"Course not! He said he didn't want to *'drop him in it'* and there was no point to it anyway because a) I didn't know him, and b) he'd left the club ages ago and moved away from the area."

"How convenient!"

"Laughable isn't it? He must have realised it was all sounding a bit lame because he suddenly changed tack and became remorseful. He admitted that having the mirror installed had been a terrible thing to do but explained it away as '*a bit of harmless fun*'. He insisted they'd only used it a few times in the early days when we'd first moved in, but swore it had been sealed up ever since. When I told him about the trap I'd set he turned nasty again. He laughed in my face and said '*why would I want to spy on you?*' So we're yelling and screaming at each other and the phone starts ringing – we tried ignoring it but it just kept ringing and ringing. It was The Marriage Guidance Council!"

"Oh dear!"

"Yeah, can you imagine? They demanded I came in IMMEDIATELY! I left the house with Carl yelling after me that I was wildly over-reacting, sadly deluded and completely nuts! I arrived at the Marriage Guidance offices and they fired me on the spot – you know, the whole thing, told to collect my belongings and escorted to the door!"

"That's when you went to your parents?"

"Yeah, I had to. I couldn't face going home. Mum and Dad were great. They didn't ask too many questions bless them. They just did what they always do at times like this – stuck the kettle on and made a nice cup of tea. They gave me plenty of TLC and as much space as I needed to figure out where the hell I went from there."

"So a bit of a breather."

"Not for long – Carl turned up the next day, hammering at the front door and begging me to come home. There was a terrible scene on the doorstep until my dad stepped in and told him he should respect my wishes and leave."

"How long did you stay?"

"Just a few weeks – I tried to make sure the boys' lives went on as normal. During the week I'd arrive at the house in time to get them up, make their breakfast and packed lunches and then drop them off to school. I took care of the house, the shopping, the laundry and was there to pick them up again in the afternoon. I'd do dinner, help with their homework and stay with them until Carl came home from work in the evening. Their weekends were spent with Carl. It worked well enough until I had to ask him for money."

"Didn't you have a credit card or anything?"

"No, I tried to get one, but because I didn't have any income of my own, the forms needed to be signed by Carl. I told him I needed an allowance for petrol money and also to pay my way at my parents, but he refused point blank and said he didn't see why he should have to support me. It had been my decision to leave, so it was up to me to sort myself out. When I tried to explain I couldn't take on a job because I was already committed to caring for the boys, he twisted what I'd said and went ballistic. I heard through mutual friends he was saying to everyone – *'what kind of a mother demands to be paid for looking after her own kids!'* Michael shook his head sympathetically. "The situation became impossible. Eventually I agreed to go back, but on the clear understanding I wasn't returning to him or our marriage, I was simply going back for the boys' sake. I made sure he understood that as far as I was concerned the marriage was over and although we'd be living under the same roof it wouldn't be as man and wife. I'd be moving into the guest suite and Carl had to

238

promise there'd be no talk of marital duties or conjugal rights."

"And he accepted all that?"

"Yep, he agreed to everything. I was given a huge welcome. Charlie and Joe were so happy to see me. Elizabeth was going crazy, tearing round the house barking his head off – it was mayhem, but a happy mayhem if you know what I mean. There were flowers everywhere and the house looked immaculate. Carl told the boys to take my bags upstairs and come straight back down so that they could '*tell Mummy their surprise*' – I asked him what was going on but he just ushered me through to the kitchen." Olivia sighed as she recalled the sight that greeted her as she entered the room. "There was a massive welcome home banner and bunches of balloons stuck all over the beams – high tea had been laid out on the table."

"Sounds like he'd made quite an effort then?"

"Yeah, he'd really gone to town which was nice… but I had this horrible feeling that something was up. Anyway, so the boys came charging in bursting with excitement. They dived straight into the cream cakes and then prompted by Carl they made their announcement. '*Opa is coming!*' I was completely baffled. I remember asking what an 'opa' was. They were all laughing… and then Carl said – '*Not what… who!… Their Opa is coming! We've found my father!! He's alive and well and still living in Vienna!*'

"Enter The Fuhrer?" said Michael. Olivia nodded grimly.

The Monster

She had been dumbstruck and sat in utter disbelief as she discovered not only had he been found, but Carl had already been out to meet him and arrangements had been made for him to come over to England so that he could meet his grandsons too. All this was relayed to her as if it were the best news imaginable. It was too much for her mind to take in. Struggling to keep even a semblance of calm, she feigned a headache and said she was going for a lie down. The boys had been told she had been staying at Nan and Granddad's because she was a bit under the weather and needed to rest, so they were not unduly worried or surprised when she headed upstairs. She went through to the guestroom and stopped dead at the door. The wallpaper had been stripped from the walls, the carpet was rolled up and there were pots of paint and decorating paraphernalia everywhere. Charlie had followed her up. "We're doing it up for Opa. Me and Joe chose the colours and Dad said we can help him paint the walls."

"Lovely!" she said, doing her best to sound bright and cheerful, "Where did you put my bags darling?"

"In *your* room silly!" he laughed as he took her hand and led her through to the room she used to share with Carl.

"Thanks sweetheart, that's fine. Why don't you go and finish your tea… and could you ask Dad to pop up please?"

She moved her stuff into one of the spare rooms over in the original part of the house. It was much smaller with twin beds and no en-suite but as she informed Carl when he got there, she would rather sleep in the conservatory with Elizabeth than share a bed with him. Their argument was conducted in squawking whispers. Liv was absolutely beside herself. "What the hell are you playing at? How could you have let me come back here without even telling me?" she hissed.

"Because you wouldn't have come back if I'd have told you!"

Carl's logic! What could you say when confronted with such single minded selfishness?

"What if I'd just walked straight out the door?"

"I knew you wouldn't do that to them." She was almost hopping with rage. She felt totally trapped. He was right of course, how could she possibly leave? Somehow the issue of the two-way mirror and the terms and conditions of her return had been totally eclipsed by the impending arrival of Carl's father.

"I won't have him here! And I don't want the boys to meet him… ever! How could you do this? Your poor mother would—"

"Liv, he's my father!" he interrupted, seemingly incapable of understanding her adverse reaction to the whole affair. "Look, come back downstairs and we'll talk about it." He took her arm, "Come on, the boys are probably getting worried down there." Charlie and Joe were fine and as soon as they finished their tea, they were sent off to play in the garden.

"How did this happen?" demanded Olivia, once they were safely out of earshot. "We agreed... you promised..." Her protestations were brushed aside. He had no recollection of any promises made and denied he had ever given up hope of finding his father. He went on to explain the reason it had taken so long and had proved so difficult was that they had been searching for a Joseph Vogel – but Vogel was Flora's maiden name.

"His name is Joseph Ljubić. I was actually registered in Vienna as Karl Joseph Ljubić, but when we came here, Mum reverted back to her maiden name and changed mine to Carl Vogel."

Liv put her hands over her ears. This wasn't happening. It was total madness.

"Shut up! I don't care! I don't want to know what his name is or anything else about him! I'm telling you Carl, I will not have that monster in my house!"

Her concerns for meeting the ogre his mother had run away from were met with amusement.

"Liv, he's no monster! Honestly, once you hear his story you'll understand. He explained everything to me – it wasn't his fault." Twenty minutes later Carl concluded with the words, "... so you see, it was all because of the metal plate!"

"So you're telling me he drank to alleviate the pain of having a metal plate in his head?"

"Correct."

"And he had this plate because of an almost fatal injury he suffered as a Yugoslav Resistance Fighter, blowing up a Nazi munitions train."

"Exactly!" beamed Carl. "He can show you the scars and everything."

Liv, who was having great difficulty replacing '*Drunken Bird Throttling Bastard*' with '*Courageous Resistance Fighter*', decided the only scars she would like to see would be those of a full frontal lobotomy.

Three weeks later he arrived. They both seemed tremendously pleased with themselves and with each other; Carl with his war hero dad, and Joseph with his rich and successful son. However, if the instincts of dogs and small children were anything to go by, Elizabeth and Joe's reaction to Joseph spoke volumes. Elizabeth growled and showed his teeth every time Joseph came near and apart from enduring the initial hugs and kisses at their first meeting, Joe avoided him like the plague. Charlie's gallant efforts to befriend his new grandfather were not reciprocated and Liv was relieved to see that before long this lack of interest became mutual.

He was a big man, heavily jowled with thick lips and dark hooded eyes; his grey hair was slicked back, accentuating his Slavic features. He looked much younger than she had expected; Flora would have been nearly eighty by now and Joseph was certainly nowhere near that age. When Liv voiced her concern over the disparity in their ages, Carl confirmed he was ten years younger than his mother and was now in his late sixties.

Any doubts Liv had over Carl's parentage were soon dismissed when he produced photographs of himself taken at a similar age. It was undeniable; Carl was almost a clone. She felt a chill as she looked at Joseph's face, realising she was staring into Carl's future. She took comfort in the knowledge there was at least one feature he could not inherit; the ugly scar that ran down his forehead, across his eye and ended at the cheekbone which appeared to be broken. He looked like a war criminal, which given the discoveries Liv had made whilst researching his story, was not surprising.

Determined to discredit him, she had immediately thrown herself into the investigation of Joseph Ljubić. All her spare time was spent ensconced in a secluded corner of her local library. With her natural interest in the Second World War, she had been in her element. Her fascination had been triggered by films she had seen as a child, in particular *Odette* and *Carve Her Name with Pride*. They told similar stories of brave young women: Special Operations Executive agents who had been dropped behind enemy lines to fight alongside the French Resistance before being captured and tortured by the Gestapo. Liv's image of resistance fighters had been born out of her love of old WWII films such as these, but her investigations would lead to the discovery that The Yugoslavian Resistance was a world apart from the resistance movements found in all other Nazi-occupied countries.

Poring over the history books she had become

completely absorbed, and by the time Joseph arrived, Liv felt she had a pretty good understanding of the situation in Yugoslavia during the Second World War.

On 6 April 1941 Adolf Hitler gave the order for German forces to invade Yugoslavia. In the remote mountain regions, resistance forces soon emerged, but before the Germans could crush them, their forces were redeployed from Yugoslavia to the east, in preparation for the imminent invasion of the Soviet Union. The resistance groups divided into two main movements – the Chetniks and the Partisans. Initially, Britain had recognised former Yugoslav Army Colonel Draza Mihailovic as the official head of the resistance in Yugoslavia and regularly sent SOE agents to the Chetniks to assist them in their effort. However, increasing Chetnik collaboration with the Axis powers finally led the British to switch their support to the Partisans. The history books revealed that the Partisan forces were a constant thorn in the side of the Wehrmacht divisions in the Balkans.

So while the Partisans had fought alongside The Allies, thought Liv, *the Chetniks were collaborating with the enemy!* As she left the library there was no doubt in her mind. *The bastard had been fighting for the other side!* Fiercely loyal to Flora's memory and determined to expose him for what he really was, Liv felt confident, that armed with this information, she was ready to do battle with Joseph Bloody Ljubić.

It was impossible to find out anything directly from Joseph, because he hardly spoke a word of English, however Carl was more than happy to act as his interpreter and was keen to persuade his father to talk about his wartime exploits.

Liv would sit quietly listening to stories of Joseph's life as a resistance fighter, as relayed to her via Carl. She knew to take most of it with a pinch of salt; the injury sustained whilst blowing up the Nazi munitions train for instance had Carl written all over it. However, throughout these seemingly innocent conversations, she would be taking it all in and filing it away as she built her case.

Finally she felt she had enough to bury him and when Carl invited some friends round to meet his father 'the war hero', she knew she had her chance. The Joseph and Carl double act ran for a while and she could see that Joseph, who had been extremely reluctant at first, was now beginning to relax into his role and was clearly enjoying himself as much as Carl. The group of friends were all suitably impressed and hanging on their every word. She had bided her time but was now deliberately leading the conversation towards specific areas that Joseph was clearly finding uncomfortable. He became cagey and she sensed he had realised she was suspiciously knowledgeable on the subject. He clammed up, but not before admitting he had been a member of the Yugoslav Army in the Homeland.

"So you were a Chetnik?" she'd asked, sounding incredibly impressed, "serving under Draza Mihailovic, that's amazing!" He had looked shocked and more than a little confused as Carl relayed this to him. He didn't know whether to admit or deny his allegiance to the Chetnik Movement. He looked at the expectant faces of his audience, who led by Liv's earlier statements, clearly thought being a Chetnik was a good thing. He gave a curt nod. "Wow!" continued Liv, feeding him more rope with every word, "So you fought *against* the partisans!"

Their eyes connected as he received Carl's translation. *Gotcha you bastard!* The look of pure evil as he gave his clipped response wiped the smile from her face – "Es ist kompliziert!" He got up and left the room. "Du denkst dass du so schlau bist," he sneered at Liv as he pushed past her, "du weißt gar nichts!"

"Christ Liv," said Carl, "what was that all about?"

"Honestly, I have no idea!"

"Well something's pissed him off, that's for sure."

"Why what did he say?"

"He said it was complicated – and then something like *'You think you're so smart – you know nothing!'* Tell you what Liv, you don't want to make an enemy of him."

"I'm not!" she protested; but she knew that the battle lines had been drawn. Clearly, she needed to go back to the library. Joseph was right; it was complicated. The makeup of the Yugoslavian population at the time of the Second World War was extremely complex. Her initial investigation had been so rushed, she had failed to recognise a crucial fact.

'Following the German invasion in 1941 and throughout the whole of World War II, a civil war raged in Yugoslavia that was both brutal and complex with many factions all fighting against each other in an ever changing theatre of war.'

As Liv had previously discovered, there had been two resistance groups in Yugoslavia, The Chetniks and The Partisans. She now realised it was not as straight forward as the distinction she had made earlier; by all accounts both sides were as bad as each other.

'Murder, rape and mass executions were all too common in Yugoslavia during World War Two – carried out by Partisan fighters as well as by Chetnik rebels and German troops.'

She discovered that ethnic cleansing took place on a huge scale with all sides wreaking genocidal atrocities against each other. The violent struggles that occurred in Yugoslavia between 1941 and 1945 resulted in over 1.7 million dead. Of these, one million were caused by Yugoslav killing Yugoslav.

'Many of the dead met a gruesome end, like the 250 Serbs who, after being locked in a church, were beaten to death by Ustase wielding spiked clubs. Such was the reality of life and death in war-torn, wartime Yugoslavia.'

"Nice house guest!" commented Michael.

"Yes, and it suddenly hit me – there was a distinct possibility that what I had living under my roof was far worse than the imposter I'd first imagined. I remembered the look in Joseph's eye and I vowed that from then on, I would let sleeping monsters lie."

"I'll Be Back!"

"Wise decision," said Michael. "He's one scary looking individual that's for sure."

"He looks like an axe murderer."

"Worse! He looks like an axe murderer who's had a run in with another axe murderer!"

Liv shuddered. "I hated having him in the house. It was like a dark presence if you know what I mean."

"And what, he just moved in?"

"No – that first visit lasted just over a month and then Carl went back to Austria with him for a few days on business. I asked him what it was about, but he was vague and said it was something he was looking into with his dad. I was glad to see the back of Joseph, but it wasn't for long. Carl made another trip to Austria and then told me that Joseph was coming back. He briefly outlined a new business venture they were setting up, but most of it went over my head."

"So what was it?"

"No idea – I still don't know now! Something to do with arranging junkets? VIPs were mentioned, and Carl's nightclub in London. I didn't take much notice to be honest – I was too busy stressing at the thought of Joseph coming back and was more interested in trying to find out how long he'd be staying. He arrived within the month and my heart sank when I saw the amount of luggage he'd brought with him."

"And that's when he took up residence?"

"Yes but thankfully, I didn't see too much of him. He went to work with Carl every morning and they were out most evenings. They spent hours holed up in Carl's study and there were frequent trips back to Austria. Carl was so preoccupied he pretty much left me to my own devices, which was fine by me."

"Not as bad as you thought then?"

"No it was okay. Life was tolerable and ticking along, when out of the blue, another fly landed in the ointment, a big fat Austrian fly—"

"Ahh! Herr Prick!"

"That's the one!" laughed Liv, "you've met him then?"

"What an absolute arsehole!"

"Bane of my life!"

"So who is he exactly?"

"Ernst! He was introduced to me as a business colleague of Joseph's who ran a string of casinos in London."

"Another Austrian."

"Yeah, a bloody über Austrian, and without doubt the most irritating person I've ever met."

"Arnold Schwarzenegger!"

"Don't!" laughed Liv, "the way he slips into role all the time – and then laughs at his own hilarity!"

"I'LL BE BACK!!!"

"Arghhhh!! – every time he leaves!"

"Prat!"

"And like a bad penny—"

"Pfennig!"

"Yeah," laughed Liv, "like a bad pfennig – he always came back!"

"So where does he fit in?"

"The casinos – Carl said they were part of the new company they were developing."

"Ah right…" said Michael thoughtfully.

"What?… what are you thinking?"

"No, nothing. Carry on."

"I remember the first time I met him," said Liv darkly, "we got off to a particularly bad start."

***

She'd pulled into her drive after the weekly supermarket shop to find two Mercedes parked up on the drive. Alongside Carl's was an enormous black S Class with the registration plate ERN 5T. Her plans for a cooling dip in the pool and a lie in the sun before picking the boys up from school were well and truly scuppered. Not only were Carl and Joseph back early, they had a visitor too. Plunged instantly into a foul mood she began unloading the car and as she slammed the last of the shopping bags

251

onto the counter she glanced out of the kitchen window. Carl and Joseph, bare-chested and clad only in shorts, were sat in the garden by the side of the pool, deep in conversation with their guest, presumably the owner of the black Mercedes. He was a big man, of a similar age to Carl, but there was something odd about him. As she peered through the blinds to get a better look, she realised her mistake. It was, in fact, a woman, albeit a very large woman, wearing a floral dress. As Liv watched, she stood up, stretched, scratched her backside and lit a cigar! Carl spotted Liv at the window and beckoned for her to join them. As she walked down the garden, the visitor turned towards her. Liv stopped dead in her tracks. Jesus Christ! It was a man! A man in a dress! He looked just like Les Dawson's Ada, the northern housewife with a penchant for gossiping over the garden wall with her neighbour Cissie. Realisation slapped her in the face – it wasn't a dress he was wearing – it was her dressing gown! She couldn't believe her eyes. Her pretty Laura Ashley robe, sheer white cotton with delicate blue flowers and a ruffled neckline was stretched tightly around his enormous torso and tied up with a bow resting on his exposed, hideously hirsute belly.

"*Vot do you think?*" he chortled as he gave her a twirl, "*is funny ja?*" He was bright red and sweating profusely. "*I hope you don't mind that I made a joke mit your bathrobe – it vos hanging in the sauna unt I could not resist – is a good joke yes?*" Words failed her. She was outraged. Her indignation finally registered and his face fell as he realised his joke had backfired. He immediately began peeling the robe from his

252

sweating bulk but it stuck fast and they both heard the rip as the flimsy material gave way. She raised a hand to silence his apologies, turned on her heel and marched back into the house. Carl followed her in and berated her for being rude to his guest.

"Rude? What about my dressing gown? The fat fuckin oaf!!"

"For God's sake Olivia, calm down! – Ernst is a very important guy. He's part of this thing I'm trying to set up with my father."

"What thing?"

"You know – the thing I'm involved in. Look, come back out with me, we can smooth things over with Ernst and then I'll explain what it's all about."

It was presented to her as just a few visitors now and then, who would be wined, dined and entertained in London. They would only stay for a couple of days and Carl would make sure they didn't intrude on their private life in any way. All Liv would have to do was provide them with a continental breakfast and then they would be out of her hair, whisked off to London by Carl and Joseph for a spot of shopping or sightseeing. The evening's entertainment would include fine dining at a top London restaurant, a chance to try their luck at the tables of one of Ernst's casinos and finally on to the VIP lounge of Carl's nightclub.

She was to be paid a proper wage from the new company for providing the bed and breakfast part of the deal and because the guests were to be accommodated in the original part of the house, Joseph would be vacating the guest suite and moving into the room she was presently occupying.

"It'll be great Liv. You're always going on about wanting to earn your own money."

"Yes but—"

"And you'll have the nice guest bedroom."

"But I—"

"It makes sense to move Dad over there with them. Much better because it keeps it all separate."

She had grave misgivings about the whole affair but as always, her opinion counted for nothing and Carl forged ahead regardless. Ernst became an almost permanent fixture and had clearly embraced Carl's invitation to make himself at home. His endless visits were driving her to distraction and were the cause of endless arguments with Carl. The final straw came when she arrived home one afternoon to find him busy at work in her kitchen. He was wearing his customary Speedo trunks but with a grotesque 'boobs and suspenders' apron tied round his ample girth. He greeted her with an enthusiastic *"Ah Olivia! Gut! Kommen! Look here vot I haff brought. Carl tells me you cannot cook – so here, I vill teach you! Ve vill make the Wiener Schnitzel!"* Liv's apoplectic response left an embarrassed Carl trying to convince the crestfallen Ernst that her suggestion of where to shove his schnitzel had been an affectionate joke and that *'Austro German Wank Chop'* was in fact a term of endearment.

Carl's plans went full steam ahead and in the blink of an eye her home was transformed into a guesthouse. There was rye bread and pumpernickel in her breadbin, German beer in the bar and her refrigerator was stuffed full with cheeses, salamis, bratwurst, knackwurst and other continental delicacies that would have put the deli at her local Waitrose to shame. She was inundated with foreign visitors, shady looking characters from all over Europe who far from vacating the premises immediately after breakfast, tended to hang around all day, lounging by the pool or playing snooker if the weather was bad. Apparently shopping and sightseeing didn't have the same appeal as 'home' with its well stocked kitchen and bar. Her complaints about the situation fell on deaf ears as she struggled to cope with this invasion of her home. To make matters worse, the visits were invariably arranged for the weekends which put Liv under further pressure to keep Charlie and Joe from getting under their guests feet and having to explain that '*no, you can't go out in the garden or swim in the pool*', and '*sorry, no, your friends can't come round to play – we have visitors.*'

"Money laundering," announced Michael.

"Huh?"

"That's what they're doing… washing money through Arnie's casinos."

"Really?"

"Yeah, I reckon. So how long was all this going on?" asked Michael. "When I came on the scene, you'd already left."

"Months! I think the first lot arrived in March. Honestly, I was at the end of my tether. The boys were due to break up for the summer holidays and the thought of trying to cope with them at home all day plus running their bloody guesthouse for the next eight weeks… I saw my life stretching out in front of me and I knew I couldn't go on. I gave Carl a final ultimatum – 'Gasthof Vogel' or me."

"I can imagine his response!"

"Yeah – '*OFF YOU FUCKING GO!*' – So that's when I made my decision. I was moving back to my parents and filing for divorce. I had to force him to accept that the marriage was over and the only way I could do that was to leave. I knew that initially the boys would have to stay with Carl because of the mayhem that would follow otherwise. The other thing I decided was that this time, I wasn't going to help Carl look after them. I hoped that by leaving him to it, he would realise he couldn't cope and would agree that they should be with me."

"Tough decision."

"It was, but I figured that with school about to break up for the summer, it was probably a good time. I knew he'd never cope with them at home all day and I was confident it wouldn't be long before he caved in. I was hopeful that once he'd accepted the marriage was over, we could start working towards a permanent solution."

"Which would have been…?"

"Well, it's laughable now, but I had had visions of living in my own little house with the boys. Carl would have full access… he could come over for Sunday lunches… Christmases and birthdays could be spent together and maybe in time, holidays could be shared—"

"And God would smile down from heaven—"

"Yeah… and pigs would fly!"

"So clearly that didn't happen."

"Course not. My plan was doomed to fail. He lasted about a week and I was getting reports from the boys like '*Dad cooked chips yesterday, but he didn't peel the potatoes*', and

'*Dad washed our trainers in the dishwasher, and they came out like Aladdin's slippers!*' I was starting to feel sorry for him, but then I reminded myself I should be pleased because the more he was struggling the sooner he'd give in. I should have known better – a week later he employed a live-in housekeeper."

"The Italian bird."

"Yes, Maria. You met her as well then? It's funny to think you know all these people too!"

"It is a bit weird isn't it? Carl was training regularly back then and we'd often come back here for a drink or a game of pool... I met them all then."

"Yeah, of course... so anyway, there I was, redundant! I stayed on at my parents and got a job."

"Doing what?"

"Temping at a kind of recruitment agency. It was okay. I was seeing the boys regularly and although I was really missing them, I knew it was only temporary."

"Sounds like you'd got your shit together."

"I had... for the first time in ages I felt in control. I instructed my solicitor to start divorce proceedings."

"Was that the first time you'd seen a solicitor?"

"No, I'd been once before, after the mirror thing. My friend Clare told me about him. He's the one she used in her divorce. We had the initial consultation, but then I ended up moving back here and calling it all off."

"So real progress this time?"

"Yeah... but all this had a terrible effect on Carl. When the first solicitor's letter arrived he went absolutely ballistic! The status quo was well and truly broken. He instructed me to tell my solicitor that the next letter that dropped on his mat would be shoved so far up his fucking arse, he'd be shitting 'afrodavids' for weeks!"

"Afro-Davids!!" laughed Michael. "What are they... little soul brothers?"

"I know, hilarious isn't it?"

"Did you pass that on?"

"I felt I had to! Fair play to Simon though, he didn't bat an eyelid. He gets threats like that all the time apparently – takes them with a pinch of salt."

"What's he like? Good solicitor?"

"He is – and he's a good guy too."

"So what was the plan?"

"Well, Simon explained that I could get a divorce on the grounds of 'irretrievable breakdown' but that it would take two years."

"Two years!"

"I told him I couldn't wait that long because until it was all over, there would be no chance for me to rebuild my relationship with the boys. The longer it dragged on, the worse it would get."

"So what was the alternative?"

"He asked me to write what he called a history of the marriage to see if there were other grounds for divorce. He told me to be really open. By the time I'd finished, the only thing I wanted to open was—"

"A bottle?" suggested Michael.

"Or the veins in my wrists! Talk about depressing!"

"Did he find anything?"

"Yes. He advised me to sue on the grounds of his

'unreasonable behaviour' which I thought pretty much hit the nail on the head."

"Sounds about right…" nodded Michael. "Anyway, back to Maria. What happened? Why did she leave?"

"She called me at work – she'd found a gun in Carl's office!" Liv paused but Michael didn't react. "Did you hear what I said? She found a gun!"

"Go on…"

"She'd been tidying some stuff away on his desk and it was in one of the drawers. It wasn't locked or anything! She showed it to me. It was all wrapped up in an oily piece of chamois leather." Liv shuddered as she remembered the revulsion she felt as Maria handed her the gun. "Ugly looking thing, really heavy, and there were some bullets in a leather pouch."

"I knew about the gun," admitted Michael, "he showed it to me before he bought it. He figured because I'd been in the services, I'd know if it was genuine."

"And was it?"

"I don't know," shrugged Michael, "I think so, but like I said to Carl, the only way you'd know for sure is if you fired it!"

"And you didn't think that was weird – him buying a gun?"

"Well yeah, I asked him what the hell he wanted it for… but it wasn't my business at the end of the day."

"Yeah well, I was horrified – and so was Maria! The thought of that thing in the house with Charlie and Joe there didn't bear thinking about."

"So arrivederci Maria."

"Yes. She gave a month's notice. She'd had enough anyway. She'd been employed to look after a father and his two sons, not run a guesthouse! This was the last straw. I had a massive showdown with Carl. He said he'd been feeling a bit uneasy about some of his houseguests and had bought the gun for added security. Apparently the baseball bat he kept under his bed didn't feel adequate anymore."

"I'm not surprised!"

"I threatened that unless he left, I would tell my solicitor about the gun. I gave him 'til the end of the week to get out. Him, his father and the rest of the bloody Mafioso!" Michael looked at her with renewed respect. "It was non-negotiable," she continued grimly, "There was nothing he could do. It took a couple of weeks but eventually he and Joseph moved into an apartment they'd taken in London. They continued to run the business from there, the only difference being they had to use hotels for their guests instead of here. Maria worked her notice while they moved out – I moved back in and carried on working until she left. Once she'd gone I had to quit my job, but they said they'd always welcome me back – so I'm thinking of getting an au pair."

"You want to go back to work?"

"Absolutely! I need to earn my own money. The thought of being beholden to Carl again is just..." she shook her head, "it's not going to happen. Loads of people round here have au pairs. My neighbour gave me the number of her agency – it's meant to be really good. I'm going to an open evening next week."

Elizabeth suddenly appeared and reminded Olivia

it was time for his afternoon walk. As he charged round the table Michael had no hesitation in turning down Liv's invitation to join them.

"No thanks mate, you crack on…" he said, heading for the door, "I've got a date with my blue book and pop-pop… I'll see you soon."

"Cheers!"

4 Chestnut Street
Beacon Hill
Boston, MA 02108, USA

30th June, 1986

Dear Clare,

So great to hear you're settled and we
can have a proper catch up at last. I've
loved receiving your little missives from
here, there and everywhere, but it's
been horrible not having an address to
write back to. I'm glad you abandoned
your road trip. Sounds like it was an
absolute nightmare! Poor Briany. Hope
you're fully recovered now?

So... Boston, Massachusetts. That's more like it! Must be a relief to get away from all the 'Have a nice day!' bollocks in LA! I've always liked the sound of New England. If ever I was thinking of visiting America, that's the place I'd go. Maybe because I've heard that Bostonians are more like us - or maybe it's just because of ' CHEERS!' How brilliant you've actually had a drink there. I bet you were you half expecting Norm or Cliffy to walk in and order a beer!

This agency sound much better than the A'holes in California. The 'Nannies Network' is a great idea - a readymade social circle and backup if you need it - perfect. So Beacon Hill... is that like Knob Hill then? Looks pretty posh in the pics. You've landed on your feet again then Briany - your English accent is still opening doors!

Talking about agencies, remember last time I said I was thinking about getting an au pair? Well... I've actually got one! Jean next door gave me the number of the agency she used and I went along to a presentation thingy a few weeks ago.

So it's all quite informal – everyone's milling around, glass of wine in one hand, canapé in the other. We go through for the talk and I find myself sitting next to a nice French girl I'd exchanged smiles with earlier. There's a slight delay waiting for the speaker. All quiet apart from a strange noise coming from behind. We turn round simultaneously and catch each other's puzzled look. There's a huge fat man spread out over two seats sitting directly behind us. The strange noise is definitely coming from him. It's his breathing – he's whistling through his nose! I steal a glance left. Her mouth is twitching. We're both avoiding eye contact – trying not to laugh. I have a pen and pad on my lap (super efficient, ready to take notes!). I also have a French phrase book but doubt that 'Nose Whistler' is in there – so I draw a big nose with crotchets and quavers flying out of the nostrils! I nudge the girl – show her the picture – girl erupts and flees the room!

It was a perfect match! Her name is Anna and we get on great. I can't tell you how nice it is to have another female in the house. She's only been with us a couple of weeks but it's like she's always been here. The boys love her. I'm back at work now and that's going really well. I'm working for a Swedish company who specialise in a new thing called 'psychological profiling'. Companies send us their shortlisted candidates for jobs or promotions and we subject them to a barrage of psychometric tests designed to measure intelligence, aptitude and personality. They're usually pretty nervous about what these tests might reveal and some of them are downright hostile! They have to work through them as quickly as possible and give the first answer that comes into their head. There's a section where they have to complete the sentence e.g. "When I woke up this morning..." Some try hard to give what they think is the 'right' answer and come out with crap like – "I embraced the dawn of a new day!" but others just take the piss! Number one on our leader board at the moment: "When I woke up this morning... I had a hard on!" Ha-ha-ha!!

All in all, I have to say that life is pretty good – apart from one thing – well, two actually – Carl and bloody Joseph! They seem to think it's perfectly okay for them to come and go as they please. They just turn up, unannounced, at any time of night or day and let themselves in. They treat Anna like she's some kind of servant and expect her to drop whatever she's doing to attend their every whim. It's seriously getting on my nerves. I have tried explaining to Carl that he should respect the fact we are now officially separated, but he carries on regardless.

In answer to your questions about Michael... ha-ha very funny... NO! I am not after his body... and NO! I do not want his babies!! It's not like that – I know you won't believe me, but honestly Clare, I don't see him that way. You know I said he had split with his fiancé – well it's not quite so straight forward. The engagement is definitely off – but I think they're seeing each other again now. He seems to genuinely love her but, for whatever reason, the idea of marriage seems to frighten the life out of him. I shall keep you posted!

Lots of love,
Brian xxx

Get Your Kicks

As Michael turned into his road he saw Hannah's car parked outside his apartment and cursed into his crash helmet. He was supposed to be ringing Olivia tonight. Since she had gone back to work they hardly saw each other but kept in touch with phone calls once or twice a week. He yanked his moped around and headed for the phone box located on the corner of a quiet cul-de-sac a few blocks from home.

"Hi, it's me."

"Hello you…! How you doing?" said Olivia brightly.

"Yeah, not bad. I've been phut-phutting round the streets of London since seven this morning so I'm a bit knackered to be honest."

"Are you still up there?"

"No, almost home now."

"Oh… I thought… you're in a phone box aren't you?"

"Yeah, Hannah's there."

"Huh?"

"Hannah's at the flat."

"Oh." Picking up on the irritation in his voice, Olivia didn't quite know what to say. "Blimey, it's nine o'clock!" she said in a bid to end the awkward silence, "that's a fourteen hour day!"

"Yeah I know, but I need to get the miles in. I've got my final appearance coming up – I don't want to cock it up at the last hurdle."

"Oh you'll be fine. How long have you been doing it?"

"Nearly four years now."

"You're joking! Why so long?"

"Because that's how long it takes! You wouldn't believe how difficult it is."

"But four—"

"There's so much to learn. Over three hundred routes across twenty-five thousand streets – and on top of that, we're supposed to know more than twenty thousand landmarks!"

"Jeez! All for a little blue badge."

"You make it sound like a Blue Peter badge! It's green anyway, not blue."

"I thought you said—"

"No, the book's blue, the badge is green. Anyway, enough of all that – how's your day been?"

"Pretty good. I got a letter from Clare today."

"Ahhh! The Scarlett Pimpernel! Where is she?"

"Well, she's in Boston now, but she's been all over."

"Did the agency arrange it?"

"No, they were hopeless. When she told them why she wanted to leave, you know, explained about the mother being a crazy cokehead and everything, they more

268

or less accused her of lying. They said she had a fertile imagination!"

"Nice!"

"Yeah, well anyway, she bummed around L.A. for a while, fruit picking, working in bars and stuff then she and an American girl she'd got friendly with decided to go on a road trip. Los Angeles to Chicago – Route 66!"

"Very rock 'n' roll! She's quite the adventurer your mate! Did they make it?"

"Only as far as Albuquerque. They both went down with food poisoning."

"Food poisoning in Albuquerque? Sounds grim – but quite funny when you think about it."

"Funny? – Why?"

"They got the shits on Route 66!"

"I wish I'd thought of that!" laughed Olivia.

"Is she staying in Boston then?"

"Yeah, they flew there from Albuquerque – her friend has family there. She stayed with them for a bit until she found another job. She's loving Boston – and guess what? You know Cheers? Well it's actually there. It really does exist."

"I know – a mate of mine's been. Apparently the outside is just like you see it in the opening credits, but inside it's completely different."

"Oh that's a shame! I had visions of Clare perched on a stool at the bar—"

"Getting chatted up by Sam—"

"And abused by Carla! Diane would have liked her though, being English and all."

"Diane isn't English."

"I meant Clare, but Diane seems like she's English too – I bet she's an Anglophile."

"You're doing it again aren't you? Books, films, TV series, you have to understand Olivia… these people aren't real."

"You started it! You said Diane wasn't English, so I said—"

"Oh alright, never mind – let's not waste time talking twaddle." He blew his frustration out in a heavy sigh. "So, what've you been up to?"

"Well… mainly writing back to Clare. Umm… are you okay, you seem a bit—"

"Oh I'm alright – just a bit pissed off with all this cloak and dagger bullshit."

"What d'you mean?"

"Oh you know, skulking around in phone boxes. All I wanted to do was get home, grab a beer, put my feet up and give you a call but…" Michael was feeling aggrieved. His relationship with Olivia was completely above board; but here it was, being viewed with suspicion from all sides. Their usual post gym visits had come to an end when Olivia went back to work. Going round in the evening didn't feel right and the last couple of times he'd popped in at the weekend he'd bumped into Carl – who'd made it perfectly clear his presence wasn't welcome. Since they had stopped training together, Carl's attitude towards Michael had turned into palpable mistrust. The fact that Michael had continued to see Olivia was proof of where his allegiance lie and with Carl's mind-set of 'you're either with me or agin me' – their friendship was toast. To make matters worse, Hannah was watching him like a hawk. Unfortunately living under suspicion was causing him to act suspiciously… fuelling her suspicions even further. Now was not the time to try and explain his friendship with Olivia so, for the time being at least, the skulduggery would have to continue. "Oh I dunno, I'm just a bit tired and pissed off with it all. Take no notice."

"S'alright… I've been a bit down lately too."

"So you've written to Clare…"

"Yep, I brought her up to date. Told her about Anna and me working… and how Carl keeps turning up here with Joseph all the time and how he's messing everything up. Michael… I think I might change the locks. What do you have to do? Do you know anyone?"

"No – I don't… but even if I did… changing the locks Liv… that's a bad idea."

"Why? Oh I don't even care! He has to accept we are separated. We're supposed to be working together to make it easier for the boys but he's causing friction all the time – making me look heartless – scoring points. I just want this to be over. This will force him to stick to the rules, to come when he's supposed to come and leave us alone in between." Michael went to say something but she continued her rant. "And another thing – I want Joseph's key back! How dare he be sat in my house in the dead of night drinking Schnapps and smoking his fucking cigars?"

"You finished?" She had. "Good. Look, I'm not saying I don't understand. I completely understand! I've got a similar thing going on myself. The engagement's off and I thought we were supposed to be having a trial separation but… it's like she's moving back in by stealth!"

"Maybe that's what Carl and Joseph are doing!"

"Yeah well like I say… I know how you feel. I get in from work and she's either there, or it's obvious she's been there."

"Maybe you should change your locks too!"

"I could just ask for her keys back… but I haven't got the heart. She comes round and has a tidy up, does a bit of ironing. Sometimes there's a lasagne in the oven or a curry, which is really nice of her and everything but—"

"It makes you feel bad."

"Well yeah 'cos I know she's trying to make a go of it – but it's not what we agreed. We were supposed to be having some time apart but… well, anyway, I haven't asked for the keys because I don't want to inflame the situation – and I don't think you should either."

"My situation is already inflamed! Let's face it – this divorce was never going to be amicable. Carl won't allow it. I just need to get it over with as soon as possible and then get on with picking up the pieces."

"Hmmmm, well just be careful. Something like this could really rattle his cage."

"Yeah well maybe his cage needs rattling! If I don't take action, nothing will change. They say actions speak louder than words don't they?"

"They do… but they've not met Carl have they? Just think it through Liv, that's all I'm saying. Anyway mate, I'm tired and hungry, so I'd better go. I'll give you a call next week."

"Okay Michael, thanks for ringing... and for the advice. I've taken it on board, I promise, but to be honest, I think it's the only way."

Pink Sands And Elephants

5th August, 1986

Dear Clare,

'Vacationing' with them in Bermuda? BERMUDA!! You've only been with them a couple of months! You jammy bastard! But let's not ignore the elephant on the page here! Bloody hell Briany - I feel ill just thinking about it! Are you flying or going by sea... mind you, by all accounts I don't think it matters! Just as many ships as planes have disappeared! Have you asked them about it? Aren't you worried?? I'm sure the photos look great in the brochure and that the pink sands are fabulous - but the Bermuda Triangle?

Sod that for a game of soldiers! Maybe you don't have to go through it? Ask them - before it's too late!

All is well here apart from Carl and Joseph who are still turning up without so much as a by your leave. It's pointless speaking to Carl about it. I've tried using the threat of going to the police about the gun, but he just said " what gun?" Obviously it's long gone now and Maria's back in Italy, so it would just be my word against his. Michael saw it, but I don't want to drag him into it. It all came to a head last night. I came down in the middle of the night to get a glass of water and almost had a heart attack when I bumped into Joseph in the kitchen. I went nuts and demanded his key back but he just laughed in my face. Anyway, that's it! - I've made up my mind - I'm changing the locks!

Thanks for letting me know you'll be incommunicado for the next three weeks... and if you disappear without a trace, it was nice knowing you!

Loads of love,
Liv xxx

King Kong

There are certain times in life when situations escalate and you find yourself on the fast track to do-do-land. For Olivia, this was such a time. It had been three hours since the deed had been done and she was strung out like Billy Whizz on crack. The tension in the house had become unbearable. Feeding off the atmosphere, Elizabeth and the boys had become so overexcited, Anna had taken them to the park to let off steam. Olivia was home alone – alone with her thoughts. She was trying to convince herself she hadn't acted hastily and realised that although she'd thought about it continuously before consulting the Yellow Pages, she hadn't actually thought it through. The ability to backtrack and identify the pivotal point of any such escalation was a useful thing; but blinding clarity moments from disaster was not. Her elation at changing the locks had nosedived into dread. What had she done! She was suddenly aware of the enormity of her folly. Carl wouldn't take this lying down. Of course he wouldn't! What would he do? As Olivia's thoughts whirled, Carl was jamming his key into the lock for the third time. She was about to find out!

"OLIVIA!!!! OPEN THIS FUCKIN DOOR!"

She leapt out of her chair in a blind panic.

"OPEN THE DOOR RIGHT NOW – OR IT'S COMING IN!"

She ran into the hall and was hopping from one foot to the other when Carl starting kicking, barging and hammering at the door.

"OLIVIA – YOU EITHER OPEN THIS DOOR OR I WALK STRAIGHT FUCKING THROUGH IT! – I SWEAR TO GOD – YOU GOT FIVE SECONDS… 1… 2…"

She opened the door and he came crashing through. He was yelling unintelligibly – something along the lines of "WHAT'S THE MEANING OF THIS???" – but what with the snarling and gnashing of teeth, she couldn't be sure. She knew she was in trouble. Everything was slowing down… and then… apparently… she grew a pair of balls!

"I've changed the locks…" she heard herself say, "to stop you waltzing in and out of here like you own the place."

He made a grab for her but such were the effects of the slow-mo, even as the words left her mouth she was skipping backwards out of reach.

"I DO OWN THE PLACE YOU FUCKING BITCH!!!" he roared, but she was already half way up the stairs and heading for the safety of her room. Everything speeded up. She made it – but so did Carl! There was no time to shut the door let alone lock it. He burst through and grabbed the front of her t-shirt as she fell backwards. He shoved her back and forth and then his hands were round her neck. He was shaking her violently, shaking the life right out of her.

Returning from the park, Anna had spotted Carl's car. She'd driven slowly past registering the fact that Bill and Jean were out on the street, anxiously looking up at Olivia's bedroom window. She'd circled back and parked on their drive. Bill gestured to Anna there was trouble next door while Jean hurriedly ushered the boys inside.

Olivia heard a shriek, and out of the corner of her eye she saw Anna fly across the room and felt the impact as she landed on Carl's back, clawing at his face and pulling his hair. Carl released Olivia and she fell backwards onto the bed. He gave a roar and like King Kong swatting planes on top of the Empire State Building, he batted Anna aside. She fell to the ground; hair all over the place and her glasses askew. Liv screamed for her to get Bill and she was out of the room like a shot. When they returned moments later the danger was already over; Carl was rocking Olivia in his arms, crying and begging her forgiveness. He looked up at Bill and sobbed "I could have killed her... I could have killed her."

Kryptonite

Olivia and Anna followed Bill as he led Carl downstairs and into the kitchen. It was quite a revelation to see Bill, the sweet natured, henpecked little man from next door, quietly taking control of the situation. He poured Carl a shot of whiskey, found him a cigarette and then turned his attention to Olivia.

"Alright love?" Olivia nodded. "Come on then, sit yourself down." He turned to Anna, "And how about you, young lady? Are you okay?" Anna smiled and nodded too. "Good girl, that's grand... so... let's get the kettle on shall we?" Coming from the same generation as Olivia's mum and dad, he was a firm believer in the healing powers of a nice cup of tea. Anna set the teapot down in front of him and after leaving it to brew for a few minutes he volunteered 'to be mother'. Liv smiled inwardly as he poured the tea and ladled in the sugar, assuring them it was 'good for the shock.' They all sat quietly sipping the hot sweet liquid and then at Olivia's request, Anna went next door to be with the boys.

"Is it okay to let Elizabeth out?" she asked, reappearing in the doorway. "He's still in the car."

"Oh God! Yes, of course, let him in. Thanks Anna."

Anna retrieved the car from Bill's drive and released Elizabeth. He came barrelling through the house like a baby rhino at full pelt, skidded to a halt directly in front of Carl and sat down at his feet. He rested his head on Carl's knees and fixed him with a ferocious glare. His lip curled back revealing a terrible smile and there was a menacing growl coming from deep within his enormous chest.

"Best put him in the garden eh love?" suggested Bill. "Don't want any more upsets do we?"

Olivia dragged him away, but he wasn't happy and flatly refused to go outside. He put the brakes on by the conservatory. With a lot of persuasion she managed to coax him in and stayed for a while to reassure him all was well before rejoining Bill and Carl in the kitchen. She drew up a chair and tuned into what Bill was saying; to her surprise, he proved to be extremely knowledgeable on the subject of emotional collapse.

"Now look old son, I think you're having a bit of a breakdown – happened to Ian, our youngest, about five years ago now. And well… me and Jean, we know the symptoms, we saw the signs." Puzzled, Olivia looked up and tried to catch Bill's eye, but he was talking again. "The weight loss Carl, that looks pretty significant. Am I right?" Carl nodded. "And sleeping – has that been a problem?" Olivia studied Carl's face as he nodded again. *'Jesus!'* she thought, taking in his sunken cheeks and hollow eyes. *'How did I not see the signs?'*

Their meetings had become brief, unpleasant skirmishes, and Olivia had done her best to keep out of his way. All hopes of an amicable divorce had long since died and it was a matter of pushing on through. He had become a figure of both hatred and fear; fear that one day he would succeed in getting her back under his control. She had been so busy staying strong and resolute, dealing with everything Carl had thrown at her from emotional blackmail to terrifying threats; she genuinely hadn't noticed the state he was in. But now… she looked across at him slumped in the chair, head bowed, tears dripping from his chin, and felt a surge of pity. A weight landed on her chest and her inner voice cried out… '*For fuck's sake Olivia! Don't feel sorry for him now!*' Letting pity in would be like sprinkling Kryptonite on Superman's cornflakes or giving Samson a short back and sides; she'd lose her strength and the game would be up. She turned her attention back to what Bill was saying.

"It's all private of course, but you'll have BUPA or something I expect?" Carl nodded. "It's an excellent place, well respected, good doctors. They were marvellous with Ian. Shall we do that then Carl? They'll sort you out, no bother, just a bit of a crisis, they'll get you through."

The weight started lifting from Olivia's chest. He was going to get help! Bill said they were going to help him through the crisis. Maybe they could help him come to terms with the divorce; maybe this madness was finally going to be over.

Bill rang the clinic and they confirmed they could take Carl straight away. They just needed a GP referral letter and details of his medical insurance. Bill spoke to Carl's doctor and it was agreed he would bring Carl to the surgery, pick up the letter and take him straight to the clinic from there. Olivia packed his case and saw them off. She couldn't believe that as simple as that, it was done.

She let Elizabeth out of the conservatory and after performing a quick sweep of the house he joined her in the garden. She called out to the boys playing Frisbee with Anna next door and indicated she was coming over. Jean met her at the front door and gasped in alarm. She ushered her through to the cloakroom and positioned her in front of the mirror. Olivia put her hands to her throat and felt the angry wheals from Carl's fingers where he had gripped her neck. Jean bustled off and found a scarf which she tied strategically to cover the marks.

Olivia brought her up to speed and Jean went to great lengths to reassure her that Barrington House was indeed a wonderful place and that they would 'soon get Carl right.' The boys were called in and Olivia explained that Daddy wasn't well and had gone into hospital for a little while to get better. At seven years of age, Joe's reaction was one of "Okay, can we play Frisbee again now!" Charlie, however, took some convincing that his dad hadn't had a heart attack and wasn't about to die. A friend in his class had lost his father recently; he'd collapsed and died on the golf course after suffering a massive heart attack. This tragic event had caused not only Charlie, but the whole of his class, to face the worrying issue of their parents' mortality.

"Is Dad gonna die?" Olivia sat down next to him and pulled him in close. He felt all arms and legs and a little stiff but thankfully, he didn't pull away. He accepted her embrace and leaned in, resting his head on her shoulder.

"No of course not silly!" said Olivia, stroking his hair, "He's just a bit unwell – tired more than anything. He's been working too hard, not getting enough sleep or eating properly – you know Dad!" Charlie nodded. "He's going to a lovely hospital. He'll have a nice room all to himself – very posh!" continued Olivia reassuringly. "Don't worry Charlie… he's going to be fine."

"Will we be able to see him?"

"I don't know darling… some hospitals are a bit funny about children visiting. Let's wait and see what Uncle Bill says when he gets back."

Karate Kid

When Bill returned the boys and Anna were in the games room playing pool. Olivia showed him through to the kitchen and closed the door.

"Right, so he's been admitted. It was quite late in the afternoon by the time we got him in, so nothing much will happen until Monday."

"How was he?"

"Okay – still very quiet and subdued. He told them he hadn't slept properly for months, and they promised to help him with that. The consultants aren't usually there at the weekend, but he'll have a full psychiatric assessment on Monday."

"Okay… and meanwhile?"

"He's going to be checked over by one of the regular doctors and written up for sleeping tablets and maybe something to keep him calm… and then I should imagine he will sleep around the clock. He looks absolutely exhausted poor chap."

"Did you recognise any of the staff?"

"Yes… there were a few familiar faces. Ian's doctor has moved on apparently, which is a shame. Mr Schroder, lovely man – he was the chief consultant and head of the facility back then but no matter, I'm sure Carl will receive the same excellent care. It's a lovely place Olivia, very tranquil… just what Carl needs."

"Thanks for everything Bill. You've been… well… just…" she started to choke up.

"Shhh… shhh, don't be silly," said Bill, giving her a hug, "I'm just glad I could help." Olivia clung to him and found she couldn't hold back the tears. It was relief more than anything. "Come on love, deep breath! You've had a horrible day but it's all over now. You can rest easy. He's in the right place and everything's going to be okay – just wait and see."

It was getting on for 6 o'clock by the time Bill left. Neither she nor Anna were hungry but the boys were ravenous so they took them to McDonald's for a treat and then on to Blockbusters. They emerged half an hour later with two videos, four pick 'n' mixes and copious amounts of popcorn under their respective arms and set off for home. They decided to watch Joe's choice first, in case he fell asleep. They were sitting comfortably and ready to go, when the phone rang. Half expecting it to be the hospital, Olivia took the call in the kitchen behind closed doors. To her relief, it was Michael. She told him straight away that Carl was in hospital.

"Hospital! Why? When?"

"This afternoon… and um… it's not a normal hospital. It's… it's a mental hospital."

"Christ! What's happened?"

"Bill next door thinks he's had a breakdown."

"But wh—"

"He lost it and attacked me."

"Jesus Christ Liv!! Are you alright?"

"Yes… honestly yes, I'm completely fine. Everyone's okay but—"

"Why did he attack you?"

"Because I changed the locks."

"For fuck's sake! I knew it would tip him over – I said didn't I?"

"I know, and you were right – but honestly Michael, I think it's turned out for the best. He's going to get help and… look, I can't really talk now – the boys are waiting for me to watch a video with them. I'll call you back later."

"Were they there when it happened?"

"No thank God. Anna had taken them to the park so they don't know anything about it."

"They don't know he's in a nut-house?"

"Michael!"

"Alright – hospital then."

"They do, but they think it's a normal hospital. I told them he's a bit poorly because he's been working too hard and not looking after himself properly."

"And they're okay with that?"

"Yes they're fine."

"How long's he going to be in there? Where is it?"

"Barrington House, just outside town apparently. I don't know how long. Bill said nothing much will happen over the weekend. He'll be assessed on Monday… oh hang on a minute, Charlie's calling me. 'OKAY CHARLIE! START WITHOUT ME... I WON'T BE LONG!'... I'll have to go... We've got two films to get through."

"Two?"

"They chose one each from the video shop and they have to be back tomorrow. The Karate Kid is all lined up and ready to go!"

"Who chose that – Joe?"

"Yeah – he's got his judo kit on and he's 'HI-YA!' and karate chopping all over the place. Charlie made him a Karate Kid headband."

"They sound alright then," chuckled Michael, "what film did Charlie choose?"

"The Goonies. He wanted The Ghoulies but it was a 15."

"What's The Goonies then?"

"P.G."

"Really? Are you sure? I took my nephew to see it at the cinema and it's pretty scary in places. There's this Sloth dude – might be too much for Joe."

"Awww, we love sloths! They're so cute!"

"Not this one, I promise you!"

"Oh, Joe will be fast asleep by then don't worry. Anyway, I must go – I'll call you later."

"No, I'm working tonight."

"Are you about tomorrow?"

"I've got some sessions booked at the gym."

"Okay, well... pop round if you get time."

"Yeah... maybe in the afternoon – I think my last one is at twelve."

"Okay… see you soon."

"Watch out for Lotney!"

"Who?"

"Mr Fratelli."

"I don't—"

"You will!" laughed Michael. "Just make sure the little fella's in bed before you put Charlie's film on."

"Okay will do. Thanks Michael… na night."

"Night."

Slothy

It was a hot, sunny afternoon and they were all out in the garden when Michael arrived. Olivia poured him a beer and they went out to join Anna who was keeping a watchful eye on The Goonies game that was in full swing around the pool. Charlie, who was wearing his Superman pyjama top and a bandana, waved when he caught sight of Michael.

"HEY YOU GUYS!"

Joe, sporting a black beret jammed down on his head and a string of Anna's beads, stretched his arms out towards Charlie.

"Come to Mama Slothy!" he beckoned.

Michael looked round in astonishment. "Joe watched it?"

"Loved it!" confirmed Olivia. Everyone was in high spirits, especially Olivia who couldn't wait to tell Michael her good news.

"They're going to help Carl come to terms with the divorce."

"I thought he wasn't seeing anyone until tomorrow."

"Well no – but Bill said that's what they would do. He knows all about it because of his son."

"Yeah but Liv, Bill's son is probably a different kettle of fish to Carl. Don't start counting your chickens."

"I'm not – I'm just… oh don't spoil it with your doom and gloom! I'm just starting to feel a bit more optimistic, that's all."

"It's not doom and gloom, I'm just trying to be realistic here," protested Michael. "I just don't think you should get too carried away, especially as he hasn't even been assessed yet."

"Yeah… okay, you're right – I know that but I just want to enjoy the moment for a bit. It's such a relief not having the shadow of Carl and Joseph hanging over me." Right on cue they were interrupted by somebody leaning on the front doorbell. Carl had fitted an amplified ringer on the outside wall and the decibel levels of the chimes echoing around the garden would have rivalled Big Ben's.

"Jesus!" said Michael. "What the f—"

"I'll go…" offered Anna, but Olivia was already on her way. She had more than an inkling who the caller might be. She slipped the chain lock into place before opening the door.

"The door – it is broken," growled Joseph.

"No – I've changed the locks." called Olivia through the crack in the door. She jumped back as he barged at it with his shoulder.

"Ver ist Carl? – Open it – NOW!!!" He was rattling the door furiously when Michael appeared at Olivia's shoulder.

"I think you should leave Joseph. Carl isn't here."

"His car!" he gestured towards Carl's car parked up on the drive.

"Look, he's…" Michael hesitated, he didn't know whether to inform him of Carl's whereabouts. Olivia pushed to the fore and took over.

"He's in hospital Joseph. There was a… an incident… he attacked me and he's had to go somewhere—"

"VER IS HE?" yelled Joseph, completely beside himself. He started shaking the door violently until Michael stepped in again.

"Listen to me Joseph – Carl is…" he circled his index finger to his temple. Joseph's grasp of the English language might not have been that great, but he understood the universal sign indicating Carl's mental condition. "They took him away."

"VER – IS – MEIN – SON?" roared Joseph, incandescent with rage.

"Now look, you need to calm down—"

Joseph pushed his face right into the crack of the door.

"UNT YOU NEED TO FUCK OFF FROM MY SON'S HOUSE!"

Olivia reappeared and shoved a piece of paper with the name of the hospital into his face.

"Carl's here… and this is MY house… so if anyone needs to fuck off – it's you!" She slammed the door and sank back against Michael as her legs began to shake. Joseph kicked at the door and ranted for a few moments before stalking off towards his car.

"MY SON VILL HEAR ABOUT YOU UNT

MR MUSCLE-BOY THERE!" he called back over his shoulder, "MAKING MIT THE HAPPY FAMILIES!" He swung round and stabbed his finger in their direction. "OH YES!! – HE VILL BE VERY INTERESTED TO HEAR ABOUT THAT!"

Michael steadied Olivia and turned her around. They looked at each other, eyebrows raised and then Michael's laughter brought some much needed light relief to this latest turn of events. "We should have let him in!" he joked. "Nice touch of reality for their game!"

"We should!" agreed Olivia with a shaky smile. "He's much scarier than dear old Slothy, that's for sure!"

"Hey... what's this?" said Michael as he caught sight of the bruising around Olivia's neck. During the kerfuffle, the scarf she had been wearing had come loose leaving the angry marks on full view. "Is this what that bastard did to you?" As Olivia nodded, rage surged through his body. He took her arm and walked her through to the kitchen. "Come on mate – you'd better tell me what happened," he said grimly.

The Lunatics Have Taken
Over The Asylum

The following morning Anna rang Olivia at work to say the hospital had called. She rang them immediately and was put straight through to Carl's consultant. He requested she came in as soon as possible to help him build a picture of what had led to the current state of affairs. Fortunately, her boss was sympathetic to her situation and said she could take as much time off as was necessary. Keen to do all she could to help and with her optimism running high, Olivia set off for her first interview with the venerable Mr Cavanah.

Within minutes, all hopes were dashed. Her nose itched as soon as she saw him – a bad sign as Olivia's nose could sniff out a pervert at ten paces. Following the initial pleasantries, she sat in confusion and utter disbelief as the esteemed Mr Cavanah, the chief consultant and head of the whole shebang, subjected her to a barrage of highly inappropriate questions.

"So Mrs Vogel... you and your husband... do you enjoy a healthy sex life?"

"Well hardly – we're separated!"

"But how was it before? Would you say you had a normal sexual relationship throughout the marriage?"

"I'm sorry Mr Cavanah but what has this got to do with anything?"

"As I explained on the telephone Mrs Vogel, in order to build a picture of what led to your husband's malaise, I need as much background information as possible."

"But shouldn't we be talking about what's going on now?"

"As I said, I need to fill in the background details first," insisted Mr Cavanah testily, "so if you wouldn't mind?" Olivia did her best to remain calm throughout the deeply personal and embarrassing interrogation, but time and time again he pushed her too far. At one point during a lengthy grilling about her relationship with her younger brother, she became so incensed by the nature of his questions she threatened to leave. "Alright, we'll leave it there for now," conceded Cavanah checking his watch, "but clearly, this is a highly contentious issue and needs to be addressed." He inspected her over his half moon specs for a moment before selecting a fresh page in his notebook. Holding her in his gaze, he smoothed the page and began clicking his pen... on and off... on and off... "One final question Mrs Vogel," he said slowly, still clicking his pen, "Do you indulge in self gratification?"

"I'm sorry?"

"Oh come come Mrs Vogel," he said tossing his pen aside, "it's a simple enough question surely? It seems that sex has been a problem throughout the marriage and I need to ascertain whether you have an aversion to sex *per se*, or if it is a specific problem between you and your husband."

"So what are you—?"

"I'm simply asking if you take matters into your own hands Mrs Vogel – I'm asking if you pleasure yourself."

Olivia sat in stunned silence. *Did he just say what I think he said?*

"Mrs Vogel?"

"Yes?"

"Do you?"

"Do I what?"

"Do you masturbate?"

"No that's it! I've had enough! I came along here in good faith because I want to help in my husband's treatment but this is just… it's unacceptable!"

"Now look… if, for whatever reason, certain questions are difficult for you—"

"Difficult? It's not difficult – it's just none of your business!"

"My my, let's calm down shall we?"

"I am calm! I just don't see the relevance of your questions. I'm here to talk about Carl. He's here because he attacked me! Did you know that?"

"I think 'attack' is probably too strong a word."

"Oh do you?" said Olivia untying the scarf from around her neck. "Look! Carl did this to me. He completely lost control and—"

"A little game that got out of hand maybe?" said Mr

Cavanah examining her neck. "There's bruising around the carotid arteries here…"

"A game?"

"… And when these arteries are compressed the brain is deprived of oxygen…"

"What??"

"… Inducing a semi-hallucinogenic state called hypoxia – which combined with orgasm gives a rush as powerful and highly addictive as cocaine!" he finished triumphantly. He grabbed a handful of tissues from the box on his desk and mopped his brow. '*Oh my God!*' thought Olivia as she took in his flushed face and glazed eyes, '*it's actually happened – the lunatics have taken over the asylum!*'

Bringing the meeting to an abrupt close, Mr Cavanah suggested she took the opportunity to visit Carl while she was there. After a brief five minutes with the barely conscious Carl, she cut a dejected figure as she made her way home. Her spirits were still rock bottom when Michael rang later to see how things were. She told him of her misgivings about Barrington House and the dreadful Mr Cavanah.

"Honestly Michael, he's a raving perv!"

"Why? What did he do?"

"It's not what he did – it's what he said! Everything was about sex!"

"Freudian," said Michael.

"What does that mean exactly? I've heard of Freud obviously but—"

"It means Cavanah follows the teachings of Sigmund Freud. I don't know too much about it except that he believed sex is the primary motivation for everything in life."

"Well that's him for sure! He managed to put a sexual spin on literally everything! Even the bruises on my neck!… *'So the bruising on your neck Mrs Vogel? Did this occur during a sexual encounter?'*

'NO!!!! IT OCCURRED DURING A THROTTLING ENCOUNTER!'

'Ahhhh! A little game of asphyxiophilia!'

'It wasn't a little game of anything! – HE WAS TRYING TO THROTTLE ME!!!'

As Olivia re-enacted her dialogue with the Freudian Mr Cavanah, Michael could feel his laughter bubbling up.

"He said the position of the bruises, the arteries on either side of my neck, indicated erotic asphyxiation!"

Michael roared with laughter. "He thinks you're a gasper!!"

"He thinks I'm a what?"

"Sorry for laughing Liv, I know it's not funny, but that's what they call them. They get off on strangling each other… or themselves!"

"Themselves?"

"Yeah… auto-asphyxiation. They stick an orange in their mouth and—"

"Oh stop! – I don't want to hear any more! I've had a bellyful of it with Doctor bloody Cavanah. Apart from wanting a blow by blow account of our sex lives, which didn't take long obviously as it's nonexistent – he then wanted to talk about my relationship with my brother."

"Daniel?"

"Yes – he began by asking if there was any history of incest in my family!"

"Christ!"

"I swear to God Michael – the whole thing was surreal. He said that during his chats with Carl my relationship with my brother had cropped up."

"In what way?"

"That's what I said! He said that Carl had suggested we were very close – too close maybe."

"He said something like that to me once."

"Really? What did he say?"

"I can't remember exactly, but it was obvious he was jealous of your relationship."

"Yeah, well anyway, I agreed we had always been close. You haven't met Daniel have you?"

"I don't think so."

"You'd like him. He's the funniest person in the world! We could be standing at death's door – facing a firing squad – anything, and he'd still make me laugh! I was seven when he was born. Mum had him at home and I remember pacing up and down outside the bedroom with my dad. It was a difficult birth – he was born with the cord around his neck and the midwife who delivered him said he was blue. Imagine that! Seven years old and you're told your new baby brother is blue!"

"Because of the cord?"

"No – they thought it was that at first, but he stayed blue! It was something to do with his blood group. My mum's rhesus negative and he was positive or something… anyway, he was rushed off to hospital for a blood transfusion and it was all very touch and go. Eventually Mum brought him home… and it was love at first sight! I was completely besotted from the moment I clapped eyes on him! Then at three months he developed bronchitis which progressed to double pneumonia. He was back in hospital and once again, we all thought he was going to die."

"Not the luckiest little fella then."

"It just went on and on… accidents, illnesses… it was like 'X' marked the spot! He became very precious to the whole family because we nearly lost him so many times. He had a motor bike accident when he was seventeen. Mum and Dad picked me up on the way to the hospital – they'd been told he had a broken leg and we were like 'thank God it's just his leg and not a head injury' – but when we got there, they were deciding whether or not to amputate the leg because it was so badly smashed – then a few days later we got the call to say he had been moved to Intensive Care. He had Fat Embolism Syndrome and was fighting for his life."

"What's that?"

"It's when the fat – you know, like the bone marrow – leaks out from the broken bones and gets into the lungs."

"Jesus!"

"I know – I'm thinking 'how can he die from a broken leg!'"

"They saved the leg though?"

"They did – but he was in hospital for over a year. I visited him every day. I was married by then of course, and Carl was pissed off about the amount of time I spent at the hospital, so I suppose the problem started way back then."

"And you told Carl's doctor all this?"

"Yes everything. I explained that when he was little, about four or five, Mum had an evening job so most nights it was me who got him to bed and read his bed time stories. Cavanah asked if my feelings towards him were maternal and I agreed that they probably were! Well that was it! He suggested we had a 'mother/son' relationship and started going on about the Oedipus complex."

"That's definitely Freud then!" said Michael. "It comes from a Greek Myth. Oedipus kills his father and marries his mother or something."

"What? How?"

"Oh I dunno, by accident I think… but basically, old Sigmund came up with this theory that all boys secretly desire their mothers or some such bollocks."

"Yep – that's pretty much what he was saying, or rather implying, about my relationship with Daniel. He suggested the conflict between him and Carl was because Daniel saw me as a mother figure – anyway, he brought up the incest thing again – he said I'd be surprised by the figures and I got so angry I threatened to walk out!"

"I don't blame you!"

"He agreed to drop it and went on to outline his treatment plan for Carl. He said that my involvement was imperative. I queried this and pointed out, yet again, that we were separated. I made it clear that in my opinion, Carl was in denial about the whole thing and needed help coming to terms with the fact we were getting divorced."

"Did he take that on board?"

"God knows! He just said 'one step at a time'. He said he knew exactly what he was doing and insisted I should visit Carl every day."

"And will you?"

"I think I'll have to initially. I don't mind visiting him, but I just worry it's not the right thing to do. I've got no faith in that creep Cavanah, but he threatened that if I didn't follow his advice, it would go down on record that I had refused to co-operate in Carl's treatment."

"How about Charlie and Joe, are they allowed to see him?"

"No, he advised against it. They're okay about it though, they've both written letters and we've chosen a nice photograph of them to take in."

"What about work? Are you going back yet?"

"No – Fiona said no rush. I've got loads of things to check out for Simon before our appointment next week. I've been working on it during my lunch breaks but what with visiting Carl every day now, there just won't be time. I might as well make the most of this time off and hopefully get it done."

"Yeah, makes sense. Okay mate. I'll give you a call tomorrow. Good luck with it all."

"Thanks Michael, see you soon."

Stitchem & Leggit

Olivia called work to let them know she would be off for at least a week and then rang Simon, her solicitor, to check if it was okay for her to pop in and use the cubbyhole they jokingly referred to as her office. "That's good timing actually Olivia. We've heard back from your husband's solicitors – they've sent copies of the papers relating to the mortgage that was taken out last year and allegedly signed by you."

"There's just no way. I'd know if I'd signed something that important."

"Well checking this signature against the ones we have on file, I don't think you have anything to worry about – it's a pretty poor attempt. I'm in court most of today but I'll leave everything with my secretary so you can have a look. Have you had any luck with the building regs?"

"No – I went to the Civic Centre but the records for the dates we needed were missing. They've no idea how that could have happened."

"Hmmmm…"

"I think somebody got there before me because it was the same at the Land Registry. Apparently I was the second person to request details on Cedars recently."

"Okay, it doesn't matter. As long as you're registered as the joint owner of the property nothing can change that. Right, so we need to crack on with the bogus builders and also the suspect valuation. Did you hear anything further from the estate agent?"

"No… they're maintaining they have no record of Cedar Avenue which is ridiculous because I know for sure Carl put it on with them briefly. He wanted to test the market after all the work was completed. Like I said, they sent people to view and everything – I remember showing them around."

"Are you sure it was with them?"

"Yes, absolutely. Carl went with them because they sold it to us in the first place. Anyway, I think I might have found a way round it. I remember them running a double page advert in The Observer showcasing some of the upmarket properties for sale in the area at the time and ours was one of them. I phoned The Observer offices and they said I could come in and look through their back issues, so I should be able to find it."

"Excellent! So that will give us a true valuation of what it was worth back then."

"Yes, and if anything, it's gone up, not down. Also, I remember there were loads of photos. The new extensions, the bar, the games room, the pool, the sauna – everything that Carl is saying he mortgaged the property to finance… this could prove it was already completed in 1983."

"That's great Olivia. Anything on the illusive builders?"

"I checked the electoral roll and there's never been a 'J.R.White' at that address. I am going to pop round there later to see if I can speak to the present occupants. Maybe they can shed some light on it."

"Good. We need to prove that the bills he's provided are phony. The more holes we can blow in his case the better. Right, must go—"

"Hang on Simon, there's something else. I nearly forgot... umm... Carl's in a psychiatric hospital. He attacked me and—"

"What??"

"He's in a psych—"

"Olivia! You must tell me these things! I have to know... it's like the gun! I only heard about that way after the event. When did this happen? Are you alright? Why didn't you let me know straight away?"

"I am! It only happened on Saturday!"

"Yes but you let me rattle on and 'nearly forgot' to mention the fact that Carl attacked you and is now in a mental institution!"

"Sorry Simon – it's not like I wasn't going to tell you, we just got a bit sidetracked that's all. And I explained about the gun. I'd used it as a threat to make Carl leave, so when he agreed to go, I had to keep my end of the bargain."

"Yes well... whilst I applaud your desire to do the right thing, just bear in mind, the other side would never have afforded you the same courtesy. Sometimes you have to fight like with like Olivia – even if it means getting your hands dirty once in a while."

"Okay, point taken… I'm sor—"

"Are you okay? Did he hurt you?"

"I'm fine honestly."

"Alright well look, I really have to go – you can tell me all about it next week."

Olivia had become Simon's unofficial personal assistant over the past few months and they had developed an excellent working relationship. She had first consulted him back in 1984 but the case had been shelved as there had been an attempt at reconciliation. He had come to spot a failed marriage when he saw one and although he appreciated Olivia's decision to try again for the sake of her children, he was not at all surprised to see her back in his office some nine months later. She seemed totally committed this time round however, and he felt sure she would see it through.

He had never had a client so hands on but it made perfect sense for Olivia to do as much of the leg work as possible; after all, she had a vested interest in helping him build the case and nobody could have had more drive. She was legally aided, but as he made clear from the start, the fees would have to be re-paid at some point, so why add the cost of a clerk when she was willing and able to do the job herself. She was an excellent assistant and he told her quite genuinely, he would have no hesitation in employing her should an opening in the firm arise. They had shared many highs and lows during the time they'd worked together and certain events along the way had led them to form a strong bond; facing mutual peril had a way of doing that! The news that Carl was in a psychiatric hospital was of no great surprise. The first letter had triggered an immediate response and Simon had been extremely impressed! *'Ooops!'* he'd thought, *'We've got a live one here!'* Things often got messy, but not straight after the first letter! There had been a frisson of professional excitement when he received notification that Carl had appointed the infamous law firm, Frobisher, Fellows and Brown; their reputation was legendary. Funnily enough it had been Olivia who had first noticed their DX address.

"*What's this Simon?*" she'd asked after spotting '*Shaft'em&Co*' on their headed paper. He couldn't quite believe their arrogance. Neither could Olivia when he explained the Document Exchange system used by the legal profession and the necessary DX code.

"*What's yours?*"

"*SinclairDoddsAssoc.*"

"*So they chose it themselves! Shaft'em & Co? That's worse than Stitchem & Leggit!*"

He was playing with the big boys now, that was for sure, but he liked the way the case was shaping up and relished the thought. Someone would be shitting affidavits by the time this was over… but it wouldn't be him!

One Flew Over The Cuckoo's Nest

The first week flew by for Olivia. She had been mightily relieved to see that the signature was indeed a forgery and as Simon had pointed out, an incredibly poor one at that. Handwriting experts from both sides would be called in but as Simon explained, this was just a formality; they had this one in the bag. This was excellent news; especially coming on the back of Olivia's crushing disappointment down at the newspaper offices. She had located the edition that carried the advert on their microfiche system, but the corresponding newspaper wasn't there. The prints taken from the microfilm were of such poor quality she feared that the whole exercise had been a complete waste of time. She'd had better luck with the builders however; the electoral register and present occupants of over thirty years confirmed there had never been any connection between 'J R White Builders Ltd' and the address shown on their invoices. There was no record of them at Companies House or with HM Revenues & Customs and Simon was confident he could prove the invoices Carl had produced were fake.

Her visits to the hospital had been going quite well. Initially Carl had been so spaced out he'd hardly known she was there, but by the second week he seemed pleased to see her and she'd been encouraged to see a steady improvement in his appearance as the week progressed. He didn't speak much about the treatment he was receiving and thankfully, apart from the initial interview with Cavanah, she hadn't seen hide nor hair of him since. Basking in the false sense of security she'd been lulled into, she waved a cheery hello to the nurses as she passed their station and made her way down the maze of corridors that led to Carl's room. She found him sat on his bed, tucking into a bucket of Kentucky Fried Chicken.

"Oh! Have you had visitors?"

"No – nobody knows I'm here do they? You haven't told anyone have you?"

"No of course not… well only your father."

"Yeah, thanks for that! He won't be back – I've told him there's no visiting. Sounds like they nearly kept him in after the hoo-hah he caused on Sunday."

"So who got you the Kentucky?"

"I did! Cavanah said I could go into town today for a wander, so I borrowed a tenner from one of the nurses and treated myself! Do you want some?"

"Err… no…" she mumbled, trying to take in this latest piece of information, "So Cavanah said it was okay for you to go into town?"

"Yep!" said Carl, brandishing a drumstick in the

general direction of the town centre. "I was going to drop in and surprise you at work, but I couldn't remember where it was. I thought about going to see the lads in the office but I didn't know what story you'd given them so I gave it a miss. I'll probably go down tomorrow. What have you told everyone by the way?" Olivia was literally speechless. "Olivia? What have you said?" The thought of Carl roaming free made the hairs on the back of her neck stand on end.

"Just that you'd been overdoing it at work and were having a well deserved rest…" she managed.

"So they don't know I'm in here then."

"Well, yes they do, but I said it was for work related stress."

"Perfect. That's exactly why I'm here. Dr Cavanah said I'd had a breakdown due to stress."

"Yes, but not related to work…"

"He said it was a combination of things, but anyway, the thing is, the treatment's working and I'm doing really well, so Cavanah said I could come home for the weekend… just the weekend at first, I'll have to be back by Monday, you know, to carry on with—"

"Home!" said Olivia aghast. "What do you mean by home?"

"What do you think I mean? I mean home. Home home!"

"Cedars?"

"Of course!"

"But that's not 'home' for you now is it? You live in London."

"Yeah well Dr Cavanah said I need to spend some quality time with my wife and kids—"

"But Carl that's ridiculous! We're separated now – we're getting divorced."

"He said it was the next step in my treatment plan. I've done so well that the next step is to spend the weekend at home."

"Carl—"

"You can't block this Olivia. Cavanah wants to see us. Together, tomorrow… you've got to go along with it alright?"

"I'm not—"

"I've got to get out – seriously Liv, you've no idea. Fuck me… it's like One Flew Over a Cuckoo's Nest in here!" There was a knock on the door and a nurse came bustling in. "See what I mean?" hissed Carl, nodding his head in her direction and mouthing 'Nurse Ratched'. "Medication Time!" he sang in a muted falsetto as she checked the drug chart at the foot of his bed. She stood over him while he made a big show of swallowing his pills and putting the upturned pot on his head to prove it was empty. The minute she was out the door Carl spat the tablets into his hand. Olivia was horrified. "You can't do that!"

"Watch me!" said Carl as he flushed them down the toilet. "Fucking bastards – drugging everyone up all the time – have you seen 'em? Poor sods shuffling about like zombies—"

"But Carl—"

"That was me the first week! Chemical cosh apparently

– bloke in the room opposite warned me. They do it to keep us quiet. Well not me! No fucking way!"

"But you said... Cavanah said the treatment was working... you can't just stop the medication like that!"

"Stop? I never really started! I only take the sleepers, the rest go down the pan."

Olivia was having trouble breathing. She tried to open the window, but it would only open a crack. Depositing Carl's cigarettes, paper and grapes on the bed she looked up at the clock on the wall.

"Is that the time?" she asked, edging towards the door, "Work... I need to... I'd better get going."

"Hang on!" She stopped dead in her tracks, heart hammering.

"What's up?"

"Two o'clock tomorrow – you, me and Cavanah. Right?"

"Oh yes, right... okay... I'll be there."

"Make sure you are – and don't be late!"

Her first thought was to phone Simon. She couldn't possibly keep her appointment with him in the morning, not with the knowledge that Carl could be anywhere at any time. It was too risky. All further thoughts centred on the need to prepare herself for the interview with the dreaded Cavanah. Her instincts had been correct; he shouldn't have included her in the treatment plan. He had done nothing to help Carl come to terms with the fact their marriage was over and she seriously doubted his competence. She would speak to Bill. If they could locate Ian's doctor, maybe Carl could be transferred. Meanwhile the Freudian fuckwit would have to be told; change the plan because this one isn't working.

Messages had been left with Mr Schroder's private secretary but by the time Olivia left for her meeting with Carl and Cavanah the next day, no contact had been made. At precisely two o'clock they were shown into Mr Cavanah's office.

"So Mrs Vogel, good news!" he announced with a tight smile. "We are extremely pleased with Carl's progress… and I believe he has explained to you that the next step is for him to come home for the weekend."

Olivia took a deep breath and steadied herself before locking horns with her odious foe.

"Yes he has – but you have to understand – Carl can't come home for the weekend – he doesn't live there. We're separated Mr Cavanah, I've filed for divorce – you know that!" Cavanah raised his hand to silence her but she ploughed on. "You were supposed to be helping him come to terms with that! The marriage is—"

"Mrs Vogel!" harrumphed Cavanah, "As Carl's doctor, my concerns are for his mental health, not the state of his marriage."

"BUT IT'S THE STATE OF THE MARRIAGE THAT'S BROUGHT HIM HERE YOU STUPID MAN!" shouted Olivia through tears of frustration. Carl was crying too, pleading with her to take him home. With all three parties trying to outshout each other, the meeting descended into chaos. Cavanah became increasingly agitated and began thumping his desk yelling "ORDER! ORDER!!" and then unbelievably, after making a big show of checking his watch, he pressed a buzzer on his desk and told them they'd have to leave. His next appointment was waiting apparently; their time was up!

A male nurse appeared and taking in their emotional state he ushered them into a nearby conference room and stayed with them trying to calm things down. It was getting very heated and mindful of their close proximity to the big chief's office, the nurse persuaded them to move to the privacy of Carl's room which was located at the end of a long corridor, probably the farthest point from the nurses' station and hub of the hospital. Halfway down the corridor, the nurse's emergency bleeper went off. Apologising, he told them to carry on to Carl's room and indicated he would join them as soon as he could. Liv stood stock still. She suddenly realised she didn't fancy being in a room on her own with Carl, especially a room so remote. Carl must have sensed her thoughts because immediately, his hand was in the small of her back. She tried to dig her heels in but they bounced off the carpet as she was propelled stiff legged along the corridor at great speed. She put up a good fight but was bundled into the room and unceremoniously dumped onto the bed. She was utterly terrified. She hit the red call button by the side of the bed but Carl lunged forward and pressed it again, cancelling the call. She tried again but he knocked her hand aside. Remembering the red cord she'd seen hanging in the bathroom, she rolled off the bed and made a dash for it. She grabbed the cord and a red light started flashing. Carl was there immediately and yanked the chord from the ceiling. There was a big scramble as she tried to get to the door. Eventually, to her enormous relief their nurse returned; but before she could utter a word, Carl got in first.

"Quick! She's completely lost it! She needs restraining! Give her something to calm her down!"

With visions of being stuck with a syringe and waking up in a strait jacket, Liv started screaming at the nurse.

"IT'S NOT ME!! IT'S HIM!!! Please help me! I'm trying to get out!"

The nurse backed out of the room and Olivia tried to follow, but Carl grabbed his case and threw it at the door blocking her exit. He began hurling his clothes into it all the while shouting at Olivia that he was coming home and 'no fucker' was going to stop him. "You're driving me home right now do you hear?" Every time she made a bid for escape he yanked her back; pandemonium ensued and then, miracle of miracles, the door pushed open and Bill's head appeared. As he came into the room Olivia took her chance. Dodging Carl, she pushed past Bill and was out… tearing down the corridor like the devil himself was after her. She didn't stop running 'til she got to the car park, then fumbling frantically for her keys, she was in the car and wheel-spinning away.

She drove straight home and gabbled out the dramatic turn of events to Anna. It was agreed that neither of them could stay if Carl was indeed returning to Cedars. Charlie and Joe were playing in the garden and were blissfully unaware of the drama that was unfolding at a terrifying pace. Liv rang her parents and quickly explained she might need to come back to them for a while, and to check if Anna could stay until her agency were able to fix her up with another position. She rang Michael but it was picked up by his answer phone. She left a quick message telling him not to ring or come round because Carl might be returning home. As she hung up the phone, it rang immediately. It was Bill calling from Barrington House.

"Olivia, it's me Bill. Just thought I should give you a quick call – Carl seems intent on discharging himself—"

"Oh God! Can he do that?"

"Well yes, of course – he wasn't sectioned or committed or anything. He's just found out that as a voluntary patient, he's been free to leave at any time. He's pretty angry! Said he'd have walked long ago if he'd known."

"I didn't know either!"

"Well that's understandable. You weren't here when he was admitted so… anyway, the thing is, he wants me to bring him home… so I thought I should… oh hang on, he's coming." There was a pause and she heard Carl asking Bill who he was talking to.

"Tell her I'm out of here! Olivia?? Can you hear me? Just to let you know alright? I'm coming home. I've had enough of this bollocks—"

"Bill – tell him he can't! We're separated – getting divorced – he can't come back he—"

Bill made a valiant attempt to relay her words but the phone was wrenched from his hand.

"I'M COMING HOME DO YOU HEAR? – TO MY FUCKING HOME!"

"If you come back here, I'll have to leave."

"FUCKIN' LEAVE THEN – GO ON! FUCK OFF YOU HORRIBLE BITCH… TRICKING ME…"

"I didn't–"

"TRYING TO KEEP ME IN HERE… IT'S A LOONY-BIN OLIVIA… A FUCKIN' LOONEY-BIN!"

"Carl… I–"

"JUST GET OUT OF MY HOUSE – AND TAKE THE FRENCH WHORE AND THAT FUCKING DOG WITH YOU!"

"Anna's coming with me, but Carl, you know I can't take Elizabeth – he'd eat Mum's dogs alive!"

"I don't give a flying fuck! You've seen the way he looks at me – I'm warning you Olivia, if he's there when I get home… I'll have him put down!" The line went dead.

Olivia helped Anna pack her case and threw a few things into a bag for herself. She gathered up Elizabeth's paraphernalia and dumped everything in her car before going to speak to the boys. They both cheered when she informed them their father was coming home but having to tell them she was leaving again was the hardest thing she had ever done. The reproach in their eyes was unbearable. Her explanation that it wasn't possible for her to stay now that their dad was coming home didn't wash with Charlie and he left the room in disgust. Even Joe was having difficulty understanding why they couldn't have both their mum and dad there at the same time. She reminded him that it was better for them not to have them arguing all the time but he said he didn't care about the arguing, just so long as they were both there. Olivia sadly shook her head and tried to pull him in for a cuddle but following Charlie's lead, he pulled away and ran off to the sanctuary of his big brother's room. She and Anna waited until they saw Bill's car slowly making its way up the dusty unmade road before quietly leaving with Elizabeth. As Bill pulled into the driveway, Liv exited from the other side.

Put The Blame On Me

Dear Clare,

I'm hoping this letter will be waiting for you when you get back from Bermuda. It's hard to believe so much has happened in the three weeks you've been away but basically, everything has changed. I'm with Mum and Dad again... it's a long story and I'd prefer to tell you about it rather than trying to put it all down in a letter. I'll just tell you the important bits here and we'll talk when you're back. Call me at Mum's ASAP!

So... I changed the locks. All hell broke loose when Carl realised what I'd

318

done. He completely lost it and ended up in a mental hospital. When he first went in, I actually started to feel a bit optimistic because I thought he was going to get help, but it all went horribly wrong. His consultant was an arsehole of the first order and did nothing at all to help Carl come to terms with what was happening in his life, you know, the divorce and everything. After two weeks he suggested Carl should come home for the weekend' to spend some quality time with his wife and family.' How ridiculous can you get! There was a big scene and well basically, Carl discharged himself and moved back in to Cedars.

Obviously I had to leave. Anna had to come too because when Carl lost it, he kind of attacked me and Anna waded in to protect me, bless her. Like I said, it's a long story but Anna couldn't stay and he kicked Elizabeth out too. He hadn't actually done anything – just a bit of snarling, but Carl said he didn't like the way he looked at him. He threatened to put him down if I left him behind. I couldn't take him with me because of Mum's dogs so he's gone to the McGuires'… remember Alison and Jim?…

they've just moved to new premises out in Hertfordshire. It's massive, four times the size of the old place - really nice. They had room and took him straight away. Alison's been great. I had to tell her what was going on because I didn't have any money or anything and I couldn't say how long Elizabeth needed to stay - but she told me not to worry about it and said we could sort it all out at the end. She said I could bring the boys to visit him and take him out for walks so that will help soften the blow for all of us. Carl told them Elizabeth was in kennels because he was dangerous. He said he'd gone for him - but I'm pretty sure they know that's a lie. They are very upset about it. It's like losing Elizabeth is the last straw.

They're very angry, especially with me, and who can blame them. Looking at it through their eyes it's me who wants the divorce, not their dad, so therefore everything that's happening is down to me. I'm angry with myself too. None of this would have happened if I hadn't been so stupid. It was all ticking along okay. It really was! Carl and Joseph were a pain but I should have just got on with it – it wasn't going to be forever. But no – I had to get all carried away – all ' gung ho ' and ' I'll show 'em!' but look at the consequences. I've lost the boys... the boys have lost Anna... Anna's lost her job and poor old Elizabeth's in kennels. I've surpassed myself this time.

Sorry you're coming back to this tale of woe. It's like I'm the one emerging from the Bermuda Triangle not you! Anyway Briany, my long suffering chum, assuming you've returned from Bermuda unscathed (!) we'll have a proper chat soon.

All my love
Liv xxx

2 + 2 = 5

As Olivia trudged home from the bus stop, she failed to notice the black cab parked at the bottom of her parent's road. She was in a foul mood. Three buses had sailed past full to the gunnels, and she'd waited over half an hour for the fourth. Public transport really was the pits. Michael, who'd been parked up for ages looking out for her car, spotted her as she walked past. He jumped out of his cab and called after her.

"LIV!"

She spun around. "Michael! What are you doing here?" Before he could answer she noticed the taxi. "Wow! Look at you and your shiny black cab! You passed then?"

"I did!" said Michael, unable to hide his delight. She walked back and gave him a hug.

"Congratulations! Is this yours?"

"Yep! I picked it up today. It's an FX4S-Plus," he added proudly.

"Wooo! An FX... SF... 4 Plus 4?"

"Nearly!" laughed Michael.

"It's gorgeous."

"Well I don't know about gorgeous, but as far as cabs go, it's pretty good. Umm… Liv, do you want to jump in for a bit. We need to talk."

"Come in…" she gestured towards her parent's house, "you can meet Mum."

"Er no, it's umm… just hop in. I'll explain. It's a bit tricky."

"Oh, okay… why, what's up?" He opened the door for her and she slid across the back seat. He pulled down one of the tip-up seats and sat opposite her.

"So… I got your message."

"Oh right. I did wonder, you know, because you hadn't phoned or anything."

"You didn't leave a number!"

"Oh didn't I? What an idiot! Sorry, I was in a bit of a state."

"Yeah, you sounded it. Anyway the thing is, Hannah was there when you rang and basically… she put two and two together and came up with a big fat five."

"What?… Why?"

"Well think about it. You leave a furtive little message in a panicky voice saying '*don't ring or come round because Carl's home*' and she's jumped to the conclusion we're having an affair. She went nuts – she even threatened to go round and see him!"

"Carl? Jesus Christ! Did you put her straight? If she… oh God, it doesn't bear—"

"Yes of course I did. I told her about Carl being in a

nut-house because he attacked you. Once I had explained the background a bit, she changed her mind."

"So she isn't going to—"

"No."

"Thank God for that! Oh look… I'm so sorry Michael. I didn't think. I've caused problems for you and Hannah now too."

"Nah s'okay. Let's face it, me and Hannah… we were in a right mess anyway. This didn't help, that's all."

"So what's going to happen? Are you—"

"Don't ask! My main concern was to nip the affair thing in the bud."

"And you definitely did?"

"Yep… but obviously, best if you don't call—"

"Yeah… no… of course."

"Anyway, enough of all that – what the hell happened? He was sectioned wasn't he – how could he just discharge himself like that?"

"That's just it – he wasn't! He went in as a voluntary patient so he was free to walk at any time!"

"And he didn't know that?"

"No! No one did, apart from Bill."

"You're joking…" laughed Michael, "that's fuckin' hilarious! I wish I'd been there when he found out."

"Trust me, you don't. Bill rang from the hospital and I could hear him ranting and raving in the background!" Despite her best efforts, she found herself laughing too. "He said that I'd tricked him and he's yelling down the phone at me – *'IT'S A LOONEY-BIN OLIVIA! – A FUCKIN' LOONEY-BIN!!'* I know I'm laughing now but it wasn't funny. That whole day – talk about a nightmare. At one point I thought they were going to sedate me and I'd wake up in a padded cell!" Wiping the tears from her eyes, Olivia looked at her watch. "Michael, I'm going to have to go. Mum will be worried. I was already late… the buses—"

"Oh yeah, I was going to ask. Where's your car?"

"The tax had run out and it needed an MOT. I rang Carl and he said no problem, he'd get it sorted."

"Really?"

"Yeah, I should have known. The guy from the garage picked it up straight away but three days later I still hadn't got it back. Every time I rang there was a different story. I got the arse because I knew they were giving me the run-around. I rang Carl – we had a big row and I ended up slamming the phone down on him. He rang straight back and said the car wasn't mine anyway. He said it was a company car and I wasn't getting it back."

"Why would he do that?"

"He's just trying to make life difficult for me. He's hoping I'll give in and go back."

"How are you managing? What about seeing the kids?"

"Well, I get the bus to work and I can borrow Dad's car at weekends to see the boys, so I'll get by – but it's such a pain and I love my car. He knows that of course, so he's probably seen it as another opportunity to punish me."

"What happened about Anna – did she leave too?"

"She had to. She came here for a bit 'til the agency found her a new family. We all really miss her but at least she's okay. The same can't be said for Elizabeth though, poor thing. He's in kennels. The boys are so upset about it all. They might have got used to me and Carl coming and going but losing Anna and then Elizabeth… it's hit them hard."

"Oh mate…"

"And you want to know the worst of it…" she said bleakly, "all of this – the boys, Anna, Elizabeth – it's all my fault." What could he say? He didn't want to trot out empty platitudes any more than she would have wanted to hear them, so they sat quietly for a while. Olivia gave a big sigh and picked up her bag. "I'd better… my mum…" Michael nodded. She found a pen and a scrap of paper and scribbled down her parents' number. "Are you sure you don't want to come in for a cuppa?"

"No, I should get going too…" he said tapping the side of the cab, "she needs to start earning her keep." He took the piece of paper. "So it's okay to ring you here?"

"Yes of course. I'm usually home by six."

"Okay mate, I'll keep in touch."

Tigger

"Okay darling, never mind, thanks for letting me know. No that's alright, I understand. Really? Fire comes out of the exhaust pipes? Wow!! Well look, you have a lovely time. Big hugs… give Joe a kiss for me… bye… love you… bye!" Liv replaced the receiver with a heavy heart. She wouldn't be seeing the boys tomorrow. Carl was taking them to a British Rallycross Championship race at Brands Hatch. He'd obviously upped the ante; up until now, the pull of visiting Elizabeth at the kennels had been enough to ensure the boys were keen to see Olivia every Sunday but with promises of flame-spitting RS200s battling it out on the track, Carl had won the day.

She tossed and turned into the wee small hours as all her grievances came to the fore. She hated the fact that Carl still had the power to mess with her life. How absolutely typical of him not to have given her any notice; they could have rescheduled for today if she'd have known. And she was still fuming about the car. What a rotten thing to do;

he knew how much she loved it. Whenever he'd suggested getting her a later model she'd always refused saying she was happy with the one she had. It's not like he needed it to sell it or anything; it probably wasn't even worth that much now because it was getting on a bit, but it was her car for Christ's sake! When she thought of all the razzamatazz when he'd presented it to her on her 30th birthday it made her blood boil.

Carl had driven her to the garage and tied a blindfold over her eyes before leading her through to the showroom. To a rousing rendition of "Happy Birthday!" from Carl and the boys, the blindfold was removed and there it stood, festooned with ribbons and bows, her beautiful BMW proudly bearing the plate LIV 1. How could he say it wasn't hers? She remembered Joe toddling up to give her the keys and Charlie presenting her with the envelope containing her card and the… *Oh My God!!! The Log Book!…* Olivia sat bolt upright in bed. The registration document was in her name! She had her proof! All she had to do was get her hands on it, give it to Simon and he would… well she didn't really know what he'd do, but she felt confident that at the very least, she'd get her car back!

She knew exactly where the log book was kept. There was a file in the top drawer of the filing cabinet in Carl's study that contained all the vehicle documentation; she just had to get into the house when Carl wasn't there. A smile broke out over her face as it suddenly dawned on her; he wouldn't be there tomorrow. She drifted off to sleep and the smile was still there when she awoke bright and early the next morning. She rang the Brands

Hatch Circuit to find out the schedule for the day's events and decided that the coast would definitely be clear between the hours of 11am and 2pm. She was too wound up to eat breakfast and kept checking her watch, itching to get going. She cleaned her dad's car to burn off some of her nervous energy and noticed the aerial had been broken. She hated having no music in the car and checked through the cassette tapes stored in the glove compartment. Realising she couldn't cope with Bing Crosby or Val Doonigan, she went in search of something more suitable. Her mum's Beatles collection wasn't quite what she had in mind either but the box of cassettes she found in Daniel's old room looked more promising. There was loads of stuff from his teenage angst years that weren't really her thing but then she came across his Pink Floyd and Wishbone Ash collections and recognised quite a few she liked. By the time she had made her selections it was almost ten thirty… time to leave!

Humming along to Pink Floyd's '*Wish You Were Here*' she was in great spirits; her bunch of keys was on the passenger seat beside her and included her car keys. She had decided that if her car was there, providing she located the log book, she was going to drive it home. She would then pick her dad up and go back for his car. She pulled into the road and drove up to the house. There were a few cars parked outside but none on the driveway and no sign of her BMW. This was a huge disappointment, but at least her mission was clear to go, and there was a fair chance the BM could be inside the garage. Not wishing to block the garage doors she parked out on the road a few houses up.

She marched boldly up to the front door and rang the bell. She knew from the boys that the new housekeeper always had Sundays off so she was confident the house would be empty. She put her key in the lock and... it didn't work! She laughed at the irony – he'd changed the locks. She walked right round the house checking all the windows and doors but everything was closed and locked apart from the fanlight window in her bedroom. *Bollocks!* There was nothing she could do. She stood there for a moment, deep in thought. She decided that if her car *was* in the garage, she was going to take it anyway. She'd heard that possession was nine tenths of the law or something, and although she hadn't managed to get the log book, she felt sure Simon could sort it all out after the deed was done.

The garage door was locked too but she knew the knack of getting past that and with a kick and a shove she started to pull it up; but before she could get to the up and over part, she was greeted by a set of snarling fangs. She slammed it shut. *Caesar!! What the fuck was he doing there!* Caesar was the enormous Alsatian guard dog from Carl's yard and although she had met him on many occasions, she wasn't at all confident as to how he would react in this situation. He was obviously in full guarding mode and there was a good chance he could view her as an intruder... or lunch! *Hmmmm... lunch!*

She drove down to the local corner shop and bought some sandwiches and sticks of Peperami. There wasn't a dog alive that could resist Peperami! Back at the house she pulled the garage door up a fraction and sat down on the ground calling out to Caesar in soothing tones. "Hello Caesar... hello big fella... there's a good boy. What's Mummy got for you then? What's this?" She stuck one of the Peperami sticks through the crack and it disappeared in an instant. Three more followed plus two of the sandwiches. With only one stick and one sandwich left, she decided to go for it and slowly pulled up the garage door. He shot out and nearly knocked her over but his tail was wagging and she was obviously his new best friend. She sat with him for a while to make sure she'd won him over before venturing inside. Disaster! The car wasn't there. Her heart sank and tears pricked her eyes. It looked like she'd be returning home without the log book or the car. She sank down onto the garage floor with Caesar enthusiastically licking away her tears. His great big paws pushed her backwards into a set of aluminium ladders that were stored in the garage. A crazy idea flickered briefly but her fear of heights soon extinguished any thought of climbing through the fanlight window.

Accepting defeat, she stood up and made ready to leave. Saying goodbye to Caesar she noticed he had knocked his water bowl over. She refilled it from the outside tap and as she set it down close to the wall, she came face to face with her personalised number plates. He had obviously put the original plates back on her BMW to back up his claim that the car didn't belong to her. She felt it unlikely Simon would be able to prove anything with just the plates, but she took them anyway. She tried to cheer herself up with the thought that at least she wasn't going home empty handed, but it was cold comfort indeed.

Pink Floyd's '*Comfortably Numb*' was making her even more depressed on the drive home, so she pressed the eject button and tried some Wishbone Ash instead. The chorus of '*Warrior*' suddenly filled the car and Liv found herself joining in with great gusto. Her fighting spirit rose like a phoenix from the ashes. She slammed on the brakes. *"FUCK IT!"* She wasn't going to give up that easily! She executed a u-turn, stuck her foot down and drove hell for leather back to the house. She parked up in the same place and without giving herself time to think, yanked the garage door open, returned Caesar's ecstatic welcome and dragged the ladders out onto the drive.

She planted the feet of the ladder into the flower bed in front of the house and then gradually extended it up towards her bedroom window. It was a triple extension ladder and she needed all three sections to reach her destination. With a mantra of '*don't look down*' she began her ascent, fixing her gaze straight ahead as she went up, rung by rung. She wobbled a bit when the bottom ladder joined the mid section and felt a wave of panic as she realised it was getting narrower. She glanced upwards towards the final section to see if that was narrower still… and then horrifyingly everything started to spin. *Sweet Baby Jesus!* She'd got her mantra all wrong; it should have been don't look up! She shut her eyes but that made matters even worse as she felt she was toppling backwards off the ladder. She clung there frozen to the spot; literally unable to move. She realised that unless she snapped herself out of it, she would still be hanging there when Carl and the boys got home; thankfully this thought spurred her on. For some reason continuing upwards seemed marginally less scary than trying to go back down, plus there was the added incentive of knowing that if she made it into the house she wouldn't need the ladder, she could exit through the front door, hopefully clutching the log book in her sweaty little paw.

One potato two potato three potato four – as she progressed upwards the wind started to pick up – *five potato six potato seven potato more* – and as she moved onto the final ladder the whole thing started bouncing in the most alarming way. As she boinged her way up, she found that counting potatoes gave way to her version of The Tigger Song! "*A wonderful thing is a tigger… a tigger's a wonderful thing…*" she intoned desperately through clenched teeth, "*his top is made out of rubber, his bottom is made out of spring.*" She was nearly there, just a few more rungs to go. "*He's bouncy, bouncy, bouncy, bouncy…*" The open window was beckoning. Could she get through it? It looked horribly small! Still holding on for grim death, she stuck her head into the net curtains and started inching her way through. One last superhuman effort, one last big push and… "I'M IN!" She crashed to the floor with an almighty great thud, leapt straight to her feet and tore around her bedroom waving her arms about and yelling "THANK YOU GOD!… THANK YOU… THANK YOU… THANK YOU!!!"

Sneak Thief

Her relief at not executing a back dive into the flower bed below caused a momentary blip as to why she was there. Gathering herself, she glanced around her bedroom. It suddenly occurred to her that this was a good opportunity to collect some of her clothes, particularly her working wardrobe. She had been recycling the same few outfits for weeks now and it was getting embarrassing. She opened the door to her dressing room and was confronted by row upon row of empty hangers. The shelves were empty too; in fact the whole room was empty save for half a dozen or so black bin liners in the corner. She took a quick look inside to confirm their content. '*Oh well*', she thought, '*saves me packing!*' and brushing off the ignominy of having all her worldly goods consigned to plastic bin bags, she headed downstairs to Carl's office.

Thankfully the filing cabinet was unlocked and to her great delight, the log book was there. Holding her breath she removed it from the file and just as she thought, the document was in her name. She sat back in Carl's swivel chair and gave herself a victory twirl. As she swung back round her eyes came to rest on a framed photograph of Charlie and Joe on Carl's desk. It was the one she had taken in for him when he was in Barrington House and was a particular favourite. Smiling at their images, she decided that now the roles were reversed, her need was greater and added it to her spoils. She went back to the filing cabinet as another thought crossed her mind. Carl had claimed she had run up some exorbitant household bills while she had been living there, particularly the telephone bill; a fact she hotly disputed. Now was her chance to obtain proof on that score as well. Flicking through the files she found the latest gas, water and electricity bills which were all perfectly reasonable, but the telephone bill was indeed through the roof; the reason soon became clear. It dated back to when Carl and Joseph were there and included a list of international calls that were clearly nothing to do with her. Feeling extremely pleased with herself, she pocketed the bills and was just replacing the file when an almighty commotion erupted outside. Car doors slamming, Caesar barking, raised voices… she ran to the front of the house and peered through the window… CARL!!!

She sprinted back to the study, grabbed the log book and photograph and headed for the back door – no key! She ran back upstairs with a view to shinnying down the ladder but arriving at her bedroom window she had to accept that even if she managed to get back out and onto the ladder, she would only get caught at the bottom.

It was a fair cop; there was nothing she could do. She grabbed a couple of the black bin bags and dragged them to the top of the stairs where she stood tall, ready to face the music.

Carl had Caesar on a lead and they were tearing around the house, going from room to room hunting down the 'intruder'. She could see Charlie and Joe peering round the front door utterly transfixed. They all seemed to spot her at exactly the same time because suddenly… everything stopped. All mouths dropped open, including the dog's, as they stared up at her in disbelief. "WHAT THE…" spluttered Carl, completely nonplussed. Charlie and Joe's eyes were like saucers. She saw them mouth the word 'MUM!!' and then Caesar, suddenly registering who she was, slipped his collar and headed for the stairs. Carl was yelling "CAESAR! CAESAR!" or was it "SEIZE HER! SEIZE HER!" Liv wasn't sure… neither was the dog, but ever hopeful of more Peperami he bounded up the stairs anyway and gave her a great big slobbery kiss.

"WHAT THE FUCK ARE YOU DOING HERE?" yelled Carl, literally frothing with rage.

"Hello Carl… hi boys!" she called out to Charlie and Joe who were now standing by their father's side. "I came to collect my things," she explained calmly, ruffling Caesar's shaggy coat, "but I couldn't get in so I—"

"YOU BROKE IN!!!"

"Well I wouldn't call it breaking in exact—"

"WELL I FUCKING WOULD!! YOU… YOU… SNEAK THIEF!!"

Liv snorted with suppressed laughter. She caught

Charlie's eye and could see that both he and Joe were trying not to laugh too.

"Sneak thief?"

"Yes!" hissed Carl, his eyes bulging dangerously. "A common sneak thief... breaking in to my home and—"

"And what? I haven't stolen anything, I just came to get my stuff. Oh, and I've taken this photograph if that's alright with you? Charlie, Joe... could you pop up and help me please?"

The boys scampered upstairs and followed Olivia to retrieve the rest of the stuff from her bedroom. They managed to drag all the bags down between them and loaded them into her dad's car. Carl followed and completely flipped when he spotted the number plates on the back seat.

"THEY'RE COMPANY PROPERTY!"

"No Carl, I think you'll find they're mine – they've literally got my name on them!" She locked the car and strode over to Bill's next door. Apologising profusely for dragging him into yet another domestic dispute, she asked him to verify the contents of the bin bags before she left. He confirmed they contained only her personal effects and agreed that the only other items she'd taken were the framed photograph and her set of personalised number plates. They were all gathered outside by the car when Olivia delivered her parting shot.

"Oh Carl... as I missed my time with the boys today I'd like to pick them up from school tomorrow if that's okay? I was thinking we could have a picnic at the kennels and take Elizabeth for a walk." Charlie and Joe looked at their father expectantly. He clearly didn't know what to say, especially with Bill standing there watching and waiting for his response.

"It's up to you…" he said at last, "do you *want* to go with your mother tomorrow?"

"Yes!" they said simultaneously. Liv almost whooped for joy. She drove off with a huge grin on her face. The log book was stuffed down the back of her jeans and she was seeing the boys tomorrow. All in all, it had been a very good day!

Silver Lining

13th October, 1986

Dear Clare,

It was so great talking to you... apart from the flippin' time delay thing. Half the call's gone in either talking over each other or waiting for the other one to speak! I was so excited to get your letter and photo of your handsome American G. I. Joe... or should I say G. I. Virgil... Virgil?? Is that really his name? I'm cracking up here! The only Virgil I've ever heard of is the one in Thunderbirds. I always liked 'Thunderbird 2' best because of Virgil's southern accent! I must admit, there's definitely something about a man in a uniform - he looks absolutely gorgeous! Ahhhh! Love blossomed on Bermuda - how romantic!!

I passed Virgil's message on to Michael by the way, and he said to tell you that he thinks you meant 'Jarhead', not 'Jawhead' (must be the southern drawl) and that marines are known as 'Bootnecks' over here anyway 'Bootnecks... Jarheads... they do love a nickname don't they? He has a message for Virgil too. He said he has two lasting memories from going on exercise with the US military. One was their ration packs, which compared to their UK counterparts, were like hampers from Fortnum and Mason... and the other was their camouflage kits. The Brits just slapped on some axle grease apparently, whereas the Yanks had a full blown make-up box complete with mirror, containing every shade of green, grey, black and brown imaginable! He reckons it took them about an hour to get it all on!

So how's that going to work then... with you in Boston and him in North Carolina? My geographical knowledge of

America is sadly lacking but somehow they don't sound that close to me? Actually, hang on a sec while I find an atlas... Ah right!... That makes sense. You are both roughly the same distance from Bermuda and a similar distance from each other - in fact looking at this you've got your own little triangle going on! Ah well, you know what they say - true love will find a way! Maybe you could conduct your courtship in Bermuda!

So... on to my news. Let's get the bad stuff out of the way first. I swear to God, the minute I start feeling pleased with myself, it all turns to shit! I have to confess though, looking back, I wasn't just pleased - I was positively thrilled with myself! I had been brave beyond measure - I had adapted and overcome - I'd faced down a wild beast, braved the elements and scaled the dizzy heights! Basically Briany, I broke into Cedars using a triple extension ladder and dived though an upstairs fanlight window! ME!!!! Unbelievable I know, but I was on a mission. I needed to get the log book for my BM because I thought it would prove it was mine.

I went to the house when everyone was out... but I couldn't get in 'cos he'd changed the locks! You've got to laugh. Anyway, after getting past Carl's guard dog from his yard, I managed to get in through my bedroom window... the little one at the top. I found the log book (in my name) but because of all the problems I'd had getting in and because I'd forgotten Carl's annoying habit of leaving way before the end of any event 'to miss the traffic'... there was a terrible miscalculation of time. I was caught bang to rights! You should have seen his face! It was like The Night of the Blue Dressing Gown X 10! But I didn't care... my mission had been accomplished! I had the log book... I was going to get my car back! Yay! Well done me! But... did I get my car back?... NO! Do you know why?... Because a log book is not proof of ownership! Arghhhhh!

But as they say, every cloud and all that... well, my silver lining came the next day. A job offer! I picked the boys up from school and took them to the kennels for a picnic and Jim and Alison offered me a job plus accommodation at the kennels... well, not in the actual kennels obviously, but with them in the new house. It's massive so we shouldn't get under each other's feet... the boys can come and visit as much as they like and I would have the use of a car. I am seriously considering it. Mum and Dad have been wonderful bless them, but I feel like I'm putting on them too much and should be moving on. It is weird living back with your parents isn't it? I feel about twelve years old half the time! I remember you saying the same when you had to move back home for a while.

It's come at a good time work wise because there's been a bit of a hiccup at the recruitment agency. You know I went there originally as a temp and then they offered me the permanent position... well I was really pleased at first, but I've just found out that if I accept, I will have to go through the profiling process myself! They said I had 'slipped in through the back door' and that every single member of staff had to be profiled... and the thing is... I don't want to do it! All of a sudden it feels like a massive invasion of my privacy which puts me in a bit of a predicament. I don't think I can carry on doing my job, because there's something a bit dishonest about persuading people to go through a process I don't want to go through myself.

This sounds more like my cup of tea anyway and as Jim pointed out, it's mutually advantageous. Alison told me they had overstretched themselves buying the new place and were badly understaffed. She said it would really help them out if I came on board so to speak. We haven't talked about money yet but they said I would have 'full board and lodging' plus a small wage. The thing is I don't need much, just enough to keep my head above water until the settlement. I would be mainly running the office, taking the bookings, seeing to the clients but where necessary I could help out with the dog walking and a bit of baby-sitting too. Their little girl has just started school and I would be involved in ferrying her about, hence the use of a car.

The other good thing is Elizabeth! They said we could try to socialise him with

their dog, an enormous St Bernard called
Nosebag. If they get on, Elizabeth can at
least be allowed out when the kennels
are closed. He wouldn't be allowed in
the house and would still sleep in his
kennel at night (Nosebag has an outside
kennel too) but at least he wouldn't
be locked up for most of the day like
he is now. And last but not least, the
boys would love it there. It's like a
farm, well more like a little menagerie
really with loads of animals for them
to play with. Horses, Shetland ponies,
a donkey, parrots, load of dogs, a crazy
emu called Rodney (I kid you not!) and
of course Elizabeth!!

As always, I shall keep you posted.

All my love
Brian
xxx

15th July

As was often the case, writing to Clare cleared Olivia's mind and by the time the letter was finished her decision had been made. She talked it over with her parents and although her mum was a bit upset at the prospect of her leaving, everyone agreed it was for the best. As she was still employed on a temporary basis by the recruitment agency, she was only obliged to give one week's notice, which meant her move to Hertfordshire was able to take place almost immediately. Michael had offered to help with her move and by the following weekend she and her belongings, most of which were still in the black bin bags collected from Cedar Avenue, were winging their way to Deputy Dog's Boarding Kennels out in the Hertfordshire countryside. Her parents' reaction to meeting Michael for the first time had been fairly predictable. Her mum had been warm and welcoming, her dad less so. He'd kept his distance and was clearly viewing Michael with more than a little suspicion. He had reassumed the role of protective father and Olivia could tell he was one step away from taking Michael aside to ask if his intentions towards his daughter were honourable. It was a similar story when Olivia introduced him to the McGuires; Alison took to him straight away, whereas Jim simply nodded as he shook Michael's extended hand, before retreating to his office in a cloud of disapproval. It seemed the men folk had difficulty with the notion that Michael was simply a friend.

She had been welcomed into the McGuire household and settled in quite easily. This felt like a good move and she was confident time would fly as she crossed off the days to the court hearing. It had been agreed she would probably be with them for the best part of a year to allow for the hearing to take place and then another six months or so for her to find a place of her own. This timeframe suited the McGuires perfectly as Jim's business forecast predicted that within a year, they would be in a position to afford the wages of a full-time office manager. Both parties felt the natural progression would be for Olivia to move into her own home, but continue to work for them at the kennels.

Elizabeth had been thrilled to be allowed out and had behaved impeccably when introduced to Nosebag. That first weekend, Olivia picked Charlie and Joe up on the Sunday and together with Lois, the McGuire's four year old daughter, they enjoyed a wonderful day picnicking in the grounds while Nosebag and Elizabeth played tag in the autumn sunshine. The boys were reluctant to leave, they'd had such a good time, so with the McGuire's blessing, Liv suggested they asked their dad if they could stay the following weekend. Her heart was singing at the thought of spending more time with them but she should have known better; figuring that Elizabeth was a major factor in the boys' desire to see Olivia, Carl decided to redress the situation. He turned up unannounced first thing Monday morning and sat in his car sounding his horn until Jim stormed down to open the gates. He informed them he'd decided to give Elizabeth another chance and had come to collect him. Olivia grilled him as to who would be taking care of him; who would walk, feed and water him? Carl brushed off her concerns and insisted he and the boys were more than capable of looking after him and that he would be happier in his own home. Her heart sank as she handed over the lead but there was nothing she could do. Even if she could fight for custody of Elizabeth, Charlie and Joe would never forgive her if she tried to block his move back home.

Disappointment at losing Elizabeth apart, she was quite happy there. Although the weekend visits hadn't yet materialised, the boys enjoyed their Sundays with Olivia and as a temporary measure, Deputy Dog's was working out fine. The job itself was a doddle and, as she'd said to Clare, was more her cup of tea. It was very much about mucking in together and apart from her actual job in the office, she found herself engaged in everything from whitewashing the latest block of kennels to mowing the lawns, walking the dogs and was very much involved in the care of little Lois. She was enjoying the novelty of spending time with a little girl and reading bedtime stories about princesses and enchanted castles instead of Roald

Dahl and the 'boys own' adventure stories favoured by the boys.

If things had run to plan, the arrangement would probably have worked out perfectly for all concerned; however the courts and Carl's lawyers had other ideas. The original date for the three day court hearing had been set for the beginning of March. Olivia had bought a 1987 calendar and circled the date, only to see that date moved time and time again. The first couple of postponements had been made by the court with no explanation given and had left Olivia bemused and bitterly disappointed. Simon explained it could have been due to the allocated judge becoming unavailable or because cases had overrun causing rescheduling along the line. Olivia put a brave face on it, tippexed out the old dates and ringed the new… only to hear that Carl's lawyers had requested a postponement of the revised date on the grounds that Carl would be out of the country at the time of the hearing. They were now scheduled for the 15th July, a depressing nine months away.

Deputy Dog's Boarding Kennels
Warrengate Hill, Barnet, Herts, EN5 3PT
01 442 4304

21st November, 1986

Dearest Brian,

Thanks for your letter – I finally got round to picking it up from Mum and Dad's yesterday! Great to hear it's going so well with your ' Airborne G.I. Joe'. That's hilarious by the way! I'm imagining a G.I. in a jet pack, hovering over the battlefield and taking pot-shots at the enemy, but I am reliably informed by Michael that an' Airborne G.I.` is in fact ' a paratrooper` and that ours are better. You can pass that on!

Well as you can see by the letterhead,
I'm here at Deputy Dog's! I moved
in about a month ago and it's just
been non-stop. It's all going well
though and I think it's going to be
okay. Alison is a sweetheart - as laid
back as ever, but Jim's a bit... ummm...
Scottish! I think the word I'm
looking for is 'dour' - DOUR: (adj) -
unsmiling, unfriendly, frowning, poker-
faced, severe, forbidding, morose, sour,
gruff, surly, uncommunicative, grim,
gloomy, dismal, sullen, sombre, grave,
sober, serious, solemn, austere, stony,
unsympathetic, disapproving. Ha ha ha!
Yes well maybe 'dour' is a bit harsh!
He's a nice enough bloke and everything,
but just a bit, you know, serious!

My court date changing hasn't helped
his 'joie de vivre'. It's been moved three
times already which is frustrating
to say the least. Jim used to be a
time and motion expert and he likes
everything to run like clockwork. He
had calculated that with a court date
of the 3rd March I would be out of
here by next October, but obviously,
these changes have put a bit of a
spanner in the works.

Simon reckons our case is more or less complete. I will meet my barrister closer to the hearing but other than that, we are all set. As you know, the case hinges on the fact that Carl is claiming he has no money to make a settlement because of a huge second mortgage he took out to fund all the work carried out at Cedar Avenue. We have the forged signature, the dodgy builder's bills and our pièce de résistance - The Midsummer Madness Party. Remember the fancy dress party we had in 1984? We have sworn affidavits from five witnesses (Daniel, Richard, Dom, Ant and Little Pete) stating they attended that party and can confirm all the building works, including extensions, swimming pool, games/party room and bar, had been completed by June '84 - long before the dodgy second mortgage had been arranged. Simon said we should have taken photos of the witnesses dressed up in their costumes and attached them to their statements! Can you imagine?

" I do solemnly declare that the attached photograph is a true likeness of me taken at a party held at 17 Cedar Avenue on Saturday 23rd June 1984. I am the bumblebee situated between ' Dennis the Menace' and ' Popeye'."

I asked if we could still do it, but unfortunately he was only joking!

Charlie and Joe love coming here even though Elizabeth is back home with them now. Carl picked him up more or less as soon as I moved here! He'd obviously concluded that Elizabeth was the reason they were keen to see me, but thankfully they still enjoy coming and haven't missed a Sunday yet. Both Alison and Jim seem quite happy for them to come, which is a relief. They are really sweet with Lois (their four year old) and she adores them, so all in all it's working out quite well.

I have to say, I really like it out here in Hertfordshire. At first, I thought I was moving out to the sticks, but in reality it's only about twenty minutes from Cedars! It's less than half an hour from central London and because it's so close to the new M25, it's ideally situated to get to almost anywhere from here – which is exactly why Jim chose it! I might decide to move out this way when my settlement comes through. It's a damn sight cheaper so I'd get a lot more for my money.

Have you thought about Christmas yet? I know we're still in October and you've got Halloween and Thanksgiving to consider first, but back home we haven't really bought into the Trick or Treat malarkey as yet, so Christmas is looming large! It's going to be a weird one for me. The boys told me on Sunday that Carl is taking them to Austria for Christmas and New Year and I have to admit I'm dreading it. I just can't imagine Christmas without them – but I suppose the one saving grace is that because they're driving there, Carl has agreed to smuggle their Christmas stockings out – so at least I can still enjoy choosing their presents and wrapping them up ready for them to open Christmas morning. I'm not sure how I'll be paying for them! Carl didn't mention anything about money, so I guess it will be added to the growing I.O.U. I have with Mum and Dad. Ah well, nearly there! The new court date is the 15th July– so it's not beyond the realms of possibility that by next

Christmas, I could have a place of my own. Theoretically at least, the boys could be spending next Christmas with me!

I'm still in touch with Michael, although it's difficult here. They don't like me taking personal calls on the kennel's line, which is fair enough, and their private line isn't in yet. He does pop in for a cuppa sometimes but Jim's not overly friendly so it's always a bit awkward. I'm not sure what's happening on the Hannah front - it's all gone a bit quiet. Last time we spoke about it he said it was 'all over bar the shouting' but I'm not so sure.

Okay, time to go - it's busy down here on Jollity Farm! I've got forms to type, calls to make, dogs to walk and an emu to feed!

Love Brian

xxx

Interest Rate

Olivia was just finishing off for the day when the phone rang; it was Michael. They had settled into a routine whereby he rang her about this time every day for a quick catch up, quick being the operative word as Liv was worried about annoying Jim.

"Hi – how's it going?"

"Not too bad thanks. Almost finished… which is just as well 'cos I'm literally starving!"

"No lunch break again?"

"Too busy."

"I'd have thought November would be quiet."

"It is… we haven't got many dogs in but the phone's been ringing non-stop with Christmas bookings, plus we've had loads of viewings."

"Makes the day go quicker though eh? When's the hearing?"

"The 15th of July."

"Not too bad then."

"Are you kidding?"

"Liv, it will fly by…"

"Hmmm… I'm not so sure. Jim's getting on my nerves already. He's so…"

"Anal?"

"What?"

"Anal."

"Why would you say that?"

"Anally retentive!" laughed Michael.

"I have no idea what you're talking about!"

"Don't worry," said Michael, still laughing, "go on… you were saying… he's so…"

"Grim."

"Grim Jim?"

"The very chap!" laughed Liv. "He's always in a bad mood lately. I think it's the court dates changing. It's messed up his long term plan."

"I don't think it's—"

"… and he's so mean! He told me off this morning for wasting teabags. We have to get three cups out of one teabag now!"

"Money's probably tight."

"Not as tight as him! He goes through the bills with a fine tooth comb and then we get dragged into his office to explain or justify them."

"Liv, the economy—"

"Oh God, don't you start! That's all we hear – the economy, the recession, interest rates… it's doing my head in!"

"Yeah well, since the recession everyone's a bit jittery.

The interest rate jumped a full percent last month and there's talk it might go up again. It's been on the news."

"I don't watch the news. Too depressing."

"It's in all the papers."

"I can't do the papers either… knowing about it isn't going to change anything and just makes me even more depressed."

"Yeah but you need to have an understanding of what's going in the world."

"No I don't! It's bad enough dealing with what's going on in *my* world. Anyway, it's not just his moods and meanness that's getting me down, he's really controlling too."

"In what way?"

"Well, for instance, every evening when we sit down for dinner he conducts a kind of debrief where we all explain what we've done that day. It's like a 'who worked the hardest competition' and then there's a finger pointing exercise at the end for anything we did wrong!"

"Sounds like fun."

"It's like he has this major plan and he has to keep checking everyone's on track all the time. He said the other day he was going to get me organised while I was here."

"Yeah well, I wish him luck with that!" laughed Michael. "He obviously doesn't realise what he's taking on. What's he like with the boys?"

"Nice so far – they've been on their best behaviour up to now but I'm always on tenterhooks in case they let themselves down."

"Yeah, I know what you mean, I have to admit, I

always feel uncomfortable when he's around. He doesn't like me much, that's for sure!"

"Oh don't take it personally – he's like that with everyone. Daniel popped round the other day and got the same treatment. It just makes it so awkward if I want to see anyone."

"What about the pub down in the village. You could meet up there."

"Yeah, good idea. Fancy a drink?"

"Wish I could," chuckled Michael, "but I'm working this evening so I'll have to pass."

"How's it all going?"

"Work?"

"Work… the gym… Hannah?"

"Work is good, always plenty of fares. I'm earning enough to cover everything plus I've got a couple of new clients at the gym."

"Recommendations?"

"Yep, which is always nice."

"And Hannah?" There was a long sigh followed by an even longer silence. "Michael?"

"Yeah, sorry… I just don't know what to say really, other than I don't want to talk about it."

"Oh right… sorry… I…"

"No don't be. It's just… difficult. Hannah's a really nice person. She doesn't deserve all this."

"So what's…?"

"Well as far as I was concerned, I thought we were pretty much over. I hadn't seen her since that row we had about you."

"When she thought—"

"Yeah. We'd agreed to have a proper break – but then last week, she rang and said we needed to meet. She said she'd done a lot of thinking and started blaming herself for the break-up. Anyway she came over and… well basically, she said she knew what had gone wrong and just wanted the chance to put it right."

"What did you say?"

"Well I was pretty flummoxed to be honest. I had in my head what I was going to say, but after her heart rending little speech, I couldn't really, could I?"

"I don't know – depends what you were going to say."

"Well, stuff like… I thought we'd grown apart… we'd always care about each other obviously, but we weren't in love anymore… that kind of thing. I was even going to say that somewhere along the line we'd turned into a boring married couple before we'd even got married."

"Jesus! That would have been hard to hear."

"Exactly!"

"So how did you leave it?"

"I started to say I didn't think it would work but she pleaded with me to at least give it a try."

"Hmmm…"

"What hmmm?"

"I think you should."

"That's your professional opinion is it?"

"It is actually!"

"Go on then counsellor."

"You need to know you gave it your best shot – otherwise you'll always wonder."

"Yeah... that's pretty much what I've been thinking. Unless we try, we'll never know."

"I reckon. Anyway... I'd better get off this line."

"Okay, but look, where Jim is... I know he's... well, he's a bit of a knob sometimes, but he's a decent bloke really."

"I suppose."

"Honestly mate, you should cut him some slack. You said they'd overstretched themselves to buy the place didn't you?"

"Yeah..." agreed Liv.

"Well there you go. They must have a hefty old mortgage on that place – if the interest rate does keep rising they could be in all sorts of trouble."

"Mmmmm..."

"Just saying... you shouldn't take it personally with Jim either. He's likely got bigger stuff going on."

"Yeah... okay."

"Alright then, take care. I'll call you tomorrow."

"Thanks Michael... bye."

Situations Vacant

Christmas came and went and was more difficult than Olivia could have imagined. The run up had been fine; she'd joined the throngs of Christmas shoppers and thrown herself into the pleasurable task of finding quirky little gifts for the boys' stockings. At thirteen, Charlie was far too old to believe in Father Christmas, but Olivia and her siblings had received Christmas stockings until they left home, so naturally, she was more than happy to do the same. They had said their goodbyes on the Sunday before their departure to Austria the following weekend. They would be spending Christmas apart for the first time and it was beginning to sink in how much she was going to miss them.

Accepting Alison's invitation to accompany her to little Lois's nativity play had been a huge mistake. As the children trooped out and assembled on the stage, memories of the boys' early nativities came flooding back and she found herself in tears. She remembered how

Charlie would anxiously scan the audience, his worried little face lighting up when he spotted her; and how Joe would march out with a cheeky grin and a big 'thumbs up' to the audience as a whole. Luckily many of the mums were teary eyed so Olivia's distress went unnoticed as she sat huddled in her chair, sadness settling around her like a heavy cloak. She got through most of the performance but the little ones singing Christmas carols at the finale proved too much and she had to leave. Many a shopping trolley had been abandoned during those final weeks before Christmas, as she succumbed to the endless loop of piped Christmas cheer in every store.

Michael's suggestion of meeting up with her friends in the village pub had proved to be a lifeline for Olivia. They would congregate there most Friday evenings and Michael would join them when his shifts allowed. He had taken the decision to try again with Hannah, but had stopped short of asking her to move back in. They would be spending Christmas and New Year together but Michael was able to join Liv and her friends at the pub's Christmas party the night before Christmas Eve. The unstinting support of her family and friends helped keep her spirits up and she saw the New Year in with optimism. She was in the home straight now and confident that 1987 would see her new life begin. Eventually Carl would accept the situation and realise that for the sake of the children they had to remain amicable. Sharing custody would be fine initially, but surely over time, even Carl would come to accept that the boys should be with their mother and would grant her residential custody. She had heard recently that one in three marriages ended in divorce. It was a shocking statistic, but it helped Olivia realise that what they were going through was not unusual and allowed her to believe that ultimately, a better future would be achieved.

She began ticking off the days on her new calendar. She had hoped to take the boys to Wales for Easter, but was soon made aware that working at the kennels meant she couldn't take time off during the school holidays. Easter was one of their busiest times; however Jim did agree to her taking a week in the less busy Whitsun break. Their trip to Wales went ahead in the beginning of June, and with no car of her own, they enjoyed the added bonus of travelling by train. As always, they had a wonderful time and she returned home in good spirits, only to see them squashed by the news of yet another postponement. Carl's lawyers had made the request on the grounds they needed more time. It was a huge blow and had a destabilising effect on life at the kennels; the atmosphere was becoming increasingly tense and her financial situation was dire.

Simon had advised her many times that Carl should be paying her spousal maintenance, but she had always rejected the idea insisting she didn't want or need his support. This latest postponement was a setback too far and when Simon suggested that forcing Carl to support her financially could discourage further delaying tactics, she reluctantly agreed. The claim was rejected immediately. The other side insisted she was capable of getting a job and therefore did not need financial support from their client, who was already under increased financial strain through needing to hire a full-time housekeeper to help care for the boys. Simon's instructions were concise. She was to apply in writing for as many jobs as possible in such a way that would ensure she received an equal amount of rejections. It took a while for the penny to drop as he refused to elucidate further. She repeated the instructions to Alison who agreed she had been told to go out there and try *not* to get as many jobs as she could, and to keep evidence of her lack of success. That night they scoured the situations vacant pages of the local newspaper and spent an enjoyable evening writing to various companies offering her services. A slew of badly handwritten letters were stacked up ready for posting the next day.

Dear Sir

I am inquireing about the job in the paper for a rec/tel/typ because I can do that job and I need the money. I no it said to ring but Im shy and not to good on the phone so I am writeing insted. I hope you dont mind.

Yours sincereley,
O. Vogel

DO NOT OPEN THIS
ENVELOPE UNTIL YOU
HAVE READ THE LETTER
AND SWEAR UPON PAIN
OF DEATH, YOU WILL NOT
SHOW THE ENCLOSED TO
ANYONE... EVER!

Gissa Job

28th June 1987

Dear Brian,

Please follow the instructions on the
enclosed envelope and do not open until
I say. I promise it will be worth it.

So I arrived back from a lovely week
with the boys at my sister's to find
that Carl had moved the court date
AGAIN!!! Honestly Clare, I am so
fed up! Things are getting increasingly
difficult here and I am sick of being
skint, so when Simon suggested
yet again that I should apply for
maintenance from Carl, I thought ' Sod
it, why not.' As it stands, Carl is in

367

no hurry to settle. Why would he? He has it all – the boys, the house, everything! It would seriously piss him off to have to support me and as Simon pointed out, could put an end to these frikkin' postponements.

Needless to say, they rejected my claim and said I was more than capable of getting a job and supporting myself. This is, of course, perfectly true but the problem is, although I could get another job that would pay more, Jim won't allow me to live here and work elsewhere. I couldn't earn enough to rent anywhere decent, plus if I left, I would lose the use of a car. Anyway, good old Simon came up with the solution. I had to prove I was unemployable by applying for (but not getting) as many jobs as possible! Me and Alison got straight on it and with the aid of a bottle of wine, spent the whole evening writing off for jobs advertised in the local paper. It was hilarious! They were full of spelling mistakes and bad grammar and said things like my reason for applying was " I need the money!"

Obviously, I didn't get many replies! We had been hoping for the usual generic response along the lines of... 'thank you for your application... blah blah... you have been unsuccessful at this time'... but unfortunately most of them made mention of the fact I'd applied for the post of receptionist/telephonist when by my own admission, 'I was shy and no good on the phone'. But then, horror of horrors, one of them invited me in for an interview! I couldn't believe it! Simon said that as we only had two letters confirming my attempts to find employment, I had to attend and fail the interview.

Cue frantic ransacking of local Oxfam shops to secure my interview apparel. My chosen ensemble included a full skirt, sporting a delightful print of Grecian figures in lilac and white on a black background, which finished just above the knee. This was teamed with a frilly blouse buttoned to the neck, a maroon cardigan and 60 denier American Tan tights. Even Jim got involved and donated a pair of horn rimmed specs that used to belong to his mother! Unfortunately, the enclosed photo cuts off my feet and doesn't show the oversized black lace-up shoes that look like their previous owner was Mr Plod! Alison had great fun frizzing out my hair with her crimping tongs. My new 'Wild Woman of Borneo' hair do was arranged in a centre parting and with my face completely devoid of make-up apart from a hint of mascara on my upper lip - I think you will agree, I really look the part!

You may open the envelope now!

You may burn the photograph now!!

But Brian! Funniest of all - they offered me the job!!!

The trouble was, once I stopped laughing, I was overcome with guilt about the whole thing. Out of the kindness of their hearts, these lovely people had decided to give her (me!) a chance and I felt really horrible about tricking them. Mind you, Jim is convinced they'd rumbled me from the start and were seeing how far I'd go with it! I prefer my version of things - but either way, it had to stop.

Word in the village has it that a boarding cattery has opened nearby and they're looking for an evening driver. Not sure what it's all about yet but rest assured - I shall be giving it a go! The new court date is the 23rd September. I just need to survive until then.

Loads of love as always,
Your industrious chum,
Olivia
Xxxx

I'm Going Slightly Mad

Landing the job as Mrs Slocombe's new collection and delivery driver had given her a boost and she'd had great fun tootling around London under the expert tutelage of George, their erstwhile driver extraordinaire. The additional money had eased her financial situation but she had wildly underestimated the demands this extra job would bring. Her working day began at 7am with some brisk dog walking over the fields and didn't end until she parked up the cattery van at around 10pm most nights.

With the court hearing fast approaching her nerves were building and she was finding it increasingly difficult to sleep. Carl had contested the divorce from day one, refusing to accept the grounds of his unreasonable behaviour; however, the revelation of the two-way mirror had gone badly for him in court and he had no choice but to give in. There was a moment of triumph when the decree nisi was granted on the 8th July but sadly, the inevitable backlash had a disastrous effect on her relationship with the boys.

The first sign that something was wrong was when she found them waiting outside for her when she went to pick them up; then came excuses as to why they couldn't visit and when they did come there was an uneasiness about them that Olivia didn't know how to handle. She eventually broached the subject with Charlie and asked if Carl was making it difficult for them to see her. He was quite upset and defensive at first and insisted their dad always said it was up to them, but then later he admitted his dad looked hurt and disappointed if they said they wanted to come. This brief insight into their weekly dilemma of choosing whether to disappoint their mum or upset their dad made her desperately sad. She knew from her own childhood experience, the gut churning misery of divided loyalties and did her best to reassure them that loving both your mum and your dad was allowed; it was how it was supposed to be. Sadly it didn't help and as the court date got closer, the situation deteriorated to such a point she had only seen them twice in the past six weeks.

Fretting about the boys, working long hours followed by sleepless nights had taken its toll. She was carted off to the doctors following a phantom stroke and Valium was prescribed to help calm her troubled mind. Her concentration was shot and she was walking through life in a daze. Silly mistakes at work resulted in constant reprimands from Jim and 'The Beelzebub Debacle', a cockup of enormous magnitude that almost got her fired from the cattery and caused George to resign, meant she was now covering central London and south of the river too. With Michael planning her routes, she had just about

373

managed to keep it all going, but she was perilously close to the edge. Cue phone call from Simon to tip her clean over.

"They've asked for a stay of execution. They're not ready."

"What? What do you mean 'they're not ready'?"

"That's the reason for their request."

"But surely they can't just say 'Oops sorry m'lud – we're not quite ready!'

"Well they can… but clearly, this is blatant. I've objected of course. Don't worry, I'm sure it will go ahead, but obviously, I had to let you know."

Mrs Slocombe's Pussies Hotel

20th August 1987

Dear Brian,

Sasha and Maurice forgave me for the cock up with their friend Alistair's cats and he's not suing me either so all is well. Mind you, after seeing their idea for new uniforms, all I can say is... George got out in the nick of time!

Silver baseball caps with embroidered "Mrs Slocombe's" emblem in pink.

Pink t-shirts with slogans printed in silver.

WE'LL TAKE CARE OF YOUR PUSSY	*YOUR PUSSY'S SAFE WITH US*
(front)	*(back)*

My days are numbered!

Sash + Mo are out celebrating their anniversary tonight so I'm here minding the shop. It's all quiet so I thought I'd make the most of it and drop you a line. Your last letter worried me a bit to be honest. I'm glad things are going well for you and Virgil and I'm really happy for you, but honestly Clare, I think you should hold your horses. You say it's been over a year but it hasn't really has it? You might have met a year ago but apart from a couple of flying visits, you've hardly seen him since! I know you've had wonderful letters and romantic phone calls that 'make you go weak at the knees' but Briany – distant memories of sun, sea, pink sand and sex isn't enough!

I can appreciate it's hard keeping the relationship going with such a distance between you, but you can't seriously be considering a move to North Carolina! Swapping the sophistication of Boston for Fayetteville? Sounds like something out of 'Gone with the Wind'! Land Sakes Miss Clara I do declare! Yo head must be full of cotton candy to come

up with such a notion! You're with a
great family there in Boston, you live in
a beautiful house, have loads of friends
in the neighbourhood and enjoy a great
lifestyle... don't chuck it all away on a
whim. Speaking as a casualty of whim,
all I'm saying is... look before you leap!
Here endeth the lesson - although I
don't know why I bother - you never
listen!

Love Brian
xxx

PS. My decree absolute has come
through - I am officially divorced!
So strange, I didn't even have to go to
court - it just happened automatically!

PPS. Carl's lawyers are trying to
postpone it again! Simon is confident it
will go ahead. I wish I was! I don't
think I can take much more of this.

The Yorkies

It was almost five; another half hour and she'd be finished. The summer season was over and both the kennels and cattery were quiet. For the first time in ages, Liv was looking forward to a couple of days off. She was just finishing the last of the booking forms when Sally, the girl from 'Dirty Dogs', the grooming parlour attached to the kennels, came rushing through to reception.

"Do us a favour Liv, keep an eye on George and Mildred. Carol's gone home and I'm desperate for a wee!" Liv went through to the salon and made friends with the two Yorkshire Terriers waiting there. Sally had finished one, freshly coiffed and loosely tied to the leg of the bench, the other was a work in progress, firmly secured by a choke chain attached to the wall. Liv was making soothing noises to the one on the bench who was getting a bit agitated with its situation. She checked the name tag. "Come on now Mildred, what's all this fuss eh? Look at George, doesn't he look—" She was interrupted by the phone ringing in reception. She waited and was pleased to hear it picked up by someone in the house. A moment later, Alison was calling out for her to take the call. It was Simon. *At last!* She had been waiting for this phone call all week; she'd all but given up hope of hearing anything by the weekend but now finally, the call had come. She picked up in reception.

"Hi Simon – thanks for getting back to me."

"Eventually," he said ruefully. "I'm really sorry Olivia, I've been in court all week and… well, you've heard it all before. Anyway, I'm pleased to confirm that the hearing is definitely going ahead. Their request for another postponement has been denied."

"Oh Halleluiah! I thought it would never happen."

"Yes it has dragged on rather hasn't it – but never mind, it's going ahead now so we need to be ready."

"Ready? I'm ready already!"

Simon chuckled but reminded her she needed to have her meeting with counsel before the hearing. She was in the diary for the following Friday; they were just awaiting confirmation of the time. She was about to go over to tell Alison the good news but stopped short when she saw her chatting to Sally outside.

"SHIT!! – THE YORKIES!"

She ran down the corridor, almost skidded past the parlour door and burst in to find Mildred hanging by her neck in her final death throes; her back legs giving their last little kicks.

"Oh Jesus, oh no!" She scooped up her lifeless form and gently shook her, praying for some sign of life. "Come on baby, come on." Mildred lay limp in her hands. Liv stood frozen for precious seconds unable to think then suddenly... a brainwave! She lay the unfortunate pooch face down on the bench, head to one side with her legs splayed and began pressing down on her back and raising her legs, lifting her tiny shoulder blades. First Aid was one of the few badges she'd earned during her brief spell in the Girl Guides; however, due to the fact that Mildred wasn't drowning, this had no effect whatsoever. Liv stared down at Mildred's little body, beseeching her to breathe. *Breathe!... Of course!* She rolled her onto her back, opened her mouth, pinched her tiny nostrils and blew. To her utter astonishment, Mildred's chest rose as her lungs inflated. "It's working!"

"What's working?" asked Sally as she came through the door. She stood rooted to the spot, momentarily struck dumb as she took in the scene. "What the f...?" Liv was too busy blowing air into a dead dog to explain. *Breathe in... and out, in... and out, in...* then suddenly, the miracle happened. With a cough, a splutter and a surprised little yelp, the Yorkie sprang back to life. Liv was all but hysterical, completely overcome by Mildred's Lazarus moment.

"SHE'S ALIVE!" she yelled triumphantly as she hoisted the unfortunate Mildred aloft. She heard manic laughter, not realising it came from her. Sally may have been young but she knew a nutter when she saw one; she leapt into action and wrestled the dog from Liv's grasp.

"WHAT THE HELL'S GOING ON HERE?" Liv spun round to see Jim standing in the doorway, his face like thunder. Sally's teenage defence mechanism kicked in. She hid Mildred behind her back and gave the stock answer of "nuffin!" Of course it all came out and Liv received the mother of all bollockings. Her ears were ringing as she ran for the house and the sanctuary of her room. Her chest was heaving. She was bursting with indignation. *He's had enough of me? Yeah well, I've had a bellyful of him!* she fumed as she paced up and down. There was a knock at her door. It was Alison.

"Liv? You okay?"

"No!"

The door handle dipped. "Can I come in?"

"No!" she said again. "Look... I'm sorry for what happened but I don't want to talk about it, okay? Please Al, just leave me alone." Liv heard her friend go back downstairs. She continued pacing, waiting for her anger to abate but she was just getting madder by the minute. The frustration of living under someone else's roof, tip-toeing around, trying not to get in the way, trying to be invisible most of the time had finally got to her. She wanted out so badly; she wanted to walk straight out that door and never come back. But where would she go? There was another knock at her door. Alison again but this time she had the phone with her; it was Michael. Liv squeezed Alison's hand as she took the phone and retreated back into her room.

"Liv?" The sound of his voice extinguished her anger and a surge of emotion engulfed her. She tried to speak but nothing came out; her throat was constricted. It felt like she'd swallowed a hairball; probably from the hairshirt she was wearing.

"You okay mate?"

Liv managed a strangled "Nope..." in reply.

"You want to tell me what's happened?"

Another "Nope" followed by the sound of her breathing heavily as she struggled to maintain the floodgates.

"Can you talk?"

She couldn't.

"Shall I come over?"

She was losing it.

"I've got to get out of here. I can't stay..."

"Pack a bag – I'll be there in fifteen minutes." He arrived in ten. She climbed in and slumped into the back seat completely exhausted.

"Am I taking you to your mum's?" He swivelled round and slid the glass screen back. "Liv?" She looked up. "Do you want to go to your parents'?"

"No... I don't know... I just need to get away for a bit and think."

"Okay. Do you want me to just drive for a while?"

"Please... that would be great. Thanks Michael, I really... you know..."

Michael kept an eye on her in his rear view mirror but left her in peace. Half an hour or so later he put U2's 'Joshua Tree' on low. He knew she liked it and hoped it might lift her spirits. Eventually there was movement in the back. Her eyes caught his in the mirror; she looked terrible. He opened the glass screen again.

"Where to M'Lady?" She shrugged her shoulders and attempted a smile. "Do you want to start heading back?" Her smile slipped and she gave a barely perceptible shake of her head. "Okay well look… it's getting on for seven. There're no services on this motorway yet so if you're hungry or anything, we'll have to come off." There was no response. "Are you hungry?" She shook her head again. "Tea, coffee?" More shaking of the head. "A drink?" She nodded. "Pub?" Vigorous shaking of the head. Liv's head movements were their only means of communication. She had her hand over her eyes, massaging her temple. "Headache?" Another nod. "Okay so… what about a hotel or something? We could check in, get a drink and hopefully something for your head. How's that sound? Maybe have a shower, a bit of kip and then decide what you want to do." She gave him a weary thumbs up, closed her eyes and rested back in her seat.

He'd been driving along the M25 for ages and hadn't a clue where they were. Somewhere in Surrey but that was about it; he was way out of his territory. A signpost was looming… he scanned the board… Redhill kind of a rang a bell but he couldn't think why. He began indicating left and as he pulled off the motorway he realised U2 were singing about the lights going down on Red Hill Town. "Liv…" he called, turning up the volume and nodding to the stereo, "… we're going to Redhill."

The Fancy A Shag Hotel

He pulled into the car park of the first hotel he found on the road to Redhill. The Wounded Stag looked like it had been a decent hotel in its time, but the attached modern buildings showed him it had gone the motel route instead. It looked okay so after parking up, Michael told Liv to hold tight while he went to check in. All the chalet rooms were taken so he took a room in the main hotel. He went back to fetch Olivia and their 'luggage'. She had a carrier bag; he had nothing. He went to his boot and dug out his old training bag. He tipped out the contents and took Liv straight up to their room.

"No mini bar by the look of it. I'll nip down and get some drinks shall I… or d'you want to come to the bar?"

"God no! Up here please – vodka and tonic and the headache tablets if you can swing it. Michael… is this putting you in a position being here?"

"No, it's fine. I was going to work tonight but I can cancel it. I could do with a night off anyway."

"Really?"

"Of course! It's up to me – don't worry about it."

"Okay thanks, I really appreciate it. I'll grab a shower now if that's okay?"

"Yeah you crack on. Ice and lemon?"

"Huh?"

"In your drink – ice and lemon?"

"Oh, probably – yes please."

"I'll get a couple, save going back down… and look what I found!" said Michael holding up a little bag of weed. "I forgot I had it! I caught a whiff when I emptied my training bag – I thought it was my kit!"

"Great," said Liv with a weary smile.

As soon as he left she kicked off her trainers, undid her jeans, unfastened her bra and flopped backwards onto the bed. She stretched out, took a deep breath and… *God, what's that awful smell?* She checked herself over and soon located the source; her kennels sweatshirt. *Poor Mildred! She must have had a Luca Brasi moment during her ordeal.* She pulled it up over her head but she'd forgotten to undo the buttons of the polo shirt underneath and everything got stuck halfway. She stood up and tried to wriggle out of it but somehow her bra straps got entangled and the whole thing ended up like a strait jacket, but with the arms wrapped up around her head. At that moment Michael came back for his cab keys. He had to radio in to let them know he'd be off call. He stood stock still, totally shocked at the sight of Liv, naked from the waist up, thrashing around like a headless chicken. She was obviously completely unaware of his presence and his immediate reaction was to tip toe back out of the room and pretend he hadn't seen her. Trouble was, her situation looked pretty desperate and his natural response was to go to her aid. He made his decision and caught hold of her by her shoulders from behind, as she cannoned about the room.

"Whoa! It's okay Liv – it's me, keep still." She went rigid in his grasp and gave a muffled scream before kicking out at him. She connected with his shin forgetting she was barefoot and yelped in pain. "Liv stop! It's me, it's Michael!" She screamed even louder. She'd clearly lost the plot. Michael frogmarched her over to the bed, shoved her face down to stifle her screams and held her there 'til she was quiet. He spoke directly into the red hot ear that was visible above the tangle of clothing, "I'm trying to help! You want me to help don't you?" She nodded, grunting an affirmative. He started to roll her over but she went ballistic again. "For Christ's sake Liv! What's wrong with you?" She was mumbling something urgently into the bed so he risked allowing her to lift her head.

"DON'T LOOK AT ME!" she shrieked before her head was pushed back down.

"I'm not you idiot! I'm just trying to sort it out!" He tried again to roll her onto her side but she fiercely resisted and jammed herself into the bed. "Okay okay, I'll try and do it from the back but I don't think I can. Your hair's all caught up in the buttons of your t-shirt." He painstakingly untangled everything and eventually she was free. Leaving the jumble of clothing beside her, he walked back over and stood by the door. Still face down and with her back to him, she slid all the way down and knelt at the foot of the bed; then without a word, she burrowed under the duvet and tunnelled her way back up to the top. Michael stared at the wriggling mound in disbelief. Eventually she emerged red faced. When she saw him standing there she nearly dived straight back under the covers. She couldn't look him in the eye.

"You okay?"

"I'm really sorry."

"You did realise it was me didn't you?"

She nodded. "I'm sor—"

"Yeah I know, you keep saying, but why would you get in such a state?"

"Because I was… because I thought you—"

"What kind of an arsehole do you take me for? I was just—"

"I know… I'm sorry Michael. I don't know what to say…"

She looked so embarrassed he had to let it go. "Alright well look, why don't we just start again. I'm getting the drinks, you're having a shower and when I get back I'm going to roll us a puff, okay?"

"Okay!" laughed Liv in relief.

Half an hour later she emerged from the bathroom wearing one of the oversized bathrobes supplied by the hotel. All she'd brought with her was a change of underwear and her toothbrush. Her clothes, the offending areas washed in the hotel's shower gel, were drying on the heated towel rack. Michael was sat at the desk engrossed in the serious business of rolling a joint. There was a tray of drinks and a couple of paracetamol on the table; she knocked the tablets back with one of the drinks, picked up another and went over to join him. She watched in amused fascination as he made a complete hash of it. "You don't know how to roll one do you?" she laughed.

"Well, I sort of know in theory, but these papers are a bit knackered..." his voice petered out as he came to the crucial bit where he had to actually roll the thing into shape. "Hold it, nearly got it – oh bollocks!" he swore as everything spilt onto the table again. "There you go then smart arse, you have a go!" he said, sliding the whole caboodle over to her.

"I can't do it either!" she laughed. "Anyway, I've got to ring Alison. I need to let her know I'm okay and to find out about Mildred."

"Who's Mildred?"

"She's a little dog that died – I resuscitated her! Don't worry, I'll tell you later."

"Resuscitated?"

"Yeah, you know," she pinched her nose and blew.

"Mouth to mouth?" She nodded. "A DOG!!"

"Shhhhhhh!" Liv made the call and it was good news.

"All fine!" she informed Michael. "Sally finished drying her off, popped a bow into her top knot and she was good as new, well almost, a bit la-la but the owners collected them and didn't notice a thing. It's been a few hours now so I think we've got away with it."

Michael had no idea what she was talking about but deciding he didn't need to know the finer details of Mildred's resuscitation, he roped her into the spliff-building mission he'd begun earlier. They sat at the desk and spent an enjoyable interlude laughing at how inept they were and then attempted to smoke some of their hilariously misshapen efforts. Pretty soon they were rolling about, roaring with laughter; misshapen they may have been, but impotent, most definitely not. Michael was doubled up, laughing and pointing to the stub held in her lips.

"S'like an exploding cigar!" he croaked. She guffawed with bits of paper and tobacco flying out of her mouth.

"Sawn-off shotgun!" she pointed back, laughing as she staggered off into the bathroom, her bladder sending out emergency signals to her fuddled brain. "We're smoking compost heaps!"

"Compost Corner!" he called as she disappeared from view. "Wha's up Liv – wha'ya doin'?"

"I'm bustin'!" she called from behind the bathroom door. She reached the loo and was about to go but was worried about making a noise; so with her knickers round her ankles, she hobbled back to the door, flicked on the main light, which fired up the extractor fan, and then turned the hotel hairdryer on full. Thrilled with the level of noise, she shuffled back to the loo and with glorious abandon, let her inhibitions flow.

"Jesus, wha's goin' on in there?" shouted Michael who could hear what sounded like Concord taking off from behind the door. She shouted something in reply which was completely lost in the roar of super-sonic engines. "WHAT?" He yelled.

"PARDON?"

"PARDON?"

"WHAT?" She started laughing.

Crawling towards the bathroom on all fours, Michael was cracking up too. For some reason they found that laughing in separate rooms, hearing but not seeing each other, was the funniest thing in the world. They had no idea what they were laughing about, let alone why! It seemed to go on for hours; all sense of time, quite literally, had gone to pot. Again and again it seemed like their mirth was abating, only to explode once more as they got to the AHHH!... NO MORE!... PLEASE STOP! state of affairs. They were almost at the point of throwing up when Liv managed to unlock the bathroom door and fell into the room. They lay on the floor in a heap, chests heaving, and their faces crimson and tear stained. When Michael saw the state of Liv he nearly started laughing again but thankfully, he was all laughed out. They made it to the bed and passed into a state of virtual unconsciousness.

Michael drifted back first. He took his bearings, still pleasantly off the head but thankfully, back in control. His ribs ached and his cheeks felt like he'd just blown up a load of balloons. Liv was out for the count, genuinely asleep, not just lying there pretending. It irritated him when girls did that. You could always tell; they arranged themselves to look as cute and appealing as possible, whereas in reality; he rolled onto his side, lifted up on one elbow and looked down. Her chin had sagged, her mouth was open and she was snoring gently. There was a little rivulet of drool running from the corner of her mouth and for some inexplicable reason, he found the whole thing, especially the dribble, really endearing. He smiled at the noises she was making as she started to stir, and to save any embarrassment, he rolled back over and waited for her to come round. They grinned at each other acknowledging the bizarre situation they'd found themselves in. Liv was aware of her aching ribs and couldn't believe how much better she felt. Laughter truly was the best medicine. They basked in the sunshine of bonhomie and had no thoughts of leaving anytime soon.

"Cuppa?"

"Love one," said Michael stretching out comfortably on the bed. Liv went over to the tea tray and flicked the kettle on. She sank into a chair and watched Michael plump up the pillows on what, she suddenly realised, was the biggest bed she'd ever seen.

"Jeez! Look at the size of the bed. It's enormous!" Michael looked from side to side.

"Yeah – it's a queen."

"Never – it's bigger than a king!"

"Queens are bigger."

"Course they're not! It goes single, double, queen, king."

"No, it's single, double, king, queen. I know 'cos I just bought a new bed!"

"Really? What size?"

"Queen!" laughed Michael.

"You lucky bastard!… you lucky, lucky bastard!" This set them off again but they managed to dampen it down; they daren't risk it getting out of hand again, their ribs couldn't take it.

"I'm bloody starving!"

"Famished!" agreed Liv. Michael rang room service while she carefully poured the tea. Her vision was far from back to normal, not quite at the 'stick your finger in the cup and pour' ploy that you see in blind films, but pretty near. *I can't understand why actors agree to play the part of a blind person*, she thought as she stirred the steaming tea. *I mean they all do the same thing – stare out into the middle distance, just off to the left or right of whoever they're talking to – so unconvincing!* In her opinion, the only actor who had successfully carried it off was Gene Hackman in 'Young Frankenstein'. She started to laugh as she remembered the clip where 'blind priest' Gene poured boiling hot soup into the Monster's lap, stuffed a cigar into his mouth and carefully set fire to his thumb.

Michael's voice broke into her rambling thoughts.

"… Yes well like I said, I'm sorry about that… yep, no problem mate. We'll keep it down." She looked over at him enquiringly. "… So if you could… yep, anything… just lots of it… and some cake."

"What's up?"

"Oh nothing, just a few complaints about the noise."

Unfortunately, although their bout of hilarity had only lasted about fifteen minutes, it had ruined the moment for the many romantic and dangerous liaisons taking place around them. Unbeknownst to Liv and Michael, The Wounded Stag was the type of establishment with an empty dining room and an extremely busy room service. It looked innocent enough but had a reputation far and wide and was known affectionately as 'The Fancy a Shag'. The switchboard had been busy with complaints about the goings on in room 137; Michael's call saved the Head Porter a trip.

Michael slapped his hand to his forehead. "Shit, I forgot!" He grabbed the phone. "Yes, me again... forgot to mention earlier... I'll make it worth your while if you could get hold of some Rizlas – or failing that a pipe." They burst out laughing and drank their tea, happily conjuring up mouth-watering images of the feast soon to be served.

Never one to miss an opportunity, the Head Porter ambled off to the kitchen with a smile. He knew exactly where to find just what they were looking for; he had confiscated it from one of the junior porters and felt sure it would fit the bill admirably. Once he had secured the said object, he set about preparing their order. No need to disturb the kitchen staff; he could manage this one himself.

Seedie Jeevsie

Fifteen minutes later, there was a loud rap on the door. They looked at each other in delight. The Head Porter had arrived bearing a tray laden with domed silver platters. It all looked very promising; no Rizlas but on the side of the tray was a large silver bullet.

"Okay cheers mate, just put it there. What's this?" said Michael holding up the silver artefact. "Full moon tonight, is it?" A blank look and sigh from the long-suffering porter. "You know – werewolves?" continued Michael, striking up a suitably scary and hairy wolverine pose. Liv turned away so that Michael couldn't catch her eye.

"It's a bong sir, an Agent Blue to be precise, which I trust you will find satisfactory. That's twenty, plus the food, and my twenty. Sixty pounds please, I thank you." He was an interesting chap in that although he looked seedy and decidedly shabby, he spoke like a pucker butler, a veritable Jeeves. Acknowledging the standard of service, Michael accepted the rip off, counted out his money, and ushered Seedy Jeevsie from the room. They rushed to the tray and whipped off the silver cloches to reveal... a huge pile of doorstep sandwiches: cheese and pickle, ham and mustard, a jar of pickled onions and a box of Lyons Lemon Curd Tarts!

"Wonderful!" said Liv with a face full of cheese and pickle.

"Ummmm," agreed Michael cramming in the ham and mustard and adding pickled onions at great speed. It didn't take long; they even ate the lemon curd tarts, although neither of them could quite believe it when they found the empty packet later. Washed down with plenty of tea made with UHT milk and sachets of saccharin, it was manna from heaven, they agreed happily. Michael was keen to try the bong but Liv felt sure she would very likely throw up if she smoked anything more than a cigarette. "Maybe you're right," said Michael. "Do you want one?" She did, so Michael lit two and flopped down beside her on the enormous bed, positioning the ashtray between them. They lay there totally content, puffing and chatting away companionably. Michael opened up a little about his relationship with Hannah. He confessed he'd never been faithful in his life and admitted he found the prospect of monogamy quite worrying.

"It'll be okay though," he said cheerfully. "It's probably like giving up drinking or smoking – when the time comes I'll just give it all up." Liv had her doubts, believing as she did that once you've cheated on someone, you've crossed that line and there's no going back; she didn't see how a wedding ring would make any difference. She found herself talking openly about her own life too and even confided in him about her brief affair with Terry. She described him as the only one brave enough to tell her the truth about Carl. Michael suspected the guy's motives but kept his thoughts to himself.

"So Liv…"

"Umm?" She was lighting a joint they'd missed in the ashtray.

"What was all that hoo-hah about earlier?"

"Oh I don't know… I'm just shy."

"Shy? That wasn't shy! You went fuckin' ape-shit!"

"I did, didn't I!" laughed Liv, "I'm really sorry. What more can I say?"

"I accidentally catch a glimpse of—" He was stopped by a pillow in his face. "Alright, only having a laugh!" protested Michael as she tried to shove him off the bed. "You don't come across as shy."

"Not that kind of shy, I'm usually alright with people. I'm just shy about my body that's all."

"Why? You're all right, I don't get it."

"Yeah well you've probably never had a hang up in your entire life."

"You reckon?" said Michael, taking the joint from her. "If you want to talk about hang ups, you should try growing up as a bloke. Jesus, you girls think you go through it, well let me tell you, so do we!"

"Nothing compared—"

"I'm telling you – adolescence for a boy is no joke. You wake up one day to find you've got spots, greasy hair and a voice that's clearly having a laugh with you. One minute you're Orson Wells and the next you're squeaking away like Pinky and Perky! You pretend you need to shave, but all you end up doing is shaving the heads off your new pimples and walking around with toilet paper stuck all over your face." He shook his head, "And then there's the constant worry about your dick. Is it normal – is it big enough – will it suddenly spring to life at the worst possible moment? You could be stuck on a bus, unable to get off because you've suddenly got a stiffy for no apparent reason! And then there was the biology lesson that haunted me for years. The teacher showed us a diagram of a fully erect penis and said that in order to produce babies, a man's penis had to become erect and stand straight up against his abdomen. Well, mine didn't, no matter what. I was convinced it was broken and that I'd never father a child!"

"Broken?" laughed Liv.

"Yeah… I honestly thought I'd broken it! Mum used to yell up the stairs, 'Stop playing those willy games, you'll break it!'"

"Is that what you called it?" laughed Liv. "Willy games!"

"Not me… my mum! I mean, I didn't know what I was doing or anything, but somehow, I'd discovered that if I kind of thrashed about from side to side like a lunatic, I'd eventually get this lovely feeling. I s'pose I was having mini orgasms, but I didn't know anything about orgasms then – all I knew was it felt nice, so I'd grab my pillows, one on either side, and off I'd go!"

"Face up or down?" laughed Liv, trying to picture his technique.

"Oh face down, of course – it was the missionary position for me!" She found his revelations incredibly liberating and found herself opening up in a way she never had before, sharing many previously untold confidences.

"Yeah," she nodded, retrieving the joint and puffing away cross legged in the middle of the bed. "It's not like you think... *right, I'm thirteen now, I'd better start masturbating!* It's more like you get to thirteen and realise that's what's been happening for the past I don't know how long!"

"So how old were you then?" he asked, "when you..."

"Well my earliest memory is... probably... when I was about... five."

"FIVE?" gasped Michael. "Jesus Christ Liv, that's worse than me! You can't have been!"

"No, I definitely was," she assured him. "I was in the infants... the nursery class I think because that's where we had the rocking horse. Don't look at me like that," she protested, "I didn't know what I was doing either!"

"That's hilarious!" laughed Michael. "So how old were you when you lost your virginity then?"

"Umm... I suppose I was about nineteen."

"Nineteen?"

"What's wrong with that?" asked Liv defensively, "How old were you then?"

"Fifteen."

"What? That's just a bit older than Charlie!"

"No, it's not, don't exaggerate. It's a huge step to fifteen when you're a boy. Trust me, I know these things."

"Yeah, well I'm sure you do but as far as girls are concerned, nineteen is perfectly acceptable. Anyway, thinking about it, I might even have been twenty. We didn't really manage it properly until after we were married." She laughed at the look of astonishment on Michael's face. "No, honestly, we had tried, quite a few times, but well... let's just say... it didn't work."

"Oh fantastic, don't tell me Carl couldn't get it up!"

"No – more like couldn't get it in!" They fell back in a heap, holding pillows over their faces to muffle their laughter. This was without doubt the funniest night of Liv's entire life. She couldn't believe the things they were saying, the secrets they were sharing; it was intoxicating. "Believe me, it wasn't funny at the time," she continued, wiping the tears from her face, "not funny at all. Carl was getting really annoyed and I was panicking. I'd heard that couples were supposed to sleep together before they got married to make sure they were compatible."

"I think you and Carl are probably the most incompatible couple I've ever met," said Michael, "and I'm not just talking genitalia here!"

"Yeah, I know... anyway, it was all pretty disastrous. I was so tense, bloody terrified actually, and him keep yelling at me to 'RELAX, RELAX' all the time didn't exactly help."

"Must be quite a sobering moment for a girl," pondered Michael.

"Losing her virginity?"

"Well yeah, obviously – but I meant her first sighting of a bloke, you know, primed and ready for action."

"Oh… right," she paused for thought, "it wasn't too bad actually. I was quite relieved."

"Really?"

"Yeah, well I had been expecting something far worse, believe me."

"So what had you been expecting? You must have had some idea."

"Not really… the only ones I'd ever seen were little babies'… and…" she pulled a face, "Lucky's."

"Who's Lucky?"

"Next door's Labrador. It's not funny – I was only little, he got into our garden and nearly raped me! He was already humping as he came towards me and when his thingy popped out, I thought I'd… urghh!" she shuddered, reliving that awful moment when Lucky's shockingly pink appendage had sprung into view. "Urghh!"

"And you thought blokes were—"

"Worse! There'd been the usual ridiculous rumours at school about the size of boys' doo-dahs and I was left imagining a ten inch version of Lucky's monstrosity! I was set to take the veil – I'd read The Nun's Story three times and seen the film twice, so I was quite keen anyway."

"Sister Olive!" laughed Michael.

"The joys of growing up eh? I hated the whole sorry business to be honest, and I promise you, it's definitely worse for girls." She shared the agonies of being, what her mum would call, 'a late developer'. She described the misery of being the only girl in her class not blossoming into womanhood; the last girl standing in the women's changing rooms. She confided her need to pretend wondrous things were happening to her too: she wore padded bras, carried sanitary pads in her school bag once a month and pretended to be pre-menstrual. It had been a nightmare trying to keep it up. A boy had stood beside her in the corridor prodding her 'breast' with the arm of his glasses; blissfully unaware, she'd only noticed when all her classmates started laughing. She even revealed her horror of horrors that still to this day, made her cringe with embarrassment. It was back in the days of long, hot summer holidays, spent mainly at the local pool; an enormous outdoor swimming pool where you could stay the whole day. She smiled dreamily as she recalled the sense of excitement as you stood in the queue; the unmistakable smell of the water, the shrieks of laughter from those already inside.

"We used to run up ahead to find out what the temperature of the water was that day."

"Yeah, we did that too," grinned Liv, but her smile soon faded as she recalled that awful day; the day she'd borrowed her nan's swimming costume.

"Your nan's?" checked Michael.

"Afraid so," she nodded. "The elastic had given out on my little Ladybird cossie and Nan was the only one who had a costume to lend me. I'll never forget it. A shiny emerald green number with a kind of skirt thing and it was boned."

"What d'you mean... boned?" asked Michael, trying not to laugh in the face of her anguish.

"It had these bendy stick things in the bosom compartment to hold you in position, but because I had nothing to put in there, it looked really stupid. They were sticking out, accentuating my flat chest, but I was so desperate to go swimming, I decided to try and pad it out. It took a hell of a lot of padding – my nan was a big lady! I started off by nicking all the falsies from my mum's bras – I'm a chip off the flat-chested block," she added wryly. "But that wasn't enough, so I chucked in all kinds of stuff… tights, stockings, socks, hankies… until I got the desired effect. Cinderella went to the pool! All was well, nobody mentioned my costume or my ample curves and just as I was thinking I'd got away with it, some boys shoved me in at the deep end!"

With her head in her hands, she recalled the awful moment when she surfaced, to find herself surrounded by a flotilla of debris still streaming out of her nan's costume. She would never forget the boys' faces as they stood at the pool side howling with laughter and just wanting to die as a couple of them scooped out her mum's foam cups and danced around with them on their heads.

"Everyone was laughing, even the girls…" she groaned, "everyone, apart from Donald Little. He jumped in beside me and helped me collect it all up. We got out of the pool and he took me to the girls' changing rooms. I waited there while he ran off to collect my towel and stuff."

"Well good for Donald Little," said Michael smiling to mask an illogical stab of jealousy for Olivia's little champion. "Was he your first boyfriend?"

"God no!" she smiled. "This was way back in primary

school. We were just mates but he always looked out for me and stood up for me if I was getting any grief."

"Did you get bullied then?"

"Yeah, I did a bit," she admitted. "I had the happiest childhood at home, loved loads by my parents and had great fun with my brothers and sisters. Not a lot of money about, but that was fine. Everything was fine at home, but outside, I was like a duck out of water. Sometimes I think my mum's only fault was that she loved us *too* much."

"Not equipped to deal with the outside world then."

"Not a chance," she agreed. "In the animal kingdom, they prepare their young to survive without them. My mum, bless her, filled our lives with love and kept all the bad stuff away. Childhood heaven."

"Until the day you were booted out of the nest…"

"Literally torn from my mother's arms at the school gates – I was completely traumatised!"

"Bloody hell Liv," said Michael, pulling her in for a hug. "No wonder you're such a fuck up." She pulled away as she felt his body start to shake with laughter.

"What? What's so funny?"

"Sorry, it's just… I was thinking about your nan's swimming costume." He stopped as Liv clouted him round the head. "HEY!" he protested, warding off her blows, "I'm not laughing at you, I promise," he caught her wrists, "I'm laughing because something similar happened to me when I was a kid." She snorted her derision. "Really, I'm being straight!" Michael re-lit the joint and took a few tokes before passing it back. "Well, not the same, obviously, and not as bad, but I sort of know how you felt. When I was

403

about eight or maybe nine, we had come up to stay at my aunt's for a while. The weather had suddenly turned really hot so we were all going to the park – it's the one with the massive paddling pool?" Liv nodded. "Anyway, we'd left in a bit of a rush as usual, my dad was playing up, and we hadn't really packed anything. I didn't have any trunks, so my Aunty produced a pair of navy blue knickers; she'd made a big thing about them being 'brand new', as if that made any difference! I mean for God's sake – I'd actually be wearing *a giant pair of knickers!*"

"Go on!" urged Liv, getting into the story.

"My cousins were beside themselves… chanting *'Michael's got Mum's knickers on! – Michael's got Mum's knickers on!'* taking the piss, big time." He ran his fingers through his hair, shaking his head, "It gets worse! As I said, it was a really hot day and the place was heaving. The paddling pool was jam packed so I waded in, fast and low, hoping to get away with it. I thought I had, but then some kids near me started pointing and laughing. I looked down, and the friggin' things had ballooned out, like they were inflating or something and the water all around me was turning blue!" Liv was guffawing, picturing him in his inflating pants, legging it from the pool, a slick of blue dye in his wake and then cracked up at her own hasty exit from the water in her deflating costume trailing socks, hankies and God knows what behind her! She lay on the bed, and with much gesturing began re-enacting his look of horror as his bloomers inflated and the water turned blue! He replied nodding as he gave a brilliant performance of her cossie collapsing and lots of slow motion underwater action as she tried to retrieve the trail of wadding blossoming all around her!

One minute they were rolling around howling with laughter, and then something truly weird happened. Liv suddenly leant over and licked a tear from Michael's cheek. She sat back in confusion and in more than a little shock. Michael was pretty taken aback too but decided to go with it… and licked her back!

***

Michael groaned inwardly as the realisation of what had just taken place came into sharp focus. He'd made love with as much finesse as a gorilla! Less in fact, a gorilla would at least have taken part in a bit of mutual grooming. Talk about 'wham bam thank you mam!' *Oh fuck, fuck, FUCK!!* He just couldn't believe it. The thought had crossed his mind, of course it had, old habits die hard, but that's not what had been going on here. How the hell? *Christ! If I'd have known I'd have…* He felt her body move in his arms and she gently turned in towards him, her head on his chest, arms and legs wrapped around him. He didn't want to look at her and couldn't think of a single thing to say. Her hand brushed the side of his cheek. He looked down and she was smiling up at him. *Maybe it's not too late!* He smiled back thinking that although it had been tragically quick; it had also been one of the most mind-blowing experiences of his life. She snuggled in closer and Michael felt himself stirring; perhaps the giddy heights of passion were still possible! He turned her face up to his, licked the end of her nose tentatively, and with a startled shriek, she leapt from the bed!

"Jesus Christ Liv! What now?"

She was sat in the chair by the side of the bed, huddled up in the bathrobe, head down, her knees hugged in close to her chest. Michael lay back down on the bed. He didn't trust himself to speak. He knew he'd end up yelling and feared that if he did, she would probably leave. He just couldn't believe this latest turn of events. He took a few deep, calming breaths.

"Was it the licking thing?" She nodded. "But you nearly licked my face off earlier, so I thought p'raps…?"

"But that was… that was an accident."

"AN ACCIDENT? How could that have been an accident Liv?"

"I didn't mean to do it… it just kind of happened."

He sighed. He knew she needed rescuing, but how do you rescue someone who thinks it's *you* they need rescuing from?

This is madness, he thought.

"This is madness," he said.

I was just inside her…

"I was just inside you…"

He was just inside me… oh God! Liv was shivering, chilled to the bone. She felt like she had a fever, her body was damp with sweat. Michael took the quilt and wrapped it around her.

"Okay Liv?" he called. No reply. "Come on mate… you're alright. Just a bit spun out that's all." The shivering got worse. "I'll run you a bath shall I? A nice hot bath... get you warmed up."

She could hear the water running and a little while later, he was back.

"It's all ready... d'you need a hand?" he asked the bundle on the chair.

"I'll be okay thanks," came the muffled reply.

"Right," said Michael, relieved that she was at least communicating with him again. "I'll go down to reception – see if I can get us a decent cup of coffee or something." She didn't answer. "Liv?"

"Michael..." he knew what was coming, "I just want to go now if that's okay?"

"Yeah... course it is mate. I'll go and check us out. I'll bring the cab round... be about ten minutes, okay?" When he returned, he found her waiting in reception, ready to go.

'Then the eyes of both of them were opened, and they realised they were naked'

Genesis 3:7

It was a long drive home; Michael's attempts at conversation had withered on the vine and the silence was killing him. He was about to turn the cassette deck on but realised that 'Red Hill' could still be playing. Having no wish to see her throw herself from his speeding cab, he decided to play it safe and turned the radio on instead. It was just gone midnight as he turned into the lane leading to the boarding kennels. Checking his rear-view mirror again he could see she hadn't moved. She appeared to be sleeping but must have sensed his gaze upon her because she looked up and caught his eye in the mirror before quickly looking away. Michael pulled over, turned the engine off and turned around to face her. Olivia stared resolutely out of the window.

"Liv? We've got to talk. We can't leave it like this." She buried her head in her arms. "Liv, will you look at me please." He got out, opened the back door and as he climbed in, she climbed out the other side. "Oh for God's sake Olivia!" he yelled after her as she scurried off down the lane, "Stop being such a baby!"

"Leave me alone!" she yelled back at him.

"I'll call you tomorrow."

"No!" she called back before disappearing from view. Alison gave her a big hug the next morning but no questions had been asked and no explanation given; everyone carried on as usual, which suited Olivia just fine. The hours dragged by until eventually, it was almost five thirty and Liv was closing down for the day. She sat at her desk – waiting for the call she knew would come.

"Deputy Dogs."

"Hi."

"Hi."

"You okay?"

"Yep… you?"

"Fine."

There was an awkward silence then they both started talking at once.

"No, go ahead…" insisted Michael. "You go first."

"Okay… right… So first of all I'd like to apologise for my infantile behaviour last night. I was blaming you for what happened when really, it was just as much my fault as yours. I was in shock and I…" she paused, "Why are you laughing?"

"You're reading that out!"

"No I'm not!"

"You are! You've got it written down in front of you, haven't you?"

"What?… No!… well, actually…" Liv couldn't help laughing too. "I've been practising all day!"

"Idiot!"

"I know… oh well look… I really am sorry."

"That's alright mate—"

"No it's not. Last night… it wasn't your fault."

"It wasn't anyone's fault, it just happened."

"Exactly, and I had no right taking it out on you so I'm sorry for that… but the thing is… I know it was an accident and everything but we—"

"It was over in the blink of an eye… literally!"

"Well yes… and we didn't mean for it to happen but the thing is…"

"We should just forget about it."

"But we can't pretend it didn't happen!"

"Why not?"

"Of course we can't!"

"Why?"

"We wouldn't be able to… there's something about it in the bible, I can't remember exactly, but it's to do with Adam and Eve after they ate the apple."

"We didn't eat any apples!"

"It's something to do with fig leaves. God knew they'd sinned because they were wearing fig leaves."

"But they hadn't been shagging had they? It was just the apple, so as long as we avoid apples and fig leaves we'll—"

"Don't say things like shagging!"

"I wasn't talking about *us* shagging—"

"Michael!"

"You could hardly call—"

"They had sex in the Garden of Eden," insisted Olivia, "It was the Original Sin."

"No – It was eating the apple."

"So why did they cover their bits then?"

"I dunno to be honest," laughed Michael, "they should've just hidden the apple core!"

"Anyway…" began Liv, determined to get back on track. "Last night—"

"It's like it never happened!" interrupted Michael. "Honestly mate, we should just forget about it."

"We can't! It's impossible – I can think of nothing else! We'd be awkward with each other – it would always be there. It's for the best anyway. Bloody hell, what were we doing? I'm on the brink of a court case to decide my future and you're supposed to be making a go of it with Hannah for goodness sake! No we should just—"

"I can think of nothing else either."

"No! See what I mean? It's always going to be there and I can't deal with that at the moment. I can't see you again."

"What never again?"

"No! I don't know! I wouldn't have thought not *ever* again… but… at the moment…"

"So do we still speak on the phone or—"

"No I think it's best we don't. I'm nearly there now. The court case is under two weeks away, I've got the meeting with my barrister coming up and I have to be, you know, completely focussed."

"Liv, you're over-reacting—"

"I'm not! Can you imagine what Carl and his lawyers would make of this? Don't you see… this is potentially—"

"You're divorced! You can do what the hell you like!"

"No I can't – I'm a mother! If he found out, he'd turn the boys against me for sure…"

"Liv—"

"… And discredit me in court."

"Woah calm down! You're getting this way out of proportion."

"Maybe I am, but that's how I feel."

"Okay, I still think you're over-reacting, but if that's what you want, maybe it *is* for the best—"

"It definitely is. Thanks Michael… thanks for everything—"

"Christ! If you'd let me finish, I was just saying, maybe it's for the best… for now! Don't start giving me the '*It was nice knowing you*' bollocks!"

"I wasn't!" laughed Liv, "I was just wanted you to know that I appreciate everything you've done."

"Okay well look, you know where I am if you need me."

"I do, thanks Michael."

"And I'm still your mate, alright?"

"I know that."

"Okay… well good luck. Ring me if you… you know, any time."

"Thank you."

Bumtwangle

Her barrister's chambers in Temple were straight out of a Dickens novel. Leaving the clamour of the city behind, she blinked as she entered the square; it was as if she had stepped into another world. Across from the beautifully kept lawns befitting an English country estate were the terraces of chambers. As she walked up the broad flight of stairs, she noticed how smoothly the stone steps had been worn away, as if gently eroded by the sea. The Dickensian theme continued as the enormous door opened and she was ushered inside by a clerk in formal attire. He was ancient, huffing and puffing as he shuffled his way along the maze of corridors with Olivia shuffling along behind him, trying to avoid stepping on the backs of his heels. Her senses were bombarded with sights and smells that furthered her feelings of otherworldliness. Dark and gloomy, old and musty, the place was literally steeped in history. They were met by the barrister's clerk who led her to a small ante-room just outside her barrister's office, instructed her to take a seat and informed her that Ms Lytton would be with her shortly.

Twenty minutes dragged by. She amused herself by imagining the names Dickens would have bestowed upon the clerks and chuckled as she pictured 'Bumtwangle & Thripplewipple' on the brass plate outside the door. She needed the loo but was afraid to move in case she was suddenly summonsed. Another fifteen minutes and she was becoming desperate. She got up from her creaky chair and crept down an even creakier corridor in search of the Ladies. She dared not venture too far knowing she'd get horribly lost. She was creaking her way back when Bumtwangle suddenly appeared from a side door. Looking decidedly miffed that she had moved from her appointed position, he led her to the 'W.C.' and then, to her great embarrassment, waited outside to escort her back.

Finally, Ms Lytton was ready for her and invited her in. She offered a firm handshake and quick apology for keeping her waiting. She explained she had just returned from her summer vacation and had needed to familiarise herself with the case. On her desk were the usual bundles of papers tied up with pink ribbon, some of which had been untied. The whole thing was archaic; Olivia half expected to see her writing with a quill.

"Your solicitor has prepared an excellent case," she assured Olivia with a smile. "Now before we start, I just need to check that nothing has changed in your personal circumstances. Is there anything else I need to know before we go to court?" Olivia gulped and felt her face redden.

"No Ms Lytton." She felt like she was sitting in the Headmistress's office and had been caught in a lie. But she wasn't lying, she told herself. An accidental sexual encounter with a friend did not have any bearing on this case; it just felt like it did.

"Hmmmm," murmured Ms Lytton, not entirely convinced. Collecting up a sheaf of loose papers, she tapped them in front of her purposefully, all the while inspecting Olivia over half moon specs that seemed to be standard issue in the higher echelons of both legal and medical professions. It was all extremely unnerving. "So you were granted your decree absolute last month?" Olivia nodded. "I see here the court had to intervene regarding the Statement of Arrangements and that you were advised to seek mediation."

"Yes."

"You had just the one appointment?"

"Yes… it didn't really help," confirmed Olivia remembering how their first appointment had also been their last. Carl's Oscar winning performance of *'broken man who loves his wife and kids and didn't want this divorce'* won the sympathy of everyone in the room whereas Olivia's look of contempt, as she witnessed the said performance, was duly noted and she knew she had been marked down as a heartless bitch. She did her best to keep her facial expression neutral but the mediator informing them there were a team of professionals seated on the other side of a two-way mirror overlooking the room brought forth an involuntary snort of laughter that left her thoroughly disgraced in the eyes of all concerned.

"And your ex-husband has residential custody of both children?"

"We have joint custody… but yes, they are living with him for now."

"For now?"

"I'm sure that once this is over and everything settles down, he'll accept that the boys should be with me."

Ms Lytton shuffled through the papers again and after much humming and harring unleashed a barrage of questions that left Olivia wondering if she knew anything about her case at all, then proceeded to outline all the things that could go wrong. High on the list was the fact that The Respondent (Carl) had made The Plaintiff (Olivia) an offer of forty-five thousand pounds. The said offer had been turned down and more recently, last week in fact, there had been a further offer, also rejected, of sixty thousand pounds. Ms Lytton expended a sigh through pursed lips and shook her head.

"You knew of this latest offer?"

Olivia bit her lip. "Yes, but my solicitor agreed we should turn it down."

"Did he indeed? Hmmmm… and was the case of 'Calderbank versus Calderbank' explained to you?" Fifteen minutes of legal jargon later and Olivia was losing the will to live. Some of what her barrister was saying rang bells from discussions with Simon, but it had not made sense to her then, and was not much clearer now. Too much legal parlance caused a leaden feeling to descend and her brain to malfunction. As new information was received, previous knowledge departed; quite literally, in one ear and out the other. Finally Ms Lytton laid it on the table in simple terms. Basically, if at the end of the hearing, the judge awarded Olivia sixty thousand or less, she would be liable not only for her own costs, but those of her ex-husband too. She pointed out that given Carl had instructed the most expensive lawyers in Christendom, his costs were likely to be astronomical and that the combined costs of both parties could possibly exceed fifty thousand pounds. She also pointed out that Carl having the children would weigh heavily in his favour. The courts would be reluctant to force the sale of the family home in order to give Olivia her settlement, the club was in Joseph's name and she was unlikely to get anything from his business because according to his financial statements, this was the only income he had to support them.

"But I don't want the family home to be sold! He doesn't need to sell it – he has plenty of money! And I don't want anything from the businesses either – it's all there in the file!" Olivia remembered feeling terribly impressed when she heard that her case file had been couriered out to her barrister in Tuscany. Clearly, her case had not figured greatly in Ms Lytton's holiday reading. With an air of irritation Ms Lytton looked at her watch and suggested they broke for lunch. She told Olivia to come back at 2pm. Upon her return two hours later, she noted with relief that all the bundles had been opened, there were papers strewn everywhere; Ms Lytton had obviously had a working lunch. Thankfully she had a much better understanding of the case and Olivia began to feel more confident; this newfound confidence, however, was soon to be shaken.

"My dear, I must be frank with you. On the face of it you *do* have a very strong case, however, the other side are in possession of all our evidence and they are still willing to meet us in court. They obviously feel confident the judge will award in their favour and as I explained earlier, this could prove disastrous for you."

"But surely the affairs, the assault, the forged signature, the lies—"

"Well apart from the forged signature, in the main it is simply your word against his. We need evidence – we need proof."

"But we *do* have proof! We have signed affidavits from witnesses confirming they were at the fancy dress party and—"

"Yes but they are all *your* people – *your* family and friends. They cannot be regarded as independent, impartial witnesses, plus of course he will be producing witnesses to counter their evidence."

Olivia sighed. It had been incredibly difficult to get any witnesses at all; Carl and his father had quite a reputation and most people were reluctant to cross them. She was eternally grateful to the few that had laid their necks on the line by signing affidavits and sincerely hoped they would not actually be required to give evidence in court.

"But the handwriting expert—"

"Yes and for every expert witness we bring, there will be one on their side to make a rebuttal. You just never know with these things. It could go either way. His original offer of forty-five would have been laughed out of court but sixty – I just don't know."

"But I can't buy a house with sixty thousand! I need a home for us – that's all I want Ms Lytton. When this is all over I need to be able to rebuild my relationship with my sons." She knew better than to start bleating on about what was fair; she had already had that conversation with Simon. At one point, when she had been heavily involved in the legwork work for her case, she had thought briefly she would enjoy working within the legal profession; however as time went on, her frustration grew, culminating in an outburst of indignation – *I thought the whole point of the law was to decide what was fair! Is it about what's fair, or is it just about... the law?*' Simon had confirmed it was simply about the law. He admitted that the next client who walked through his door could be another Carl and that even if Simon knew he was lying through his teeth, he would have to represent him and regardless of his personal opinions, he would be duty bound to achieve the best possible outcome for his client. Olivia had been shocked to the core and knew that the legal profession was most definitely not for her. Mr Bumble was right; the law truly was an ass.

"Dear girl I *do* understand your situation, but it is my duty to point out the pitfalls in turning down this latest offer." She tilted her head back and closed her eyes in contemplation for a few moments. Decision reached, her eyes snapped open and she slapped the desk in front of her. "Right! We are going to approach this in a different way. We're going to force an out of court settlement. We need to push him into thinking *he's* the one who can't risk going before the judge; now is there anything else we can hit him with to bring pressure to bear?" Once again, Olivia was the subject of intense scrutiny from above the half moon specs. "Can you think of anything, anything at all that could make him think twice about going to court?"

Olivia sat bolt upright and with butterflies rising, chased the thought that had flashed through her mind. "Actually Ms Lytton," she said gripping the desk and resisting the urge to give it a hearty slap of her own, "I think I can!"

Ms Lytton

18th September 1987

Dear Clare,

I hope everything's okay out there?
It's just you haven't replied to my last
letter and it's really not like you. I'm
not overly worried because I'm thinking
it's probably a case of 'Thunderbirds
Are Go!' with your Mr Tracy, but even
so, a little note or even a postcard
would be nice!

I've just got back from the pub -
everyone was there, Karen, Anna, Daniel
and the whole motley crew - well almost
everyone - Michael wasn't but I'll
explain about that later. It was good

to see them and great timing because I had the meeting with my barrister today. She's a frosty old bird that's for sure - thank God she's on my side! She reminds me of Miss Grimley! (Was that her real name do you think or did she make it up to sound more scary!) Remember how she'd peer at you over her wire glasses, her beady little eyes stuck on either side of her enormous beak? Ms Lytton hasn't got the beak but she's got that same look that strikes terror to your heart and turns your bowels to water!

Anyway, I was telling them what she'd said about all my witnesses being friends or family and how it was a bit of a concern and suddenly Daniel jumps up, convinced he's solved the problem! He reminds us about Simon's jokey suggestion of taking photos of them in fancy dress and sticking them to their affidavits and says "That's it! We'll get photos of us dressed up in the costumes that Carl's lot were wearing - he'll think they've changed sides!" Sadly, I had to pour cold water on his brilliant wheeze because a) Simon was only joking and b) even if he wasn't, they couldn't swear affidavits in someone else's name.

I'm finding it hard to believe that after all this time it's finally going to happen. Wednesday 23rd September - this Wednesday in fact - as in five days' time! Crikey Blimes! Did I tell you it has been set for three days? How could it take that long? It's beyond me! Anyway, hopefully Ms Lytton knows what she's doing and can get it over with on day one. She said we had to try and force him into an out of court settlement and that we needed to come up with something that would make him think twice about going before the judge. I sat there racking my brains and then suddenly it came to me! Something Michael said ages ago - he reckons Carl and Joseph are running a money laundering syndicate!

She looked really interested at first - started scribbling it all down and nodding encouragingly, but in the end she said she couldn't use it! She explained that she's not allowed to just spring something like that on them in court (I know that's what happens in the

movies but really, you have to inform
the other side of any developments in
your case before it comes to court)
and more importantly of course, we
have absolutely no proof. Ah well... it
was worth a try! Simon thinks we have
a strong enough case to go to court
anyway - I just hope he's right.

Now we come to the difficult part
of this letter - I've been trying to
write it all week! I haven't been able
to speak to anyone about this and the
only reason I'm telling you is because
you're thousands of miles away and
can't come round and give me a slap!
The thing is - I accidentally slept with
Michael. Honestly Clare, I know what
you're thinking but please believe me, it
really was an accident and should never
have happened. I've tried to explain but
it all looks so ridiculous when I write
it down! There are screwed up balls of
paper everywhere! I'm sorry Briany, I
just can't do it so we'll have to wait
until we can talk. Ring me when you can.

All I can say is, it happened last Friday
and we haven't seen or spoken to each
other since. Michael seemed to think

that because it was unintentional and 'over in the blink of an eye' we could just carry on as if nothing had happened. As if we could! Well, it's clear he could! It obviously meant nothing to him whereas everything's changed for me! I can't think of him in the same way. If I picture him now, instead of just seeing his face, I see the crinkles at the side of his eyes and the dimple on the left side of his mouth when he smiles - and then I'm looking at his mouth and remembering the feel of his lips on mine - Oh God! Do you see what I mean?!? How could it have meant nothing to him? It was wild and passionate... he basically ravished me... or did I ravish him??? Oh God Briany, I think I did! Nothing like this has ever happened to me before! With Carl, it was always like I' did my duty' and with Terry it was tender and comforting... but this... this was... Oh God! I can see this letter getting binned with the rest of them if I don't get a grip!!!

So anyway, I told him we couldn't have any contact until the court case was over - he thought I was over-reacting but agreed to respect my decision. I'm sure it was the right thing to do, especially when I was sat in Miss Grimley's office this afternoon getting the third degree. She asked me point blank if there was anything I thought she should know! I nearly confessed right there on the spot! I didn't of course, because it has no bearing on the case - but it shows how much it's bothering me.

Not speaking to Michael has been hard - much worse than I could ever have imagined. I miss that daily contact. It's made me realise how much I've come to depend on him. To be honest, I don't know how I'd have got through all this without him. Whenever I get jangled he calms me down. He has this way of keeping me on an even keel - a minor miracle considering how up and down I am. One minute I'm convinced it's all going to turn out fine and the next I'm in the depths of despair, equally convinced I'll lose the boys and my life will be over for ever. Manically high or rock bottom low - borderline manic depressive methinks!

When things were getting tricky here, he gave me an old cassette player so

I could have some music in my room.
(I don't watch tele anymore because I
can't concentrate on anything, but music
soothes the soul.) He lent me some
headphones and a selection of tapes
including one I think he made himself.
There's lots of uplifting tracks like
'Don't Give Up' (the one Peter Gabriel
did with Kate Bush) and stuff like
'Lean On Me' by Bill Withers and James
Taylor's 'You've Got a Friend'. I've been
listening to it a lot this week and it
feels like he made it for me, but now
I'm thinking, 'With or Without You'
and 'Alive and Kicking', are they there
because he knows I like them, or is
there a message there too? But then
there's Fleetwood Mac's 'Sarah' and
the theme music from Formula One
where the lyrics mean diddly squat –
so it's probably just a coincidence!
Arghhhh! I can't stop thinking about
him and it's driving me mad!

He said I could call him anytime, but
I don't like ringing him at home in case
Hannah's there. I can't remember if I
told you – she picked up a message I'd
left on his answer phone once and all
hell broke loose so I daren't risk that

again! I've told Alison that if he rings, I'll take the call. I know I told him 'no contact' - but surely he'll ring to wish me good luck or something - he knows the case starts next week.

Anyway, I've just got to stop all this nonsense and concentrate on what's ahead. My goal has always been clear - get through the divorce, get my own home and get my boys back. This crazy thing has happened and I'm - well I don't know what I am but one thing's for sure - I can't let a moment of madness derail everything but I fear that it could! Please call or write back soon Briany - I am cast adrift!

All my love
Liv xxx

Should I Stay Or Should I Go

Unfortunately, Jim hadn't been told the ban on Michael's calls had been lifted, so when he rang on Tuesday evening, Jim wouldn't put him through. Disappointed at not getting the chance to speak to her, Michael made a snap decision to drive up and see her instead. Olivia, meanwhile, was in her room agonising over what she was going to wear to court the next day. There were clothes everywhere and her room was starting to resemble the backroom of a charity shop. She had settled on a much loved French Connection suit but there was a problem; the cut of the trousers meant she couldn't wear heels and she didn't have any decent flats. She was trying to decide if she could get away with the Mr Plod lace-ups from the interview fiasco when there was a tap at her door.

"You've got a visitor," said Alison with a struggling Lois in her arms, "HE'S OVER IN THE OFFICE…" she shouted over Lois's protests that she didn't want a bath, "I THOUGHT YOU'D PREFER SOME PRIVACY!"

With her heart thumping, Olivia rushed downstairs and over to the office but stopped dead in her tracks as the figure at the desk turned round to greet her.

"Hello Tuppence! Long time no see!"

"TERRY!"

Liv had asked her parents not to give out any information as to where she was. *'Just take their number'* she'd said, *'then if it's someone I want to speak to, I can ring them back.'* Terry laughed as he described his phone call with her mum.

"She was very tight lipped about your whereabouts. She said something like *'I'm not at liberty to say!'* I gave her the old flannel about being a dear and trusted friend but she wouldn't budge, so I offered her my number and bingo… she says, *'No sorry, I'm not allowed to take it… but I can give you hers!'…"*

"Ah bless Mum!"

"I couldn't believe my luck!" laughed Terry. "Anyway, it was easy to track you down after that. I rang the kennels, got the address and here I am!"

As Michael neared the end of the lane he was surprised to find the gates were open. It was getting on for 7 o'clock; the kennels should have closed ages ago. He pulled up alongside a black Range Rover in the car park and gave a low whistle of appreciation; it was a brand new Overfinch and with its beefed up body, blacked out windows and massive wheels it was one hell of a mean machine; a bit flash but impressive none the less. He parked up and walked towards the house but noticed the lights were on in reception. He could see Olivia engaged in conversation with a client he assumed to be the owner of the Range Rover. He hung back and lit a cigarette… then a second… and a third. *What was taking so long?* He wandered in a bit closer and realised something was wrong; Liv looked flushed and agitated as she stood talking to a heavyset man with cropped grey hair.

"Everything all right in here?"

Terry swung round.

"Well fuck me! Look who it is!! Alright mate?"

"Mitchell you old bastard! What the hell are you doing here?"

Laughing, the two men began to spar, feigning left hooks and uppercuts before coming together for a hearty backslapping embrace. Liv looked on horrified. Not only did they know each other, judging by their joyous reunion, they knew each other well! When she'd confided in Michael about her affair with Terry, she'd obviously had no idea. She came out from behind her desk and toyed with the idea of making a run for it, but Terry was blocking her exit, regaling them with stories of when Michael had worked for him on the door.

"Remember Mama?"

"Yeah, but—"

"Fucking funny!" laughed Terry turning to Olivia. "I'd stuck him in at The Hippodrome. He looked good all tux'd up on the door and they loved him, but he'd only do a couple of nights a week. Wasn't really your thing was it mate?" Michael didn't reply. "They didn't know how best to use him so I've told them it's obvious… Gay Nights! I've sold it to Michael saying it's a doddle – no rucks, good tips – anyway, there's this big fat sheikh, Mama, absolutely minted and completely besotted with Michael here. It's love at first sight and he's determined to have him, so I'm straight in there negotiating. I should have been a pimp! Five grand I could have got him – five grand! Mind you, just as well you turned it down Michael – the poor sod died of AIDS!" Partway through the telling of his tale Terry had picked up on a vibe; a certain frisson in the air. He realised he should do the decent thing and leave. He caught Michael's eye and smiled; he had no intention of doing the decent thing.

"So…" said Michael, "are you collecting your dog or…"

"No!" laughed Terry, "I just popped in to see Livvie here."

"You know each other?"

"Oh yeah, we go way back don't we Liv," said Terry, ruffling her hair affectionately, "way, way back."

There was an uncomfortable silence as Michael processed this information.

"Right… well look mate, nice seeing you and everything, but—"

"And you know each other too then?" said Terry pleasantly.

"Yeah… we do," said Michael, "and to be honest mate, your timing couldn't have been worse. We're in the middle of something here—"

"Is that so?" said Terry, still smiling. "Seems to me *we* were in the middle of something when *you* walked in!"

"Look Terry… I need a word with Liv, a private word,

432

so if you wouldn't mind…" he moved aside and nodded to the door.

"Really!" said Terry, his smile stretching into a broad grin. "I think that's up to Olivia don't you?" He turned towards her, "What's it to be darlin'… should I stay or should I go?"

Olivia stared at the ground.

"Do you want me to leave?"

She nodded silently.

"Okay sweetheart," he said taking her face in his hands and planting a kiss on her forehead to show there were no hard feelings. "I'll be in touch. But meanwhile…" He gave her his card and lifted a cumbersome looking briefcase with a coiled lead and an aerial onto the counter. "Mobile phone." He said, giving it a tap. "Number's on the card. You can reach me anytime." And without a backward glance he was gone.

They stood in silence, watching the taillights of the Range Rover disappear down the lane.

"So that was Terry was it?"

She nodded.

"Your Terry… is actually that Terry."

"Yes."

"Polar Fucking Shagnasty!"

"Huh?"

"How could you have been taken in by that whoring scumbag?"

"It wa—"

"And he's the one who told you about Carl?"

"Yes."

"The only one brave enough!"

"That's right, he—"

"Oh for God's sake Olivia – how could you be so naïve?"

"What do you mean?"

"He used that to get you into bed!"

"NO!"

"Of course he did! He's worse than Carl ever knew how to be – he's worse than anyone I know!"

"No, you're wrong… it wasn't—"

"Oh spare me the *'it wasn't like that'* bollocks BECAUSE I MIGHT JUST FUCKIN' EXPLODE!"

They stood there in mutual shock; his outburst still ringing in the air when Jim appeared at the door. His sharp reminder she had a big day ahead of her and suggestion that Michael should leave was unassailable.

"You're absolutely right Jim. We're nearly finished here. Five minutes… alright Olivia?"

"Yes… five minutes please Jim. We're fine."

Aware that Jim's inbuilt stopwatch had been set, they both started talking at once.

"I'm sorry—" began Michael.

"No it's fine."

"It's not. Jim's right. I shouldn't even be here – I tried ringing but he wouldn't… oh look, I just wanted to wish you good luck!"

"I'm glad you did – well apart from—"

"Yeah well we could have all done without that."

"I've missed talking."

"So have I…" admitted Michael.

"It's been horrible."

"Yeah… and look, this thing with Terry. It's none of my business so I shouldn't even… I'm just worried you might be taken in again by—"

"No… I'm—"

"… Billy Big Bollocks with his Overfinch and wanky mobile phone – who's he trying to impress?"

"He wasn't try—"

"So why was he here?"

"Oh I don't know! He's been in Ibiza. He's got a club there now… he was back in London and heard about the divorce. He fluked Mum into giving him—"

"Oh Christ!" interrupted Michael, "Here comes Jim McGrim!" He ran his fingers through his hair in frustration. "Look, I'll shoot. Give me a ring in about half an hour."

"What about Hannah?"

"She won't be there… it's over."

Back in the house, Alison helped Olivia with her preparations for the next day. Order had been restored to her room, a suitable pair of shoes had been found and her outfit lay ready on the back of the chair. She collected the cordless phone, hugged both Alison and Jim and retired to her room for the night. Michael answered at the first ring. He sounded a bit gruff.

"Michael… can I ask you something?"

"What?"

"Who's Polar Shagnasty?"

He hung up.

Laughing, she rang him straight back.

"It's an old joke," Michael explained. "I can't

remember… something about a marauding polar bear that shags everything in its path."

"And that's what they call him?"

"Yep."

"The polar bear?"

"And Terry!"

"You don't know him."

"No Olivia… *you* don't know him!"

"He's a good man," she insisted.

"Do you really think so?"

"But you're mates. You were—"

"Yeah he *is* a mate – and I like him. He's a funny guy, but Liv, you shouldn't be anywhere near him."

"I'm not! Terry is the last thing on my mind at the moment, can't you see that? The court hearing begins tomorrow… after all the delays and bullshit postponements, it's actually going ahead!"

"Yep… and that's all that matters right now," agreed Michael. "So how are you feeling?"

"Strangely… I'm feeling fine. In fact, if I could choose how I'd be feeling the night before the hearing, I'd choose this."

"Excellent!" smiled Michael into the phone. "Well look… good luck tomorrow, keep your wits about you, stay focussed… listen to Simon, he seems to have your back."

"I will."

"And don't get rushed into anything. At the end of the day it's your future that's at stake – you make the final decisions."

"Yes I know."

"Listen to their advice, but follow your instincts."

"What if my instincts go against their advice?"

"Well, then you're fucked!" laughed Michael.

"That's no good! What should I do? Follow my instincts?"

"Ignore them at your peril!"

They said their goodbyes and Liv promised to ring him as soon as she could the next day. She lay in bed unable to sleep, which under the circumstances was no great surprise. At one point she convinced herself Carl had probably been staking out the kennels from day one; he'd done it before. If he'd been there tonight he'd have had a field day! Supposing they questioned her about her private life. She hadn't mentioned Terry in the history of the marriage because it was such a long time ago and it didn't feel relevant… but him turning up here… and after what happened with Michael… she could imagine how it would be presented in court; she'd stand accused of a fling and a one night stand! She eventually fell into an uneasy sleep around 2am, tossing and turning under the weight of her guilty secrets.

Courtroom Steps

Carl was the first to arrive. He parked up and with a spring in his step he strode towards the courthouse. He was feeling supremely confident. He had the best legal representation money could buy, Bartholomew Frobisher QC, head honcho of Frobisher, Fellows & Brown; lawyers to the rich and famous, lawyers to the stars! Like Olivia, he had been quick to spot '*Shaft'em & Co*' on their headed paper but had taken it as confirmation his choice of barrister had been sound. He didn't have a clue what to expect here today and had no real understanding of his case; he'd left that all in the hands of the experts. Christ knows he was paying them enough; they *had* to be good to command those prices! There was no doubt in his mind; with old Shafty-Boy at the helm, Olivia and her Legal Aid crew didn't stand a chance.

There had been the odd wobble along the way of course; the last minute business with the two-way mirror had been a disaster! A 'slight hiccup' they'd called it.

'Slight hiccup? More like "Spectacular fuckup"! His barrister had laughed it off as 'high jinks' when it came up in court but the judge didn't see it that way and the next thing he knew, she'd got him on the grounds of his unreasonable behaviour!

The forgery had been unfortunate but apparently for every expert witness she had, they had one to counter their evidence. Quite how that was going to work with the forged signature was beyond him. *'You don't need a handwriting expert to spot that one',* he thought, *'going to "baffle 'em with bullshit" by the sound of it.'* The sworn affidavits from guests at the fancy dress party were a bit of a worry too, but Carl stayed resolute in his trust in Shaft'em & Co; they exuded confidence and he was happy to be swept along by it. They assured him he needn't worry about anything that came up in court because in the main, Olivia's witnesses were family and friends and could not be deemed impartial. *'Yeah… her little Band of Brothers sticking their heads above the parapet – bastards! They probably think they're in with a chance with her once this is all over. Why else would they risk helping her? Yeah well, what goes around comes around',* he thought darkly. *'Mind you, I'll have to watch the old man.'*

Joseph was getting increasingly out of control. Carl was beginning to think Olivia was right about him; he was definitely showing alarmingly psychopathic tendencies. Carl had no problem with a bit of menacing here and there but threatening to blow people away was going too far! Joseph had already hinted at how easy it would be for Olivia to meet with an accident and said he only had to give the word and she would disappear; given his so-called business associates and their ever-present henchmen, Carl could well believe it. '*He'll be telling me she sleeps with the fishes next!*' Carl had made up his mind; once this lot was over, he was going to take steps to distance himself from his father's business. As far as he was concerned, the sooner the mad old bastard went back to Austria, the better!

The foyer of the court house was starting to fill up and pretty soon was positively heaving with members of the legal profession and anxious 'civilians' in court for their day of reckoning. Amongst the throngs of wigs and gowns, bespectacled solicitors and clerks of the court, Carl spotted what appeared to be a French onion seller! He blinked. His eyes were obviously deceiving him. In order to get a better look, he attempted to push his way through the hive of legal activity but found himself shouldered out to the periphery. As he inched his way along the side of a large plate glass window, a bright splash of colour caught his eye. He glanced left. Outside on the street, the Incredible Hulk was waving at him. He shook his head '…*just a weird dream, that's what this is… I'm still asleep. Any minute now I'll wake up laughing… any minute now…*' A bumblebee joined the bizarre group of characters gathering outside the courthouse. He sat down heavily and put his head between his knees. He felt horribly sick but was still trying to convince himself he was dreaming. Suddenly, pandemonium broke out at the front of the court house. He looked up to see a pantomime cow attempting to negotiate the revolving door. Realisation scored a direct hit in his solar plexus and he had to accept the awful truth; this was no nightmare, this was for real! Where was his brief? He spotted his legal team homing in on him, their silk robes fluttering as they came swooping down the corridor like a swarm of vampire bats.

Watching in disbelief from a far corner was Olivia, her heart almost thumping right out of her chest. This had Daniel written all over it! They must have got together and hatched a Plan B! She applauded her friends' ingenuity and couldn't believe their gall, but was terrified of her barrister's reaction. She kept scanning the hall, looking for Simon and Ms Lytton. She checked her watch again. She had been instructed to get there by ten thirty and it was almost that now. Relief washed over her as she saw them come through the main door but her blood froze at the look on Ms Lytton's face as she picked her way through the mêlée.

"What the hell is going on here?" she spluttered. "Have you lost your mind, this is a Court of Law, not a bally circus!"

Simon's grim demeanour did nothing to mask the amusement in his eyes.

"Honestly Ms Lytton, I had no idea they were coming," insisted Olivia, "It was all just a joke!"

"A joke! A joke??? Well you can forget any notion that they can be called as witnesses—"

They were interrupted by an emissary from the other side. Ms Lytton went to meet her counterpart. A brief exchange and she returned with the news they were keen to negotiate.

"That's good isn't it?" checked Liv. She assumed it was but Ms Lytton's grim face suggested otherwise.

"Yes of course it's good – but we shall let them stew. Now then Olivia, did you bring the estate agent details I requested?" They adjourned to a quiet corner away from the madness unfolding in the main hall. Olivia handed over the property details of suitable houses that were near the boys' schools and Cedars but within easy commute of the boarding kennels in Hertfordshire. "Excellent!" said Ms Lytton flicking through the details. Simon drew Ms Lytton's attention to what looked like a full scale argument going on in the opposite camp. "Discord in the ranks eh?" she observed, "Always good to see!" Ms Lytton's opposite number signalled and she strode back out to meet him. Another very brief exchange and she was back.

"Seventy thousand."

"Huh?"

"They've upped their offer to seventy thousand pounds," explained Simon.

Olivia's face lit up in delight. Daniel's crazy plan was working!

"God's teeth!" hissed her barrister, absolutely furious at Olivia's reaction. "Wipe that smile from your face, turn your back and start shaking your head!" She did as she was told and began shaking her head vigorously. Ms Lytton took hold of Olivia by her shoulders and with a fixed smile, whispered directly into her ear. "Get a grip! You'll scupper any chance of a courthouse steps settlement if you don't calm down!" Ms Lytton may have been smiling but the fingers digging into her shoulders told Olivia her barrister was not best pleased. "Get a coffee or something and leave this to me." Olivia was only too happy to oblige.

"Should I meet you back here or are we going out on the steps?"

"Back here is fine Olivia," said Simon quickly as Ms Lytton rolled her eyes and walked off bristling with frustration, "It's just a figure of speech – it means settling out of court." He hurried after Ms Lytton who was about to enter the ring for round three.

The Lone Ranger came up behind Olivia as she stood at the coffee machine.

"Alright Liv? How's it going? Carl's looking a bit grey!" She nearly jumped out of her skin, sloshing coffee in all directions.

"Shhhh! Don't talk to me! You'll give the game away!" She spotted an Egyptian mummy shuffling towards them with a slow catatonic gait, arms outstretched and trailing crusty old bandages behind him. "Go away!" she hissed, "You're unravelling – he might figure out who you are!"

Even as they spoke, their huge bluff was coming to an end; the pantomime cow was being ejected from the courthouse, along with Zorro and The Caped Crusader. Carl was over in the corner surrounded by his legal team and Olivia was relieved to see they were far too preoccupied to notice the eviction of her 'star witnesses'. Carl's lawyers were trying to convince him that no surprise witnesses could be called; if Carl had been more involved in his case, he may have had a better understanding of the situation, but he had lost confidence in them and didn't believe a word. If the characters in fancy dress couldn't testify, why were they here? *'They've turned on me, the dirty bastards.'* He was already panicking over the forged signature, the invoices from the phony builder, the valuation on the house… and now this!

Both barristers were operating independently of their clients now, hell-bent on thrashing out a settlement. It was high drama with offers and counter offers punctuated by the Clerk of the Court calling their names, and insisting they take up their places in front of the allegedly impatient judge. Meanwhile, back in his chambers, the judge was rather hoping this case was going to come before him. He was more than used to the frantic, last minute negotiations going on outside and as was customary, he was using the time to bring himself up to speed with the case in hand. From what he had read so far, this one was shaping up to be an absolute corker!

Back outside in the main hall Ms Lytton was still trying to achieve her out of court settlement. They were up to seventy-five thousand pounds now and her advice to Olivia was that it was far too risky to hold out for more. Simon was inclined to agree with Olivia who was convinced they should take their chances in court. She felt sure the judge would see through Carl's tangle of lies and award a fair settlement. The courthouse clock was ticking. Ms Lytton tilted her head back and closed her eyes. It was almost 11 o'clock and it was clear the silly girl was not going to change her mind. Simon and Olivia exchanged a quick glance; they knew the signs. With bated breath, they awaited the result of Ms Lytton's deliberations with eager anticipation. Suddenly her eyes flashed open. "Right!" They looked at her expectantly. "Once more unto the breach dear friends, once more!" she announced, before turning on her heel, marching back to the middle of the hall and beckoning to the other side with an imperious crook of her finger.

The whole of Carl's legal team plus Carl hurried to meet her as the Clerk of the Court reappeared and demanded their immediate presence in Courtroom Three. As soon as Ms Lytton had finished speaking, Carl's team huddled around him, all the while casting furtive glances in Olivia's direction. Carl's face was ashen; his life's blood sucked right out of him. Ms Lytton was sauntering back towards them with a satisfied smile; secure in the knowledge the little bombshell she had dropped was having the desired effect. She didn't get far before Carl chased after her and attempted to haul her back.

"UNHAND ME YOU RAPSCALLION!" she bellowed, yanking her robes from Carl's grasp and brushing herself down in disgust. "How dare you manhandle a member of the Bar?"

A wave of black silks descended upon their wayward client and dragged him back into the fold. They did their best to calm him down but he wasn't having any of it; his instructions were clear.

"SHUT THE FUCK UP AND GET THIS SETTLED – NOW!!!"

Desperate to find out what the hell was going on, Simon and Olivia almost grabbed hold of Ms Lytton themselves when she eventually returned.

"Well that rather set the cat amongst the pigeons…" she began.

"What did you say out there?" asked Olivia. "Why did he—"

"They're going to settle. Is the figure of one hundred thousand pounds still acceptable to you?"

"Yes of course! But how—"

"We've got him on the ropes – do you want to push for more?"

"No – just accept! What happened? How did—"

"I simply told them we were considering an adjournment."

"But—"

"All in good time," said Ms Lytton, silencing their questions with the raise of her hand. "I need to get this signed off before dear old Barty succeeds in changing his client's mind!"

Dirty Money

"Michael? It's me."

"What's happening?"

"It's all over!"

"Christ! Already?"

"We settled out of court! Oh God – you won't believe what happened. Daniel and Co. turned up in fancy dress! The court house was full of them – even the pantomime cow!"

"You're joking!"

"No I swear to God, it was total carnage! My barrister was doing her nut but the funny thing is – it worked! He upped his offer straight away. He must have thought his mates were going to testify against him!"

"Brilliant!" laughed Michael.

"Yes but we stalled at seventy-five thousand. We were running out of time and Ms Lytton was advising me to accept because of the Calderbank thing I told you about."

"So you accepted?"

"No, because it wouldn't have been seventy-five by the time my costs were deducted."

"I thought you had Legal Aid."

"I do – but you still have to pay it back. It's taken out of the settlement at the end."

"Oh right… I didn't realise."

"Yep – that's how it works. After costs, I'd have been left with under sixty so I trusted my instincts and turned it down! The Clerk of the Court was calling us in because the judge was waiting and all of a sudden Ms Lytton stomped back over to the other side, said a few words and Carl totally lost it! He grabbed hold of her and she was yelling 'GER'OFF ME!' and his lot are trying to calm him down and we hear him screaming 'SHUT THE FUCK UP!' and me and Simon didn't have a clue what she'd said and—"

"Liv!… Slow down!"

"Sorry… I'm rushing 'cos there's only one payphone working and there's a massive queue. Hang on…" He could hear her trying to placate the next in line. "Oh God, they're turning ugly! Anyway, so just quickly… guess what it was!"

"I've no idea."

"THE MONEY LAUNDERING! She told them we had fresh information concerning Carl's business association with his father. She said we were considering an adjournment to investigate considerable sums of undeclared income that could have huge implications for the case."

"And they swallowed it?"

"Carl did – hook, line and sinker!" laughed Liv. "Sorry,

I'll have to go… we're all meeting in the pub tonight to celebrate. Can you make it?"

"I'm working, but I'll definitely get there at some point."

"Okay great, see you later!"

Home Sweet Home

24th September, 1987

Dear Clare,

Thanks so much for ringing! It was great talking to you but so frustrating when the money ran out! I know it's a pain trundling off to the payphone with saddlebags full of change, but please ring again - I need to know where you are! I'm still writing to the Boston address but I've got more than a sneaking suspicion you've moved on. If my hunch is correct, hopefully the Boston family are forwarding your mail and this letter will get through.

Oh my God Briany, I still can't believe

it's all over — it's just not sinking in!
I'm not entirely sure what happens next,
I was in a bit of daze to be honest,
but I'm sure Simon will be in touch
soon. That figure of £100,000 is clear
by the way. Thanks to Ms Lytton, Carl
is paying all the costs so there won't
be any deductions. I'm pinching myself
because this means I can afford to
buy that lovely house I was telling you
about — the one overlooking the park. It
has three double bedrooms, a big garden,
loads of fruit trees and a fish pond
for Joe. It's a proper family home and
has a wonderful feel to it — I know
we could be happy there. The boys will
love it — I can't wait to show them!
It's such a relief knowing I can give
them a home that won't feel like a huge
disappointment after Cedars. Charlie
could have the main bedroom with the
en-suite, it's massive so it could be like
a teenage bedsit, and I was thinking, the
garden is so big I could get one of those
summer house/log cabin things so they
could have a pool table out there!

I'm sure that once the dust settles,
Carl will see the sense of letting them
live with me. I could take care of day to

day life, you know, school, their clubs, seeing their friends etc and they could spend time with their dad at the weekends and in the school holidays. Surely that's got to be the right way, and who knows... maybe in time, for the sake of the children, Carl and I can be friends. Anyway, I mustn't get too excited and carried away (wise words from Jim) but it's hard not to. He's been great actually. He's going to help me with the house purchase and everything which is a relief 'cos I seriously don't have a clue!

We covered most things on the phone but I didn't get to tell you about the bizarre conversation I was having with Terry before Michael turned up. He seemed to think we could pick up from where we left it all those years ago, and disappear into the Ibizan sunset! It was strange seeing him again, like a dream I used to dream. He looked the same, in fact he looked great, those ice blue eyes sit well in a tan, but he's not the Terry from my dream – and I'm not that Olivia. When Michael appeared at the door, at first I felt relief, but that soon turned to horror when I realised they were old pals! Could it get any worse? I'm afraid it could! Michael asked Terry to leave, and the minute he was out the door, Michael went ballistic! I don't know who was more surprised - him or me! He explained it away by saying he didn't trust Terry and was worried I'd get hurt again, but that didn't explain his rage!

Alison knows by the way. She already knew something was up, obviously, she's lived the last few weeks with me, in fact, the last year and a half - but she didn't know what, until last night. I told Michael we'd be different with each other but I didn't think other people would notice too! I swear to God, he was only at the pub for about fifteen minutes but apparently that was enough! She said she'd noticed me checking my watch and keeping an eye on the door until he arrived, and that when he came over and gave me a hug I ' went all swoony!' - her words, not mine! I have to admit though, when he passed me a drink and our hands touched I nearly dropped the bloody thing! She reckons I could have got away with it up 'til that point but then Michael did something that completely gave the game away. Jim had arranged a little buffet and Alison, bless her, had baked a cake. Naturally I'd been stuffing my face and allegedly, for I have no recollection of this, Michael leant over and wiped a splodge of cream from the side of my mouth and absentmindedly sucked it from his thumb! That was it – caught bang to rights by the old ' cream on the side of the mouth play!' She reckoned ' it showed a level of intimacy that went far beyond friendship'. I could only but agree!

So, like I say, Michael wasn't there long but we spoke briefly in the car park before he left. It's over with Hannah. He said that after what happened that night in the hotel he knew he couldn't be with her. He ended it straight away. She was very dignified about it apparently and he's hopeful they can stay friends. Hannah thinks not but as I said to Michael, it's early days.

We spoke about us and all we know is that our feelings are mutual – I can't imagine life without him now and he feels the same. We know it's going to be difficult, especially with the boys and even more so with Carl, but we'll cross those bridges when we get there. He understands my situation, he's lived it too, and he respects my priorities. He said there's no rush, he's not going anywhere, but that we should see where this is going - and I agreed!

The future is beckoning for both of us Briany, and it's looking bright, but I feel you should proceed with caution here, especially in matters of the heart. You think you're in love with Virgil, but you don't know him yet. I know he's gorgeous and funny, and you get on great and the sex is amazing, but Clare, that's not enough! Sorry to sound like your mother - well maybe not YOUR mother! Ha! Imagine your mum saying something like 'the sex is amazing!' Seriously though, I know I'm clucking away like a mother hen but I do worry about you out there. Please listen to me because this is important. You need to know who he is - to share the same values and look at the world in the same way. Trust me, there's something wonderful in knowing that whatever the situation, you can trust in that person to do the right thing. It's great to be in love - all the great love songs were written for you and the world is a beautiful place - but I'm just saying, please make sure you're safe in that love before you surrender your heart.

I told Michael last night he made me feel safe and he laughed and said 'Christ that's a first!' - but I could tell he was pleased. I didn't tell him this, but the only other person who's made me feel that way is my dad - and a certain character in a book I'll be sending you. I can hear you groaning 'Oh no! Not Atticus again!' and okay I must admit, I did get a bit evangelical about it all and giving everyone a copy for Christmas that year probably was a bit over the top! I know you read it at school but honestly Clare, you should read it again - everyone should! It will stay with you, and remind you of the person you wish to be.

Okay matie, time to bring this letter to a close. I have places to go, people to see and houses to buy!!! There's a wonderful sense of optimism in the air, on both sides of the ocean - so let's join hands and raise our glasses in a toast!

'To New Beginnings!'
' Out of the darkness and into the light!'

Loving you always, missing you loads
and eagerly awaiting your call (cluck
cluck!)

Liv xxx

Acknowledgements

Seeking Atticus takes its title from Harper Lee's *To Kill a Mockingbird*. The quotes taken from this novel were chosen to portray the profound effect Atticus's words had on both Olivia and the author. I wish to pay homage to Harper Lee and acknowledge that her wonderful book was not only a resource, but a source of inspiration too!

I would also like to acknowledge the following song titles and thank the artists for providing the legendary soundtrack for this book: Carly Simon; *You're So Vain:* Steve Harley; *Make Me Smile (Come Up and See Me)*: Ian Drury and the Blockheads; *Reasons to be Cheerful, Part 3*: Madness; *Baggy Trousers, One Step Beyond*: The Beat; *Mirror in the Bathroom*: Pink Floyd; *Wish You Were Here, Comfortably Numb*: Wishbone Ash; *Warrior*: The Fun Boy Three; *The Lunatics (Have Taken Over The Asylum)*: U2; *Red Hill Mining Town, With or Without You*: The Clash; *Should I Stay or Should I Go?*: Simple Minds; *Alive and Kicking*: Peter Gabriel and Kate Bush; *Don't Give Up*: Bill Withers; *Lean On Me*: James Taylor; *You've Got a Friend*: Fleetwood Mac; *Sarah, The Chain*.

My thanks too, to everyone who knowingly, or unknowingly, contributed to the telling of this tale, especially those who read the first draft on reams of A4 paper (complete with post-it notes, paper clips, letters, envelopes and illustrations) presented in a big cardboard box!

And finally, thank you to: Richard for Humble Bumbles: Dave for Bumtwangle: Howard for Polar Shagnasty: Kelly for her 'kell-check' and Adam for all things black cab related; any inaccuracies in this respect are completely mine!